Desperate Dispatches

Mike Mollman

First Edition

Beaver Castle Media

Cover by Dmitry Yakhovsky

Desperate Dispatches

The Protectors of Pretanni Book Four

ISBN   *978-1-958265-97-0*   *Hardback*

       978-1-958265-01-7   *Paperback*

       978-1-958265-02-4   *Ebook*

       978-1-958265-03-1   *Audiobook*

Jeff Davidson is my self-appointed Agent of Chaos.

Dr. Wyatt Johnson is my fantasy hating alpha reader.

None of my books would have been possible without their friendship and support. Bleck! Don't make me be sincere again.

 TABLE OF CONTENTS

Book One: Glasna

Book Two: Crisa

Book Three: Blachstenius

Book Four: Arthmael

Book One

Glasna

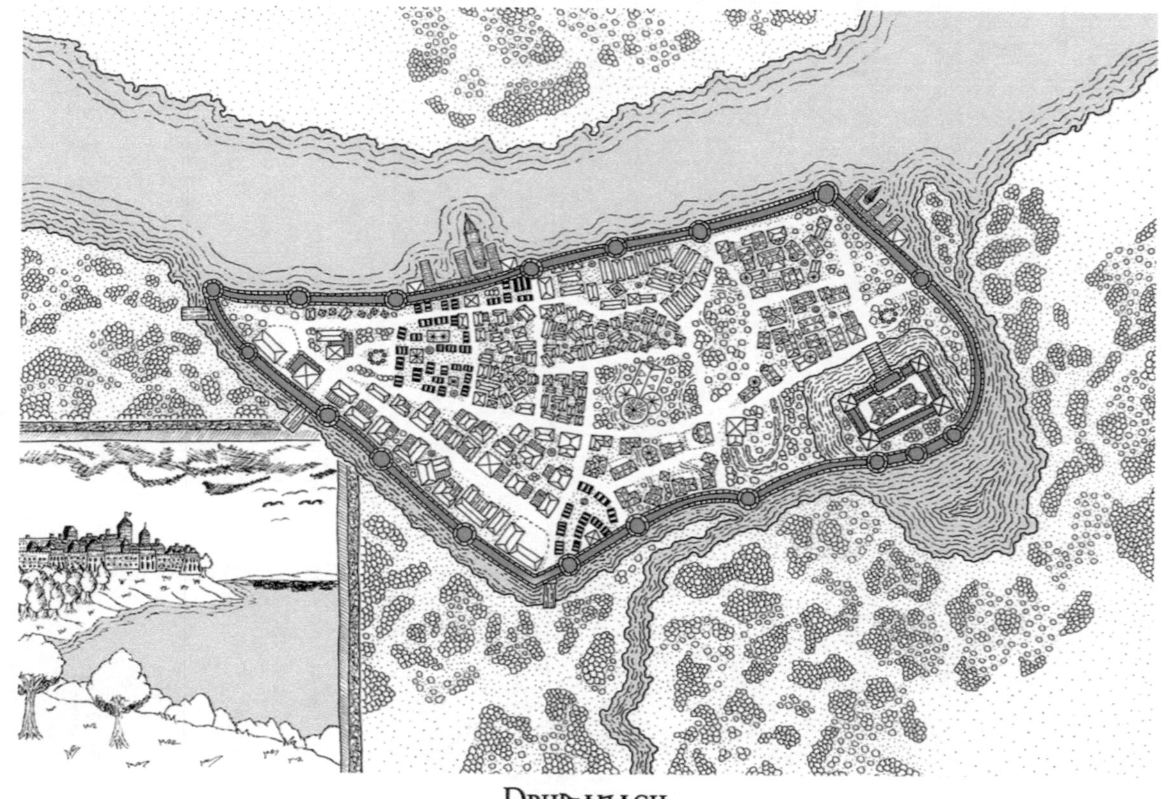

Drumanagh

Chapter One

The New Normal

After the community meal, a contented quiet takes hold as the children are finally still and the grandmothers and grandfathers take charge. Their repeated observations about me being too thin, too tired, or too withdrawn grate on my nerves.

As a refugee, I retreat to the cave entrance and watch the shadows lengthen as the day ends. Crisa is much better at this communal life, so she stays within and builds connections with the manwolves.

Outside, the clouds have come in, and something between a fog and a drizzle waits for me. In times like these, I wonder what I'm even doing here in Ossory. I was a princess; now I watch children.

"Come away, you silly girl," Frewyn calls. "You'll catch your death standing there in the cold rain."

Before I turn around, I close my eyes and take a deep breath. She means well, but as the fianna's toothless grandmother, all she can do is warn, cajole or complain. She used to cook, but she rendered carrots into orange mush too many times. Frewyn can't even watch the little ones without help, so that's where I fit in.

I resign myself to join the others for after supper talk. I must remember to compliment the old ones again for their wonderful stew.

Can they prepare anything else?

I do like the dandelion and curly dock, though. Father would never have allowed those at his noble table. I snort. I'm not nobility anymore.

"Please come in before Frewyn faints," Crisa whispers. She puts her arm across my shoulders and steers me inside. "I know that you're accustomed to better—"

"—if you apologize one more time, I will hurt you, druid lord or not." I look up at her and dare her to continue. "I was a willing participant in everything that happened, and honestly, I would choose to do it all over again."

Crisa's face brightens, ignoring the false threat. "In that case, would you like to forage for mushrooms tomorrow? It would get you out of the den."

I squeeze her arm. "Do you mean it?"

As a princess, I would regularly tell Father what I would do each day. Now, as an outlaw and a guest of the manwolves of Ossory, I must answer to tired old women like Frewyn.

"Spring is here. It won't be long before the women are with child and won't be allowed to forage in the forest."

"Do the men really think that pregnant women are helpless?"

"Who can say what men use their brains for?"

"Everybody! Everybody knows what men use their brains for."

Crisa chuckles. "Unless you plan on producing a child," she stops and looks at me for a breath, "you should learn which mushrooms are edible and abundant."

"Oh, thank you. I don't know who will make me lose my mind first, the children or Frewyn."

As if on cue, pretentious little Anulf stands up and declares that he is going to challenge Odmard for fianna leader tomorrow. Being all of nine years old, Anulf hasn't even undergone the ear shaping yet.

"Do you mean it?" I sound desperate, even to my ears. "Do we have to come back?"

Crisa laughs at my half joke. "Let me be the one to break it to Frewyn."

* * *

Now that spring has arrived, the demands of communal life slow down well before dusk. People gather in groups to play games, tell stories or gossip. It's times like these when I feel most comfortable.

There are raised voices coming from the cave entrance. That's odd. As a rule, the manwolves don't get into many fights amongst themselves.

"Odmard!" can be heard clearly as a man approaches, running fast. "Anach has been taken prisoner!"

Leony pushes past Crisa, the children, and me as he rushes toward the back of the cave.

Crisa and I share a glance. It's not like the males to speak of anything important before the children are fast asleep. Crisa slams her arm into my chest, forcing me back away from the children and against the wall into the shadows.

"If Frewyn sees you, she'll insist you take the children to the sleeping rooms."

"Frewyn is worse than any child," I say in a low voice. "The children would keep quiet at least. She's likely to scream about the fates being against us again."

"Where is that Glasna?" Frewyn's nasally voice echoes off the walls. "Glasna!" she calls. "Sometimes I think that girl is as useful as a three-legged wolf on a hunt."

I roll my eyes and press myself tighter against the wall.

"She went out to relieve herself," Crisa says once she controls her mirth.

"Frewyn," Odmard says, cutting off her next lamentation. "Please take the children to the sleeping rooms. Perhaps a story from you will keep them amused."

"Come along, lit'l ones," Frewyn calls. "Poor Frewyn's work is never done."

Crisa and I wait, counting our breaths to ten. Odmard's wide shoulders and jet-black hair rounds the sharp corner.

"If you two would like to join us," he says with a slight smile, "Frewyn and the children are gone now."

The senior men and women are seated around the fire. Only Leony is left standing, though he's too busy pacing to notice.

"Leony," Odmard says, "please tell us the news." He raises his finger. "But slower, and in order this time."

"Anach has been seized!" Leony blurts. "Gorann is now the Head Druid, and no one has seen Anach since he was escorted into Drumanagh."

Odmard does his best to slow Leony down, but the extent of his knowledge was expended in his initial outburst. Numerous pointed questions go unanswered as an increasingly flustered Leony makes apologies.

"You did well," Odmard says. "You chose to deliver this news immediately, which is right. We can speculate on the whys and hows for days on end. The important point is that Diardoc is making his play for power."

Diardoc has always been the most ambitious of the Eriu kings, but to jail the head druid and place his own druid, Gorann, as the new head of the order? That is beyond belief. Does he think he could possibly get away with this?

"What does that mean for us?" a small, quiet woman asks.

"Only time will tell," Odmard says. "They could try to rid themselves of us once and for all, or they could focus their sight on the other kings. I think it'd be best that we halt our raids for a bit so we don't provoke them."

The others nod their agreement. This is why this fianna is so successful. Odmard is aggressive when he needs to be, yet he will still his hand when he must. The nobles from my former life consider the manwolves to be a mix between savages and animals. I know they would never embrace such a measured response.

Odmard declares it best to sleep on this news and to reconvene at daybreak. Reyny, Odmard's wife, signals for Crisa and me to stay.

The others wander out in silence. At last, everyone has gone to their sleeping rooms, save the four of us. Combined, the manwolves are too few to face any of the kings in an open fight, so the end of their lifestyle always hangs in the balance.

"The rain has stopped," Reyny says.

"Good. Let's go outside then," Odmard responds.

As we leave the cave, we ignore the scurrying footsteps in front of us. I smile at the thought of our would-be eavesdroppers stumbling over each other to avoid being discovered. Odmard is a very wise leader. He slows his pace, so no one is caught. Once outside, we round a thicket of hemlock and continue to the central glade. This is where the pack will assemble during the day, as needed. It also gives us a clear view of the path to the caves, so no one can get close enough to overhear.

"What do you think is happening?" Odmard asks.

"It's not unprecedented for an older Head Druid to exchange roles with another member of the council; though it's considered bad form for an individual to decide the next leader rather than the council," Crisa says. "Now Anach certainly doesn't care about the niceties, but that man would never relinquish power, and to Gorann least of all."

The chill in the air is brisk enough to keep us all alert. After Leony's news, the busybodies will want to be the first to know Odmard's thoughts.

"So, Diardoc has imprisoned the head druid?" Reyny asks.

She's always the direct one.

"It would seem so," Crisa says.

"Diardoc would never do it unless he knew the other kings would let him," I add.

"Then we must find out what the other kings plan to do," Odmard says.

Reyny turns a questioning eye toward Crisa. "Will any of the druids speak with you?"

Crisa rocks her head sideways. "Maybe? They were there when Anach declared us outlaws. Had we stayed and fought the charges, my chances would be better, but once we ran for it, our expulsion became permanent."

Odmard turns to me. "Do you have any channels to the kingly courts?"

It's my turn to pause and consider. "It's no use going to Invernis; Caohin has withdrawn from nearly everyone. He's a creepy old man who's fixated on the dead and dying. And if you've ever smelled his breath, you'd wonder how he's not joined them yet."

"Fessach is not much better," Crisa adds, adding Caohin's druid to the growing list of those who will offer us no assistance. "I always tried to stay away from him during the council meetings."

Rhalthan is Diardoc's biggest rival amongst the kings, but the man is so loud and ill-mannered that none are likely to follow him. No one even suggests his name.

"Oshid is the druid there, and he has a good head," Crisa says. She wraps and unwraps her hair around her finger. "Oshid takes his duty to the holy place of Allcashel very seriously. If I were to meet him there, instead of at Rhalthan's hall, he may choose to speak with me."

At least there is one potential option. No one even asks about me going to my father's hall. Ulothin is far away, and his renunciation of me in front of all the other kings and druid lords has tied his hands. I know that Father loves me, but he would lock me away until they found a fishmonger to marry me.

"Crisa," Odmard says, "would you leave tomorrow for Allcashel? Our best scouts can listen in on trading caravans all they wish, but no one save the nobles will know the entire story."

"As you wish."

She shoots me an apologetic look. Once again, I'm to be trapped with Frewyn and the children.

Chapter Two

Trapped, Part One

Crisa left before first light, leaving Frewyn to wake me. Now I will spend all day listening to her jabs about being a lazy sleeper. Reyny told me that in her day, Frewyn was the finest female warrior. It's just that her day was a long, long time ago, before the elder races left, maybe.

"Hurry lit'l ones, or the cleavers will go to flower before we can pick them," Frewyn calls.

The children and I are off to pick weeds for one of her tonics. At least she has sense to keep the group on a narrow path. Otherwise, the children would spread out like bees at first light. The ponderous dragino bushes grow into the path from both sides. The children can walk under the blackthorns, but they're right at eye level for me. The bushes are beautiful at this time, as they are in bloom with perfect white flowers. However, the flowers cover the darker branches and hide the sinister finger-long thorns.

Frewyn points out the cleavers to the children, and they harvest them with smiles and excitement. Frewyn walks over to me while the children boisterously slap the cleavers on each other's clothes.

"It's nice when children can laugh while doing their chores," she says. "It makes everyone happier."

I smile despite myself. Frewyn is overprotective, and I don't need that, but she does know a few tricks. Unfortunately, some of the children are as headstrong as I used to be.

"Anulf, come back here," Frewyn calls. He strays to the end of the path and disappears around the bend.

We look at each other and frown.

"It's my turn," I say.

"No, let me go. I can pop him a good one if need be."

She stalks off around the bend in search of our intrepid explorer, leaving me with the rest of the children.

It's silly really, but at last, I'm in charge while Frewyn's away. Sure, the children can act like feral creatures at times, but for now, they are well behaved, doing their chores and smiling. Wistfully, I think about the day when I'll have my own children.

There's a very shy girl who can barely look at me before growing nervous. Not once has she spoken to me. She's Anulf's little sister, I think. I watch as her eyes grow big with Frewyn's departure. I spot a couple of cleavers the children missed and hide them in my left hand.

I stare at the girl and beckon her to me. Her eyes are big, and she has to grab one hand in the other to keep from trembling. I squat down, so we're eye to eye, and I stick the cleavers to the front of her frock and smile.

She giggles a couple times and I reciprocate. I tousle her hair.

"I'm not giving you anymore," I say. "So, if you want to win, you better get picking!"

Her eyes light up and she runs to the nearest cleaver patch.

Little Anulf runs around the bend, not stopping at his sister, but coming straight to me.

"What is it?" I ask.

"Bad men." He grabs my left hand as tight as he can.

I furrow my brow, but he doesn't volunteer anything more.

"Children, come to me. We need to find another patch of cleavers."

"Where's Auntie Frewyn?" One of the children asks.

"She'll be along shortly. Now find a partner and line up."

It's always Frewyn who gives the children direction. As a group, they pause only for a breath before they follow my instructions.

I'm getting the hang of this.

Behind the children, Frewyn backs into view with a knife drawn. She glances at us only once before returning her attention to whatever is in front of her.

"Move," I tell the children. "Go to the big ash tree in the glade."

The first six children leave, but the rest follow my eyes to Frewyn. They gasp and freeze in place.

Frewyn makes a feint with her big knife before giving ground.

"Get the children out of here!" she yells.

Anulf runs toward his Auntie. I break into a sprint and grab the child by the waist.

"Anulf, I need you to lead the children, while Auntie Frewyn and I take care of this."

He looks at me with earnestness.

"None of the other children can take charge. You have to be the man of the group. Now take the others to the big ash tree in the glade. That's where your sister and the rest of the children are now."

He looks once at Frewyn's back before sliding out of my grip. He runs to the others, barking out orders. To my relief, they follow him without question. Now I can see to what Frewyn is doing.

"Are the children gone?" the old grandmother shouts, without looking back.

"They are." I approach even as she continues her retreat.

Two Laigin soldiers turn the corner, spears pointed at Frewyn. I expected a bear, or maybe wolves. If Diardoc's soldiers are here, the fianna must be warned.

Five more soldiers follow them onto our path. The men look at the two of us and smile.

"Glasna, get the children back to the cave," Frewyn says. She's pulled out the hatchet she uses for cutting branches to go along with her paring knife as her only weapons. She won't last four breaths against the men.

"Frewyn, you know the paths better than I." I stand next to her. She's about to argue. "And I have anger issues when dealing with soldiers."

I give the men a malicious grin. *"Lichiul srenc Elruzon."*

My imp appears, and Frewyn recoils in fear. I've kept this ability secret from the manwolves. They were bound to find out sometime; it might as well be in defense of the children.

"Elruzon, feast on them." I point at the now seven soldiers.

The imp flies at the closest man. He panics, drops his weapons and waves his arms above his head. Imps are the smallest of the demons and the easiest to dispatch. They fight by diving and retreating from their target. It doesn't take many blows to dispatch the least of demon kind.

Frewyn is staring open-mouthed.

"Go!" I yell. "Get the children to safety." I grab her hatchet. "But leave me this, just in case."

Eyes wide, Frewyn nods at me before she too vanishes in the brush. "Children, evacuation drill!" she yells, steel in her voice as she runs after our charges.

"You've all been drilled in demon tactics," a gray-streaked bearded man says. He points at me. "Forward!"

Elruzon circles the men, but they keep their spears pointed outward, like a hedgehog. I give ground slowly. The more I delay, the better chance Frewyn and the children have of getting away.

One of the men drops his spear slightly. Elruzon dives for the man's face. The soldier breaks the formation and waves his spear desperately in front of him.

The graybeard swings his sword and clips Elruzon's foot, making the imp scream out in pain. It flies out of range before circling the soldiers again. I throw my hatchet, but graybeard must have been expecting it. He knocks it down easily.

"Form up and don't lose your water this time," Graybeard orders. The grim-faced men reform their hedgehog.

Another man lowers his spear, and Elruzon falls for the ruse. He rushes in to attack, only to be skewered by the man to his right. The little imp gives off a wail of despair.

"Pin it to the ground!" the graybeard yells.

Before Elruzon can get free, the spearpoint and imp go crashing to the ground.

"Everyone, stab at the infernal thing. Let's send it back to the underworld, where it belongs."

He's wrong, of course. My imp would be killed, not returned to its own hellish home.

"Elruzon!"

I throw my knife at the graybeard and rush the men. One of them knocks me to the ground, but that was my plan all along. Kneeling over the imp, I place one hand on the spear and one on Elruzon. The imp's flesh sears my palm as I yank out the spear.

"*Favin cepen*," I whisper before the killing blows can be delivered to my imp.

I look up at my captors and see the butt of Graybeard's spear racing toward me.

CHAPTER THREE

Trapped, Part Two

The hard stone floor steals the warmth from my very bones. I grew up in my father's keep, so I know instantly where I am, Drumanagh Castle. While the weather has turned warmer, the stones have not caught up. There is only one source of light, and it is from a small slit in the thick stone wall. It's an arrow slit, really. I shake the iron bars; but they're newly installed, well-oiled, and without a speck of rust.

When my brother Roisair and I were little, we'd play in Father's dungeon, at least when it was empty. Father's cells were used so infrequently that upkeep was never a priority. Every cell door squealed with even the tiniest movement.

"They're scared of you," a weathered voice calls out from the shadows. "They built that cage special, and even put a ring of heavy stones around it."

So, they prepared for my summoning of demons.

I study the rubble pile ringing my cell. Sitting on the floor, I try to reach the stones with my foot. For seventeen years, I've told my brothers that being short doesn't matter. I stretch as best I can, but for once, my lack of height is a liability.

The old man laughs at my exertions. I glare at him and his dirty white robes.

"Are you a druid?" I ask.

He scowls and turns his back on me.

"You *are* a druid! Why don't you change into an animal and escape?"

"You're a silly girl. What do you know?" he says harshly.

"I know that I will not accept being caged." I inspect each bar, more carefully this time, but it's no use. "Are you content to rot here? I thought druids were paragons of virtue, not defeated cowards."

"Watch your mouth!" The old druid rises off the floor and walks into the light.

"Anach?"

"Lord Druid Anach," he corrects, though his tone is not as harsh.

"We need to get you out of here."

He raises his hands from the folds of his robe, revealing his manacles.

"How do you plan on doing that?" he asks.

"I don't know. Turn into a bird and fly away."

"The art of animorphing is a lost art," he says dismissively.

"Grahme and Figol could do it."

"There are none on Eriu who can do what they do."

"No," I say. My sadness surprises me.

Figol wasn't that cute.

"Why do they have a ring of stones around your cage?" the head druid asks.

"I went to Laleah and learned to summon demons."

"Treacherous girl," he scolds. "Why would you learn those foul arts?"

"Because the Tusci were taking over the north, and you and your fat, lazy druids did exactly nothing!" I shout. "Only Crisa was willing to serve the people."

He stalks back into the recesses of his cell and out of the meager light. He moans slightly as he sinks to his bench.

"I was wrong to trust Diardoc," he snorts. "That's obvious now."

"Then let's break out of here and you can set things right."

The heavy wooden door scrapes along the floor. I approach the cell wall closest to the guards.

"Look, the flame-haired one is awake," the first guard says. "Careful, don't go inside the circle or she'll summon a demon to rip you apart."

"But she's just a little girl," the second guard says.

"I saw the little horror when we captured her. But don't trust me, enter the circle. Just don't scream out my name so I catch the blame."

"How do we get food to her?"

The first guard snickers. "Take the food to the druid. I'll handle her."

The guard throws the bread at the bars. It hits sideways and drops outside the cell, too far for me to reach.

"I can't reach that."

"Too bad. Here's your water." With a quick, underhanded motion, he flings the contents of the cup in my face. "Is that better?"

The second guard at least looks ashamed as the two leave the room. I listen until I can no longer hear them.

"How stale is the bread?" I ask.

"I haven't chipped a tooth yet, but I fear that day is coming," Anach says.

"Good."

I sit on the floor again and grab the loaf between my feet. I slide it to the nearest corner and push it up against the stone circle. I can't get enough contact with both feet to push the loaf any farther. I twist a little so that my left leg can reach just a little farther. I give it all the force I can muster, and the loaf turns sideways. My shoulders slump in defeat.

"That was foolish. That's your only meal for the day."

"It was foolish alright, for them." I stand up and extend my hands outside the iron bars.

"Lichiul srenc Elruzon."

My little imp appears and scowls at me, clearly angry at being skewered by an iron weapon the last time he was summoned.

"Elruzon, push the loaf of bread and break the circle of stones."

He curses at me in demontongue.

I have no time for his tirade. "Elruzon, do as I say."

The imp cautiously approaches the circle and breaks the plane with one finger. A puff of smoke appears as he snatches his hand back.

"The loaf of bread," I remind the infernal thing. "Push the bread until you break the circle."

Elruzon gingerly grabs the loaf and turns toward me as it turns to ash in his hands. It gives me a taunting smile.

"Tuthu mini fase!" I call the demon to me. I thrust my arms backward as far as I can and, like a puppeteer, I pull the demon toward me. The demon screams as it makes contact with the cell's iron bars. Greasy black smoke emerges as the impetuous imp is literally being burned by the iron.

I wave my hand dismissively. *"Favin cepen."*

The demon drifts away from the iron bars and vanishes into a cloud of dark smoke.

Thick boots are approaching the prison door. Anach grunts once and returns to his bunk. The guards must have heard Elruzon's screams.

The key turns in the lock and the stout oak door opens inward.

"Keep quiet in here or else I'll give you something to scream about."

"There was a rock in my bread. I think I chipped a tooth."

"Aw, the little princess chipped a tooth?" The guard smiles, showing his misaligned, yellow teeth. "Then I won't give you one tomorrow. You can't chip your tooth if you have nothing to eat." He slams the door shut.

Anach starts laughing. "Looks like you're going to lose weight. If you get thin enough, maybe you can slip between those bars."

The bars are only a hand's width apart from one another. "At least I'm not going to give up, like you, old man."

* * *

Hunger forces me to consume the next few loaves of bread, but the time has come to break the stone circle. I call forth Elruzon.

"Defy me and you will feel iron against your skin again. Now, use that stale loaf of bread to break open the stone circle." My words are slow and clear.

He speaks too fast in demontongue for me to catch the individual words, but his meaning is clear. No demon wants to risk losing their essence.

"Elruzon, do it now," I say in a firm tone.

His argument is cut short when I raise my arms out wide. One backward stretch and the demon will be pulled toward me.

His tone turns plaintive.

"Do it."

It grabs the loaf and pulls it away from the stones. Wrapping both hands around it, the demon transfers enough heat to over-cook the bread and make it hard as a rock. Elruzon lands on the ground and pokes the rocks on top with his tool. The first tumbles, and the imp gives a grunt of triumph. With a few more jabs, the circle is broken. The imp flies over the rocks and back in obvious relief.

"Move a rock from here so that the circle is not complete." I point to the part of the circle farthest from the door. The imp, now in better spirits, does as I ask. Next, I have it replace the rocks it initially moved with the loaf.

"You have done well, Elruzon."

I sit on the floor again and stretch my legs toward the hard loaf of bread. Rock hard or not, it's my only meal. Elruzon sees me stretching and flies over to the bread. He picks it up in his hands and transfers his heat to the loaf, turning it black in two heartbeats.

"Elruzon!" I yell.

The foul creature smiles at me as it dissipates itself from this realm.

Foolish Glasna, demons are not your friends. When will you learn this?

"As interesting as that was, what did you accomplish?" Anach asks.

"More that you think. I'll trade an explanation for part of your bread."

Chapter Four

Jail Break, Part Two

Demons are not your friends. How many times did my instructors tell me that? Mosech and Cara are good people, and try as they might, they couldn't get me to think of Elruzon as anything other than a pet. For the nine hundredth time, I see my error. Elruzon had to taste the iron bars several times before he became compliant to my wishes. But that is in the past, for now.

"You can call forth that demon spawn," Anach says. "So what?"

"Shh," I wave at him to be quiet. "The big nose guard likes to check in on us before they throw dice."

"He's only done that twice," Anach counters.

I wave for him to be quiet. It's not two heartbeats before we hear the clop of Big Nose's heavy boots on the stone floor. Anach hurries to his bench and moans slightly while leaning against the wall. He's way overdoing it, but Big Nose is not on guard duty because of his brains. I pace back and forth, shooting the guard angry glares.

Big Nose smiles and blows me a kiss. I huff and turn my back to him. He chuckles and returns to the table with the other guards. Little do they know that one day soon, all of them will suffer from terminally bad luck.

Anach has been busy in the shadows of his cell ever since I broke the stone ring. Any time I question him, he yells at me to be quiet. For all I know, the man is losing his sanity.

A mouse scurries from Anach's cell, and he cajoles it to return. It's great that he's got a friend, but I need him to focus on bigger issues. I can't break out of here by myself.

Idly, I watch as Anach's little friend goes into a rubble pile and emerges with a piece of wood that more resembles an oversized needle than anything else. The mouse struggles to bring it back to Anach, but once it's in reach, Anach rises to his feet and raises his arms in victory.

It's sad watching the old lose their minds—even Anach.

The old druid gives the mouse a few scraps of bread before turning his attention to his new toy. He gnaws on the wood, inspects it closely, then gnaws on it again. It's as if he's becoming a mouse in his head.

Happy with his work, he retreats to his bunk and works furiously at something in the shadows. There's a thumping noise from his cell. This is how sad my life has become. I'm left watching a doddering old man injure himself.

Anach comes to the wall of his cell that is closest to me. He sticks his hands between the iron bar and wiggles his fingers at me.

"What are you doing?" I ask, annoyed.

"You're not a very observant child, are you?" he quips. "You haven't even noticed that my manacles are nowhere to be seen?"

"You used that wooden shard to pick the manacle?" I ask, amazed.

"I did. And maybe" He inserts the shard into the cell lock. Try as he might, he can't get the lock to open.

"No worries," he says after giving up. "Now that I'm not bound by iron, I can call an entire legion of rats to my service."

Great, he's going to have a whole party now.

"What good will that do?" I ask, plopping back down on my bench.

"The rats can carry larger pieces of wood. With a whole pack, they can scavenge the castle until I find a piece capable of defeating this lock."

"The clouds are hiding Belenos from us, so it's hard to determine how late in the day it is. You should wait until after they bring our food."

"Thank you. In all my years as a druid, I never once considered the path Belenos takes across the sky," the old druid says sarcastically.

*   *   *

I summon Elruzon while Anach summons a pack of rats. Elruzon takes up his post at the door, since demon hearing is superior to humans'. Anach directs the rats to gnaw on the scrap of wood they found on their journey through the castle.

Anach lets out a whispered cheer as the rats have managed to shape a wooden key for his cell door. He tosses them their reward—the remains of his stale bread. He opens his cell door and stretches theatrically in front of me.

"We don't have much time. Open my door."

He rubs his chin. "Do I need a demon-summoning traitor at my side?"

"Yes, you do," I say without raising my voice. "Because that demon summoner has her imp ready to tear your throat out if you double-cross her."

While Anach watches me, I compel my imp to fly right behind the old druid.

The flutter of Elruzon's leathery wings gives him away. Anach jumps away from the imp, who is hovering just off his left shoulder.

"Get that vile thing away from me," he demands.

"As soon as you uphold your end of the bargain." I swipe my hand, and the imp retreats back to the door. The old fool grudgingly opens my cell door. I take his hand as I step over the rock circle.

We lean against the heavy oak door that separates us from our captors. Their table is around a corner, so we can't see how many are there.

Anach raises three fingers and nods toward the door latch. I get a whiff of brimstone and rest my left hand on his, stopping his motion.

"Izrak is troubled," a new voice says. "He seems to think your prisoners are free."

"*Favin cepen.*"

I dismiss Elruzon as I race back to my cell. The guards are pushing their chairs back, so I close my cell door and pray they don't notice the difference.

"The key!" Anach hisses as he points to my cell door. Thankfully, the guards are in no hurry, since they *know* we can't escape. I race to the front of my cage and yank at the key, to no avail.

The heavy prison door opens, and three guards and one strange little man in red Tusci robes enter. Last of all, his imp flutters through the door.

I lower my head to hide my surprise. Imp hearing is far superior to human abilities. It has heard everything. It looks at me, then notes my hands obstructing the lock. Its toothy maul is revealed as its lips widen out in a smile. I can't let it speak in demontongue.

I close my eyes and recall my lessons. Cara was more adept at summoning, but Mosech could make demons dance. Few learn these fine control commands anymore, he told me. The Tusci seek only the most powerful demons to control.

"*Phersu,*" I whisper.

The demon opens its mouth, but no sound comes out. It opens its jaws until all of its teeth are pointing at me. It slams its mouth shut, and the tooth-on-tooth clacking draws the attention of its master.

"*Suthina,*" I say, while looking down at the floor.

Only the slightest chirp comes out of the hellspawn until its body is forced to be still. It drifts to the floor as it gives me a baleful look.

If this Tusci knew of these fine demon controls, my actions would be transparent to him. But he has no idea that I have commandeered his demon. Still, all summoners learn the small oddities of their summoned, so it won't be long before he suspects my tampering.

I lower my head as I gamble one more time. I must wrest total control of this demon.

"*Lucumu Izrak.*"

I glance up and see that the demon is enthralled to me. I know the look. The hate-filled eyes promise retribution if ever Izrak breaks free of my control.

"What was that?" one of the guards asks. Clearly, he heard me mutter something.

"Free me now or you will feel my full wrath once I reclaim my proper status!" Anach bellows, as he bangs his manacles against the iron poles of his cell.

Good, he's used his time wisely.

"Shut up, old man!" A guard trudges over to Anach's cell. "I told you once before that you're a nobody now. And nobodies don't talk." He jabs Anach in the stomach with the butt of his spear.

Anach groans in pain. That's all the distraction I need.

"Izrak, *tur lein avil.*"

Literally, I've told the demon to die for one year. What it means is that he will be unable to be summoned for that length of time. I smile at the stone floor. The little Tusci has been emasculated, and he doesn't even know it. As soon as he tries and fails to summon his little imp in the presence of other Tusci, they will see his weakness and torment him with their demons.

"Where'd your demon go?"

The little man looks at me. "She sent it away!"

He strides toward me. Once he's inside the circle, I smile at him. *"Lichiul srenc Elruzon."*

The little imp is not happy to be recalled so quickly, so it fights me for control. It's all I need, however. The strange little man realizes my imp can tear him to pieces, and he scurries back over the circle.

"*Favin cepen,*" I say, waving away my imp with one hand before he, too, exits the circle and gives away our secret.

"Did your skirts knock over a rock while you were running away?" I ask in a mocking tone.

"Shut up, Eriu scum!" he shouts.

"Well, did you?" A guard asks the demoralized Tusci.

"Why don't you come over here and find out?" I taunt.

"Summon your demon back and see if it can cross the circle," Big Nose grumbles to the smaller man.

"*Lichiul srenc Izrak,*" The Tusci commands. Nothing happens. "*Lichiul srenc Izrak,*" he says again, this time in a higher pitch. He glares at me. "You did this!"

"Did what?" I snort. "You call yourself a Tusci, yet you can't even reliably call forth a demon?"

"Give me the name of your imp. What was it? Elrusic?"

"Cross the stone circle and I'll be happy to summon him. Or are you afraid that my little pet will overpower you?"

"She's trying to get us to step over the circle again and again until someone kicks a stone and breaks the trap," the Tusci says. "If it was already broken, her imp would be upon us already."

"But what about your demon?" Big Nose asks.

"That is not your concern." The Tusci spins with a flourish and leaves the jail.

"No bread for either of you for a week," Big Nose says, grinning.

I shriek incoherent noises at him. He ignores me and follows the inept demon summoner out of the room. The stout door slams shut, and I open my right hand, revealing new bruises from gripping the wooden key so tightly.

Chapter Five

Jail Break, Part Two

The fact that we can now get out of our cells is nice, but the novelty of it doesn't last. The thick wooden prison door can only be unlocked from the other side. Even if Anach could direct a horde to attack the guards, how would that help us?

The old man has taken to peering out the arrow slit at night and basking in Aine's pale glow. I tap him on the shoulder, but he ignores me. Agitation flashes across his face, so I know it's not a trance.

I spend my time at the door, listening to the guards. Other than dubious advice at throwing dice, I learn nothing.

"Aine will be at her full brilliance tomorrow," Anach says.

I jump at the sound of his voice next to my ear and slap him on the arm for surprising me. "What good will that do? Are you going to stay up all night staring?"

"The impatience of youth," he says. "Did you think I was merely staring up at Aine? Get extra sleep during the day, for you shall witness something truly amazing tomorrow night."

What else do I have to do?

* * *

Napping during the day is just not happening. My head says I'll be underwhelmed by Anach, but my heart is holding onto hope. We just got our bread rations back, and I'm afraid we'll lose them again. I'm too nervous to banter with Big Nose, so I devour my bread without a word.

"What is it you're going to show me?" I ask again.

"Aine will rise soon." Anach keeps his self-satisfied smirk. He beckons me to the back of the room, where there's nothing but rubble. Whoever was charged with building my cell wasn't too keen to clean up. Old, rusty iron bars and loose rocks are strewn across the back wall.

"I can't see the individual blocks of stone; there must be plaster covering them'" Anach says. "Grab something from the pile and help me remove it."

It's not as if there's something better I could be doing, so I join the fun.

"This one," Anach points to a stone as wide as my arm and as high as from my elbow to fingertip. "Help me clear away all the plaster on this one."

"What good will this do?"

"Patience," he councils me.

Once our job is completed, the old fool goes back to the arrow slit and sits in the moonlight. Only after the last rays retreat from view does he move.

"Don't be afraid," he says.

I manage not to laugh.

He faces the stone block we so carefully cleaned and mutters in a language I've not heard. Before my eyes, dust starts to fall from the fissures in the stone. The grating of stone on stone is so loud, surely Big Nose must hear it. The entire wall quivers, and dust starts pouring down. I watch the prison door, but there are shadows from the guards' feet beneath the door. Glancing back at the wall, I watch as a squarish arm and leg sticks out. Ponderously, the other arm and leg extend into our prison, and the elemental pulls its way out of the wall.

The stone is only as wide as my extended arms, which isn't a lot, however it is as deep as my elbow to wrist. The giants who built this citadel were not taking any chances.

"Well, don't just stand there," Anach says. "Go explore!"

"What?" I say. "You want me to just walk around the castle like I own the place?"

"Yes." He nods his head and looks at me like I'm a child.

I cock my head and try to find an objection. I can't, so I hoist myself up and roll through the rather large hole.

"If you see someone coming, you'll have to alert me somehow so I can fill in this hole in the wall."

Thanks, Anach. You'll be safe in the prison while the guards are hunting me in the halls.

The hallway is deserted at this time of night. By the lack of hanging crests or animal heads, this must be a servant's passage. Scrambling through, I look back at Anach.

"What should I search for?"

"Just get your bearings. We'll take advantage of whatever you find as you explore each night."

Great, I get to repeatedly walk alone and unarmed in the enemy's fortress.

"What could possibly go wrong?" I mutter to myself.

"Call when you're finished, and I'll let you back in."

"What?"

The elemental swings one leg across the bottom of the hole and bends forward until its chest touches its knee.

"I'll have it leave a small opening in the top corner. Call through there when you're finished."

It's worse than I thought. I'm still likely to get skewered as I wait for that lumbering rock to move. I inhale a deep breath. So, I have to rely only on myself. Isn't that what I would prefer?

The corridor goes dark, and I feel so very alone. I start to my left and move toward the only light. Pressing up against the wall, I hear Big Nose's unmistakable voice.

I can't have the guards see me walking the halls, so this way is off limits.

I head back the opposite way and hear voices approaching. The barest glimmer of a torch alerts me to a darkened room. I dive inside and wait for the servants to pass.

Stupid, stupid me.

Of course, servants are going to be up when Aine is at full brilliance. This is the time when they can get ahead of their chores.

I befriended several of the staff when I was a young girl, and this is the way of them the world over. Scouting will have to wait a few days until Aine grows more dim.

"Remember," an older woman is saying to her charge, "if a demon approaches, say '*Ei alpan. Ei al mi.*'"

"Are you sure?" the girl asks, wringing her hands. "What does that mean?"

"It means, 'Not an offering, do not approach me,' or something like that. I have used it, and as long as you're firm, they will leave you be."

How long have the Tusci been here? If even the servants know demon protection phrases, this castle must have been infiltrated for quite a while.

The girl grabs the older servant's arm and draws closer to her.

"You have more to fear from the guards than from the demons," the matron says. "That's why we don't go past this next room until their snores are evident."

I wait for the light to fade in the distance before I emerge from hiding. With much more effort than I'd expected, I find the small hole and peer into our prison room. Anach is nowhere to be seen.

"Anach!" I whisper as loud as I dare. "Anach!"

Nothing.

"Anach!" I say through my cupped hands.

Where is he?

"Back so soon?"

I check both ends of the corridor for any flickering lights. The guard's room illuminates the wall across from it. Otherwise, there's no one about.

Anach repeats his gibberish, and stone scrapes upon stone.

"I can't pull him out on my own," Anach says.

Never have I felt so stupid as now, when I must push against a stone wall. The noise grows louder. There will be no chance of hearing anyone approaching. I check the hall again. Is that a flickering light coming from the direction of the guard's room? Thanks to their light, I can't tell.

"Hurry!"

While standing idly in the servants' corridor, unarmed and with no story prepared, I focus on the hall past the guard's room. There is definitely a bobbing of light from someone's torch in the corridor.

The grinding noises are even louder and the stone sluggishly moves inward, toward the cell. At the halfway point, the scraping rises to new levels as the elemental frees itself from the wall.

"What's that noise?" A woman's voice echoes down the hallway.

I plop onto the bottom stone and spin my body so my feet can go first. The woman with the torch is running now.

"We've been discovered!" I whisper urgently. "A servant saw me coming through this wall just now." I press up against the side of the wall. "We'll have to kill her somehow."

"Leave this to me," Anach says.

"Hello?" The servant says from the corridor.

Anach walks into view and rests his hands on the opening. "Hello dear child, what is your name?"

"Are you Anach?" The woman asks, unbelieving.

"I am," Anach says kindly.

"Oh! My name is Bondua, most holy."

The old druid shoots me a triumphant look. "Bondua, that is a lovely name," he purrs. "Please rise, dear child. Are you a believer in the old and true ways?"

"Yes, head druid," she says quickly. "I did not believe that you had been imprisoned here. Had I known, I would have—"

"—Don't worry about that, dear one. I allowed myself to be captured so that I could learn about the traitors from within their midst."

I roll my eyes at that lie.

"All I need for you to do, under the blessings of the gods, is to go about your business and tell no one of my efforts," Anach says.

"It will be as you say!" Bondua declares. "I will take over the chores in this area so that the other servants do not discover your plan. They are a good lot, but some of the younger ones can be loose with such knowledge."

"Bondua, may Brigantia smile upon you." Anach reaches out into the corridor and draws her hands back through the opening. "I want you to see Glasna, my apprentice."

He releases his right hand and draws me toward the encounter.

"If you see her, know that she is following my orders."

His apprentice? It's all I can do not to scoff. I glance at the servant for an instant before I avert my eyes. I'm not sure I can keep the annoyance off my face.

"It will be as you say, holy one."

"Then go back to your work. Continue as if nothing is amiss. That is the greatest contribution you can make for our righteous cause."

Bondua hurries on her way and Anach commands the elemental to reform the wall.

"Your apprentice?" I ask with some heat. "The cause of righteousness? You were laying it on overly much, weren't you?"

The old druid ignores me as he falls against the wall. "I don't know how many more times I can do that."

Chapter Six

The Heat Rises

It's taken time, but we perfected our system. Diardoc's guards know nothing of demon magic, and the inept demon summoner never returned, so we're able to expand our roaming by having Elruzon scout ahead of me. I even raided the kitchen one night.

Everything was going well, but then I let my anger get the better of me. It was stupid. I let Big Nose provoke me, and the next thing I knew, I was questioning his manhood. We went a solid week without food. In the intervening two weeks, I've recovered, but Anach has not. His sunken eyes contradict the assurances he gives me.

Anach had the elemental leave an opening in the upper left corner. I'm able to summon Elruzon on the other side of the wall, but the only way I can communicate with the hellspawn is by inhabiting its head. The effort is exhausting and thoroughly uncomfortable.

Demons only see red hues and the heat given off by bodies or fires. Their hearing is tuned to the drum of heartbeats. This is what makes them so dangerous; they sense the flushing of the skin or a racing heartbeat long before a person would notice. Human speech sounds like high-pitched warbling, so they're keen to ignore it.

From the beginning, my goal has been to escape, but with Anach so weak, that plan has been set aside. Instead, through my imp, we spy and disrupt wherever we can. Elruzon has the ability to travel farther and faster on his own than I could ever do. The problem is that in the darkest hours, everyone's asleep, so there are no conversations to be overheard.

Tonight, Aine's glow will be at full brilliance. I've convinced Anach that if he bathes in the goddess' light, he'll have the strength to call forth the elemental. I would normally be willing to forego the excursions, but Anach needs substantive food.

"Wake up, Anach." He sleeps most of the day and all night now. The week without food has laid bare just how weak he has become.

"Hey, old man," I call. "Are you sleeping or dying?"

"A little bit of both, I think." He rises to a sitting position.

At least he's being honest. From the deep shadows, the old druid rises, stretching and groaning noisily.

"The servants will be about, so you'll have to be extra attentive tonight," Anach says.

Old people. They tell you the obvious and call it wisdom.

"Yes, Anach, we've gone over this."

"Extra careful," he says while wagging his finger. "Unless you're willing to reconsider sliding down the castle wall to make good our escape."

I sigh heavily. We have a version of this conversation every night.

"We are three floors up in the castle, and the ditch is another two floors deep. If the wall of the castle doesn't kill us outright by tearing off all of our skin, the fall into the ditch will certainly lead to numerous broken bones."

"I can summon eagle owls to grab us and slow our descent," the old man volunteers, again.

"No, Anach." Visions of puncture wounds from the owl's talons, loss of whatever skin comes in contact with the wall, screams of pain from the broken bones as we sit at the bottom of the ditch and guards shooting arrows down at our wrecked bodies fill my mind. That's what Anach's plan will deliver.

The old druid unlocks his cell and shuffles over to do the same for me.

"What would you like to eat tonight?" I ask in my most cheerful tone. He always grunts at me, but they're more a formality now, rather than a repudiation.

"The lamb was good."

"Then let me find more mutton." I pat him on the cheek and smile.

Anach animates the elemental, and I'm able to help pull it out of the wall. All the scraping between the elemental and the wall has loosened the extra snug fit. Either that, or I've become stronger. It still makes terrible grating noises as it frees itself from the wall, and every time I hold my breath as I wait for us to be discovered. Thank the gods that our guards are such sound sleepers.

Even though Bondua says she'll help us, I think it's best if she doesn't know about Elruzon. What little chatter we've heard revolves around demons and human interactions. Her loyalty would be severely tested if she saw me with my very own imp.

Once I can confirm that the corridor is empty, I send Elruzon to the throne room. There have been numerous late-night meetings lately between Diardoc and Lar Crespe, the envoy from Ynys Manaw and the real power here. Since Lar's arrival from the demon isle, one more imp in the room will hardly be noticed. The Tusci have arrived in force in Drumanagh within the last month. Diardoc still pretends to be the power here, but the fool has invited wolves into his flock of sheep.

I close my eyes and focus on Elruzon's vision. Mosech taught me that demons know when we become flustered well before we do. That is how they know when to challenge their summoner. According to my teacher, one must find an inner calm when commanding demons. Eriu kings are not aware of these facts.

Mutton to do about it now.

I'll have to remember that one. It will make Anach groan when he hears it. I head to the kitchens, since they're deserted at this time of night. The banquet hall, which is favored by the Tusci for these late-night meetings, is only a single door away. I've never come this close before, but now that I'm here, I have to take advantage of it.

I can listen to what Elruzon hears, but I've always found it difficult. Instead of listening through the imp's ears and getting a terrible headache, I creep closer to the banquet hall door. The Tusci are not a quiet people, unlike we natives of Eriu.

Peeking inside, I see Lar Crespe leaning over a map and growling at Diardoc. Poor Diardoc, he won't even make eye contact with his overseer or any of the Tusci. He stares at the floor a lot. This is what happens when the sheep invites the wolves to dinner.

"You said that the druids would accept the change and the kings would fear attacks from one another. Yet now there is word that this druid lord, Oshid, is rallying people to his side."

"Oshid is no leader," Diardoc says. "He's soft and is in the Goidel court of Rhalthan is the king and he's crude and belligerent. No one will follow either of them for long. If we just wait them out, the whole siege will melt away by Beltane, or midsummer at the latest."

"How did they know to attack the convoy of fresh Arevacen horses on the road between Menipia and here?" Lar demands. "How did they even get into this territory without your men knowing?"

"The manwolves of Ossory are vermin," Diardoc says, still inspecting the rug. "If you would just send your demon summoners out, the nuisance could be exterminated once and for all."

"I find that explanation too convenient," the Tusci lord says. "I think there is a spy in this castle."

A chill runs down my back.

"Elruzon, quietly leave the room, now."

"Lord Crespe," Diardoc begins, even more obsequious than before, "since more of your men have arrived, none of my men have been able to leave the castle, much less the town."

The Tusci snorts at the pathetic display. He surveys the men in the room. "It could not be anyone present here. However, many of you have the ability to summon lesser demons or imps. And I know that every one of you covets my position."

"Metusthurasi! Repinthi sa."

My eyes go wide as I mouth his words. "Servants of Metus, bend to me." He's calling every hellspawn within the city to obey him.

"*Lucumo heva fler zichu mlusna.*"

"I command you to offer up your summoner's name," I say aloud, making sure that I translate the order correctly.

More frightening than the order, if possible, is that fact that I was ejected from my imp's mind by the force of Lar's command. I reestablish contact with Elruzon's mind. The sheer force of Lar Crespe's command has stopped the imp in its tracks. As is natural for his kind, the imp is fighting the urge to return to the banquet hall and report.

Being in the imp's head during such a command has demonstrated how little power I have compared to a Tusci master.

"Elruzon, I respect the greater power, but Lar did not command you to return to him. Stand firm where you are and report that I am your master, as requested."

I sense a flicker of will within the imp. It hovers in place and clearly states my name. The pressure within the demon's mind lessens after he complies with the order. I can't help but smile.

"Elruzon, *favin cepen.*"

The imp dissipates immediately, and I sigh in relief. I was that close to being discovered.

Lar becomes more irate as he interrogates the demons one by one. He' unable to find the spy in his midst.

"You are the last, De' Pari," he thunders.

"Lord," the demon begins its deep rumble, "I have not been ordered to convey any words from this hall. Indeed, none but you have the power to command me so."

"No one shared our plans?" Lar pounds the table. "The manwolves are just that lucky?" He looks around the room. No one is willing to look him in the eye.

"Lord," the demon says, "that door is warmer than the surrounding wall. Perhaps the human vermin are the guilty ones, after all."

Through the crack, I see the demon pointing in my direction.

"Really?" Lar says.

He motions his demon to stand between him and the door. He must fear an assassin's knife. The man rules by fear, and that makes him willing to believe any number of conspiracy theories.

That could prove helpful. One more reason why I need to escape from here.

Diardoc barks out an order for his guards to investigate. By the sound of it, he's going to join them in their march. Poor Diardoc, looking for any excuse to leave Lar's presence.

I run silently to the opposite kitchen door. Once there, I forgo stealth for speed. In their heavy armor, I should easily outdistance Diardoc and his guards.

I make my way through the servant's hallway, barely able to hear my feet slapping the stone floor over my ragged breathing. Finally, I make it back to our corridor and scramble into our prison room.

"Why don't you try to be louder next time?" Anach demands crossly.

"No time," I gasp. "Guards behind me. Close hole now," I say between pants. I race for my own cell and take care to close the door silently while Anach orders the elemental back into the wall.

"We're safe," he says in an attempt to calm me.

"No," I say. "Demons will see the excess heat from me after all that running."

I wipe away the sweat from my forehead. "If they come in here, we'll be discovered."

"Lie down on you bench," Anach says as he grabs his manacles. "And whatever you do, don't scream in panic."

What could he possibly be planning?

I do as I'm told and I watch in horror as Anach summons a whole pack of black rats. He points in my direction and the rodent horde scampers toward me.

"Act as if you're sick. I'll tell them that you were cold, so I summoned the rats to warm you. That will explain your sweat."

I quell the panic rising up within me. I squeeze my eyes shut and try to ignore the constant sniffing and squeals around me.

I can do this. I open my mouth, take in a deep breath and feel whiskers touching my tongue. Violently, I shake my head and roll over so I can wedge my nose in the corner.

The rats leap off of me. I turn to see them gathered around the stone ring. I hear stone scraping stone. Anach is having them reestablish the stone circle.

"They're in the guardroom now," Anach whispers.

Lar is screaming at the guards for sleeping while at their post. I have no love for the guards, but we're in an ancient giant's castle, surrounded by incredibly thick walls. It would be reasonable to assume that no threats are forthcoming.

"Anach," I say, swallowing hard. "Send the rats back to me."

I know better than most what a demon as powerful as Ni' Pari would do to me.

Anach closes his eyes, and I hear the patter of little paws scurrying toward me.

From the other side of the door, one of the guards rattles the keys on his keyring as he hurriedly tries to open the door.

"Perhaps my demon will encourage you to hurry," Lar says impatiently.

"No, Lord," the guard says. "That will not be necessary." His voice rises higher, and the keys rattle all the more.

I hear the click of Anach's manacles.

The door bursts open, and Big Nose runs into the room. The demon, Ni' Pari, stands in the doorway, glowing a malevolent red. Big Nose turns to the demon, and I can see the singe marks on the back of his uniform. It must have been pressed up against him as he fumbled with the keys.

The demon ignores Anach and points to me.

"She is unnaturally hot."

I wipe away the sweat from my brow. "It is so cold in here," I add as I pull my arms tighter around me.

"She is sick," Anach declares. "Release me and I will heal her."

Lar and Diardoc stand on the outside of the rock circle. Diardoc holds his nose. "And why are there rats all around her?" he asks.

"You leave us no blankets, so I summoned them to warm her," Anach says.

"But you're bound in iron!" Diardoc exclaims.

"The ability to speak with animals is a talent anyone can master," Anach says. "And with the incentive of bread placed strategically around her, the creatures could hardly resist."

"If she is cold, I will have my demon share its warmth."

"I feel much better," I blurt.

"Show us your imp," Diardoc says.

"I'm surrounded by a stone circle." I shake my head dismissively.

"Do as Diardoc says." Lar says.

"But the iron bars inhibit me as well."

Lar's face relaxes. "Ni' Pari, bring me the druid."

"No!" My eyes lock with Lar's. "I will try." I keep my eyes down and stumble to the cell door. I gulp down the extra-large lump in my throat as I stretch my arms through the iron bars.

"Lichiul srenc Elruzon."

Lar studies me, rather than my demon. The slightest smile crosses his face. "Elruzon is your name?" he asks.

The imp lands inside the circle of stones and bows to the Tusci master.

"I have not seen you before."

I try not to show my relief, but my shoulders drop noticeably.

"Tuthu mini fase, come to me," Lar interprets, for Diardoc's benefit.

Elruzon tries to slow its approach, but Lar is a powerful summoner. As the imp reaches the stone circle, it shrieks out in pain. Its body smolders and black smoke collects at the boundary.

"Cel, rasna fase," Lar says before directing the essence of my imp to his demon. "You have served me well, Ni' Pari."

I tremble silently as the demon inhales poor Elruzon's essence. Yes, the imp is always testing his limits with me, but he is my demon to command. Any plea from me though, will likely cause my imp to be destroyed.

"If I ever see you again, imp, I will feed you and your summoner to Ni' Pari."

"Favin cepen." Lar waves his left hand dismissively as he leaves.

Both Ni' Pari and the badly charred Elruzon turn to smoke as they return to the demon realm.

Chapter Seven

Separated

Aine's rays are once again shining through the window. So, it's been a month since they moved Anach to a new cell. I've nothing to do now but pace. But I can't pace for long, since I can't augment my measly rations. Rising from my bench is taxing enough.

The wooden key to unlock my cell door has gone to wherever Anach now resides. The stone circle was remade that fateful night, so a summoned Elruzon would be as much a prisoner as me. And of course, there's no Anach to open the wall up for us in any case.

After a month of using my charm on the guards, all I have to show for it is that now they make sure the bread makes it through the bars. Well, and they don't throw the water in my face anymore. They make the new, timid guard enter the circle and hand me the cup.

Dawn is not too far off, but Aine has put an end to my fitful sleep. What really galls me is that I can hear the snoring of the guards outside. For the first few nights, they remained awake, fearing another visit from Lar Crespe. But the old routine soon returned.

A high-pitched chirp from below makes me nearly jump out of my skin. A rat scurries several strides away before turning and chirping at me again. Down at my feet is a wooden key.

My shoulders melt as I bend down to get the present. Anach is safe, and the attention on him must have diminished as well.

"Thank you, little one." I feel foolish speaking to a rat, but I do anyway. I regret finishing my bread now; I have nothing to give this brave little rodent.

"I don't know if you understand, but tell Anach thank you, and to hold on, I'll be coming for him soon enough."

I grab the key and free myself from my iron cage. Once through the door, I feel taller somehow. Before I forget, I move one of the rocks bathed in shadow, breaking the circle. There's no Anach to create a hole in the wall, but I will still find a way to create mischief while I search for an escape.

"Lichiul srenc Elruzon."

The state of my imp takes my breath away. Typical of most demons, the overall size tells you how powerful the demon is. Elruzon is half-sized; about the size of a tawny owl. He hovers in front of me, listlessly.

"Lar Crespe hurt you, bad," I say. "You will need to feed tonight."

The imp dives for the brown rat and kills it before it can complete a squeal.

Stupid!

Mosech told me over and over that as soon as you think of a demon as a pet, or a friend, it will show you its true nature. Now Anach's trained rat is dead.

Will Anach even try to reach me again?

"Right, bigger problems." I quietly walk to the prison door. There is a flickering light coming from under it. I lay on the floor and listen to the rhythmic, untroubled breaths of my guards. I push on the door, but no luck. They may be sleeping, but they still lock the door.

Elruzon is hovering much too close to me. I can feel each hot, dry breath on my neck. This is not the same imp from before. He's hungrier and more calculating. And I'm weak and exhausted.

"*Favin cepen.*"

I sit up against the door. My prison has become a little larger, otherwise I've not improved my lot. The door has no give at all, no matter how hard I bang the back of my head against it. No one in the next room reacts to my constant thumping.

A strand of hair makes its way into my mouth. I spit my dull, dirt-coated hair out. Even the servants looked better than I do. If I could just get past this door, I could walk out the front gates looking like this and no one would look twice at me. But I can't get out of this room yet. I will not let one stupid door stop me.

Rolling down on my stomach, the cool floor feels nice, but that's not what I'm after. I slip my hands as far under the door as I can. My fingertips clear the barrier and stick out in the guardroom. That's all I need. Since part of me is past the door, I can summon Elruzon to appear in the room with the guards.

"*Lichiul srenc Elruzon.*"

The imp appears and I immediately force it to share its vision with me. It darts for the shadows up around the ceiling. He flies up above the guards, inspecting them and the rest of the room.

I try to get my bearings, but the imp is darting his head too quickly. Finally, it stops and dives at the exposed neck of one of the guards. The man only gets out a muffled yell before his body goes slack. Elruzon stares above his fresh kill, denying me any information. A couple of flecks of blood splatter on the white stone wall. I shudder. Elruzon is drinking the blood as fast as it spills out of the man.

"No, Elruzon!"

The imp ignores me while it gorges on the fresh feast. It's worrisome that the imp can put aside my commands. Mosech had said that this day would come, when it would test my control.

I can hear my instructor's voice now, "One, calm yourself. Two, gather your will. Then three, hold nothing back and command the imp to obey you."

Big Nose's scream is cut short. I look through Elruzon's eyes and see the large man fall, never to get up. Behind him is the timid guard's inert body. As guards go, I liked him.

"Elruzon, stop!" The imp ignores me.

If I don't regain control, it will go on a killing spree. I lie on the floor so my voice will carry. "Elruzon!"

The imp eyes me warily.

"*Favin cepen.*"

It responds with an amused grunt.

From this vantage point, I note the glowing red feet approaching the door. Black scorch marks are left in the demon's wake. I try to look through the demon's eyes, but it blocks me. The blood gorging has increased its size and power substantially. It pounds against the door, but to no avail.

He's coming for me.

Horrified, I listen as Elruzon returns to the guard's table. I hear keys jingle with every step as it returns to deal with me. The metal will burn the demon as long as there is contact. Elruzon has always been afraid of pain; not any longer, it seems.

On the other side, a step away, I hear a body fall against the door. The demon snorts and I feel something, a head most likely, thumping into the door.

A weak stream of blood oozes from the demon's victim, finding my hand. I pull it out from under the door just as Elruzon's claw swipes where my fingers had been. My heart races while the demon laughs from the other side of the door. The body is discarded off to the side, and the demon pounds on the door with its fists. I hear the jingle of keys again and the slow sizzle of demon flesh. The imp only grunts from the pain. The key is inserted into the lock.

Throwing off the yoke of its summoner is the first goal of every demon, and a terrified summoner is easy to defeat. Rising to my feet, I backpedal toward my cell. The door crashes open and I kick the stone circle with my left heal. I bolt for my cell and slam the door behind me.

Stupid! I watched the demon's antics instead of reassembling the circle.

Elruzon looks down at the stone I kicked. If it thought the circle had been intact, it now knows otherwise. It kicks several stones at me, but the bars keep any from getting through.

A deep, booming chuckle emanates from the hellspawn as it advances to the cell door. Cautiously, it touches the iron door before withdrawing its finger.

If I don't dispel him now, he'll kill me and the castle staff. Calmly, I face it.

"Elruzon, *favin cepen.*"

It laughs at me.

I gather my will and stare down my would-be predator.

It gives me a menacing smile.

"*Tuthu mini fase!*" I shout as I throw my arms back.

The order catches the demon off guard. It must have expected me to try to dispel it again. Unprepared, it lurches forward until it makes contact with the iron bars. Greasy black smoke boils off the demon, obscuring its body. I can sense Elruzon is unable to focus its will. The baritone howls of the demon hit my ears like physical shocks, but I don't lose focus.

I continue forcing my will upon the foul creature as the howls get higher and higher in pitch. At last, the tone is one I'm used to hearing. Elruzon has been diminished. Back to its imp size, the threat is over, for now.

"*Cel, rasna fase.*"

The demon's essence rushes toward me, giving me the sustenance I've been lacking. I glare at the feeble imp as I recall Mosech's words.

"Stealing demon essence can grant unbelievable power, but you also take on the demon's hate. If you attempt it, you must be able to control your impulses, lest you be as evil as the hellspawn itself."

"*Favin cepen.*" I wave the foul thing away.

Chapter Eight

Rescue

The guardroom is worse than anything I ever wished upon my captors. Poor Big Nose? Can I really feel that? My chief tormentor is nothing but a mangled body and a detached head. I give a gruesome chuckle, as his head is only partly face down, because of course, of his nose. There are scorch marks on the clothes of the guards as well as blackened spots on their arms and faces. Fluids, but not blood, are starting to leak out. There is so very little blood that the room still looks clean, considering what has happened.

I can't be here when the guards are replaced.

Elruzon's murders have unsettled me. Knowing I have to run, I stand frozen in place, looking at the carnage. I'll never make it out by myself. I'll most likely never make it out of here, regardless. Epona, please search elsewhere tonight for newly dead souls.

If escape is too much, at least I can still create havoc, and recalling Elruzon will cause the most disruption. My training tells me to never summon that hellspawn again, but I'll just have to be more vigilant. Besides, I know only one other true demon name, and I banished Izsak for a year.

Retreating to my cell, I sit on my bench and calm myself. I can't stay here, but I can't run aimlessly in the corridors either. Resummoning Elruzon as my scout is what the ingested demon essence is telling me to do. I will use that demon aggression, not the other way around.

The dried husk of a rat from hours ago sits outside my cell. I can't try to escape without Anach, and to find him, I must find Bondua. I toss the key to my cell on my bench. I won't see the inside of this cell ever again.

Now, where would a housemaid be at this hour of the night?

The corridor to the left of my prison door is where Bondua always emerged. Without a source of light, I'm forced to keep my left hand sliding along the wall.

If I remain still, I can hear bustling from a nearby room. I approach slowly. There's a telltale flicker of light from the door on my right. I lean forward until I can see inside.

It's Bondua, sweeping out the fireplace.

"Bondua," I say in a raised whisper.

Startled, she drops the fire iron and the clangs on the floors. The noise bounces off the stone walls and I'm horrified by the clamor. We look at each other, each afraid to add to the noise.

"What's all the racket in there?" A man calls from farther down the corridor.

I raise my finger to my mouth, urging her to be quiet. Footsteps bring the perturbed man closer.

I scurry into the room with Bondua. She picks up her fire iron and is ready to strike.

"Bondua, you have to help me get out of here." I walk toward her, and she raises the iron, arms trembling. I raise my hands in front of me. "I'm Glasna, the woman who was imprisoned with Anach."

"You there!" the man shouts from the doorway. "What are you doing skulking around the castle at this hour?"

My shoulders freeze up on me. I watch Bondua's inscrutable face for a clue about what comes next. One word from her and my escape will be over before it even began.

"She's the healer I sent for," the housemaid blurts out. "Master druid Anach is in urgent need of her skills."

"What's your name?" the guard asks.

Slowly, I turn to face him. "My name is Crisa," I lie. "And I don't have time to waste." Hopefully, he doesn't ask about my flaming red hair.

The guard looks over my shoulder at Bondua. Whatever was communicated relaxes the guard's posture.

"Follow me," he says.

"I'll come too," Bondua says.

"Bondua, how many of your girls are down with the grip?" the guard asks. "You stay and get the chores completed before the lords rise."

She grips the fire iron tightly. "It's just that I promised Anach that I would bring a healer to see him."

The guard motions for me to walk with him. "The passageway is unlit, so take my hand."

I have to nearly sprint to keep up with the guard. How Bondua manages to tag right behind us on her tired old legs, I'll never understand. We reach a thick oak door and the guard gropes for something off to the side. Just by the size of the door, I can tell that this is Anach's prison. Only the strongest doors for little women like me and old men like Anach. The guard strikes a couple of stones together and ignites an oil-soaked rag wrapped around a stick.

"One of these is left burning outside when the druid is being interrogated." He withdraws his hand quickly. "It's still warm to the touch."

The door opens, and poor Anach has his wrists bound in manacles which are hanging from the ceiling. There's no way for the man to sit, much less lie down.

I slap his cheek a few times. "Anach? Anach!"

His eyes flutter open.

"Glasna?" he asks.

"Glasna!?" the guard repeats.

Thwack!

Bondua's fire iron connects with the side of the guard's head. The man collapses to the floor. The housemaid drops the fire iron again! Unaware of the noise she's made, she tends to her victim.

"We have to get you out of here," I tell the old druid.

"Did we win?" he asks.

"What are you talking about?" I search the room for a thin piece of iron or wood. If nothing else, I've learned the fine art of picking locks during my time here.

"The assault. Has Oshid taken the city?"

"What assault?"

"Lar Crespe and his foul demon interrogated me about it. He thought I was behind all of it." His voice trails off and his body slumps again. I hear the chains above snap taut as the old druid tries in vain to lower himself.

I find the metal shard I need and go to work on the manacles. Off to my left, I hear Bondua's quiet sniffling.

"Is he dead, then?" I ask.

Under better circumstances, my voice would have carried the concern I feel, not the emotionless query that springs forth now.

Bondua's head sinks into her hands and her shoulders bounce spasmodically. I lower Anach to the floor and approach the guard. I feel for his life's blood in both his neck and arm, but there is nothing. I put one arm around Bondua's kneeling form and close the guard's eyes. I kiss his forehead and whisper the prayer of the dead.

> Epona, righteous goddess
> Escort this man to a tranquil place
> Until his rebirth.

"Bless him, goddess," Bondua says. Even with her eyes scrunched shut, tears find a way onto the man's uniform. She whimpers over the man.

So Epona's attention will be on the castle this night.

I pat her shoulder a few times, but I can spare no more time. The castle change-over will happen soon, and I'll have to deal with Anach's fragility. I grab the torch from the prone guard's hand and head back to the old druid.

Anach tries to walk, but his left leg can barely hold his weight. I pull back his robe and see that a large portion of his thigh is missing.

Anach slaps my hand. "When I wouldn't give up any information, the demon took a bite out of my leg," he growls.

I lift him up and put his left arm around my shoulder. The man weighs almost nothing. Still, the simple act of placing one foot in front of the other is a challenge for him. I'm half tempted to throw him over my shoulder, except that would be hard to explain to any guards we meet. I'll save that for our last desperate sprint if we make it that far.

"We're on the fourth floor," I tell the old druid. "Can you make it down the stairs?"

Anach coughs, and spittle flies into my face. "If I can't, what are you going to do? Carry me?"

He starts coughing again, but this time, he looks away.

"Let's move," I say.

He slaps my hand away. "I missed Beltane." He stares at me as if that should mean something. "Beltane!" He starts coughing again. "Ever . . ." he draws a jagged breath. "Ever since I can first remember, I celebrated Beltane." He grips my arms tightly as I start moving him out of the room.

"But I missed it . . . I missed it this year. I forgot when it was, but warring season doesn't start until after Beltane." With unfocused eyes, he stares down the hallway.

As much as I feel pity for the man, I can't stop and comfort him. He leans further and further onto my shoulder. I guide him down the corridor without issue; the man weighs almost nothing. I should have asked Bondua directions. But with the state she's in, I wonder if she'd even hear me.

CHAPTER NINE

Collapsing Plans

There's no sense going back toward the corpses of Big Nose and his timid partner. I try giving Anach the torch, but he's in a daze and can't hold it upright. He'll only catch his robes on fire if I leave it with him.

We find a large spiral staircase. Of course, this castle was built by giants, so it probably only looks grand to us humans, especially us short ones. Like the rest of the castle, it's unadorned gray stone. Both the inner and outer walls of the staircase twist around one another in perfect circles.

Anach is breathing heavily by the time we reach the third floor. His constant complaining tells me that he's out of his mind fog.

"You! What are you doing outside the sleeping chambers?" a man calls.

I turn my head to look down the hall at the are six guards, each outside a different doorway. This must be the royal wing. The leader motions for the nearest two guards to investigate.

"Hurry, Anach," I say in a low voice as I point him down the stairs. "Give me everything you have left." I take his arm off my shoulder and rest it against the wall. His legs are shaky, but I have my own problems.

I climb back up the handful of stairs.

"I'm sorry," I say, head down. "The old one is shaky on his feet."

"There's no one in this castle that frail," the first guard says. "Any servant so infirm would have been retired. Who is that man?"

Behind them, two more guards have halved the distance, waiting to see if they'll be needed. One of them looks to be the leader of the group.

The second guard looks at me. "I haven't seen you around here before either; and I like red hair." He gives me a lurid smile.

It's all I can do not to wretch right there. The guards behind them are all watching with interest. I don't like my odds, one against six, so I throw the torch at the nearest man and run down the stairs.

Anach has only made it down another five stairs before dropping to a seated position against the wall. I pick him up and throw him over my shoulder.

"I am the head druid," he says through rasping breaths. He even tries to feebly kick his legs a couple of times before his energy gives out.

"Spear at the ready," one of the guards says from the top of the stairs.

I turn to face the guards, but in my haste, Anach slips off my shoulder and slides down several stairs. I don't have the time to check on him, not with the city guards coming. I steady myself for what I must do.

"*Lichiul srenc Elruzon.*"

The imp appears, hatred spilling out of his mouth in the foul language of the demons.

"Kill all the men above us," I command.

It looks at me with predator's eyes. We both know that a challenge is coming, but it flies up the stairs more than willing to kill indiscriminately. I scramble down to Anach and throw him back over my shoulder. He grunts once, so I know he's alive.

I hear a scream of pain from the imp. It must have flown straight into the spearpoint.

"Demon!" one of the guards shouts.

We barely make it to the bottom of the stairs before I feel Elruzon's bloodlust ramp up. I stop and look through the demon's eyes. It's too busy fending off the second guard's spear to stop me. Through the red haze of the demon's vision, I see the second guard giving ground up the stairs as he abandons his downed comrade. I can hear the man's heart thumping louder and louder, faster and faster. The man's voice sounds more like a chirping bird to the demon's ear.

Elruzon fakes left, then rolls over the top of the man's spear and goes straight for the neck. Man and demon crumple to the gray stone steps. Within the span of a couple of heartbeats, the man's dead eyes stare aimlessly at the ceiling.

"Hold!" a guard calls from the top of the stairs. "We wait and all go down the stairs together, spears at the ready. None of us will be open to attack."

Through Elruzon's eyes, I see two men standing side by side, spears pointing at it. The imp flies over to its first victim and gorges on the dead man's blood. It looks up again to see four guards standing two by two. The demon kicks me out of its head.

Just as well, I don't have the luxury to stand here and wait for whichever bad outcome prevails. Anach starts to wiggle his way off my shoulder. The man's at death's door, yet his pride still takes precedence. I hear someone hit the floor other than Anach, followed by the jangling of a spear on stones.

"To me! To me!" a man yells to the remaining men.

There are panicked shouts from the men and a low rumbling of a proper demon's voice.

There's a clang of metal on stone, then a soft gurgling noise.

That makes four downed guards.

"Go, Anach! Don't wait for me," I say.

I try to look through my imp's eyes, but he blocks me. It gives a soft growl of pain before screaming in demontongue.

"Hold," one of the two remaining guards says. I can't wait any longer. I rush down the stairs, grabbing Anach by the shoulders as I go. All I've done is remind the demon that there is easy prey below it.

By the smell of it, we've reached the level with the latrines. There are two torches lit on either side of the stairs. I take one, though I know it will do no harm to Elruzon.

The demon lets out a low, throaty chortle as it makes the final turn. It is already as tall as I am, and it is relishing our showdown. It approaches slowly this time, ready for whatever trick I may throw at it. This is not the imp I knew; it is bigger, much stronger and on the hunt.

Anach has fallen onto a small table placed against the wall, and he makes no attempt to rise.

"Come then, you foul hellspawn!" My anger is rising at the unfairness of it all.

Knowing full well that the demon will go for Anach first so it can feast on an easy kill, I slowly backtrack between the demon and the druid.

Elruzon takes two great strides and smashes into an invisible barrier. It begins losing its essence as dense, acrid smoke fills the space between us. I look, disbelieving, at the staircase. Both the inner and outer walls are complete stone circles, even if they do span four floors of the castle.

"*Tuthu mini fase!*" I shout, pulling the demon toward the invisible barrier.

My strength is not what it was, though, and the demon is able to break free.

"Enjoy your cage." I wave at it.

The demon bellows its defiance.

That will wake everyone. Stupid of me to taunt it.

"*Cel, rasna fase.*" I direct the demon essence to Anach rather than myself.

"What have you done?" he demands.

Right, I forgot about the attitude adjustment that comes with the consuming of demon essence.

"We must find another stairway," I say.

Even with Elruzon's diminished state, I don't like my chances of facing it.

"I will run no longer," the old druid says. His raspy voice is gone and the arrogant man I despised so much at the beginning has returned.

"Anach, don't destroy the stairway. It's the only thing keeping the imp away from us."

The old druid walks toward the wall opposite the staircase. Placing his hand upon it, he chants quietly.

"This ends here." Anach says defiantly. He takes a step back and makes grand gestures with his arms while yelling in some foreign tongue. The whole castle shakes beneath us. The wall in front of Anach moves, and two massive arms push the elemental away from the castle proper. Anach is forced to jump back several steps to keep from falling with the floor that was beneath him.

As the elemental takes a step away from the castle, it tumbles into the water below us and water splashes up to our level and higher. The gaping openings in our floor as well as the levels above and below us expose a fair number of people to the brisk night air. Loose stones continue to fall from overhead. Through the gaping hole, I can clearly see Aine sinking into the trees in the west.

Anach approaches the opening and compels his gargantuan element to rise from the inky black pool.

I back up until I'm pressed against the wall. Without taking my eyes off the druid, I trace a large crack in the wall. My heart sinks when I discover the staircase has taken damage. I can hear my former imp grunt in displeasure from the floor above us.

It's only a matter of time before he discovers this outer circle of the staircase is broken at our level. If we don't flee now, we're dead.

Much of the floor has fallen since Anach's elemental pulled itself away from the castle. Anach is perilously close to the edge as debris falls down around him. He pays it no mind. Again and again, he has the three-story elemental bash the opening of the hole it made. Screams ring out in the night as people run around, confused and afraid.

"More! More!" Anach rages. The elemental itself is slowly disintegrating as it takes as much damage as it gives. The old druid goes down to one knee. Gasping for breath, he rests his right hand on the ground while holding his chest with his left. He shakes his head and sweat goes flying. From his knees, he raises both hands and in a raspy voice says, "Come to me."

The elemental stops its attack and leans toward us. Anach falls forward and his momentum carries him over the edge. I pick my way as best I can to Anach's perch, but I'm too late. The elemental begins to creak as it transforms back into lifeless stone. It tilts toward the gaping hole it created and breaks in half. I sprint back toward the center of the floor. A wave of dust overtakes me and I'm forced to breathe through my sleeve. Falling to my knees, I wait, eyes closed, as my fate is determined.

Chapter Ten

Escape

The entire castle shakes, releasing more stones and debris both inside and out. A fine powder falls from the ceiling. I've more than enough experience to know what that means. I dive for the only cover I can find: a thick wooden table just before the heavy stones above come crashing down. The cacophonous noise gives way to silence, as if everyone if everyone is holding their collective breath, waiting for the next disaster.

When the dust filled air thins, allowing me to see shapes, I crawl out of the newly formed tunnel. All around me, cracks run up the walls. The spiral staircase has been demolished; hopefully burying the demon.

I hold my breath and listen carefully for any movement. I stand and shake off as much dust as I can. It's silly, really. Never have I heard of someone worrying about their fashion sense while fleeing for their life.

I wonder if the royal rooms are still above or if they came crashing down as well. Diardoc could well be dead in the surrounding rubble. I get on top of the toppled floor from the level above and leap and peer outside into the night.

On the opposite shore, several torches have appeared from the forest canopy. The slope of the rubble pile that was once an elemental, is pretty steep, but it's the only exit I have. It looks as if I'll have to try Anach's plan of sliding down the wall. Poor Anach, buried under his own creation.

A turtur dove flies up, lands at my feet, and begins its gently purring. I'm no druid, but birds in general don't fly at night. The air goes hazy before an old woman appears where the bird had been.

She pulls her hood tighter around her face. "I've been wondering when you and Anach would make your escape."

"Who... who are you?"

"That doesn't matter now. Ask again once we're away from here." She surveys the shattered wall, and the collapsed floors as if they are common place. "Where's that fool, Anach?"

"Who are you?" I ask again.

"Would you like to stand out here in the open while I give a full accounting of myself?" she asks acerbically.

From the shadows behind us, rubble is being pushed upward as something tries to free itself.

"Elruzon?"

A deep bass laugh responds to my call.

"We have to go!" I grab the woman's hand and look for the least likely spot to give way in the rubble beneath us.

"Did you call forth that demon?" The stranger jerks her hand from mine. "It's bad form to leave it for someone else to banish."

"It's too powerful. I can't control it any longer."

Elruzon tosses off the last of the stones and walks into the open space, its gaping mouth open wider that any human could. It creates flames over its entire body, removing the soot. Now a head taller than me, it thrusts out its chest and eyes me hungrily.

"Silly girl, you shouldn't play with things you don't understand." She raises her hand. "Elruzon, hold."

"You must use the demontongue to control the hellspawn," I say, amazed.

The woman cuts her eyes sidelong at me. "So much knowledge has been lost."

Elruzon growls in frustration.

"Hintha lautn a sa Elruzon," the woman says as she waves her hand.

A fiery explosion of tiny black pebbles erupts from where Elruzon used to be. When they find my robe, they burn through, singeing my skin.

"What did you do?" I ask the woman.

"I unmade the demon." She pats at the new holes in my robes. "That's brimstone and it will cause a terrible burn if you're not careful."

Several arrows rain down upon us. I move back, away from the ledge.

The old woman gives me an amused look. "Yes, that is problematic." She nods her head once and looks down at the dark pool below us. She raises her arms and mutters words in a strange tongue.

Fog rises from the pool, and it's not long before it rises to the height of the castle.

"That should stop the archers from making a nuisance of themselves." She stretches out her hand to me. "They can't see us, but that doesn't mean they won't get a lucky shot. Come with me and be quiet."

"It's a good thing that tonight is a cool night," I say.

The woman gives me an amused look and stretches out her hand. Together, we gingerly tap on the stones before transferring our weight to them. My nerves are in tatters by the time we reach the bottom. The legs of the great elemental stick out of the pool of water. The torches are still on the opposite shore, and manwolf voices accompany them.

Torn between a swim to safety and following my unexpected guide, I decide to follow this strange, powerful woman. She's bends down at the top half of Anach's body; the rest has been crushed beneath his greatest summons.

"You grumpy old fool," the woman says tenderly as she caresses his cheek. "You redeemed yourself, after all."

"Did he?" I ask. "He was trying to bring the whole castle crashing down upon itself."

"Of course he was," she says quickly. "Had he succeeded, we'd be rid of Diardoc and the demon summoners."

"And countless innocents whose only crimes are working within the castle."

"Cowering people make would-be tyrants like Diardoc possible. You fight, or you flee. Any other choice only strengthens the despot."

There are voices calling out to the injured from the first level. The old woman puts her finger to her lips before jumping into the fog. She makes a small splash in the marsh grasses below. I follow her and land on a rock, rolling my right ankle and tumbling to the ground. I let out a surprised yelp of pain.

"There's more outside the wall!" a man shouts above us. "Call to us," he orders.

The old woman gives me a harsh look and signals for me to follow her. She picks her way through the submerged chunks of city wall as if she's known the path her entire life. I scurry to catch up and notice that she's walking with her eyes firmly closed. We ford the dark pool where it meets the River Poddle. Looking back, I can just make out the gaping hole in the castle wall.

"Who are you?" I ask the old woman.

"I have had many names over the years, but in this time and place, people call me Mistress Red."

"I've heard of you." She was the healer of Grahme and Osion. "You are more than just a healer."

She winks at me. "The fog is letting up. It would be best if no one knows that I was here."

From the forest, several men run toward us.

She retakes the form of a turtur dove and flies to the branches above.

From the forest, a pack of manwolves breaks their cover.

"Odmard!" I whisper urgently. I jump into his arms. Never did I expect to see his beautiful, scarred face again.

"Glasna?" he asks, dumbfounded. "How did you get out?"

From above, a turtur dove lets out a rumbling call.

"I don't know if I'm able to explain it." Overwhelmed, I laugh, a loud and uncontrolled laugh.

Odmard looks on with concern. An arrow splashes into the river, and the manwolves escort me deeper into cover.

I'm free!

EPILOGUE

Odmard insists I spend my first night of newly found freedom in the healer's tent. It's not bad, I guess, but I have too many questions to just lie here. Did Frewyn and the children make it back safely? Is Crisa back? Is Oshid really leading a rebellion? What of the other kings? Surely they will march on Drumanagh now.

I try to rise, but find that my arms are bound to the sides of the bed. Yanking my arms does no good, other than to have the cot lurch from side to side.

"Easy girl," an old lady says as she enters the tent. Her hood hangs down low, obscuring her face. "We can't have you land face-down on the ground again today."

The old healer removes her hood. Mistress Red stands before me.

"What are you doing here? Didn't you just tell me that you wish to not be seen?"

"No one looks at healers, especially old crones."

She sets a small cup on the table next to my bed. She searches her pockets of her robe and finds a small, wax-sealed vial. She holds it near the fire until the wax melts away.

"This will give you a deep, restorative sleep. You'll feel good as new in the morning."

I eye her suspiciously. I desperately want what she's offering, but nothing so good comes for free.

"It's a shame you're the only one to inherit brains from your mother." She unties the cord holding my right arm. "I will answer your unspoken question. In exchange for this, you must agree to sing Anach's praises as the hero who freed you from captivity."

My disbelief causes my face to contort in strange ways. I stare at her, waiting for more explanation.

"If you want the other kingdoms to join your insignificant revolt, you will need a heroic figure for everyone to rally around. Personally, I prefer dead heroes. You don't have to worry about the stupid things they'll say or do. You can prescribe whatever persona you need upon them, and they can't get an over-inflated sense of worth."

"But he was such an overbearing, self-righteous demagogue."

"That he was, but if it makes you feel any better, his spirit—wherever it resides—will be howling mad at what we will do to the memory of him."

"It's better than he deserves," I say in a flat voice. "He was nothing but a bitter old man." I'm too tired for anger to spill out of me.

"That's how you'll remember him, no doubt, but those of us who knew him when he was younger can tell a different tale." She grunts as she reaches across me to untie my left arm. "But there are few enough of us left, I suppose."

I sit up on the cot and massage my arms.

She grabs the small cup. "Do we have a deal?"

Just the act of sitting up has sapped my energy. "I am a royal princess. I will do what needs to be done for the good of the kingdom."

"Good."

I raise the cup to my lips. "But first, tell me of Crisa."

"She returned just before Beltane," Mistress Red says slowly, "with friends."

"Where is she?"

"A very good question. I believe she is off in the Mantan mountains to the south." She points at the cup in my hand.

"One more question," I say hurriedly. "What is the day?"

"It is five days until midsummer." She places her hand underneath my cup and gently raises it up. I know that look. I won't be getting anymore answers tonight. I down the concoction in one gulp, and the warming liquid coats my throat. I feel like I'm six once again and buried beneath several thick, warm blankets.

Why is Crisa in the mountains?

Book Two

Crisa

Kathno Briga

CHAPTER ONE

The Resistance Begins

At the very edge of Allcashel, the steep cliffs plummet down into the sea. The wind buffets the waves up against the rocks, and the spray quickly drenches me. There's not a tree or even a bush in sight to break the wind. Only a desperate fool would be out here at dusk.

Since Anach stripped me of being a druid lord and named me an outlaw, my resources have been greatly diminished. Of all my fellow druid lords, I've only met with Oshid since my banishment. In the intervening months, I've managed to teach him to animorph, making the two of us the only druids on Eriu who can. Now the time has come to ask for a favor. He's always been the most timid of the council, so his cooperation is far from guaranteed.

"Of all places for this meeting!" Oshid yells over the wind.

"I didn't want us to be overheard," I say, smiling back at him.

His mantle catches in the wind and snaps with each gust. He tries to catch it and pull it tight, but the wind is relentless. "If you could say your piece before I freeze, it would be appreciated."

"You know that Anach has been seized by Diardoc and Gorann is now set to rule the council?"

"Of course. I am still a druid lord."

I frown at his dig. Removing me from the council was as unorthodox as it was unjust. If Oshid won't help me now, then all hope of returning to the order is lost.

"What are the other kings, and for that matter, the druids, doing about it?" I ask.

"What can we do? Caohin won't leave Invernis for any reason. And that means that Rhalthan can't afford to leave our lands unguarded. No one is going to allow the northern kingdoms to march through their lands with an army, so we sit and do nothing. You could say we're frozen in place." He turns his back to the wind, and his mantle blows over his head.

I pull his mantle back down. I've gone from freezing to completely numb. We stand with our backs to the sea. It was a mistake to meet here. Oshid loves his comfort and it won't be long before he leaves me and this cruel wind.

"Could you lead a small force and disrupt the northern trade roads?"

He smiles at me. "You've been hiding out in Ossory, haven't you?"

I cast my eyes downward. "You know I can't answer that question."

"So, you'll block the southern routes?"

"Yes."

"Even if we block the land routes, Drumanagh has the largest trading fleet of anyone."

"If we can start blocking trade, maybe the other kingdoms will join us and we can overthrow Diardoc and Gorann."

"I will do as you ask, if only to stick a thumb in Gorann's eye. But even if all you say comes to pass, there is still Drumanagh and its impenetrable city walls."

"They said that Laleah was impenetrable as well."

"We are not willing to butcher an entire city, like your half-brother did." Before I can respond, Oshid begins to turn hazy. He's trying to animorph, but he's painfully slow. His essence shrinks and reforms as a lesser auk. Without bidding me goodbye, he flies away.

"Not a bad choice, considering the weather."

Oshid's aid is less enthusiastic than I had hoped. And he's right, even if we cut off the land routes, they still have the sea. None of the kings would be willing to wait out a siege, even if we could close down Drumanagh's docks. No, we must do the impossible and surmount the city walls.

I follow Oshid's lead and change into the black and white sea bird. I flee the bitter wind and circle the nearest copse of trees, in hopes that Oshid retreated here to get out of the wind. I thought that teaching him how to animorph would earn me more sympathy, but that was clearly wrong.

The trees lessen the wind, but it's still miserable. I change into an owl and fly inland, away from the brutal wind. Perhaps my next move will occur to me during flight.

*　　*　　*

Do I go back to the manwolves? Odmard and Reyny have been nothing but kind to Glasna and me, but I can't go back with nothing. It's not the best idea, but I'm off to Drumanagh. If I can't find a way to get inside, all is lost.

The wind remains at my back as I fly toward the dreaded city. There is a small homestead below me which is putting out quite a bit of smoke. I circle around and land at a small gap between the thatched roof and the wattle and daub wall. I ruffle my feathers once to dislodge the cold, wet mist, and the couple within both notice and leave me be. The three of us settle down for a warm, dry night.

I'm up before dawn and crossing the breadth of Eriu as a swift. I settle in a tree on the opposite shore from the massively walled city. The city walls extend into the depths of the River Poddle, and they tower up over the landscape. Even from my perch, I must look up to see the guards patrolling the wall. Such heavy, high walls are unbreachable on Eriu.

Father told me of a time when his grandparents' city was taken by subterfuge. A company of dwarven miners had delved deep into the earth and dug a tunnel below the city walls. They could never invade with such a small opening, but they could open the tunnel to a nearby river and flood the city. I never knew the name of the city. He promised to tell me the rest when he returned, but I never saw him again.

If only I had a cohort of dwarves to command. That's foolish talk. Dwarves are famous for their full beards, love of drink and an absolute terror of the open seas. Even if I could conjure up dwarves on these shores, their price would be beyond anything I could provide.

Still, Oshid's support is lackluster at best. If he actually undertakes the raids, it won't take much to dissuade him from continuing. Such is my curse; of the druid lords, only timid Oshid would meet with me, but for that very reason, his commitment cannot be relied upon.

What did I accomplish?

Any resistance has to start somewhere. Even if I had the full-throated support of the remaining druid lords and the kings, it would still amount to nothing. Unless the walls are overcome, the situation is hopeless.

Telling Reyny there is no path forward will surely break my heart, but I see nothing to give even a glimmer of hope. At least I can arrive as a peewit; it's her favorite bird. It's not much, but maybe it will soften the blow.

*   *   *

I give the customary *pee wit, pee wit* call outside the cave's mouth. It's our way of speaking without Frewyn finding out and eavesdropping. Frewyn's a kindhearted woman, but she frets about even the smallest details in that loud, piercing voice of hers.

The other women of the fianna know the call's meaning, and it's not long before Reyny appears. She extends her right arm and I take up my new perch. She strokes my feathers from head to tail and I cock my head at her. This is new.

"I dread being the bearer of this news," she says. "Perhaps you should take your human form."

I hop off her arm and animorph into my human form.

"What is it?" I get out in barely a whisper.

"While you were gone," Reyny begins, tears already forming in her eyes. "Diardoc's men attacked Frewyn, Glasna, and the children as they were harvesting cleavers. Frewyn's account is garbled, since she can't decide if she fought the guards all by herself or if she fled with the children."

We share a quick chuckle. That's just like Frewyn; she's the only one to ever take action, the way she tells it.

"Glasna was captured," Reyny continues, her voice catching. She looks at me with tear-filled eyes. "According to Anulf, Glasna conjured a demon to harry the guards while Frewyn and the children escaped. For all her bravado, Frewyn refused to go back to the place. Mala, Hydie and I had to look for clues. There were signs of a struggle, but no blood, or . . . or worse."

I grab the fianna's beta and pull her into a fierce hug. "I feel sorry for Glasna's jailors."

Reyny lets out a surprised laugh before hugging me back just as tight.

"Diardoc will not let any harm come to her. She's a princess after all," Reyny says. We separate and Reyny dries her eyes.

"I'm afraid there is more bad news," I say. "Oshid has promised to block the northern trade routes, but he wouldn't say for how long. If Drumanagh's port remains open, then blocking the land routes is an annoyance at best."

Reyny exhales slowly, digesting the news.

"I flew to Drumanagh after my meeting. There is no way to scale or topple those walls."

We look at one another, neither wanting to state the obvious—that we've lost before we've even begun.

"If only I could bring back the dwarves from father's stories. They could bring the walls down."

"Do you mean that?" Reyny asks.

"What?"

"That you could bring the dwarves back here and topple Drumanagh's walls."

"They were just stories father told me between his voyages. I always wanted to meet a dwarf, since I would have been taller than a *real* adult, but that's the only reason I still remember the stories."

"But they could bring the walls down?"

"I don't know. Maybe. They were just stories to amuse a little girl who liked to fight the boys. He left on a trading vessel and didn't come back with the crew. Mother and I left Hiberia shortly after that. I saw my first and only dwarf as the ship left Kathno Briga's harbor."

"Then you know where to find them. You need to get them and bring them back here." She holds up her hand to stop me from interjecting. "Because if we can't bring down Diardoc, we will have to give up this home and move further west. We're between the hammer of the Invern and the anvil of the Laigins."

"But they're just child's tales."

"Then you're not even willing to try?"

"Reyny," I say, annoyed, "you know me better than that. I would try anything, anything that had a hope of succeeding."

"Your dwarves are the only hope we have left. Mortas and his men were our best fighters, and they were slaughtered at Laleah. The Wyot and Gotfrith clans have been decimated by disease and years of fighting the Inverns. We are the last fully intact fianna, and if Diardoc has his way . . .."

"This whole idea is madness," I say, shaking my head.

"What else do we have?" Reyny asks.

"If madness is what is needed, I will try."

Chapter Two

Feeling Salty

I never liked harbor towns. I thought it was because of my dislike of Diardoc and Gorann, but coming back here, smelling the salty water and rotting fish, it brings my memories back. This is where father abandoned us.

Mother asked a handful of the crew from the *Leaping Dolphin*, and everyone agreed father didn't perish, but none could tell us what happened to him. It was only much later that I realized he must have moved to a new port and a new family. Mother and I weren't good enough for him.

How fitting that decay reminds me of father. No, he doesn't deserve that title. It reminds me of Tesair, the betrayer of his family. I embrace my anger; it will help me focus.

A squat, auburn-haired man nearly knocks me into the water and grunts his displeasure with me standing here. I see a steady line of sailors leaving a beat-up ship. There are scorch marks along the ship's sides, and most of the sailors bear a fresh scar.

Raiders. Why did I land here?

I follow the disembarking sailors and their hard-won prizes into a warehouse. A small, officious man is there with ink and parchment, scribbling his little symbols down as fast as he can.

"What ship are you from?" he asks, holding out his arm to stop my progress through the dingy building.

"I came on no ship."

"You just flew in, did you? On the easterly breeze?" Sarcasm is dripping from his every word.

"Exactly." I show him my white druid robes.

"A ratty dress like that is not going to bring paying customers, unless the men are drunk and desperate."

Bringing myself up to my full height, I slap the man. "I am a druid lord, and if you mistake me for a sailor's toy again, I'll drop you into the harbor."

He grabs my arm. "You need to learn some manners."

I look down at the man's hand, then back at his eyes. He holds firm, daring me to try something.

If he insists. I change into a cave bear. We're at eye level, with him sitting and me on all four legs. He quickly snatches his arm away from me. I rear up, placing my front paws on his desk, and it creaks under my weight. His eyes . . . they're as big as my palms as he stares at me, petrified. I headbutt his chest and send him sprawling. Before he can gather himself, I bite down on his smock and pull him to me. Bodily, I drag him as he kicks and screams.

The dockworkers stay well clear of us despite his cries for help. Once his top half is suspended above the water, he decides to address me.

"No! No! I can't swim!" he shouts. I raise my head, forcing him into a sitting position. He surveys the smiling sailors on the dock and his anger returns. He babbles something about me letting go of him. So I do. He continues to shout all the way to the cold water below.

I animorph back and dust off my hands as I look down at him. He lied. He can swim. I give him a smug smile and a wave as he makes for a piling. The docks are silent, and everyone is staring at me. It's enough to make a girl self-conscious.

"You need to get off the docks," a short, bald man says.

A chain mail circlet looks as if it would slide down to his neck if not for his protruding eyebrows. It's all I can do not to gawk.

"I'm going." I finally manage to say. "I just couldn't have such disrespect go unanswered."

"Colla is a jerk, sure, but everyone here would sell their best friend if it meant being in his favor. How long do you think it will take these salty fools to decide to tie you up?"

"Oh," is all I can manage. I look around at the men as they slowly form groups of four to six.

"Follow me." He turns quickly and puts distance between us.

I give one last look at the sailors before turning into a seagull and flying after my new, strange friend. Despite his short legs, he reaches the sea keep faster than I could if I weren't flying. He looks worried as he searches for me.

I retake my human form several steps in front of him. His very blue eyes stare at me, confused.

"Gobannus' hammer!" He yells. "Why did that little thief send me for you? I'd rather kiss a dyowl kaballo than step foot on the docks."

His accent is much thicker than I'm used to hearing. "I'm sorry, young sir, I don't understand. You want to kiss a demon horse?"

"Young sir?" He raises to his full height, which only comes to my chin and he pokes me in the chest. "I'm a dwarf! And a woman twice your age besides!"

"You're a dwarf?"

"I'll tie you up and take you back to Colla myself if you don't start to listen."

"No, I heard you, it's just, I always wanted to meet a dwarf, you know, face to face."

"I'm going to hurt Sornei," the dwarf says, shaking her shiny head. "This has to be a prank of his."

"I'm sorry we got off on the wrong foot—"

"Say one thing about my feet," she says with venom in her voice.

I bow my head. "Forgive me, I mean no offense."

"Are you sure? 'Cause you're doing a great job at it."

"Perhaps we should find Sornei," I suggest.

"No, I have done as my goddess commanded."

A teenage boy with hazelwood colored skin exits the keep's gate. "It's alright Lapis, she's no threat."

"She may not be a threat, but I will be if you pull another prank like this."

"It's no prank," he squeals. "I swear by Ilurbeda Doomgiver." He reaches out to take my hands.

"You should not invoke the goddess' name in front of non-believers," Lapis says.

"Then how will the Doomgiver ever gain more followers if her name can only be spoken to those who know of her?"

The dwarf swipes her hand in the air, dismissing his obvious question.

Sornei takes my hands and his eyes roll up in his head. His body goes limp, and it's all I can do to lower him slowly to the ground. I look at Lapis, but she only shakes her head in annoyance.

"The little fool. He has to learn that he can't go helping everyone he meets."

"Is there anything that needs to be done for him?" I ask.

"No, he has received a vision from our goddess. It knocks him low, but he'll recover."

"Is it typical for dwarves to shave their heads?"

"No." She draws her knife and points it at me.

The child tugs at my hand. I bend down and he whispers in my ear.

"Look for Feldspar, and you can save one another."

I furrow my brow. What does that even mean? I try to pull away but he shakes his head no and pulls me closer.

"Your father didn't abandon you."

I snatch my hands away from him.

How dare he?

I scowl at the odd pair before leaving them. I have urgent business in the city.

Chapter Three

Wound Up Tight

Leaving the keep, the streets become darker and more congested. There are occasional fights between drunks and thieving child pickpockets who continually bump into me, but these are not what give me pause. The mix of hurried glances and long stares feeds my unease.

Another child runs into me and I grab her dirt-stained arm and yank upward.

"You're hurting me!" she screams.

"That's enough of that," I say as I give her arm a shake.

She gives me her best innocent face, but I'm not buying it. She looks around the street, and I realize everyone is waiting to see what I do next. Nervously, I lick my lips.

"You can tell your little friends that I'm an Eriu druid, so I don't carry any coin. No metal at all, in fact."

Child or not, she looks up at me with a calculating eye. If I let her speak, I don't know where it will lead.

"So, if you point me to a reputable tavern, we'll call it even."

"The *Culebre's Hoard* is straight down this street," she says.

I release her and she runs several steps away before showing me my former pouch. I check my left hip and my thousandleaf stores have departed. It's easy to harvest and of little to no value. I nod my head at her before she vanishes down an alley. The banter picks up again and everyone goes about their business. I guess I passed my first test.

I take a greater interest in my surroundings, including the group of men to my left who are staring at me. I give them a 'Is that all you got?' look as I pass. One of them calls after me, wanting me to please him.

"Come close, and I'll put you to sleep for the night," I say while shaking my staff.

The other men laugh and push him forward.

"You can walk away without a knot on your head," I tell him.

I know how to fight, but when there's six men and only me, I don't like the odds. I put on my confident face. Weakness will only encourage them.

"Now, you just come over here and I promise to be gentle with you." His friends laugh at his attempt at sweet-talk.

"You want me to come running to you and plant a kiss on your lips?" I ask playfully.

"Now you have the idea," he grins like the drunken fool he is.

I flash a nervous smile. It's a risk, but what is life if not a series of trials?

"Then catch me, big boy." I take one step before turning into a wolf and leaping at the man's face. His eyes and mouth both go wide in fear. My nose smashes into his and we tumble to the ground. He screams and tries to run back to his friends, but his foot slips in the dirt and he lands on his stomach. I growl once before animorphing back into myself. His friends have to catch him and slow him down.

"You have to buy me a drink before your tongue gets involved!" I call after him. His friends erupt in laughter.

Keeping my face impassive, I pretend my heart isn't pounding. If his friends had decided to join in . . ..

The man is getting jostled by his friends. He throws a couple elbows as his friends try to calm him down. He stares directly at me and points. He's leading his friends now and picking up the pace.

Why did I stay here gawking?

I can't animorph on a whim, like Grahme; I need time to settle my mind and I'm unlikely to get it here. I bolt through the nearest door to a potter's workshop. I don't try to explain, I just run past the couple toward the back. The ruffians have begun their hunt.

In the back, by the ovens, I see a small girl fanning freshly fired crockery.

"I need an exit," I whisper.

The girl points to a half-sized door to the left of the ovens. Pots crash heavily on the ground behind me, and the girl goes wide-eyed.

"Hide, little one."

She scampers between the two kilns. It's too small of a space for even me to fit through. I head for the half-door. One of the men sees me leaving out the back. There's no latch for me to secure on this side.

I look down the strangely long room and notice men laying down bundles of atocha grass. I'll never forget that smell, even though I've not experienced it since mother and I left here. Everyone agrees that Kathno Briga rope is the finest in the world.

There are teams laying down the long grass in consistent piles in two very long rows. The first lays the bundles down, the second flips half of the grass the opposite way and the third staggers the bundles so there isn't a sudden stop.

The first man struggles to get through the half door. How I wish I could linger, but I would only endanger more people. He bursts the door open with his shoulder and lands on his face. Another drunken fool is right behind him.

I take a breath to settle myself, and change into a swift. I dart back and forth above the first man's head. The second one grunts as his gut gets stuck in the narrow door. At the end of the hall, three men walk with purpose in my direction. I don't care to explain myself, so I take off in the opposite direction and squeeze through a crack between the wall and roof.

On the other side is a tight alley leading out to the main street. A number of black rats busy themselves scurrying in the shadows. No one in this part of town has seen me transform, and I'd rather not identify myself as the druid woman in the wild tales that will no doubt be told, so I leap from the ledge and retake my human shape. It's less than a shoulder length wide, forcing me to slide sideways between the walls. At my insistence, the vermin stay away from me as I squeeze through.

I return into sunlight at the end of the alley. I'm back on the main street, but in a nicer section. On my right there are smooth stone benches on either side of a thick, oaken door. I hear a group of men belting out a ditty. If ever you're in doubt, go toward singing men and you will find a pub.

As I pass the first bench, I glance at it and see my reflection in the polished stone. I'm both amazed and appalled—my forehead is filled with wrinkle lines, and my eyes look as if they're falling into my head.

No wonder the dockmaster mistook my profession.

My stomach flutters a bit, which is foolish, since this is why I came all this way. Perhaps if I thought I had a chance of succeeding instead of being laughed out of the hall, I'd be more confident. I close my eyes and enter the hall.

Chapter Four

Striking the Right Chord

The oaken door glides open easily into a room filled with music and laughter. The tavern is filled will low tables and chairs. Each chair has an animal's likeness carved into the seat back, and the appropriate feet or talons resting on the floor. Above are wide wooden circles with some sort of magical light emanating from glass jars. Behind the bar is a carving of a proud dwarf standing atop the body of a dragon. This tavern exists in the middle of this city?

The ceiling is low enough for me to touch with my hand. The thick wooden beams support immaculate stonework, and the sturdy tables are laughably low. Looking around the room, I am the only human. Furry-faced dwarves sit at several tables, listening to the performers next to the central fireplace. The three musicians are armed with flutes and a lyre as well as a harp standing unused behind them.

I make my way to the entertainment and motion for permission to play the harp. The oldest one, a male, I think, nods his head. Lowering myself onto a stool lower than my knees, it takes me a moment to get settled. The test strum of the strings delivers a rich, sonorous melody. The old one on the lyre nods once and barks out a couple of words in dwarvish.

The tune changes, becoming slower and more melancholy. Gently at first, I join the musical conversation, following the lyrist's lead. I nearly fall off my stool when every man and woman belt out the words of some old dwarvish dirge. I stay true to the melody and let the others lead. The echoes from the bare stone walls provide a haunting harmony. At last, the voices grow quieter and the lament ends with a few mournful notes from the flutes.

I wipe the tears from my eyes for this unknown person. To a dwarf, they all stand and face me with boisterous cheers.

"You did Gulden's Demise proper justice. You are welcome here anytime," the lyrist says as he grabs my right hand.

"It was so beautiful and sorrowful at the same time," I reply

The old dwarf smiles contently. "Barkeep! A tankard of mead for this fair lass!"

"Thank you, kind sir," I take a chance that I guessed his gender correctly. "But I came here looking for Feldspar. Do you know where I can find him?"

"Feldspar the dwarf?" The man chuckles once. "Of all the dwarves here, his life most closely resembles Gulden's Demise, I'm afraid." He stands on his knee-high stool to look over the crowd. "He's there, the red-headed one in the corner caressing his beer like he's trying to keep it from wandering off."

I make my way to the downtrodden dwarf with a bit of difficulty. It seems everyone wants to shake my hand and thank me for the performance. When I reach his table, he looks up with unfocused eyes.

"May I sit?"

He frowns and gestures toward the unused chair.

"I am Crisa, a druid lord from Eriu, and a seer told me to seek you out."

"So now they're sending humans to laugh at my plight," he says, slurring his words.

This won't do. I did not come all this way to hear a drunk whine about his life. The fate of people I love depends on me.

"I'll be back." He doesn't even look up when I turn and make my way to the barkeep. My face must radiate trouble, for no one steps in my way.

"Barkeep, can you get me a cup of boiling water?"

Whatever he was about to say dies on his lips. "I'll bring it to you as soon as it's ready."

"Thank you." I wink and smile at him before returning to the drunken sot.

The piping hot mug arrives and I drop the milk thistle and water mint I've been crushing into the cup. Feldspar's knife is lying on the table, so I use it to stir.

"Drink this." I slide the cup over to him and remove his beer. He gives me a confused look, but I've worked with difficult patients before. I stare him down until he mutely drinks from the mug.

He smacks his lips a couple of times after the first sip. Then he downs the remaining mix, crushed leaves and all. He looks at me in astonishment.

"What did you put in that?" he asks, noticeably more sober.

"I can't give away my secrets to just any stranger."

"It seems you know who I am, whereas I do not know you. That makes you the stranger."

"My name is Crisa, and a seer told me to seek you out so that we can help each other."

It's not entirely true, but he looks so depressed that I have to believe almost anything will make it better.

"Come on, Feldspar, you stay here much longer and you'll fall off the bridge going home," a kind voice says from behind me.

"I'm fine, Tephra," he says as he waves the dwarf away. "I'll be the first on the cliffs tomorrow, waiting on you as always."

Tephra, the brown-bearded dwarf, looks at me questioning. "He's had fourteen beers tonight. What did you give him?" He can't decide if he should be amazed or suspicious.

"I'm a druid lord from Eriu. Herb craft is one of my specialties."

"You're a long way from home then." He turns to the barkeep. "Wacke! Come over here."

The barkeep sets down the mug he's been cleaning and trudges over to us. Feldspar watches his friend with a big smile.

"Look at Feldspar!" Tephra says. "He's not even drunk."

"I didn't know you were so gifted," Wacke says, slapping the dwarf on the back.

"He's not," Tephra adds. "It was the drink this lass gave him that brought him back from his semi-conscious state."

All three dwarves turn to me.

"I suppose I should mention now that druids of Eriu refuse to use metal, so I have no coin." Before they can react, I'm ready with my proposal. "But if you're willing to give me free drink in this establishment, I'll tell you what very common ingredients I put into that mug of hot water."

"Done!" Wacke says.

"So, what are these magical ingredients?" Tephra asks.

"No." I wag my finger at him. "I owe Wacke, so he's the only one I'll tell. If he wants to share—"

Both Tephra and Feldspar scoff at that.

"Just come over here to the bar and show me exactly what you did," Wacke says.

Feldspar waits for me at the door. He opens it, and I'm accosted by the smell of salt air and rotting sea life.

"You've done me a kind service tonight." He looks me up and down. "I'm willing to bet that you haven't found anywhere to stay for the night."

"I have not," I confirm.

"Then come with me and you can be one of the rare humans given proper dwarven hospitality."

With Feldspar as my companion, no one bothers us as we leave through the southern gate. A guard hands him a torch on his way out. We make our way up the mountainside.

I match the dwarf step for step, though he never seems to tire. Once we reach the top, the dwarf turns to me and smiles. "Now, the hard part. Stay close behind me or you won't have any light to see."

He turns and the meager light shines on a narrow metal bridge spanning the chasm between mountains. His smile looks almost predatory now. "There are handrails, but they're made for our young, so they're much too low for you to reach. If there's a gust, hunker down until it blows itself out or you'll be sent over the side."

"Lead the way." I smile right back at him.

He sets off at a brisk pace while I turn into an owl and fly just below the bridge. I land on the other side and watch him in my avian form. He makes it across before turning back.

"The silly lass, all that bravado and she's too scared to follow."

"I don't follow, I lead."

Feldspar nearly jumps off the ledge when he hears my voice.

"What did you put in that drink?"

"If you provided better hospitality, maybe I'd tell you."

"I like you," he says with a laugh. "Can't remember the last time I said that about a mud-crawler." He waves his torch back and forth while looking upward into the cloud-covered sky. "Let me lead now, or you're likely to find an arrow lodged in your chest." He hugs the left wall as we enter into the cave.

Light from Feldspar's torch reflects off the walls of the cavern in an unsettling red hue. "It feels as if we're being swallowed."

The dwarf chuckles. "I guess to a newcomer the throne room can feel ominous."

He veers away from the entrance and heads for the back wall. Holding his torch up, the seat before us looks imbued with life as the flickering reflections dance within the crystals.

"This is the throne of our King Hornfel, first of his name, the Dragonslayer."

"It's exquisite," I say in a hushed voice.

"Follow me." Feldspar takes me behind the throne. One by one, dagger-sized teeth appear in the gaping maws of five monstrous creatures. I shudder at the terrible, majestic weapons of carnage. "These are the heads of the five great wyrms that our founding king has slain."

"How does one hunt such a beast?"

I can see Feldspar's teeth as he grins at me. "Hunting is what the loremaster calls it, but in fact, the creatures are baited into this cavern and ambushed." He draws a circle with his torch. "Above us, on the walls and ceiling, are the skins of the five red dragons that had the misfortune of encountering the Burntbeards."

He scratches his head. "Now that you mention it, it does feel as if we're in the giant throat of some fearsome beast."

"Never have I seen anything like this place." I look up at the ceiling and the glistening red scales one more time.

"Bah. The smaller the person, the more they need impressive surroundings. My home is nowhere near as grand, but my hospitality is second to none. I'm guessing that a soft, warm bed would be welcome to you."

"That sounds better than even the beautiful dwarven music from the tavern."

Chapter Five

Dwarven Hospitality

For the interior of a mountain, Feldspar's home is blindingly bright. A shaft in the ceiling brings forth a flood of sunlight. Reaching my hand toward it, I can feel heat from Belenos.

"We have silvered clearstone at all the right places to bring the sunlight down," Feldspar says with obvious pride. He slips his gray armor overtop his head. He shimmies his torso, and the scales catch the light and practically glow. He sees me watching and gives his hips another shake. "It's culebre scale armor."

"I've never heard of such creatures."

"They look like serpents with wings when they're freshly hatched. Later, when they become bloated with gold and silver, they are more like giant wyrms with tiny wings." He puts his hands against his shoulders and wiggles his fingers to demonstrate.

"And that is when you hunt them?"

"Of course. The precious metals are nice, but we use their slime as well. Boil the right amount with water and you create a glue that will last a lifetime."

I have no interest in learning about the slime of any animal. I stare at the light streaming down upon us instead.

"It's truly a wonder," I agree. "You could grow plants down here."

"Bah! Why would we want to do that? Plants are for livestock."

As the dwarf speaks, the light grows dim.

"I told you to fix the stone ring," Tekti says. "But you went to drown your sorrows instead. Now the goats have got in and we're in the dark."

"Yes dear," Feldspar says. "I'll go take care of it before the hunt."

Tekti gives me a quick smile. "Good, because if he gets started on his stories, you'll still be in that same spot come sunset." She hands him a stone maul that's three quarters of his height. "Do you need a weapon as well?"

"No, thank you. As a druid, we refuse to use any metal."

"Oh, dear!" Tekti says. "It's best you keep that to yourself in this city."

With a hug for us both, Tekti walks us to the door. The tunnel outside their home is dimly lit with torches. I blink several times to help adjust my eyes.

"Today is the king's day. Once every seven days, we are given a day to rest and be with family," Feldspar says. "When we return, the throne room should be empty, so I can show it to you in all its glory."

He quickens his pace.

"If you thought it glowed red with just my torch, wait until the light of midday."

"Why do dragons enter your throne room?" I ask.

"The throne room is an open cavern facing east. There's gold set out to catch the eye of the dragons. When they come for the treasure, the Burntbeards ready their ballistae and the trap is sprung on the great beasts.

"Hornfel II, the crown prince and head of the Burntbeards, hasn't been able to add to the dragon scale collection yet, and it's eating him alive," Feldspar says with obvious delight. "His father killed all five beasts in his first forty years here. The second Hornfel has failed to kill a single one in the seventeen years he's been in charge of the force."

"You don't seem too happy with your crown prince."

Feldspar shakes his head. Sometimes I can be so thick. Asking him to badmouth his ruler while in the city has to be one of the least thoughtful comments I've made in a while.

"Tell me about the culebres."

My friend's countenance brightens.

"Each spring, the great sea serpents lay thousands of eggs all at once. It's always at high tide, just before daybreak. The eggs have a thin veneer of firestone, or fool's gold, to you mud-crawlers. We have to muster our army each spring to ensure that at least half the eggs are allowed to hatch. The cocas, as the just-hatched culebres are called, are only as long as my elbow to my fingertip, and they can fly wickedly fast. We collect the eggshells, which we use as tribute to our patron goddess, Ilurbeda."

"They sound harmless enough," I say.

Feldspar chuckles. "Once the creatures make it up the mountainside, they eat any living thing they can swallow. For reasons no one can explain, they also sniff out gold and hoard it in their nests. They grow to the weight of ten or twelve dwarves by the end of the summer. It's in the autumn, you see, when the rains hit, that they prepare for their trip back to the sea. They'll consume all the water they can, so they can make an ample amount of slime coating. Then they travel down the mountains, eating every living thing that will fit in their mouth."

He points to the tunnel on the right, and we go down again. There are no torches this way, just the pale glow of some sort of algae covering the walls.

We reach the end of the passage and he turns to me. "The next part is a natural seam in the rock. It's low, tight and gloriously dark. We're made to memorize this exit passage when we're children. Because we fear humans may find this secret entrance, no light or excess sound is allowed. Hold on to my hand and be ready to duck. The last thing we want is for the mudders to discover it."

He can't see me, but I smile as wide as I can. For him to not think of me as a mud-crawler is clearly a good sign.

It takes about forty paces, but we finally emerge from the darkness along a goat path. There's a small outcrop of weathered stone between us and the sea; just enough to keep us hidden from the city below.

"Now," Feldspar fixes me with a wary look, "I can speak of our *illustrious* king." He kicks a rock over the edge before taking the path upward.

"There are four culebre lanes on this mountain, and each has a dedicated team to harvest the creatures when they migrate. Upon his ascension to crown prince, Hornfel II decided that the royal family needed one of these lanes for themselves. So, they took the first and richest lane. Everyone was bumped over one lane, and my group—which had the fourth lane—was left with nothing."

"Didn't Hornfel at least try and accommodate you and your team?"

"Well, he invited me to serve in the Burntbeards, but only because my family line held more prestige than his did in our ancestral city. But once I joined, he was always pranking me. Once, he jumped on my back and I slammed him into what I thought was the wall behind me. It turns out it was the lime liniment vat, and we managed to knock it over. It's what we use to treat burns, especially from dragon fire." He snorts. "You can guess who was blamed for the whole disaster."

"What happened?"

"I kept my mouth shut, and he allowed me to resign. It's for the best, really. My men had been forced into rubble clearing and other menial jobs, so I rounded up my crew and we're going to make a go of it by looting the culebre nests before they fatten up."

"Why doesn't everyone do that?"

"Oh, culebre are quite deadly. Their wings can't lift them off the ground by this time of year, but the scaly hulks can move much faster than you'd guess."

"Don't listen to him," a voice from above says. "He's still afraid of the dark passageway out of the city. I bet he had to hold your hand to keep from getting scared."

"Tephra is second in the group, by a wide margin." Feldspar says as he reaches out to shake the dwarf's hand. "No one listens to what he says if they're smart."

"Are you ladies going to just sit here while the rest of us hunt?" Tephra asks.

If I've learned one thing from being with the manwolves of Ossory, it's that to gain the trust of the males, you have to brag outrageously and cut everyone else down. I have no idea why.

"Tephra, you seem like a loud, empty-headed dwarf. I can more than hold my own in your little band," I reply.

"Well, if the culebre spots us while we're looting its nest, we run upward so it can't catch us. Being a mudder, you'll be far outpaced on the mountainside by the rest of us."

"You think so?" I ask. Feldspar tries to interrupt, but I won't let him. "I wager I can beat you to whatever spot you choose on these slopes."

"Crisa, don't," Feldspar warns.

"It's a bet!" Tephra says. "See that rock formation on the southern peak?"

I look at the formation and nod. "When do we start?"

"Now!" Tephra laughs, and he takes off in a dead run.

"Crisa," Feldspar says, exasperated.

"No need to worry." I change into a golden eagle and take off after Tephra. I hear Feldspar laugh behind me. I lazily fly up to Tephra and notice the throwing axes strapped to his back. I grab the left one with my talons and fly away with it. I race past him and his shouts to the top of the peak.

His pace is impressive, but I'm able to easily outpace him. I drop the hand axe in front of the rock formation before changing back. When he finally approaches, I'm lounging idly while turning his axe over in my hands. He stares at me, dumbfounded.

"Before I return your axe, let's talk about what I've won from you."

Chapter Six

Beginning the Hunt

Tephra and I wait as Feldspar and six other dwarves make their way toward us. The air is thick with moisture, and despite the altitude, the wind is nonexistent. Already the heat of the day has me uncomfortable.

"It's strange for the air to be so still," Tephra says. It's the first thing he's said since we completed our challenge. "It means the culebre won't smell us coming."

"Is this the entire crew?"

"Not hardly," Tephra says. "There were forty of us, until we were displaced. Four have found work with other culebre crews. Soon, others from our band will leave us as well. That's why Feldspar and I do this, so that our men can gain reputations and find better work."

"There won't be a fifth lane created for you?"

"Hah," Feldspar laughs bitterly, "there won't."

"Did the king compensate you for the loss of your lane?"

"No. He had the official scribe change the numbers of kills for the last three years to make us look incompetent." Tephra snorts.

"After that, he was able to make the change 'for the good of the city.'"

"Then, after the men all leave, what will you do?"

Tephra looks at me side-eyed. "We'll just have to cross that iron bridge when we get to it." He turns to welcome Feldspar and his men.

"It's a good day for a hunt!" Feldspar says in greeting.

"Indeed, it is," Tephra replies.

The men silently form up into two teams of four. Standing between the two squads, I look for some indication of where I should go. Feldspar waves me over as he addresses the group.

"Alright men, with the winds nearly dead, we'll take the high routes and signal when our prey is spotted."

"We'll be stuck way behind with her in our group," one of the dwarves mutters.

"Crisa can keep up," Tephra says. "Trust me on that."

We form up in single line with me in the back, since I'm the tallest. That's the first time I've warranted that place. I spot a green blur below us, scurrying across the high meadow. I watch as it raises its head over the tall grass and surveys the surroundings.

"Is that a culebre?" I ask Feldspar as I point at the bright green creature.

He takes a closer look.

"No," he whispers, "That's a ramidreju."

He raises his left hand and with two quick jerks forward, alerts Tephra to move forward.

"There's no culebre around here if a ramidreju is present," he says.

I look at him, confused.

"Both species love their gold," he explains. "When the cocas come up the mountains in the spring, the ramidreju feast on them. Once the culebre grow to full size, the situation is reversed, and the ramidreju become the hunted. If that creature is here, you can bet there are no culebre near."

"You don't try to capture the ramidreju for its gold?"

"We would if we could, but they are intelligent creatures who bury their treasure. They're too quick to capture, or else we'd harvest their venom." He sees my puzzlement. "Ramidreju venom knocks humans right out, but dwarves get a pleasant numbing effect, at least at first. If we could catch it, the venom would be worth a few shiny coins."

"Do you have to kill it to get the venom?"

Feldspar shakes his head.

"Then I'll catch it for you."

"Wait! How?"

It's easier to demonstrate. I morph into a golden eagle and take off high above the dwarf's head. I circle around the ramidreju, making sure my shadow is not visible. I hear Feldspar and his men shout as I make my dive. The ramidreju looks up at the dwarves, but I'm coming from the opposite side. I grab the creature with both talons, fighting against the urge to impale it. Once it's pinned to the ground, I spring up and fly back to the awestruck dwarves.

The creature is half tail, and it uses it to try to wrap around my wings. All in all, the creature is longer than my human form is tall. I take to the sky and hope that the creature is intelligent, or else we'll go crashing into the rocky earth below.

I land in front of Feldspar and two of his men grab the weasel-like animal's tail. The ramidreju's coat changes from bright to dark green. Retaking my human form, I step back and watch.

Feldspar strokes the thing's head and talks in low, reassuring tones. He grabs a waterskin and places it at the mouth. After it sprays the venom in the skin with a noise that sounds much too much like a man peeing, Feldspar orders his men to release the green weasel. It takes a couple of hops to get clear of us before turning and hissing. It gives me one last look before springing down the mountainside.

"I hope she doesn't go too far down, or she's likely to run into a ravenous culebre," Feldspar says.

"If you know there are culebre down there, why don't you hunt in that location?"

"If the culebre are already down in the trees, then they are much too large for us to deal with. Even the ones we hunt up here are lethal if we're not careful."

Before I can ask any more questions, he orders his men to line up and continue the march. I retake my golden eagle form and scout ahead. There is a green-scaled, legless lizard monstrosity below me with two totally ineffectual wings. Rising high above the mountain top, I circle the beast. Both Feldspar and Tephra spot me and race to find their quarry.

With the vision of an eagle, I follow the dwarves' movements without issue. With mere human eyes, their grayish cloaks would render them virtually invisible. With four on either side, they coordinate the attack, and eight blades come crashing down before the creature can react. The attack is over as soon as it begins. Feldspar severs the culebre's head before his men roll the body over. Tephra cuts through the belly and climbs into the viscera. He emerges bloodied from head to toe, but he's pulling on part of the digestive track. He drops it outside the body and the men hack through it excitedly. Gold nuggets spill out, and the men let out a cheer.

Feldspar orders Tephra and one other to cut up the beast. I keep circling from above. I'm not squeamish about dressing out an animal, but if I'm not going to benefit, I see no reason to get my hands bloody. Four of the men are ordered to follow the slime trail back to the nest and collect as much of it as they can. At least they use the entire beast. I land next to my friend and watch as he pulls out pack after empty pack.

"This is a great haul! No doubt this one was heading down to the forest to fatten up before his trek to the sea."

Off to the east, I catch a slight bit of movement in the sky. Looking into the rays of Belenos, it's difficult to see, but there is a red, flying lizard coming toward us.

"Feldspar," I say with a bit of urgency. "When the culebre get bigger, do their wings start to grow again?"

"Nah, the wings on this one are as big as they get. They're long past the time when they can fly."

Pointing at the flying lizard, I say, "Then can you tell me what that is?"

Feldspar shields his eyes as he follows my finger.

"Dragon!" he shouts as loudly as he can. He grabs my hand. "Run!"

The rest of his men have already started running toward the tree line. Two of them run side by side, carrying the stomach and all the gold within it.

"They'll never make it," I say.

"Follow them!" Feldspar pushes me downward before taking off toward the top of the mountain, where there is no cover. He brandishes his maul and curses at the dragon.

The fool! I change into a golden eagle instead and take to the air.

Chapter Seven

The Early Wyrm Hunts the Bird

The other members of Feldspar's crew hunker down and let their culebre scales hide them in the crags of the mountain. Only their fearless, stupid leader is racing along the mountain path, attempting to lead the dragon away.

The creature circles once and rises in the air. It snorts smoke from its nostrils and lazily dives toward the dwarf. The monstrosity belches out flames, bathing the land in fire.

As the fearsome beast pulls up and the smoke clears, I spot Feldspar in a gully with scorch marks on his scale armor. His maul's wooden handle has ignited, causing the dwarf to fling it away.

The dragon roars, circling overhead. It's playing with its food, and I won't stand for it. I beat my wings feverishly to gain altitude. Once I'm above the dragon, I dive for its eyes with my outstretched talons.

It ducks its head just in time, and I only make contact with its well-armored brow. My attack produces the barest of scratches on the dragon's scaly hide. The great beast flips up its head, tossing me away and spinning me wildly. It turns toward me and lets out a malevolent roar. My entire body shakes under the concussive assault. It banks to its right until it's facing me. I dive downward and to the left initially before turning to the right.

I can feel the heat of the dragon's breath. Below, several pines explode into flames. I gain altitude, but the brute is closing in. One blast would be the end of me. Head druid Anach was not a good mentor, but one piece of advice I took to heart was 'when in trouble, do the unexpected'.

I circle around and head straight for the beast. It rears back its head, readying for another blast. I beat my wings faster, heading straight for its gullet. As its head comes forward, I surge upward. The blast misses me, though the following wave of heat robs me of my breath.

As I fly overtop the creature, it tries to impale me with one of the bony horns on its head. I circle around and grab hold of the left one. The dragon bellows in fury as I attach myself to the side of its head. Its baleful eye rotates toward me as it banks hard to the left. I only just leave my perch before the beast's left arm strikes the spot where I was perched.

It lets out another bellow of frustration. It is stronger and faster, but I'm more agile. While it tries to turn into me, I fly straight to the west, putting a fair amount of distance between us. To my surprise, the beast continues the chase, wings beating loudly as it makes up the distance. Once again, I must time my desperate dive to the dragon's fiery attack. Too soon or in the wrong direction and I'm dead.

Feldspar and his men should be out of danger now. If I had the time to focus, I'd confirm this with my superior vision, but I've no such luxury. I break to the left, but there's no flame. Realizing it tricked me, I rise as fast as I can, mostly avoiding the flames. I make a tight circle, but my scorched tail feathers let me down. It's hard to see, but it looks as if several tail feathers are charred and fused together.

We play this mortal game for quite a while. I find my best move is to dive as if hunting. It's too sudden for the dragon to mimic. At last, I'm free of it. I circle once to confirm my auspicious fate. Even if it left, I should be able to spot its retreating form.

Sunward attack!

As a bird of prey, it's natural to attack with the sun behind you. I dive just as the dragon bites the air where I had been. Its leg swipes at me, sending me flailing side over side. I tuck my wings to convert my tumbling into a dive. Once my body is righted, I spread out my wings and pull out as quickly as I'm able.

Over the course of the chase, we've descended halfway down the mountainside to a level where trees are prevalent. I take cover in the forest and slow my flight.

The dragon soars past me, igniting vast swaths of the montane forest. Still not willing to give up, it rises and hovers above, waiting to incinerate or pounce, whichever it desires.

I skirt through the inferno in front of me, taking refuge in a meadow. The dragon roars, and I'm forced to turn back to the forest fire once more. The smoke hides me from mortal peril even as it robs me of full breaths. I make it back under the canopy and bleed off much of my speed. Above, the beast still hunts.

One more mistake like that and I'm dead.

To my left is a circular temple of white stone gleaming against the brownish-green land around it. I make for it, if for no other reason than to seek shelter inside.

A tall woman with long, curly blond hair exits the temple and raises her hands to the sky. Thick fog rises from the ground and obscures her and the temple from view. The fog continues to rise and I make a beeline toward where she is standing. The crimson dragon reacts to my desperate gamble and moves to intercept me.

From out of the fog, fiery arcs emerge, exploding in midair. The dragon cries out in pain and I risk a turn to see its left wing has been blackened. It pulls its wings in tight and makes a suicidal dive right at me. Guessing that it wants me to pull up, I, too, dive toward the ground. It's a matter of who will pull up first.

I enter the fog and turn abruptly to the right. The dragon releases a fiery breath that dissipates in the fog. More fiery arcs come from in front of me, and the dragon gives out a thunderous bellow in frustration. It has lost sight of me as well as its best weapon. At last, it gives up the chase.

I flare my wings to slow my momentum and land with practiced ease on the front stairs of the temple.

"Welcome, druid," the woman says. "You are safe now."

I change back to myself and have numerous questions vying for primacy. The noise emanating from my mouth sounds more like the bleating of a sheep than actual language. The woman smiles serenely back at me. I swallow once and regain my composure.

"It was you who called forth the fog," I declare instead of asking.

"That is true."

"I have never seen one pull the moisture from the ground before. Are you a druid lord?"

"I am Ilurbeda," she says.

I stare at her blankly.

A brief chuckle escapes her mouth. "Then, formally, I am Ilurbeda, the goddess of paths."

"The goddess of paths," I repeat back slowly.

Feldspar had spoken of her, but I hadn't focused on his words.

"I am also known as the traveler's goddess, the goddess of miners, and the voice of fate."

"You're an actual god?" bursts from me. I cover mouth is a panic.

"Goddess," she corrects me.

I drop to my knees and avert my gaze. In truth, I'm using this time to figure out the proper decorum when speaking to an actual goddess.

"Rise . . . Druid Lord Crisa. I require no such homage from anyone." She turns and walks toward the temple doors. "Are you injured?"

"No, my lor—" I stop myself. "Would you be so kind as to instruct me in the proper way to address you?"

"I place no value in formality, so Ilurbeda will do."

"As you say, Ilurbeda."

That is never going to feel comfortable.

Several women, who are also in flowing white robes, come forth and hold the gleaming bronze doors open.

"My adherents take a vow of silence, despite my protestations, so actual conversation is a treat for me."

"Your followers don't obey you?"

The goddess caresses the face of the woman off to her left. The dark-haired woman drops to one knee and averts her gaze.

"Most of my adherents come from the Arevaci, to the south, and they adhere to the rigid belief that they should not speak in my presence. For this reason, most choose to have their tongues removed. Others adherents wear the lace neckband, signifying their choice of silence." She sighs. "I do not require it, but they are petrified to be in my presence otherwise.

I nod to the women as we pass. Two of the women lower their heads, while the one with a neckband looks up at me in awe? Surprise? I'm not sure what her expression conveys.

"As it is, my scrying this morning alerted me to your arrival. I did not, however, see the brute Diablori arriving with you." She nods toward me. "I must commend you on your flying. I have never seen one fly as deftly as you."

"Diablori?"

"The crimson dragon that chased you. He's very old, older even than me, so the very fact you stayed alive indicates your immense talent."

"I fear it was luck born of desperation," I say.

When I was in eagle form, the dragon singed my tail feathers. Now in human form, my tail end is still burned, but there is no way I'm going to mention it here, no matter how accommodating the goddess is.

"In any case, you are to relax here for as long as you wish, to recover your nerves, if nothing else."

Does she already know of my injury? I've never been in the presence of an actual goddess before.

"That is overly kind."

We enter the center chamber of the temple, which has a high, domed roof made of small bricks placed in shrinking circles until one final square stone caps the structure. How so many bricks can remain in place and not fall on the devotees is beyond my comprehension. The room is much cooler than where we came from. I refuse to rub my arms for warmth. Instead, I lower my gaze and try to focus on anything else. White tiles cover the floor from wall to wall. We have nothing so fine in Eriu.

"In truth, it is not all driven by kindness. I would ask a favor of you," Ilurbeda says.

"What do you wish of me?" I ask in a hushed voice. The enormity of receiving a doom from a goddess is overwhelming.

On some unseen signal, a dark-skinned woman approaches with an object wrapped in a fine linen cloth.

"This is Gaddah. She is the finest wood carver in all of Hiberia. Many months ago, I had a vision that this should be made."

Gaddah removes the cloth to reveal two exquisite hand axes made of ash. I nod my head at the woman before running my hand over the works of art.

"It is the Grey Wolf Axe," Ilurbeda says.

I look at her, then back to the axes.

The goddess takes the two weapons and slides one handle into the other, creating a battleaxe. Once combined, a mosaic-like pattern appears of a grey wolf leading its pack from one blade to the other, with its mouth open wide at the slightly larger blade. The pattern is repeated on the opposite side.

"It is beautiful."

"And it is yours to give to a worthy recipient."

"Glorious Ilurbeda, why would you trust me with the likes of this?"

I lift up the axe and gaze upon the lifelike wolf carvings. I close my eyes and run my hand over the snout and along the fur coat of the leader. It gives off heat, as if I am touching a live wolf.

Ignoring my protest, she continues. "It is not finished yet. Behold." The goddess takes the battleaxe from me and lays it at her feet. She drops a runestone on the weapon and mumbles a word of power too low for me to hear. The weapon transforms from new yellow ash to a gray, metallic hue.

"I would ask you to take this to Gobannus, the god of the forge, and ask him to sharpen and bless this weapon."

"Why would he do that?"

"At the request of another immortal, he will be persuaded." Her smile reassures me.

"But I do not know the way to Gobannus."

"Fly west, over the mountains. You cannot miss the smoke that comes from his forges."

"But I can't—"

"—fly with metal?" she finishes for me. "This is not metal, but ironwood. Since it was made from nature, it will not affect your abilities."

"I don't understand why you would ask this of me. It is fit for a king."

"Aye, a dwarven lord would be honored to receive such a gift. But which one will you choose?" Ilurbeda gives me an impish look. "The ways of the gods are rarely clear to mortals."

She notes my misgivings and addresses me sternly. "I would advise you not to refuse the will of a goddess."

Chapter Eight

Divine Instruction

The goddess insists that I stay the night, despite my misgivings. At first light, I strap the ironwood axes to my back. Ilurbeda gives me a benign smile as I shake my arms out, as if limbering up for a flight while still human. I push the goddess and everything else from my mind, focusing on the golden eagle form. I surprise myself when the transformation occurs. I had doubted the ironwood would allow me to transform. With Belenos at my back, I head west, toward what looks like another forest fire.

In the valley below, smoke emerges from several tall, thatched-covered workshops. One of the brick-walled structures on the outskirts of the area has had its thatch roof burned away. Well away from the smoking buildings are small homes and a mead hall. The largest of the workshops is in the center, which I assume makes it the god's temple, if indeed it can be called a temple.

The reddish-brown brick walls of the structure make it look more like a fortress than a temple. It's as big as any mead hall on Eriu and the amount of smoke streaming from the roof makes me think that this building too is on fire. A large wooden wheel is attached to the building and dipping into the river, lazily turning in the current.

I land outside the entrance and retake my human shape. I wait for someone to greet me. The lintel above the entrance has images of hammers and anvils carved deeply into it. This place lacks any of the polished finishes of Ilurbeda's temple, though I find the serenade of hammer strikes oddly peaceful.

A tall, lanky man in a simple linen tunic and trousers greets me at the entrance. His clothes are singed, and he lacks any rings, necklaces or other ornamentation. If not for his confident bearing, I'd think him a servant.

"Welcome to the forge of Gobannus. May I help you?" On each of his hips are unadorned bearded axes.

"Thank you, sir," I start. "I have been sent here by the goddess Ilurbeda—"

"She is no goddess," he interrupts curtly.

I start again, "Ilurbeda has sent me here, asking that Gobannus sharpen and bless these axes so that it may be presented to a dwarven lord."

The man holds out his hands and I give him the weapons. "Ironwood?"

"Yes."

He eyes the handles and nods approvingly. Without being prompted, he slides one axe haft into the other, forming the battle axe.

"Follow me."

I look questioningly at the man's back. He neither gave me his name nor asked for mine. He didn't even bother to consider whether I was telling the truth or not. This is an interesting place.

Inside the workshop, the reddish glow of heated metal and the forge fires are the primary light sources. Shadows dance on the walls at a frenetic pace. All around me, the striking of metal on metal rings out in a disjointed tune. What little light exists only illuminates the rising smoke, and the heat reminds me of the dragon fire I barely survived.

At the center of the temple forge is a single fire with several anvils positioned around it. The ringing of hammers is constant as shirtless, sweaty men shape the glowing metal to their needs. Young apprentices maintain the bellows and run errands for the smiths.

"I do not see a dwarf in this forge," I say.

"You are correct. We denounced their false goddess as the charlatan she is. The dwarven king decided to salve his wounded pride by ordering all his smiths from our halls rather than face the truth. Hornfel's weaponsmiths are quite capable of making sturdy blades, but they lack the finesse for fine work. They cannot duplicate our expertise, so they pay us in gold and iron to temper their blades in the Smith God's fires. So far, Gobannus has not forsaken the fool king's emissaries."

"Is your god here?" I ask. On Eriu, the gods never mingle amongst the people.

He raises an eye at me. "True gods live not in this realm. It is we, his priests, who are a conduit for him. Vettones, like Ilurbeda, may have learned to forestall death, and even to restore their youth and vigor, but they are not true gods. They play the part of charlatans, enticing the gullible to lavish them with gifts."

I think of Rhedna of the Sorrows. "Ah, we have ones such as that on Eriu as well."

Charlatan is perhaps too strong a charge for Mistress Red, but the similarity in abilities is obvious.

"Can you sharpen and bless this weapon?" I ask.

He looks the weapon over closely. "Is it destined for the new king?"

"It is not."

"Then we shall place it within the hearth and let the will of Gobannus be done."

"I thank you. What is a proper tribute for such a gift?"

"Do you have gold or iron?"

I smile at him. "I am a druid of Eriu, and we have foresworn metals in our lives."

"Fear not, Gobannus is a wise and fair god. You will receive that which you deserve."

"The weapon was given to me by Ilurbeda, though the person I am to gift it to was unclear," I start.

The priest waves his hand back and forth, cutting off my explanation. "Save your words. I am not the one to judge." He holds the ironwood weapon above his head and approaches the central fire.

Word spreads quickly and the ringing of hammers stops. The smiths have formed a loose circle around us. The tallest, strongest man steps forward with iron tongs, and the priest lowers the weapon and allows the tongs to grab the blade. Everyone, including me, watches as the axe is placed directly in the fire.

I look at the priest with obvious concern. "That fire will not ruin the axe?"

"Oh, it may, depending on our god's decision. We worry not about being fooled, for Gobannus will consume any weapon brought here with ill intentions."

He tosses a fine white powder onto the blade, and whatever the substance is, it turns orange and embeds itself within the weapon.

The large smith turns the glowing white axe over and the priest again repeats, tossing the powder.

"That is a good sign. You have come with a pure heart." He nods to the smith, and the axe is removed from the flames. The priest grabs the glowing white handle and hoists it above his head again.

I freeze in place, astounded by his audacity.

"No need for that. It is quite cool," the priest says. "Our god protects us."

The priest holds the weapon up and the color fades back to the metallic gray from before. The priest lowers the weapon and stares down the shaft.

"It is perfectly straight, and has been tempered." He offers the blade to me. "By the will of Gobannus, this blade will never dull."

I hold my breath as I take the weapon. It is cool and suffused with flecks of clearstone within the blade.

"How . . . what does this mean?"

"The incorporation of glassrock in the blade means the weapon is destined for a true leader, and it will protect the wielder from fire. All who see this weapon will be awed by its aura and inclined to follow the one who possesses it."

"It is exactly what is needed," I say, amazed. "But how does one sharpen it?"

"Gobannus has seen to that." The priest chuckles. "Did you expect less from a god?"

"It is not right to receive without giving in return. I must give something back."

"Go in peace." He pats my hand. "Your goal, whatever it may be, has the backing of Gobannus."

"But . . .."

The priest rests his hand on my shoulder and gently spins me around. "What can you offer a god? Go, and may you be successful in this endeavor."

I look back at the priest and the gathered smiths. They placidly return my gaze, waiting for me to make the next move. I bow low to the assembled men and boys and take the shape of a golden eagle. I leap into the air and circle the forge temple once before turning east.

*   *   *

I have partaken of no drink, yet my head is addled. What my next move should be, I have no idea. I don't believe I can find the secret entrance to the dwarven realm by myself, and I wouldn't be able to navigate the tunnels on my own in any case. An unescorted entrance to the throne room isn't appealing either.

I continue east until I spot the head of the dead culebre. I circle the scant remains. If life is going to be taken, it should not be wasted. The eagle eyes may have sharper vision, but I'm easily distracted by rabbits and songbirds. I land and retake my human form in order to find the dwarves' trail. While inspecting the ground, I hear my name on the wind. The next hill over, Syen, one of Feldspar's men, is waving at me.

"Well met, Syen," I say once my feet carry me to him.

He takes my hand and looks earnestly at me. "Crisa, you must leave here."

Furrowing my brow, I look closer at the worry lines around his eyes. "What has happened?"

"The dragon, well, Tephra insisted it must have killed you, but Feldspar wasn't so sure. We agreed to man this hill for five days, to either mourn your passing or to welcome you back."

"Well, we know which one it is now," I say. "So why are you so uneasy?"

"It's Feldspar. He has been condemned. His life will end in four days."

I shake my head before clasping my hands together. "Tell me everything."

"After you and the dragon flew off, there was nothing we could do for you."

I nod, and the tension in his shoulders eases.

"So, we went to work harvesting the culebre. As we made our way to the secret entrance to the city, we spotted the dragon flying toward us. We feared the worst for you," he says, refusing to meet my eyes. "The dragon circled and spotted the golden bait in the throne room. It entered, and the Burntbeards, well, they didn't perform as they should. Someone fired prematurely, and the dragon was alerted to the trap. It breathed fire throughout, and several dwarves were badly burned. Once it realized the bait was mere fool's gold, it left with hardly a scratch."

"How many were injured?" I ask.

"Three Burntbeards have died so far. And Feldspar is being blamed, because the crown prince claims that Feldspar tipped over the curran oil, even though everyone knows it was the prince who did it. The king has declared that the deaths are due to Feldspar, and not his son" He wipes his eyes. "Feldspar's been imprisoned."

"What will happen to him?" I ask, my heart in my throat.

"He won't be killed," Syen says. "Killing our own is never an option."

I let out a sigh.

"No, his family will have to pay restitution, which no one in the caves can afford, so his entire clan will be dissolved and they will become servants of the city until such time that the debt is repaid. Feldspar himself will be ostracized and never be allowed to enter dwarven lands again."

"At least he'll live."

"Not for long," Syen shakes his head. "A lone dwarf will be attacked for the gold that everyone believes we carry. His wife and children will be slaves of the city for the rest of their lives. An honorable death would be better, but Hornfel won't allow it."

"What happens in four days, then?"

"In four days, he'll be let out of his cell. Like any good dwarf, he'll dive off the iron bridge and end his life."

"Why would he do that?" I ask, startled.

"Because his sudden death will allow the king to cancel all familial debts. His family will be allowed to maintain their homes, and the shame will end with Feldspar."

"But it's misdirected shame," I add.

"True, but his family will be unscathed."

"What if he left with me? He could find a prosperous life away from these mountains."

"No dwarf would leave the safety of the northern mountains."

"But there is no life for him here."

Syen shakes his head. "Once one's honor is lost, it cannot be reclaimed."

"Where's Tephra?" I ask.

"Most of the crew are in the tavern in Kathno Briwa. None of us dare show our faces until after Feldspar's fate is determined. As it is, the king has forbidden any further culebre hunts, so our crew will be disbanded. At the moment when our men need to be seen as necessary, the opinion of us could not be lower. How are we to find work to support our families?"

"How is the relationship between Tephra and Feldspar? Does Tephra wish to be in charge, or is he content to follow?"

Syen chuckles. "Those two have been inseparable for sixty years. I fear for Tephra when Feldspar is gone."

"Thank you, Syen. Please join Tephra in the city."

For the first time, I see a path to success.

Chapter Nine

Longshot

I land on the path at the far end of the iron bridge and change from my golden eagle to human. I don't relish walking this bridge in a shifting wind, but if Feldspar's description of the dwarven king is accurate, it's important that I look the part of the penitent. If I extend my elbows as far from my body as I can, they would be outside the span of this "bridge." There are knee rails along either side. For dwarves, they may be useful, but for humans, they are more likely to be tripped over. I suspect that is the point of having them. Besides Feldspar, his family, and his crew, these dwarves are far from hospitable to strangers like me.

At the eye of the Grey Wolf Axe, where the handle meets the twin blades, is the hammer symbol of Gobannus. How it got there is a divine mystery, but it brings me comfort. Gripping the axe at the eye, I use it as a walking stick. Halfway across the bridge, a dwarf blows a deep, resounding horn that makes my heart skip a beat.

"A penitent human approaches the storied city of Isarnobriga!" he yells a breath later.

There is some movement from inside the cavern, but I'm too focused on my feet to see what is happening. I get two steps from the end when a dwarf blocks my path.

"It would be a shame to get blown over the side now," he says. "Perhaps you should give me that axe to lighten your load."

"It would be a shame," I agree. "So, why are you blocking my way?"

"What is your business here?"

"I have come to request that the king release Feldspar, the mountain ranger."

The dwarf smiles as he looks past me. "Just wait a couple days and you can join him as he leaves the city." He looks down into the rocky valley below, in case I needed help to understand his meaning.

"I'd rather discuss this with your king than with you."

A gust hits us, and I'm forced to use the axe to brace myself. As quickly as the wind comes, the air reverts to a temporary stillness. The dwarf laughs at my balance and slowly moves out of the way before escorting me into the cavern. Once I'm within the shade of the great cavern, the motion within the room is apparent.

The king sits on a thick stone chair with a rounded top and jagged purple amethyst crystals pointing inward toward him. Only the armrests and presumably the seat have been smoothed. A thin band of inlaid gold demarks where the crystal ends and the rough rock begins. Reflected purple light bathes the king in an awe-inspiring radiance that is simply stunning to behold.

My escort bangs his axe on the floor next to me, breaking my trance.

"The king has asked you why you have come," the dwarf barks out.

I have dealt with the unruly kings of Eriu and their fops for many years. These dwarves are in for a surprise if they think they can cowl me so easily.

"Forgive me, your highness. I was struck by the opulence of your hall, and I needed a moment to gather myself in the presence of such wonder." An outrageous compliment always plays well to the overly vain. "I have come before you . . .."

I gaze at the five red dragon skins covering the walls and roof of the cavern. It bathes the rest of the court in a reddish light, making them appear more threatening. Thankfully, Feldspar had pointed them out and let me know that these were the king's proudest achievement.

"Yes?" the old king asks.

"Forgive me." I give the monarch a shy smile. "I have come before you to plead for the release of the mountain ranger, Feldspar. I was present when the dragon attacked, and I can vouch that his heroic actions saved the lives of his men from otherwise dire consequences."

The old king bobs his head several times as he takes in my words.

"I do not doubt Feldspar's bravery. It was his decision to hunt culebres before the appointed time that has doomed the dwarf. Had he and his men not slain the culebre and piled the gold on the mountaintop in plain sight, the dragon would not have been drawn to it, so it is his poor choice which endangered his men."

This is not, in fact, what happened, but contradicting the king will not benefit my cause.

There are grunts of agreement from a contingent of dwarves suffering from multiple burns. Several have lost their beards and have shiny, blistered chins which will never grow facial hair again. One wears an eye patch, and his left arm is bandaged heavily.

"Your highness," I say as I bow low. "I am new here, but I wonder if you can afford to lose brave, stout men of courage such as Feldspar. Would you consider letting him join me as I return to Eriu?"

An undercurrent of laughter fills the cavern.

"We dwarves will always choose death on land rather than death on the cold, uncaring sea," the king answers.

I bend forward, as if I'd been punched in the gut. The axe is pushed forward, and the glassrock in the blade comes to life, glowing like miniature white flames.

The king and his court grow silent as everyone stares at my weapon. I grip the eye ever tighter.

"That is truly a kingly gift; one that can only be meant for me," the king says, regaining his composure. "I thank you for bringing this weapon to me."

I give the king a knowing smile. "Hornfel Augite, the first of your lineage, King of Isarnobriga and slayer of terrible dragons, this axe, the Grey Wolf axe, was given to me by Ilurbeda's very hand and blessed by the priests of Gobannus. I am but a caretaker until the worthy owner of this great axe can be found."

The king gives me a smug smile. "Then your mission is accomplished, for none but I could wield a weapon so great."

"With respect, your highness, I do not believe this to be so."

"You dare slight my honor?" Glaring at me, the king rises from his seat, spitting out his anger. "You and Feldspar so enraged the wyrm that it not only withstood the Burntbeards' attacks but also inflicted horrible wounds to my elite guards!" he yells. "This is the crime which cannot be forgiven."

He nods to the Burntbeards, and they move to surround me.

"But fear not, you will join Feldspar and experience the same fate."

Am I so off-putting that royals will forever be demanding my capture?

I raise my right hand in a gesture of surrender. With great care, I stow the great axe in the holder on my back. The Burntbeards approach, but before they can reach me, I change into a bat and fly up toward the ceiling. There are startled shouts, and in the confusion, I find shadows and follow them deeper into the dwarven tunnels.

* * *

Tekti is an impressive woman. Even after showing up at her home unannounced and breathlessly reliving my tale, she listens until the end before deciding what needs to be done. She studies the axe closely while peppering me with questions.

"I'm afraid my plan is ill-conceived, but it's the best I could devise since fleeing the throne room."

"Bah, Hornfel, first of his name and first in shortsightedness, baits the terrible wyrms into an ambush. Does that sound like nobility to you? We dwarves face our opponents head-on, not hiding in the shadows like spiders."

She tears her attention away from the axe as I finish explaining my plan. "First, you need to eat and rest," she says.

"But what if the guards come here looking for me?"

"The guards are all male. What do they think would be gained by going to the family of the condemned? They think we're helpless in Feldspar's absence and sitting in circles, crying on each other's shoulders. Why would anyone want to come here?" She waves me to follow her past the receiving room.

"Males are good at following simple orders, especially if you let them think it's their idea." Tekti snorts. "They think women swoon over their honor. In truth, the best mate is one that is dim and faithful. There are plenty to go around."

*   *   *

I thank Tekti before I put my ridiculous plan into action. It's a new morning

"For your plan to work, you must go to the city first, then to the mountains. I fear talking sense into the men will be the most difficult." Tekti rests her hand on a standing safe which is as tall as her. "You will need this." She opens the door and reveals a small hoard of gold.

"I can't take it. It will interfere with my powers."

"Then how will you pay off the humans?"

"Is Syen trustworthy?"

"He and Tephra are my husband's most trusted. Of the two, Syen is the most rigid in his thinking."

"Then I'll send him to collect the gold from you before he makes the arrangements in town. I'll tell him that Feldspar's life depends on him following the plan exactly."

"I will go see my husband tonight after I inform the wives of our departure. Like most men, Feldspar will be wrapped up in his honor and planning every step of his noble death." She shakes her head in exasperation. "He's not getting off that easy."

"Here Tekti." I hand her the axe. "Give it to Feldspar when you leave. He'll be so transfixed on this that he'll follow whatever you say."

"This is a noble gift," she says softly. Instead of taking it from me, she runs her thumb along the edge, drawing blood.

"Worthy of the first dwarven king of Eriu?"

"Aye," she says, without taking her eyes off the weapon.

CHAPTER TEN

Preparations

Syen was a blubbering mess when I told him to go see Tekti. First, the guards would be waiting for him. Then it would be improper to be with Feldspar's mate while he was imprisoned. After that, the excuses grew even more outlandish. I should have known better, but once I mentioned Feldspar's honor rested upon him following my directions, Syen changed his temperament completely.

Ah yes, males; they are fearless against a visible enemy. But tell them to enter their very own city without being detected and they fall to pieces. Why do I have to explain to use the secret back entrance and further, to avoid going near the throne room? Shouldn't that be obvious?

Honestly, are all dwarven men so helpless without a weapon in their hand? I shake my head as I fly toward the mountaintops where the culebre was killed. Jerking my head this way and that while flying destabilizes my flight. Unwittingly, I take a nosedive, and am lucky to not crash into the hard stone below. I'm not so bright either, it seems.

I spot a ramidreju, possibly the same one as before. I land near it and retake my human form. I could compel it to obey me, but there shouldn't be any need. Reaching out, I touch its mind and make our bargain. I'm surprised at how intelligent these creatures are. I soar into the sky and lead it to our prey.

A man-sized culebre is marauding its way through the montane grass. I circle it as the ramidreju gets into place. Once the beast sees its gold-hoarding nemesis, it moves with amazing speed. I dive at it and sink my talons into its rotund neck. It ignores me and continues after the ramidreju. I animorph back to my human form and hang on with all my might. The creature takes note of my extra weight and rolls over in an attempt to crush me. I dive off and regain my feet at once.

The culebre decides to go for the ramidreju. Whether it is because they both collect gold or because the animal was downhill from it, I'll never know. Try as I might to read the thing's mind, I cannot.

With breathtaking speed, it slides toward my partner. The ramidreju realizes that something is amiss, and it tries to run from the beast. That is a losing bet. I spot a large rock farther down the slope. Animorphing doesn't solve every problem. I force the boulder to rise from the ground and engage the culebre. It places itself between the two and braces for a collision. The beast propels itself headlong into my elemental and bounces off it. That's all I need. The elemental springs to life and pounds on the creature's head until the body goes still. Thanking the stone, I send it back to its place and return it to slumber.

I slash the belly open and reveal a pile of gold ore the same size as my sly accomplice. I remove a waterskin and hold it next to the ramidreju's mouth. It spots the gold and runs excitedly in circles before returning to me. It takes the skin into its paws and forces all the venom it possesses into the container. Stretching upward, it looks at the gold again and strains even harder.

I take the waterskin from the creature and reassure it that all the gold is for him. He immediately rips out several grassy clumps and lays them over the prized metal. Then, taking all it can manage, the ramidreju scampers to its den. I grab a few more clumps of grass and add it on top of the treasure.

I smell the venom; it smells rich and exotic. No wonder dwarves are willing to capture such elusive prey. Even the aroma is intoxicating. I grab a small ceramic jar and carefully pour two fingers' height of venom into it. Once I'm back on Eriu, it will be interesting to study this. Once more, I change into an eagle and fly toward the seedy port of Briga Kathno.

*   *   *

Syen and Tephra are making animated gestures at a sea captain and the same dockmaster I'd dropped into the harbor. Landing behind the two humans, I grab a coil of rope and approach. I loop the rope around the dockmaster's neck and bend him backward over my hip.

"If you would like to avoid swimming in the harbor again, I would suggest you be more accommodating to these dwarves."

He waves his hands helplessly in circles while his face goes red. He sputters out some unintelligible reply, so I pull harder. The ship's captain reaches his weapon, but Tephra hooks the man's hand with his sturdy bearded axe. The captain raises his hands and takes a step backward, letting the dockmaster fight his own battle.

Releasing the rope, I spin the man around and explain exactly what is going to happen. With two armed dwarves behind him, the dockmaster is reluctant to argue. I order Tephra to hand over the gold, and it's the dwarves' turn to act aggrieved.

"Don't make me throw you into the sea," I tell Tephra.

He shakes his head, as if clearing up a mental fog.

"Ask him," I point behind me to the dockmaster, "if you don't believe I can."

I hear the dockmaster backing away. That won't do; I insist on fair negotiations. I look directly at Tephra, daring him to stop me. I lift the cover on his leather pouch and withdraw a thumb-sized nugget of gold.

"Thank you for overseeing these negotiations." I hand it over to the dockmaster. Payment in hand, he flees us for the safety of the sea keep.

"Now pay the captain exactly what you agreed upon."

The dwarves explode into outraged shouting. I let them go on until their emotional scree runs its course. They wait for me to respond.

"Does Feldspar mean so little that you would risk his life for a few coins?"

That stops them cold.

"Give the captain his due and let's move on with the plan."

"I'm afraid," the captain interrupts, "that dwarven fugitives on my boat will increase my price."

I raise my hand to forestall the dwarves from arguing.

"Captain," I say with a sweet smile, "did you hear about him—" I nod toward the retreating dockmaster, "—being dropped into the harbor a couple days ago?"

"Aye. What of it?"

"I am the one who did it to him."

"The sailors say it was a barrel-chested, hairy man the size of a bear, not a mere woman."

Tephra puts his arm across Syen's chest and they back up a couple of paces. Syen looks confused, but Tephra is all smiles. I nod to the dwarf before I change into an elk. I lower my head and my horns cut off any path except the water behind him. The sea captain's mouth hangs open. I wobble my horns and he shields his head with his arms.

What is it with sailors that they always freeze in place when scared?

Raising my head, I spot the dockmaster in an all-out sprint toward the nearest defensive tower. He'll be back with a dozen or more men, and soon.

Retaking my human form, I pat the poor ship's captain on the cheek. "I can also turn into a wide variety of birds, or a bear, so if you decide to take sail without us, I will find you, land on your deck and not be as restrained as I've been today."

"Of . . . of course. Here, you can keep your gold."

"No!" I say before the dwarves can reclaim the payment. "A deal has been struck and everyone will honor their part."

"But if he doesn't want payment . . .." Tephra starts.

Making a slashing movement with my hand, I silence Tephra. "What time can we depart?"

"At . . . at high tide. Just as Aine rises above the waves."

"We'll be there." I turn to the dwarves. "Let's go to the tavern. I have to meet with the barkeep, and you two must keep your men in the tavern and out of trouble."

Tephra begins speaking again, but Syen cuts him off.

"We still have work to do."

"But . . .." Tephra says.

"It's no use. You can argue as much as you want with the druid, but you'll end up doing it her way in the end," Syen says.

Only I find the declaration to be funny.

Chapter Eleven

First Problem with the Plan

The *Culebre's Hoard* is already crowded this morning. By the reaction Tephra and Syen get, it looks like Feldspar's men are all present. Tephra announces that they have a plan to free Feldspar. He raises his hands and waits for silence.

"In order for this plan to work, we all have to do our part." He has their full attention now. "And for all of us here, our part is to wait here and drink for free all day!" He raises a fist-sized gold nugget in each hand.

Several dwarves demand to know more, but they're drowned out by the cheers. Tephra and Syen work the crowd, assuring the confused that everything will work out.

I amble to the bar and nonchalantly drop another gold nugget into the barkeep's hand. Wacke slips it in one deft move before wiping down the bar with a dingy cloth. I slide the venom-enriched waterskin over to his waiting hand.

"We need these men to be drunk when Aine rises. Can you make that happen with that amount of ramidreju venom?"

He opens up the neck and inhales. "With this amount, I can have them all passed out."

"Nah, that would be too many to carry. We need them to be willing to follow directions without hesitation and march where we tell them to march."

"Easily done," he says. "But what do you want to do with them until then?"

"You saw the two gold nuggets Tephra had?"

"Aye."

"Between those two and one I just gave you, that should be ample pay to keep them here and in good spirits."

"What happens at nightfall?" Wacke asks.

"You're welcome to come along and see."

"No thanks," he slides his dirty cloth along the bar until he's out of speaking distance.

Syen comes over to me. "We're good?"

"As long as you can pry those gold nuggets from Tephra's hands. Wacke will keep the men drunk and happy."

"What's next?" he asks.

"I have to check on how your wives are faring." I pat him on the shoulder and slip out the door.

So far, everything is going according to my plan.

* * *

Entering the dwarven throne room is my biggest concern. It's just past midday, so a bat won't do. There's a small band of swifts circling each other and vocalizing their high-pitched trills. I always thought it sounded like one long, squeaky argument.

I assume their shape and ascend the mountain. Grabbing a spindly root, I land on the side of the cavern and discreetly change into a field mouse. The ones here have a yellow band of fur across their necks, which I find adorable. More importantly, they have big ears and a brownish-gray coat along their backs—good hearing and perfect camouflage in a dim cavern.

I slink along the wall of the throne room and marvel as the dwarves shoo bats out of the caverns. With the diminutive people all looking up, I have no trouble making my way through the tunnels to Feldspar's home. What I didn't count on is how long it takes when your steps are only the width of two fingers.

Outside the home, I wait for the tunnel to clear before animorphing back to myself. My heart is pounding after my knock on the door, as breath after breath, there's no movement from within. The tunnel feels both gigantic enough to be easily spotted, yet too incredibly small to escape. I bounce from leg to leg as I wait for my presence to be discovered. I hear steps coming, but from where? Down here it's hard to locate direction of sounds. I try to settle my mind and imagine the yellow-necked mouse again.

The door flings open, and Tekti waves me in. I nearly fall through the doorway. She slams the door and rests up against it.

"How did you make it here without being spotted?"

"I changed into a mouse. With everyone obsessed with bats, it was no hassle."

"Well, if you were a mouse, why didn't you enter through the crack in the door?" She points down to where the door and wall meet.

"I didn't want to just enter, unannounced. How rude would that be?"

She squints her eyes at me. "We're planning on freeing a royal prisoner and spiriting away an eighth of this kingdom—without the king's knowledge—to strange lands, and you waste time obeying proper etiquette?" She throws up her hands in annoyance.

I follow her into the kitchen, which looks like it has been ransacked. Last time, there wasn't a single grain out of place.

"We don't have time to clean up either," Tekti says, frowning. She goes to the Grey Wolf axe. "I just haven't found a way to get this to my husband." Her hand slides up the handle. At the blade, she gives it a couple knocks before looking at me and my smile.

"Are you bringing a bag with you to the jail?" I ask.

"They'll search it."

"Just bring a small bag that will fit a mouse, and I'll take care of the rest."

She grabs a small pouch that fits across her neck and shoulder.

"Got anything with longer handles? I'm going to have to jump out of it once we're in the prison, so the closer to the ground I am, the easier it will be to go undetected."

"I have just the thing."

She disappears into the sleeping area and returns with a small leather pouch on a long strand.

"What is that?"

"It's Feldspar's hammer pouch."

"I repeat my question. What is that?"

Tekti throws her arms up in the air again. She pushes past me and starts shoving all sorts of utensils into a large bag.

"When our beards first come in, it's a signal that we've obtained our full height. It happens quite early, and those enjoying their first

Beard Day are quite thin and gangly for dwarves, especially the males. With females, the transition is more gradual."

She strokes her short beard as she stares at her shelves.

"The proper gift in either case is a hammer that is equal in weight to the youth."

She tosses the strap over my left shoulder and squeezes by me and the table. She waves her hand at the spice rack hanging on the wall. "Pick out whatever spices seem strange to you. No sense bringing them all if we can get them in this new land of yours."

I open up the ceramic jars one by one and inhale the intoxicating aromas. Seeing Tekti fly from point to point in the kitchen, I have to speed up so I don't cause offense.

"The youth are stupid," she begins again. "I think that's a universal truth of the young from all races. So, the youths insist on dragging their hammer with them everywhere they go. We make these small pouches on long straps so they don't ruin their hammers."

"Perfect! I'll bring the axe with me and jump out once we're inside the prison."

"Dear, the axe won't fit in the pouch," Tekti says, as if she's talking to a little one.

"Watch this." I grab the battle axe and separate it into its two halves. Tekti raises her eyebrows, but says nothing. The two halves are still too large for the hammer pouch. I spin and ask for help to get them strapped to my back. Before she can voice her doubts, I change into a mouse again.

Her eyes go wide and she blinks at me several times. "I don't understand," she says. "Where did the axe go?"

I change back. "It stays with me."

"But you were no bigger than my hand."

"No one can explain where the axe, our clothes, or any of our other possessions go. As long as nothing is living or made of metal, it will accompany us when we transform and be right where it was when we change back. Most call it the Earthmother's blessing."

"Skarn, Topaz!" Tekti claps her hands. Two dwarves come running at her call.

"Pack up the rest of this." She waves her hand to what's left on the table. "Then leave for the mud-crawler's town and make sure you use the back tunnel, not the throne room. Once you arrive, find Beryl and Pearl. They'll be organizing the families."

"Who are they?" I ask.

"Skarn and Topaz are clanless siblings. Only clans have the resources to build homes in the rock. The clanless have to fit in where they can. It's cruel, really; the only thing they're guilty of is being born to the wrong parents. I gave them the choice of leaving with us or staying and finding new work."

I grab the axe, change into a mouse once more, and jump into the hammer pouch. Tekti chokes up on the strap so she can whisper to me as we walk.

"Beryl and Pearl are the wives of Tephra and Syen. They both have good heads and will get all the families and supplies loaded on the ship well before sunset."

She nods at a couple of women as they pass in the hall. They nod back with smug smiles on their faces.

"I will not miss those two," she whispers. Once they pass, Tekti increases her pace. "The king has summoned everyone to the throne room. Since my husband will be condemned, I'm excused."

She snorts. "They assume I'll break down and sob uncontrollably, or some such nonsense if I show up."

After the two women, the tunnels are empty. We descend the next two levels, where the tunnels are only lit with a glowing fungus. It's too weak to cause shadows.

"We're at the prison level now," Tekti says. "The top two levels are nearly full, so it won't be long before they'll have to dig down another level and make that the prison. This level will become another level of homes. Of course, with our mass defection, it won't be quite as soon as everyone's expecting."

We approach a metal-studded door. Tekti lowers the hammer pouch to the ground and kicks her dress up to cover it before pounding on the door.

The guard opens the door partially before wordlessly opening it up the rest of the way. I scamper out and hug the wall while Tekti makes a show of running to her husband, half hysterical. Her wails are unintelligible to everyone but Feldspar. He strokes her hair and keeps repeating, "I know, I know."

"You know we have to inspect that pouch, so come away from your husband," an annoyed guard says.

Tekti milks it for all it's worth. She takes two steps toward the guard before going red-faced and running back to her husband. Feldspar has to push her away to the waiting hands of the guards. There are six dwarves in total watching their lone prisoner. We were expecting one, maybe two.

"You need so many to protect against a loving wife?" Feldspar asks.

"It's the druid; she's still unaccounted for," the guard nearest Tekti says. "With all of that," he motions to the point where Tekti was carrying on, "I guess you've heard the news."

"What news?" Tekti asks as she dries her eyes.

"Oh!" the dwarf says as he walks to his commander.

"Are we a child, then? Running to your pops?" Tekti's voice drips with scorn.

The commander eyes the guard for a second before stepping forward. "Because the druid cannot be found, your husband's time has been moved up to today at dusk."

I let out a chirp of astonishment, though no one can hear it over Tekti's protestations. She goes red-faced again. This time it's not an act. Her fists pound the commander's chest. He gives her a few moments before he grasps her wrists.

Looking her in the eye, he speaks ever so softly, "We will give you time to say goodbye to your husband. Not all of us think he has done wrong, but this is where we find ourselves, nonetheless."

Tekti races to her husband and buries her head in Feldspar's chest. The commander ushers his men out of the room. Before closing the door, he does one last scan of the ceiling, looking for that troublesome druid.

As the door slams, I retake my human form.

CHAPTER TWELVE

Jailbreak

"Crisa?" Feldspar asks with narrowed eyes.

"What do we do now?" I whisper to them.

Tekti pats her husband's cheek and turns toward the door. "There's too many of them for the three of us to take on, especially when we only have two weapons."

Feldspar looks at the two axes I'm carrying, but it rates far down on his list of questions. "Why are you here?" he asks me.

"We're going to spring you from jail."

He looks at me like I'm a simpleton.

"Listen to me, dear," Tekti says. "We've got your whole crew at the *Culebre's Hoard* in the mud-crawler's town. At high tide, we sail for Crisa's lands to start our own kingdom."

"Did they slip something in the water they gave me? Neither of you makes any sense," Feldspar says, slapping himself on the cheek.

Tekti stabs her finger at the door repeatedly as she signals Feldspar to keep his voice down. While she's getting control of her husband, I venture to the guard's table. It's clear they were throwing dice and drinking dwarven ale.

I race to Tekti's side and pull out my ceramic vial. "I have ramidreju venom."

A slow smile creeps across Tekti's face. She reaches for the vial. "You'll be too heavy-handed," she says. "I know just the right amount."

I replace Tekti at her spot next to Feldspar. "Once they fall over drunk, we'll get you out of here and to the ship."

"I'm not getting on any ship!" Feldspar says, indignant. Both his wife and I signal for him to keep his voice down.

"I'm not getting on any ship, and neither would any of my crew," he says more softly.

I take the axes out and combine them together before handing it to the caged dwarf. It's enough to shut him up while he admires the craftsmanship.

"Did they really move your time up because of me?" I ask.

"From what the guards said, you nearly made King Hornfel belch fire."

Times are desperate, but I can't help but smile. "The pompous ass deserves a much fuller telling of his deficiencies. If not for your short-sighted king, everyone could have come out of this a winner."

A guard pounds on the door.

"Give us a bit!" Tekti shouts. "We've barely had time to undress!"

There are chuckles from the other side of the door and someone says, "play acting," before laughing with his mates.

Good, let them think that's what's happening here. I get a chill in my spine. They're not really planning on that, are they? There's no other exit and I don't care to witness that.

"Grr," Tekti says, rolling her r's. "Yes."

She's still over at the table. Feldspar and I look at one another. Tekti waves at us and rolls her hand, telling her husband to play along.

"Ah," he says.

His wife scoffs at him. "Really?" she whispers. "It's your last time to make love to your wife, and the best you can do is to mimic sitting down after a hard day?"

I bite my fist to keep from laughing out loud.

"That's it, that's it!" Feldspar says, getting a little too into the acting for my comfort.

"Don't go to the big finish! I need more time." Tekti whispers. She's dosed four of the cups.

I look back and forth at the two of them, grinning like a fool. Never could I have dreamed up this situation.

The two continue their low-pitched groaning. Outside, the men are nervously laughing at the exertion.

Finally, Tekti fakes her ending as she returns to Feldspar and me.

"Crisa will keep the axe and turn back into a mouse." She looks at me. "Once all the men are out, give the axe to my husband and let him splinter those iron bars. You'll need to open the door and see if the tunnel is clear. I'll be out of sight, so I don't raise suspicion."

She turns back to Feldspar.

"You take her to the back exit. Anyone who raises a weapon against you must be dealt with, but try not to injure them too badly," she says, caressing his cheek and kissing him on the lips. She gets down on one knee in front of her husband. Feldspar and I look at each other. She unties one of his boots and gives him an impish smile.

"How did your shoe get all the way over here by the door?" Tekti shouts. That's my cue to shrink from sight.

*　*　*

Six nearly passed out guards are no match for Feldspar and his new axe. He only hits them with the sides, though, bruising their pride and sending them to sleep.

Once in the hall, Feldspar refuses to use a torch. The dwarf squeezes all the blood from my left hand as he drags me around behind him. He's afraid if we get separated, I'll get lost in this byzantine maze of tunnels. I can't argue with him. He chuckles when I hit my head on a stalactite, but I take it in stride because this dwarf doesn't know what the night has in store for him.

"All I'm saying," he whispers, "is that you could have changed back much earlier and brained the last two. You wasted a lot of time waiting on the commander to finally drink his ale."

"Ouch," I say as another stalactite unleashes its attack on me. "Tekti wasn't anywhere along the path. What does that mean?"

"I don't know," Feldspar says in a worried voice. "It has to be close to dusk by now."

We navigate through the keyhole passage and reach the tall grass outside. Below us, Tekti has been captured, but she's still putting up a fight with three guards. There's a long train of dwarves and their children running for the city.

"*Tekti!*" Feldspar yells as he brandishes the Grey Wolf axe.

One against seven doesn't make for good odds. Two against seven won't change the outcome either. But one against none works! Closing my eyes, I focus on the culebres I've encountered. I push against my physical limits and expand into a behemoth of a wyrm. Without conscious thought, my scales start releasing an ooze that makes sliding down the mountainside unavoidable. My body starts to rotate to the side and my ineffectual wing slams into a boulder. I give out a yell of pain as I right myself. It echoes down the slope. Who knew the creature could roar so loud?

All the dwarves below crane their necks up toward me.

"Culebre!" shouts go up all over and the guards scatter left and right. Only Feldspar remains, protecting his bound wife. Try as I might, I can't stop my slide.

The gray eyes of the dwarven hunter are trained upon me. He holds the axe up high, waiting to strike. With effort, my mind calms and I'm able to animorph back to myself. My speed downward doesn't change, however, and I'm pounded by every rock sticking up from the ground.

Feldspar rams his shoulder into mine, spinning me around, and more importantly, stopping my momentum. Dust and grime make my hair stiff and matted even as it obscures my vision. I try to push it back, but my grime-filled locks have a mind of their own. After two more tries, I give up and turn my head so I can see out of the tangled mess.

"I could cut that for you," Feldspar says.

"Look up there!" Tekti shouts, pointing with her chin. Above us, an unbroken line of dwarves stretches across the bridge and down the mountain path toward Kathno Briwa.

Feldspar cuts his wife's bonds and the pair survey the scene. "Do you have any more tricks up your sleeve?" Feldspar asks me.

"Against a dwarven army? Not hardly."

"Then we need to run!"

With longer strides, it's not long before I pass the dwarven couple. "Go straight to the ship! I'll get the crew from the tavern."

Without waiting for a reply, I change to a golden eagle and soar on the wind to my destination.

CHAPTER THIRTEEN

The Plan Goes Out to Sea

The tavern door opens as I'm preparing to land. There's no time to change. I stay on the wing and fly over the dwarven patron's head. Hopefully, that wasn't one of Feldspar's crew. I flare my wings and land next to the bar. All eyes are on me.

"Where's Tephra?" I ask the barkeep.

"I'm here," comes a reply from halfway across the room.

I stand up on a stool. "There's no time to waste. Get to the ship now!"

Pandemonium erupts as most were still unaware of tonight's surprise finish. Looking down at Wacke, he shrugs.

"You said to get them in a stupor at dusk. I've just started to serve your concoction."

Tephra approaches us. "What's going on?"

"The short version is that King Hornfel is sending troops down the mountain to apprehend Feldspar and, most likely, your entire band. The last of the families are making their way down the mountainside as we speak. It's a race, so everyone here has to get to that ship now."

Tephra's face lights up and he steps onto his seat, then the table. I suddenly feel uneasy.

"Defend the gate!" He cries. "Repel the invaders! Form up in your lines."

Before my eyes, the dwarves line up in rows. One dwarf from each group runs to the front, turning to face his dwarves.

"Syen!" Tephra calls.

"Here!"

"Go to the human magistrate, tell him invaders are coming down the hill."

"Aye! My men and I will persuade the magistrate to fit us into his schedule at once."

Syen and his giddy crew leave to the cheers of the remaining dwarves.

Tephra smiles. "Breccia!"

"Here!"

"Take your men and help the last of our families get inside the city."

"Aye!" The second line of dwarves breaks out into a cheer before marching out in unison.

"Gypsum! West gate. Rhyodac! East gate. Hold them until we say otherwise."

The soldiers hoot and holler for a moment before leaving on their missions.

"Dacite and Diorite!"

"Aye!" the two remaining commanders answer.

"Since I can never tell you two apart, you and your men are to secure the south gate and repel all who try to enter."

The two dwarves slap hands above their heads while roaring in pleasure. They and their men leave at once.

Dwarves.

Only a handful of patrons remain, but Wacke encourages them to go home and not to come out again until morning.

The barkeep pours Tephra and me a drink. I give him a look before I grab it.

"No ramidreju venom," he assures me. "What will you do now?"

"One way or another, those soldiers are going to make it into the city," I say. "Wacke, why don't you tell the incoming soldiers that you've never been happier than to see the last of us?"

"True," he says with a smile.

"And offer them free drinks on the house."

"What?"

"You're going to give them the envenomed drinks," I say.

"Why? You'll already be gone or in custody before they come in here."

"Because we've paid for those drinks already. And if the commanders come in here for a quick drink before reporting back . . .."

"It will be daybreak before the king will be apprised of the situation," Tephra finishes my thought.

"And anything he might try will be much too late," I say smugly.

*   *   *

Feldspar paces the gangplank. "Where are they?" he asks for the fourth time.

"The tide is turning," the captain says.

"Just a bit longer!" I say before Feldspar can explode. Between the dwarf and the captain, neither is handling the stress very well. I look up at Aine and beg for her to calm these two.

"I see dwarves running this way!" I point at the amorphous mass moving toward us. From this angle, it's hard to tell one bearded dwarf from another.

"Who are we?" is called from the approaching crowd.

"Culebre hunters!" is the answer.

"Those clueless twins," Feldspar smiles in relief. "They are forever trying to get the party to shout that out while we're on the hunt."

Syen is running with the twins with a big smile on his face.

"Is it me, or are there more of your crew than there should be?" I ask.

"Aye, that's nearly the entirety."

I turn to the captain. "There, you see? The rest of the passengers will be here shortly."

He turns from me and starts barking at his crew to get ready for launch.

Feldspar races down the gangplank to meet his men on the docks. He holds the Grey Wolf axe up high, and his men form a blob around him, each trying to touch the weapon.

The twins lift Feldspar up and chant all the way back to the ship. They set him down on a mooring hook and his foot slips. If not for Syen grabbing his beard, their fearless leader would be swimming now.

"Feldspar!" I call from the ship. "There's another group of dwarves coming fast."

"Let's fight 'em!" one of the twins calls out. The dwarves give a cheer.

"There are men with the dwarves!" I call.

"To the ship!" Feldspar roars. "Let's wave at them from on board." He brandishes his axe above him, and it glimmers like the night sky. "Follow me!"

The dwarves follow him up the gangway.

The doors of the sea keep burst open, and men file out. They line up and turn to face Hornfel's dwarves.

"Get us out of here," I tell the captain.

The last line is pulled away, and the ship puts distance between us and the dock. The dwarven army is hopping mad, but the men of Kathno Briwa turn a deaf ear to them as they line up five deep across the dock.

Feldspar and his men rush to the side of the ship and blow kisses to their former countrymen. Only when Prince Hornfel gives up and leaves the docks with his men do the twins and Syen open up.

"We barred the gate!" one twin says.

"Yeah, Dacite distracted the gatehouse while the men and I closed and barred the gate."

"Two of the guards were still outside when the gate was slammed shut," Dacite chuckles.

"They started banging on the stout oak doors," Diorite adds.

"That's when the gatehouse guards came pouring out—"

"—demanding that we open the gate."

"Then Diorite told them an enemy approached."

"They scurried up to the top to see that it was Hornfel II leading a contingent of Burntbeards and others."

"Hornfel acted all uptight and threatened the guards—"

"—but Syen came at just the right time with a contingent of guards from the palace and the dwarves from the east and west gates."

I've lost track of which dwarf is Diorite and which is Dacite, much like everyone else I'd wager.

Syen gets pushed into the center of the dwarven circle.

"I told the palace guards that a small army was streaming down the mountainside. In his panic, the magistrate failed to ask who exactly made up this force. Once we arrived, he told the gatehouse guards to man their posts," Syen says.

"That's when Syen told Dacite and me to get our men together and inconspicuously make our way to the ship. Once the head human saw Prince Hornfel, he started looking around for answers."

"That's when we broke into an all-out run," says one of the twins—Dacite, maybe?

"If Hornfel had not demanded an apology from the guards quite so vociferously, the humans could have caught us," Syen says.

"That's truer than you know," I say. "Even with your head start, the humans could have caught you, but they were content to run side by side with the prince and his men."

"So, the real hero of our escape is Prince Hornfel!" Syen says.

"No, no, no," Feldspar shouts. He raises his axe as a call for silence. "There are many heroes to this tale, and they are all on this ship. In battle, there will always be mistakes. Our job was to be better prepared and a little smarter than the royal court. And we succeeded!"

Cheers go up again, and the dwarves jump up and down. It's not until the captain comes and tells us that the ship is listing to our side that they stop.

"Spread out so the ship doesn't lean!" I shout.

"Why are we on a boat?" one of the twins asks.

EPILOGUE

Despite my best efforts, none of the dwarves are willing to join me on deck now that the excitement is over; they insist on huddling together in the dark underbelly of the ship. Every creak spooks them into holding each other tighter. Even the fiercest of warriors have weaknesses.

I'm left topside by myself as I try to reconcile why dwarves don't become sailors. They're low to the ground, with short, powerful legs. If they can run back and forth on the iron bridge without difficulty, they can surely walk on a deck, even in a tempest. They would be naturals. Whatever the reasons, they're not going to change on this voyage.

I stare up at Aine one last time tonight. I'm honor-bound to go below and educate the dwarves as best I can about their new home. I bow my head to Aine and go below deck.

* * *

"It's done," Tekti says again. "Stop worrying about us dwarves. There are none in this realm that are made of sterner stuff."

"Wait until you meet the manwolves," I tell her. "Your peoples will become either the tightest of allies or the fiercest of enemies."

"See, you should worry about that," Tekti says. "That's in the future. It makes no sense to worry about what's done."

"You're right. I'll go speak with the captain and see when we'll reach Eriu." I jump up and head for the stairs.

Once on the deck, there is a faintly glowing area where the clouds are thin and some of Aine's radiance breaks through. I head for the captain.

"Will there be storms tonight?"

"Aye, somewhere there are bound to be storms tonight, but not here."

The tension in my shoulders lessens. "And when will we arrive?"

The captain laughs. "This is your first time aboard a ship?"

"Am I that obvious?"

"You are, but you paid me handsomely, so I don't mind. We will arrive at Menipia tomorrow, two days before Beltane."

"Beltane?" I'd forgotten about the calendar. That means the time for war is nigh. "I don't know if the dwarves celebrate the holy day or not. It will be an opportunity to integrate them into the island life."

"Good luck with that. You'd be better off letting them dig into the earth somewhere and leave the surface to us humans."

Since the ship has departed, my unease has been fed by my restlessness. It's been a whirlwind, and I'm unable to relax. The captain has walked away, probably because he's guessed that I'll ask him questions throughout the night if he doesn't escape from me.

It makes no sense to aggravate the captain. I suppose I'll return to Tekti and see if the dwarves are familiar with Beltane.

Tekti waves me over and hands me a drink.

"You've been milling about ever since the boat left the docks," she says. "Relax, there is nothing else you can accomplish tonight."

"But there's so much to plan. You haven't even seen the lands yet, much less picked a spot to settle."

"And that's a problem for later, not now. Here, drink up, it will calm you."

I'm not really a fan of dwarven ale. I'm hopeful that they'll take to Eriu's mead.

"Is this an herbal drink?" I ask.

Tekti smiles. "It is. It comes from all the favorite plants of the ramidreju, blended together."

I try it and it has a spicy, exotic tang. "This is really good."

"I'm glad you like it. Give me the cup and I'll pour you some more."

"No, I couldn't," I say with a yawn. My head feels so very heavy. It's all I can do to keep it up.

"Just settle down for a bit," Tekti says, as she takes the cup from me.

Why not? The sack of smithy tools I'm sitting upon is nice and cool. I wedge myself between them and an anvil.

Tekti gives me a warm, knowing smile. "Worry about tomorrow's problems tomorrow." She tosses a blanket over me, and I feel totally at ease.

"I'll just rest here for a moment. . .."

BOOK THREE

Blachstenius

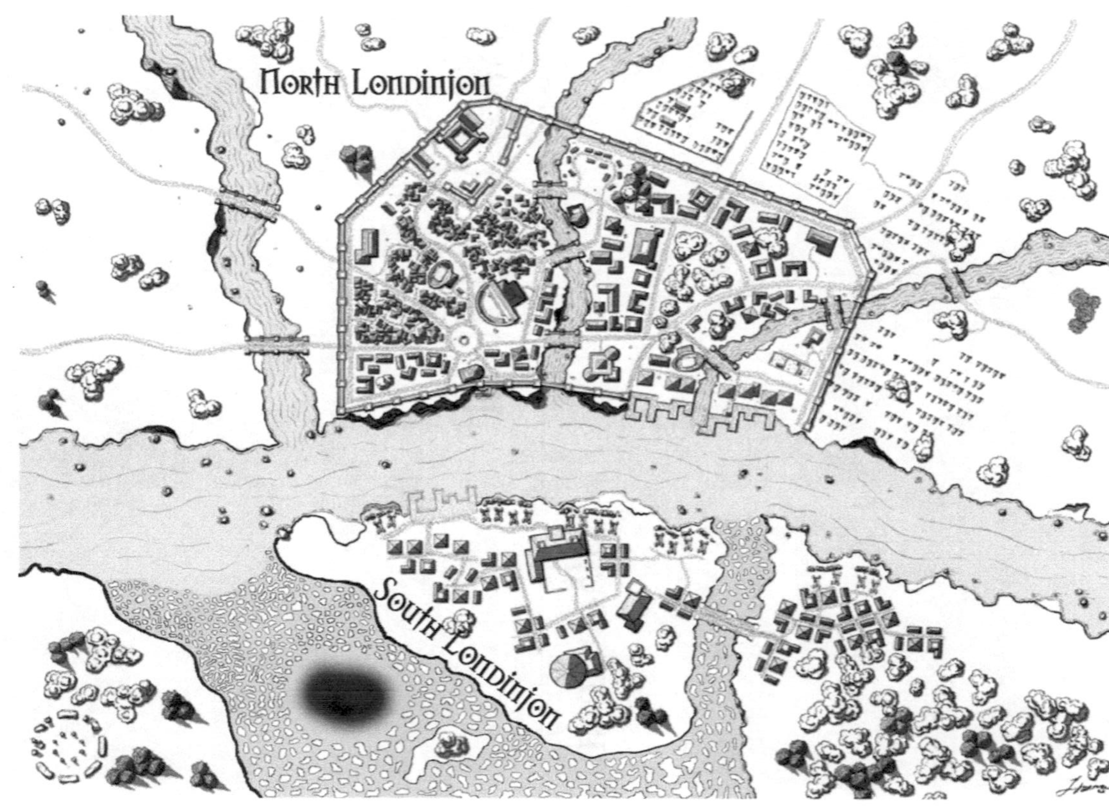

North Londinjon
South Londinjon

Chapter One

Starting Over

It's only been four hours since I left Solent Keep—and Koni—and I can't get it out of my head. I'm grateful for the wagon and the ponies, but why? Why did she fill the wagon with her husband's swords? She knows I abhor violence. I could have been the head of the Obsidian order by now had I chosen that life.

Then, there's that other thing. I've known that woman for over three decades and I still don't understand her. After all these years and all the secrets we've shared, she keeps her curse private from me? Gods, I will never understand women.

I'm glad I left the swords on the ground. It was the right thing to do, and it reaffirms what I stand for. But right now all it means is that I'm hungry and I have nothing to eat or anything to trade for a meal. Women.

At least Mai Dun is only a four-hour ride. Before Koni and I started on our mission to free Solent Keep, I gave all of my possessions to Lowen, the lowly gatekeeper of Mai Dun. Now I'm just a short ride away from seeing if he's willing to invest in my trading endeavors.

* * *

A youth is asleep at the gate. I stop my wagon and cough several times, but he's out cold. Dismounting, I walk to him and shout, "What is your name, child?"

The youth bolts awake with his eyes as large as his fists.

"I've come to invade the city!" I yell while raising my arms.

He takes in a sharp breath and backs against the wall. His arms are halfway up in a position that would be useless in a fight.

"I'm only teasing you." I grin.

He's still too shocked to register my jest. I rest my hand on his much-too-thin arm and give a gentle squeeze.

"What's your name?"

"I'm Miacha," he stammers.

"Good to meet you Miacha. Can you tell me where Lowen would be?"

"Master Lowen?" he stammers. "Please, good sir, don't tell Master Lowen that you found me sleeping." There's real fear in his eyes.

"Rest assured, I will not. I only wish to rehash old times with him." I wink at Miacha. "I promise not to mention your . . . relaxed posture."

The boy smiles shyly at me. "Thank you, sir. Um, may I have your name?" He bows his head. "I'm supposed to announce any newcomers to Master Lowen before I let them into our community."

"Well, it seems you provided me a warm spot to sit and wait while you do your duty."

Without another word, the youth runs into the city center. I wait by my ponies and begin counting, waiting for his return. I don't get far before I notice him round a corner toward me, his limbs splaying out in all directions. One would have to stay at arm's length to avoid being hit.

"My name is Blachstenius!" I call, sparing him a few extra steps. Oh, to be young and gangly and have a whole glorious future planned out for one's self. It's hard to believe, but I was once so naïve.

I do my best to mimic his sleeping posture. I won't tell Lowen of the boy's transgression, but that doesn't mean I can't make the boy a little nervous.

I ignore the first couple of calls from Lowen. Let him think I'm really asleep. Once he's within reach of me, I open my eyes and clap my hands on his face. Lowen nearly ends up in Miacha's lap. The boy is a head taller than Lowen and still looks scrawny compared to the former gatekeeper.

I stand up and stretch. "This is mean of you, Lowen, making this strong boy sit in the sun and wait for vagabonds like me to arrive. With the warming rays of Belenos shining down here, it's amazing that Master Miacha could stay awake."

I see the boy flinch. I don't dare smile or even acknowledge it.

"Well, Miacha *has* had an issue with remaining awake," Lowen says.

"Not this time, I'm happy to report. The boy had me quivering in fear with his stern address."

"I'm sure," Lowen laughs. "What brings you back to our fair city?"

"Word is that it's your city now, since you own nearly everything."

"Never trust what a trader tells you." Lowen looks up at his young charge. "They are always playing one advantage or another." He climbs into my wagon and looks at me expectantly. "The least you can do is give me a ride home."

"As you say." I smile broadly back at my friend. Miacha is smiling too, more because he wasn't caught sleeping by Lowen, I'd wager, but I'll take a smile for whatever the reason.

* * *

"Blachstenius, I've never seen you like this. It doesn't take your mind-reading skills to know that you have something to say even as you dance all around it."

I look around in his hut before responding. It was Conwenna's hut once, and I can't help but think what could have been.

"You're right, of course. I've never had to ask for such a favor before, and I'm afraid you might think less of me."

My old friend explodes in laughter. "You gave me the contents of your wagon. You made sure Isla gave me a fair price for the fabrics. You convinced Ferroth to give me his home and his forge, and now you expect me to become cross?"

I raise my hands in surrender. "Here it is, then. I've had to start over, and as you noted, my wagon is empty." I look my friend in the eye. "Would you be willing to provide me with something—goods or coin—to get me started again? I promise to repay you by Beltane if I can, Lughnasa at the latest."

"Of course," he says. "And there is no repayment necessary." He wags his finger at me. "Without you, I would have ended my days a poor, cold gatekeeper. How little you must think of me," he shakes his head, "wanting to be repaid."

"Thank you. That is one burden off my shoulders."

"There's more?"

I hadn't meant to bring up my other problem, but Lowen is so unassuming that I tend to share more than I normally would.

"Do you have anyone to leave all your wealth to?" I ask.

Lowen frowns. "My wife and child died some years back. Wet lung hit our village hard, and neither of them made it. Since then, I've been alone."

"Well, I too am the last of my family," I say. "My line is the founding noble house of Ynys Luko. We are considered the first family of the island."

"You have no sisters?" Lowen asks.

"None. It was only Rhunior and I. Now it is just me." I raise my eyes from the floor. "On the mission with Koni—Conwenna to you—we were cornered by a hag and each of us were cursed." I take a deep breath. "Strigula rendered me sterile."

We stare at one another.

"I hate to ask, but what curse did Conwenna receive?"

"I don't know." I look out the door as I blink away a tear. I close my eyes and take a deep breath. "She would not tell me."

"Oh, Blachstenius . . .."

I rise to my feet, wishing for this meeting to end. In my most businesslike voice I say, "If you could lend me the money, I will be on my way searching for an undeclared child of my brother."

Lowen is on his feet as well. "I don't know much," he says. "But in all these years since my wife and beautiful daughter left me, the one thing I know to be true is that without a family, it is vital that you have strong friendships. Otherwise, you will struggle to find a purpose in this world."

I look away, even though I'm unable to hide my tears this time.

"I hope you find what you seek." Lowen moves to his bedroll and retrieves a heavy coin purse. Daring me to say something, he plops it in my hand.

My voice is raspy with emotion, but some words can't be left unsaid. "I have crisscrossed this island many times over, and I've met the important, the self-important and the powerful, yet I think the former gatekeeper of Mai Dun is the wisest amongst them."

"Don't tease me so, you old trader. I'm but a humble man." He slaps me on my shoulder as I leave. "Where will you go first?"

CHAPTER TWO

Regnorum

The palace of Regnorum is one of my favorite places in Pretanni. The last time I visited, Noviomagus Gisgo threw a lavish party for me. It was at the behest of Astal, his concubine, who is another of my favorite people. And in the city of Regnorum is Bodo, the hardest bargainer of all the traders I know. It will be good to spar with him, even if he does have the upper hand this time.

I peruse the market for cheap dates and olives. Both will keep for quite a while, and they are exceedingly rare away from trading cities. I get a bushel of each. If only they end up being traded instead of eaten by me. That will be the real test.

Just smelling my goods brings a smile to my face. Sure, olives and dates can be found in Londinjon as well, but they always taste bolder and more flavorful when they come from one of our Sorim ports. The Wigesta don't treat them with the respect that the products deserve.

First, I'll meet with Bodo. He still thinks he can replace me as the best trader on the isle, but with his paunch, his traveling days are over. I'll have to pay way too much for his goods and trinkets, but that just means I'll have to work extra hard to turn a profit. I'll likely never hear the end of it. It will be good to be challenged again. I have to direct the ponies to Bodo's shop. My old pair knew their way here from the city gate.

Once all that is finished, I'll ask Astal to help find any undeclared children of my brother. She always says that each Sorim mind is as unique as the person's face. Hopefully that extends to offspring as well.

The street is not half as busy as it should be. I spy Bodo's shop in the distance, and for some odd reason, it's closed. It's not like Bodo to take a day off from profits. That's why he's nearly as good a trader as I am.

"Where is Bodo?" I ask a passing man.

"He was killed in his shop months ago. His widow is trying to sell the place." He brushes past me.

"How was he killed?" I ask, but the man doesn't break his stride.

I try the door, but it's locked. There's not even a little wiggle in the door, so it must be braced from the inside. Bodo was the only trader in this city willing to do business with me. The rest knew they were outclassed. I'll miss haggling with my old nemesis. I bow my head as I touch the door to his trading shop.

If nothing else, I can make sure that Bodo's wife gets the income she needs. I'll go see her and offer a fair price for the merchandise after I take care of my business in the palace. She'll be able to live comfortably, and I'll have my position as the unquestioned first among traders reestablished. I stable my ponies and wagon behind the shop. That would have infuriated Bodo.

* * *

The palace is filled with snakes of one kind or another: scheming generals, predatory merchants, and other ill-intentioned people. And not one of them is a match for me except for Astal. She entered the palace with only her wits and her considerable talents. Now she's the mistress to tired old Gisgo, and the true ruling voice of the Sorim on Pretanni. I project to her several times, but she refuses to answer. She's done this before. When Astal is like this, it means she's up to some game.

Local men are drilling in military formations on either side of the road. That's new. Astal despises the Obsidians. She sees the military as a waste of money. By playing the Obsidians off the Tyrians, she's been able to weaken them both. In fact, my brother was pushing for Solent Keep to become the new capital, since Tyrians—Sorim traders like me—were not welcome there.

"Halt!" an overly serious man calls. Oddly, he's dressed well, like a tax collector, but he has the bearing of a fighter. He has several silver rings on his fingers and a large silver cloak pin. That pin is the hallmark of tax collectors. Three guards sit off to his right, laughing amongst themselves.

Does he need such help?

"I have no goods to declare," I say, without stopping. I have no time for tedious men, regardless of their stature.

"That will be one silver to enter." He rises and bars my way with his brawny arm.

I take a breath and speak slowly, as if to a child. "I am Sorim and have no goods to declare."

He looks me up and down and sneers. "You fat traders have to pay your own fair share now. That was the first change of the new noviomagus."

"Gisgo is dead?" This is not so surprising, he was old. However, I've found that asking obvious questions to simple people will cause them to lord their knowledge over you.

"We finally have a real leader, Jebel dar Arqan. He respects the Obsidian ways." The man puffs out his chest and glares at me, daring me to disagree.

I grunt in return. I don't remember much of Jebel dar Arqan from the Academy days, but I've never met a member of that family whom I respected. My thoughts turn to Astal. Would she even remain here? I must find her. Perhaps I'm not the only one in need of a friend.

"Here, leech." I flip him a coin.

I make my way down the orange tile walkway and stop at the central fountain to calm myself. If Astal is still here, I can't let her know that I just came from Solent Keep and Koni. Since they first met, those two have been rivals at everything they do.

Even if Astal doesn't have the noviomagus' ear any longer, she'll still be able to get me into the royal records. It's common enough for Sorim to register their offspring here. It ensures that any harm to the children is punishable by our laws, even if they lack the mental gift of a true Sorim.

Wetting my hands, I run them through my hair. Astal's courtyard is empty, and by the lack of a flowery smell, she hasn't been here today. Perhaps she did leave after Gisko's death. I shield my mind; in case it's warranted.

The door to the servant's quarters is unlocked; some things at least will never change. I sneak in like always. I hear Arisha before I can see her ample frame. She's a big woman with a bigger voice. Whoever she's scolding will be scared to death if they've any sense.

I slip through the door and sneak up behind her. Mimicking her, I put my left hand on my hip and wag my finger at the two servant girls. Neither dares to laugh. Instead, they stare at me, causing the big woman to spin around.

"Blachstenius," she mouths. She hurries over and pulls me into her chest. "You must get out of here," she whispers urgently.

With her left hand, she waves the girls away.

"But I just arrived."

"Since Mistress and the noviomagus died, their friends are not welcome here."

"Astal is dead?" My legs turn to pudding, and I have to support myself against the door.

"Some say that Bodo did it."

"Bodo? Nonsense!" I wave my hand to make Arisha stop. "Bodo cared only about his profits, and maybe his wife."

"Oh, but master Blachstenius, I'm not one to tell tales, but Bodo's daughter was getting very, very close to the noviomagus. The mistress took notice and was not pleased. Being that they're all dead, I'm thinking it's alright to come out with their secrets."

Arisha wrings her hands and studies the floor.

"Is it wrong of me?" she blurts. "Am I, am I speaking ill of the dead? Oh, poor Arisha doesn't know about these things. I'm a simple servant, not a high-minded noble like you, Lord Blachstenius Dar Mot Dariik."

I place my hands on her shoulders. "Arisha, you have done your best, and no one can ask more of you than that." I lift my left hand to forestall any doubts. "And I have told you many times to call me Blachstenius. I am just a simple man, not a noble."

Her shoulders bounce, and she grunts and smiles at me. "Master Blachstenius, you must think I'm daft. Old Arisha knows when she's in the presence of greatness, no matter the title. Mistress was also a great lady."

She stops to wipe her eyes.

"And so are you," she whispers to me. "A great man, I mean, don't be offended. I dare say you and the mistress were better than either the old or new noviomagus." Her head sinks into her shoulders as if she's afraid she'll be caught.

Arisha is a kind woman, but if I don't put an end to this, I'll be stuck here all night hearing her lamentations.

"Arisha, I need to speak to the new noviomagus about an urgent matter. Where may I find him?"

Her eyes go wide. "Oh no, Master Blachstenius, you don't want to go into the noviomagusstudy. He has surrounded himself with bad-feeling people. Poor Arisha doesn't know what they have done, but they feel like bad people. No, I don't like going in there at all. Poor Arisha must get up well before the sun to clean the room. It's a bad place now, a bad place."

"Thank you, Arisha. I had planned on giving this to Lady Astal, but I can think of no better person to have it than you." I remove a glass bottle from inside my robe and present the honeysuckle perfume to the servant.

She cradles it with both hands and shyly sniffs the top.

"It's honeysuckle water! Like the mistress had." She stares at me, unable to speak for once.

I tenderly touch her left hand and guide it overtop the present. "Thank you for always being my friend."

I slide past her before she can find more words.

Chapter Three

The Confrontation

The anteroom to Gisgo's study is open. Piled up within are all of Gisgo's treasures, as he called them, even the giant clam chairs. The old noviomagus loved his seashells. Somewhere in the deep, deep ocean, a giant clam had been harvested. Pried open, the shells were each big enough for a person to lounge comfortably. He and Astal would each sit in one half during their nightly reads.

I've always been fond of the dar Cuthos, Astal's family, especially since her grandmother—also named Astal—was the deciding vote for me to be reinstated within my own clan. The family, however, were not big believers in the military, and the army officers were always irate that they were made to give their reports in front of her.

It's only now that my heart has grasped the meaning of Arisha's words. First Bodo, then Gisgo, and now Astal; three of my dearest friends are all dead. Seeing the chairs shoved into a dark corner makes me feel the loss all the more. I take a moment to come to grips with this. Have I ever needed a friend as badly as I do now?

The wavy insides of the great shells are cool and smooth, a harsh counter to the prickly barnacles underneath the lip of the seats. When I would provoke Astal into a reaction, she would say I was as helpful as a barnacle.

I run my hand underneath the seat and cut my pinky. I smile in spite of my melancholy. If Astal were still here, she'd tell me that there's no sense wallowing in self-pity.

I pull the tiny shell sliver from my finger with my teeth and spit it onto the floor. There's nothing left here anymore. The list of places where I once found joy but now only misery has increased rapidly these last couple months.

I came here to see if there is an official record of children sired by my brother. All Sorim are supposed to report children, even illegitimate ones, to the noviomagus. Not all do. The Tyrians report their offspring to the Lord of Commerce in South Londinjon rather than here, but Rhunior was an Obsidian through and through.

The idea that Sorim could be left to their own whims, far away from their official indoctrination, scares those in power on Ynys Luko. Rhunior aspired to supplant Gisgo as the supreme military leader, so the chances of him complying is small. Still, I must look, to be sure.

The study door creaks open, and a servant emerges carrying a huge tray of picked-over food. Several strident voices fight for supremacy within the study. There's a loud thunk, and the tray crashes to the floor. I stoop to help the servant up. Only now do I notice the hand-ax embedded at head-height in the thick oaken door. The people inside jeer at us.

"Don't come back here again tonight." I tell the frightened man as I place the last of the spilled food on the tray.

He quickly nods and sprints down the hall with the large tray over his shoulder.

"I expect members of noble Sorim families to refrain from acting like drunken sailors newly arrived in port." I glare at my countrymen.

"It's him!" Zianni calls. "Kill him!"

I curl my lip at the bleating fop. "Zianni, I thought you'd run all the way back to your mother's teat once you left, screaming your empty little head off."

The warriors in the room laugh at the deposed priest. Warriors the world over are all the same. Introduce yourself by insulting one of their number, and they'll sit back and watch the entertainment.

He turns to a tall, black-haired woman. "You're called the cleaver! Take his head!" His voice goes up an octave, and the woman snickers in response.

I grab the monkey's paw within my robes. Since Conwenna was so effective with it, I'd bought my own. I'd rather not go up against an ax-wielding warrior woman with it, but it's better than only my fists.

A man with oiled brown hair steps forward from the crowd. "Zianni, stop your whining." He places a hand on the ax-wielding woman to still her hand. "You are Blachstenius, I presume?"

I notice the golden armbands on his left arm. "I am, and by your reputation, I'd guess you're Jebel dar Arqan, the new noviomagus."

He flashes me a quick smile. "They say you're a clever one."

I look around the room. Ynys Luko is a small island, and the number of Obsidians from noble houses is smaller still. I recognize several of the faces, but their names escape me. They all are younger than me, an unfortunate side effect of advanced years.

"Are you afraid of my challenge still?" the woman asks.

Squinting at her, it finally comes to me. "Is that little Amma dar Eppon?"

She points with her one remaining hand ax. "You lied to me and told me there was a rule against challenging too many times."

"I did, but only because my father would have been outraged by his son losing to a girl."

"I took it out on Rhunior. I have a winning record against the house of Mot Dariik," she says with pride.

Amma was about four years younger than me. Her ferocity was legendary, even at the Academy. Clearly, nothing has changed. In her eleventh year, she challenged me for the first time. At that age, four years is a huge difference. I beat her then and the next nine times as well. I knew she would not stop until she won, so I made up a rule that if you challenge and lose to the same person ten times, you lose your right to challenge that person.

Once I finished at the Academy, I walked out and followed Koni's steps to Pretanni. Father had been livid; however, the Tyrians were all too happy to accept and train me in the ways of commerce.

"I had no idea that Rhunior was so humiliated. My compliments to you."

Jebel clears his throat loudly. Amma bows her head ever so slightly, as protocol dictates.

So, Jebel is not held in high esteem by the Yatiim Jabbur, the head of the assassins.

"The matter at hand," the new noviomagus says, "is how you should be punished for your crimes."

"Crimes? You'll have to tell me which ones you mean."

The room remains silent.

So, humor is not going to work.

"Pardon my flippant tone. I am tired after a long journey." I bow my head much lower than Amma. Perhaps I'm not too late to make amends.

I feel a pressure on my forehead, a subtle but a steady presence. Looking up, Zianni and two others are chanting under their breath. Does this man know of any trick other than the *nimr nessek*?

I push back against the mind crush, aiming my attack at Zianni. I use the *Rosh Sekab*, the mind razor. It's a simple but subtle attack that Zianni never could grasp. It severs the mind's conscious control of the body for a heartbeat or two. Unless your balance is perfect, you tumble to the ground.

Zianni falls into the back of one of his cohorts and they both lose their concentration. The third, sensing he's alone, raises his hands and looks away from me.

Jebel eyes me intently, but doesn't intervene. As much as I'd like to slap Zianni around some more, it won't win me any supporters in this room. I raise my hands and look away, the universal Sorim signal for disengagement.

The room falls silent until Jebel begins clapping.

"That was most instructive," he says. "Tell me, Blachstenius, how long have you been sterile, and in what cities have you searched for your brother's unnamed child?"

My whole body freezes as I stare back at the man.

He waves his hand at Zianni and his cronies. "They were a perfect distraction, and you let your guard down."

I desperately want to smack his smug face. Instead, I stare at the noviomagus, waiting for him to tip his hand. It's too late now, but I form a *hemyet*, a mental fortress to protect my thoughts from further prying.

"Come now, the legendary Blachstenius is speechless?"

His cronies laugh. If they all band together for the *nimr nessek*. . .. I take a half-step backward. He would discover that Grahme killed his cousin, my brother's second, at Solent Keep, and another friend would be put in danger. My arms are extended backward, feeling for the door as I take another retreating step.

"No!" Jebel shouts. "First, we must discover all of your crimes, then we will punish you accordingly." He makes a gesture of putting a noose over his head.

"Everyone!" He points at me, and now eight people in the room are attacking me with the *nimr nessek*.

My legs feel wooden as they work against my will and bring me closer to my enemies. If I succumb, what's to stop them from killing me outright and ending the house of Mot Dariik right here?

My arms are becoming rigid. It won't be long until I'm completely within their thrall. They're startled when I give into the compulsion and my gait quickens. It gives me an instant of respite. Grabbing the monkey's paw, I throw it underhanded at Jebel. He sees it at the last instant and tries to duck. The iron ball connects with his breastbone, perhaps leaving a bruise, but that's all I need. His sudden motion has broken their concentration.

I turn and sprint to the door. Compulsion spells are only effective if there's a line of sight. I feel something skim by my ear and hear the thump. Next to me, wedged deeply within the door, is another hand ax. I turn to see my attacker.

"*Nice move,*" Amma projects to me. She smiles and blows me a kiss. "*Exit through the courtyard and don't stop running for any reason.*"

Chapter Four

South Londinjon

It could always be worse, I tell myself as I alternate between standing and sitting in my wagon. I've traveled through the night to put a good distance between me and Zianni's lackeys. The bite of the bitter wind on this unusually cold night is my only ally against sleep's siren call. Once more, I ask the unknowable question of why Amma didn't kill me outright in Gisko's old study.

Bodo, Askal, and Gisgo are all dead. My plans are shattered, and my desperate plight has been revealed to my enemies. How could everything have gone so wrong?

*   *   *

The smell of rotting plant life is unmistakable. Londinjon can't be far off now. The Wigesta control North Londinjon, a truly worldly city filled with baubles and oddities from every known trade route. Stone buildings tower three levels or more above the street, especially in the warehouse district. The city wall is two levels high, with a wooden palisade atop it. The sprawling city has two rivers running through it and a third just outside the wall that keeps the city clean and provides a safe water supply.

The Tyrians, Sorim traders like me, control the run-down, depressing city of South Londinjon. There is no flowing river for our city, only a swamp. The only time the city is bearable is in winter, when the mosquitoes are dormant. I make it a point to avoid this fetid city, but this once, I cannot.

Soon winter will end and the little bloodsuckers will reawaken. Only here do we Sorim build thatched-roof homes like the natives. A constant hearth fire in the homes provides the protection needed from the pests. Of course, when the Wigesta decides to attack from across the river, these homes will burn very quickly and very brightly.

As the road reaches the marsh, there's a stable and warehouse for traders. An old man with stooped shoulders waves me to him.

"The next flatboat won't ship off until tomorrow morning. Leave your ponies and wagon with me and I'll see that they're taken care of."

I slide down from the box seat and slip him a silver coin.

"Melqart bless you," he says.

"Don't you mean Dagan? I would think the god of good fortune to be more fitting."

"Good fortune is in rare supply these days, and I fear Melqart will be needed when the Wigesta bring war upon us."

I pull at the neck of my robe. Suddenly it feels tight. "I don't know that Melqart will see fit to bless me."

So, it's not common knowledge yet that Conwenna and I defiled Melqart's temple in Solent Keep.

He nods. "A pacifist then, wanting only to wander the island and sell your wares. I've seen more than my share of men like you."

"Yes, that's it." I cough into my hand. "How is the ale here?"

* * *

In the long-honored tradition of Sorim traders, I don't wait for my wagon and ponies to be shipped across the marsh to the main island of South Londinjon. I pay a fisherman to ferry me across instead. The boat I chose smells of day-old catch, so there mustn't have been any fishing today.

Because of the fisherman ferries, I must adhere to the most ridiculous of rules. The Tyrians in charge of South Londinjon insist that all travelers head to the baths upon arriving on the island. Whoever heard of traders afraid of road-worn travelers? I do enjoy a good bath, but here, the baths will soften my skin, making it easier for the mosquitoes to drain the blood from me.

I spend the absolute minimum amount of time in the baths. There can be no dawdling here. I shake out my robe to remove as many signs of the road as I can before I approach the hall of records. Both my brother and I arrived in Pretanni here, in South Londinjon. I chose this city because it's ruled by the Tyrians; I'll never know why Rhunior chose this port over Regnorum.

It's highly unlikely he registered any of his unnamed children here; that wasn't my brother's way. Perhaps the mother of my niece or nephew was wise enough to come here to secure protections for their child. The hall of records is a dimly lit hut, without a hearth fire. Scribes the world over fear the fire that would consume their life's work, but this old one is the worst I've seen in years. Pale, flickering light from the two candles at a man's desk try to displace the shadows on the walls and largely fail.

"I wish to see the records concerning Rhunior dar Mot Dariik of Solent Keep," I tell the master scribe.

The scribe is hunched over some old, musty tome and busy stroking his hair sideways while doing whatever it is they do. His gray hair is quite stiff and remains extended away from his head when he stops the odd habit. The candles are placed on either side of his tome, perilously close to his disheveled hair. The way he sits, I wonder if the hunched posture is permanent, or if his eyes have begun failing.

I clear my throat. Nothing. I clear it again and toss a gold coin on the table. It rolls into one of the stubby wooden candle holders and flops over on its side. Still nothing. It's rude, but I extend my mind toward him, gently probing him to converse with the living.

He finishes the line of text and slams his hand down. The candles are bright enough to illuminate the dust billowing up between them.

"Yes," he says, drawing it out in an exasperated fashion.

"I do apologize, but I have urgent business."

"Urgent business in the hall of records?" he asks, incredulous.

"Yes. I need to see the records immediately."

"A handful of years ago, there was one offspring registered as a child of your brother."

"I did not claim relation to this Rhunior."

"Even us old, musty scribes know of the Mot Dariik brothers. In fact, I was the one to log both you and your brother into the records when you arrived."

"Is that so?" A smile emerges on my lips for the first time in days. "Can you show me the record?"

"I cannot."

He follows my gaze to the gold coin. He reaches for it and tosses it back to me. "I am an old, simple man. There is no need for this."

"I don't understand. I thought all the Pretanni records were kept here."

"They were," the man says, pushing himself away from the table. "Until your brother came here and burned everything pertaining to Solent Keep."

"Why was he allowed to do this?"

"Did you expect me to stand up to Rhunior and his men?" The old man laughs as he again drags his fingers through his tousled hair.

"Then any records of unnamed children are lost for good." I try to keep the disappointment out of my voice and fail.

"On that score, I possess some knowledge." The man gives me a smug smile and shakes his head back and forth. "It was that knowledge specifically that he wanted destroyed. When I wouldn't give him that page, he decided to burn all the Solent Keep records just to be safe."

"So, you know of this child?" I dare to hope.

"A woman came in here three years ago, holding a toddler. She claimed the boy to be Rhunior's child." He rubs his chin. "Her name was Bara. She was a striking woman, tall, with long brown hair down to her waist."

"She was a native, then?"

"Oh, indeed she was. She had the most colorful robes dyed in many different colors and a deep voice that brooked no dissent."

"Where was this Bara from?"

The man grimaces and shakes his head. "I'm afraid I don't recall."

"Was it a Sorim city?"

The man appears to shrink before me. His tired eyes look up at me. "In my youth I may have recalled such detail, but I'm afraid those days are gone."

I pound the table with my fist before turning away. "Is there a chance you might recall if I give you time to consider?"

"I'm afraid I have been doing little else this day."

"You were randomly pondering about my brother's offspring today?" I ask, perplexed.

"Oh, no. You are not the first to ask me this. A follower of Zianni, the High Priest of Melqart, came but a few hours ago."

I freeze. "Did the man arrive earlier today?" I ask. There's no way he could have outridden me.

"Oh no, he has been here for months, overseeing the new temple to Melqart."

"Could you point him out to me?"

The scribe remains hunched over when he leaves his chair and wobbles around his table. He thrusts the door open wide, slamming it against the wooden wall of his hut. Short of screaming, there is no better way to call attention to us. With his gnarled writing hand, he points to a man with short blond hair who is staring back at us.

The priest's eyes widen, then he continues his conversation as if he didn't recognize me. It was only for an instant, but it will take more than that to fool me.

I send a mind whip strong enough to punch through his defenses. He drops to his knees, but that's all. I don't know how many Sorim he has here with him, and I don't care to find out. The southern docks are empty of boats, and I don't have time to call a fisherman again. I run for the eastern docks instead. That's where the ships are repaired. It's a gamble, but I'd rather swim the mighty River Thames than face a small mob of Melqart's devotees.

"Are there any boats available here?" I ask, breathless.

"I can take you," a man says with badly slurred speech. "Right after I finish my mead." He raises his wooden cup to me, spilling plenty of it on his hairy chest.

"Where's your boat?"

He points to a single fishing vessel at the end of the pier. I have to hope that he didn't do the repairs himself.

The blond-haired priest has assembled three others, and they are racing toward me. I use considerable suggestion toward the drunk to get him to his feet and his free arm around my shoulders. Being drunk, he has no defenses against me, so I take control of his legs and move us along at a decent pace. Once on the suspect boat, I compel him to launch.

The priests of Melqart yell for us to return, but using my powers, I block their mental commands. The boat rocks as my ferryman tries to stand and relieve himself. I grab his shoulder and compel him to sit and row. A wet spot grows on his trousers. One more foul odor can hardly make a difference. My control over him is so complete that he doesn't even notice. From south Londinjon, the priests stamp their feet as we get smaller in the distance.

I drove my cart over all the roads of Pretanni for twenty years before it broke. Now I lose my second wagon in less than a month. Someone will no doubt enjoy my figs and olives, but it won't be me. I jingle my coin purse. I'm going to have to do some work to live up to the title of best trader in Pretanni.

Chapter Five

North Londinjon

My drunk ferryman is a pugnacious man. He vomits over the side of his boat and begins to sober up. His mental skill is not great, but he never stops fighting me, so I must maintain my compulsion the whole time as he ferries me across the river.

The Wigesta control North Londinjon, and they're not about to allow Sorim boats to cross the River Thames at will. Their favorite ploy with fisherman is to wait until the catch is finished, then they sail out and steal the fish. We have no catch, but there are still huge trading vessels sailing up and down the river which consider it a sport to ram fishermen's boats.

It's all about the timing. An enormous trading vessel is launching from the docks of North Londinjon. We keep to the shallow, swampy area until they turn east, toward the sea. We race directly for it and let it hide us from view of the city walls. East of the city are the graveyards. For obvious reasons, they're not guarded.

My guide puts us so close to the trading vessel that the crew can hurl items at us. We're spotted, and one of the crew calls to his mates.

"Get closer to it!" I shout.

My guide sits, slack-jawed, as valuable time is lost. A dagger lands in the boat, just missing his knee. One of us could be dead now. I give up my control, since even his drunken instincts are better than mine in this case. He pulls with all his might, taking us closer to the ship. We miss running into it, but not by much. Looking up, no sailor can be seen over the bulge in the side of the behemoth.

We're no match for the speed of our shield, so it's not long before it leaves us in its wake. The big, wide world beyond awaits the ship. The muddy, low-lying cemetery of Wigesta Londinjon awaits me.

Disembarking is just as treacherous as my legs sink knee deep in the muck. I find small, flat stones at regular intervals. I slosh from one to another, only able to get free of the muck for a moment before my stone perch sinks. It's only when one is laying face-up that I realize these are overturned gravestones.

A shiver goes down my spine. Those many hard objects my feet encountered beneath me must have been the remains of the dead. This swampy land is where the poor are forced to bury their loved ones. I know the ones beneath me can't feel anything, but I'm appalled at what I must do, nonetheless.

There are a dozen people gathered around a small stone between me and the city walls. They've dug the grave too shallow, probably in hopes of keeping their loved one away from the river's high tide. I suspect this is the best they can do.

My robes are caked in mud, and I realize that a fetid smell is coming from me. I close the distance to the mourners and enter the city at the rear of the group. No one is interested in questioning the mourners, least of all me, the most odiferous member of the group.

Once inside the city walls, I break off and head northward. The walls encircling the city never cease to amaze me. There are taller walls on Eriu, but those cities were built by the giants. Northern Londinjon's walls were completely built by the Wigesta, and they have no human-made equal.

It's been many years since I've been in the city. The faces change, but the game of commerce never does. I'm without merchandise and my coins are few, yet I can't stop grinning. It's invigorating. With the help of some old friends, I'll regain a leading spot in the game. But first, I need to bathe.

*　*　*

Turec and Sibwine are a wonderful couple and the best silversmiths on the isle. Turec's delicate hammer-work and Sibwine's bold designs should be the envy of all the elites. However, they are guilty of being low born.

I skirt past the potters, the blacksmiths, and the tanners to the couple's work studio, which is pressed up against the northern wall of the city. Workshops closer to the main road are the coveted spots. Their shop is within smelling distance of the stables.

From the back of the studio, I hear the delicate striking of a hammer on metal and a soft but determined woman's voice. I approach the counter and see a polished iron hand mirror sitting out. Lifting it, I gaze at my own weathered reflection.

"This mirror is defective!" I shout toward the back.

Sibwine rushes through the thin curtain, expecting an unruly customer no doubt. She stops in her tracks when she sees me.

"I might have known." She puts her hand on her hip. "Turec! Come out here and clear this miscreant from our property." She turns her back to me.

Head down and fists balled, Turec swats the curtain out of his way. He looks up at me and freezes for an instant.

"Surely I don't deserve that look," I say.

"Blachstenius!" he shouts. "No one has put a dagger into you yet?"

He reaches over the counter and grabs me in a bear hug.

Sibwine yells at her excited husband not to break my spine in his enthusiasm. Thanks to her level head, I suffer nothing other than a couple of thumps to my back.

"I don't know why you haven't left this clod for some young man like me," I tell Sibwine.

She rolls her eyes. "What brings you back to our shop?"

I nod and smile. "Straight to negotiations." I hold up the mirror. "Is this promised to anyone?"

"No," Sibwine says cautiously. She always takes the lead in negotiations. It's one of the reasons I'm so fond of them. They don't let convention or egos get in the way of business.

"I find myself short on coin," I say. "And I decided I would let you help me remedy that."

Turec chuckles, but Sibwine is unmoved.

"What are you proposing we do for you?" she asks archly.

I smile at her, though she doesn't reciprocate. "Can you draw interweaving vines along the outside of this polished mirror and have Turec lightly engrave the pattern?"

"Sure, but why would we want to mar the perfect outside edge of this mirror?"

I glance at Turec. I can see that he wants to do it for the challenge, if nothing else. "If you are successful, and you give me a small amount of coin to buy some good Hiberian wine —"

Sibwine snorts in derision.

"—then I'll take you and the mirror with me during my audience with the Walda of Londinjon." I finish.

"When do you see him?" Turec blurts.

"Well, I haven't announced myself to Tilbert yet, so it will be a few days."

"Are you going to go see the Walda dressed like that?" Sibwine lets out a disgusted sigh. "To be clear, you want us to risk ruining a fine piece of workmanship *and* give you money to buy a drink for an empty promise?"

"We'll do it," Turec says.

Sibwine backhands her husband in the chest.

"Ouch!" He rubs the spot and looks at his wife, mystified. "We both know you're going to say yes. Blachstenius has probably used his mental gift and knows your answer too, so why be difficult?"

Sibwine grabs the mirror off the counter and slaps her husband's stomach with it. "This is why I don't let you come out when we get new customers."

Turec gives us a big, goofy grin before hurrying back to his workshop.

Sibwine nods toward the back. "You might as well come back and inspect the pattern."

The big man clears his bench and places the mirror in the center. He's like a child, waiting impatiently to play with his new toy.

Sibwine taps his chest with the back of her hand so she can have her space.

"What vine do you want?"

"Edennos. It symbolizes friendship and connection, and we'll need both."

"Right," Sibwine says. "You two go to the mead hall for a drink and leave me be."

*　*　*

The vines are masterfully done, complete with intricate leaves wrapping around the outside of the mirror. Despite her protestations of poverty, Sibwine has a fine new dress made for our audience with the leader of the city. I spend what little I have left on new robes as well.

"It's important that you let me do the talking, at least at first," I say. "Once the formality is lifted, it will be your job to explain your work to Tilbert."

Turec shallowly nods his head. His eyes stare off into the distant lands of the pixies.

"Remember to breathe, Turec," I say.

"What?" He looks quickly between his wife and me. "Right, breathe."

Sibwine backhands him in the chest once more and sighs. "Let me do the talking."

Chapter Six

A Formal Audience

My gift fits snugly between my elbow and hand. Whether it be a lack of coin or Sibwine's thriftiness, I've never had so little to offer a man of Tilbert's station. He's likely to drink it all before our audience is over and that's not nearly enough to get him drunk. I dare not push him with my mind. The Wigesta cannot abide being mind-controlled.

Who can? I smile at myself.

Turec and I stand by the door, waiting on Sibwine. She emerges wearing a rich blue and white fleece mantle over her best linen robe. I don't think it's a coincidence that the colors match Tilbert's family crest. I note two faint stains and a small hole, but it will have to do. Turec gawks at his wife, mouth open.

She's blushing and refusing to meet her husband's eyes. "Don't just stand there; we'll be late for Blachstenius' audience with the Walda."

The big man places his hands on his wife's shoulders, kisses the top of her head and follows her out into the street.

I probably should have told her that I don't have a scheduled audience.

"It seems everyone is a bit nervous about this meeting," Sibwine says as she hugs her stout husband. Turec leans down and kisses her forehead this time. She looks up and picks something out of his mustache.

"We should go," I say.

The sparse trees within the city are decked in fresh spring growth. I must be spending too much time with the druids, for I wish there were more trees around us.

My one good fortune is that Tilbert will be at the trading hall today and not his palace. I've teased the man mercilessly about acting so stern and unapproachable when he's on his throne. The Walda will be on the raised platform overlooking the tree-lined park. The trader's complaints are heard there, rather than at the palace.

Mature trees and shrubs line the street opposite the trading hall. The park is a long and narrow triangle. The traders block the street at these meetings. The residents, if they take any interest in the proceedings, show up here. The master traders are all seated on either side of the podium, where Tilbert will speak.

There are a dozen columns topped with statues in front of the hall. One day, after he's passed, Tilbert's likeness will certainly be added to the row. Steps run from the street level up to the plaza where the wealthy sit. This is where Tilbert will stand to hear the endless complaints of the traders. I select a spot directly in front of the podium.

He arrives and his eyes drift unseeing across the width of the park. That's unfortunate; I was counting on him seeing me. He thanks the noble traders and the good people of the city before he drones on about construction projects within the city.

I start to cross the closed-off street, but the guards intercept me. Tilbert looks down and we lock eyes. Abruptly, he signals the public time is up and retreats back into the hall. What little crowd assembled leaves in confusion at the canceled speech.

A young page runs from the trading hall and stands rigidly to the side of the guards. "The Walda has requested the presence of the scoundrel Blachstenius," he says nervously.

"A scoundrel?" I ask, affronted. "Only to hopeless cheats like Tilbert."

Lifting my robe from the ground, I lead us up the steps. The trading hall is nothing more than four covered hallways forming a square around a tree-filled garden. The hallway roofs rest upon a double row of columns. In driving rainstorms, it's not uncommon for men to stand underneath the trading hall roof for hours until the rain desists. No trader worthy of high stature would leave the hall and have their clothes dampened by mere weather.

I turn to my friends. "Remember, let me greet Tilbert and only speak if you are spoken to. Follow me, but stay a step behind. After I've presented the gifts, he'll want to know more. Answer him honestly and succinctly. Once he smiles and lobs an insult my way, you'll know the formal audience is over."

Sibwine grabs Turec's free hand. She stands on her tippytoes as he leans down to kiss her. I turn away and grin to myself. What snarky comment would mother have said if she saw this? Only commoners partake in such public displays of affection. I repress the barest twinge of jealousy.

Along the sunny south side of the hall, Tilbert has maneuvered so his back is to Belenos. Traders are confident, and over-familiar, so Tilbert's move is sly, as it keeps the traders' heads low while they speak to him, not giving them a chance to look him in the eye while they avoid the glare of the sun. I smile as I approach. I taught him that trick. He has a dozen guards stationed around him, but they're standing far enough away to allow his conversations to remain private. Unless, of course, one can read the surface thoughts of the petitioner.

Tilbert talks to another two traders while we wait behind him. He's playing games with me, by making me wait.

I scan the guards until I find the commander. I deaden his mind enough so we can walk past him. None of the other guards will dare step in if he remains still. Turec slows his pace and is pulled along by his wife. The trader speaking to Tilbert looks at us indignantly. I stare back impassively.

There's the slightest trace of a smile on the Walda's face. "I will look into this, good trader. Allow me a month and I will provide you with an answer."

The trader's lips curl up in a sneer as he looks at us. I hear Sibwine whispering to her husband to stand still. I bow low to Tilbert to acknowledge his station. As I rise, he fixes me with a formidable stare.

"Oh wise city elder, through the many, many years of your wisdom and guidance, this great city has flourished like never before. I beseech you to focus those aged eyes upon my plight and grant me some grandfatherly advice." I bow low a second time and hold myself still, so he can see my full head of hair.

Tilbert and I stare impassively at each other. Turec takes a startled breath. The big craftsman tries to maneuver Sibwine behind him, but she throws off her husband's hands. At last, Tilbert cracks a smile.

I should have thought about this address more. Surely, I could have come up with more ways of calling him old.

"One day you will rue that barbed tongue of yours," Tilbert says.

Turec sighs loudly behind me.

"May I present the most talented metalsmiths in your city? Master Turec and his wife, Sibwine, have gone unnoticed for far too long."

I reach for the gifts, but both Turec and Sibwine are still bowing low.

"Rise," I whisper.

First Sibwine, then her husband, do as I bid, though they refuse to look directly at their Walda. I take the mirror from Sibwine and give her arm a little shake. She looks ready to faint. I turn and stride toward Tilbert. He signals the guards to hold their places.

"Tell me truthfully. Have you ever seen finer workmanship?" I ask as I give him the mirror.

Despite his efforts, I can see that he's excited to receive the mirror.

"Consider this a gift from Turec and Sibwine, to their honored Walda."

Tilbert looks around me at the nervous couple. "This is truly exquisite workmanship. If I give this gift to my wife, she will demand similar items for the rest of our days. Will you be able to match such work?"

"Yes, Walda Tilbert!" Sibwine blurts.

Turec nods his head in agreement with his diminutive wife.

"Then I will send a man to you soon to commission another work in the coming days."

The tradesmen start chattering to themselves. Discovering such skilled craftsmen under their collective noses is sure to be the talk of the city.

I lean toward Sibwine. "You are about to be inundated with requests. Raise your prices and hold firm to the time you need to produce the goods. They'll complain vociferously, but they'll pay."

She gives me a guilty look. "Thank you, Blachstenius, I'm sorry I doubted you."

I give her arm a gentle squeeze and face Tilbert as he turns his attention back to me.

"And what do you want?" he asks, not even trying to hide his delight at the gift.

"Me? I merely wish to present you with some fine Hiberian wine and ask for the privilege of walking back to the palace with you."

He snorts once.

"This audience is over," he announces. "I will return next month to discuss the city's future with the noble trading houses."

"Give your names to the head guard," I tell Sibwine with a wink. "He'll make sure Tilbert's order reaches you."

The traders voice their disappointment at the sudden conclusion, and the guards watch the crowd as it slowly disperses. The traders all stare at my friends, memorizing their faces.

"Don't be alarmed if several of them follow you home. They'll need to know where to find you for their orders," I say to my friends.

Sibwine and her grinning fool of a husband have taken their first steps to a higher social station.

* * *

Tilbert's study is on the second floor of his palace, and his one small window overlooks the River Walo. The solid stone wall of the kitchen is below us. That's another trick I taught Tilbert. The heat from the kitchen will keep the floor warm, even in winter.

If my memory can be trusted, there are two guards stationed below this window to ensure that no one can overhear what is said. Unlike most, Tilbert doesn't require grand gestures of his power, but he does insist on privacy.

I place my feet on Tilbert's table. Bemused, he stares at me, then shrugs and follows my lead. A servant comes into the Walda's private study and pours two glasses of the fine Hiberian wine. If he's surprised by our slouching, he never shows it.

"I can't have this," I say. "There is but a small amount."

"Blachstenius, drink, so that there is less for me to suffer through."

"But this is your favorite?"

It's Tilbert's time to smile at me. "I hate this stuff. I lied and told you otherwise so that I could see if you were busy up here." He taps the side of his head. He takes a sip and makes a disgusted face. "I much prefer ale, or now that we're alone, I can admit that Pretanni mead is a favorite of mine."

"All this time, I've been spending a fortune getting you a gift that you secretly can't stand." I can't help but laugh. I finish my glass and grab his. He rises and walks to one of the walls.

The study is decorated with giant maps. There's one of Londinjon, one of Pretanni, and one of the trading routes to Hiberia and beyond. I presented that one to him years ago.

"All this time, I thought you were a man of culture," I press. He lets my good-natured barb go unchallenged. "Have your servant bring mead, and I'll be happy to drink with you."

"As if I could. What would the traders say if they knew I drank the peasant's drink?"

"Why do you care?"

"Because I wish to be proclaimed the Bretwalda of Pretanni." He motions toward the map.

The head of every decent-sized town insists on being called a Walda. A Bretwalda is the equivalent of a king. Rendell only wants to be the First Wickner, the leader of our army, but my friend Tilbert has much more imagination.

"Is this map accurate?" he asks. "And why doesn't it show the location of the druid's base on the plains?"

"It is as accurate as any trader's map, and I've only been to the plains druid camp a couple times."

Per year, I add to myself.

"I have given my word not to divulge the location. Unless you wish to bring war upon them, there is no need to know."

"Don't pretend you're not aware that war is coming," he says.

I take another drink of the wine, encouraging him to continue.

"Everyone knows that Rendel and I are the two leading contenders. Andrei was also being considered until he died—"

"—he died?"

"Where have you been hiding?" Tilbert demands. "Andrei died last month in Calleva. It seems that this Loris has risen from the weeds and leads the Verlamion faction now."

"Loris? As in the leader of the Pretanni druids?"

"The former leader, yes, him. I've spent fifteen years cultivating favors and groveling to traders, and this pompous fool appears from nowhere and now contends for the title of Bretwalda. I can handle Rendell. I'd even allow him to keep what he wants, the command of the army, as long as he's pledged to me. Now this Loris comes out of nowhere and claims a religious mantle. I move against him, and he'll claim I'm not pious."

"But you're not pious."

His face contorts upon itself. "How do I handle him?"

"Then the troops are assembled?"

"Blachstenius," he says exasperatedly, "it's hardly a secret that we will move during the battle season next year. Personally, I want to negotiate with the Sorim, and the druids, if I can. We'd leave your lands alone as long as a yearly tribute is paid. There's no need for thousands to become food for the crows."

I take a moment to let Tilbert's news sink in.

"Do you know who the new leaders of the Sorim are?" That gets his attention.

"At Regnorum or Solent Keep?"

"Both."

He makes an almost purring noise. "Go on."

"Jebel dar Arqan is the new noviomagus."

Tilbert grunts. "That's not welcome news."

The servant arrives with our mead. I scan the walls. He must have a secret spot to observe us so our needs can be seen to without interruption.

How private is this conversation?

"The leader of Solent Keep is Lady Koni dar Surby."

"The fleeing princess? You mean that wasn't just a servant's tale?"

I chuckle. "Whatever you do, don't let her hear you say that."

"Do you know what she's like?" Tilbert asks, all joviality gone.

"Better than any other person alive," I say. "We've been friends since I started pulling on her ponytail."

"Can she be negotiated with?" he asks excitedly. "Talking with Jebel is a waste of time. Please tell me this Lady Koni is different."

I nod. "This is wonderful mead. I'll have to return here after my trip to Solent Keep to sample it again."

The Walda smiles. "That would be most welcome."

"Are you aware of my station within my house, the Mot Dariiks?"

"I know that it is an old house—the founding house of Ynys Luko, if I'm not mistaken," Tilbert says cautiously.

"Correct." The drink in me wants to let out my whole sorry tale, but I can't give Tilbert all that information for free. "Are you aware that Rhunior and I were the last of our line?"

"I was not."

"Well, now Rhunior is dead, and there is no heir to the Mot Dariik house."

Tilbert gives me a broad grin. "Then you better get to it, man!"

I down the last of my wine in one gulp. I gather myself and I look at my friend. "I am unable to make a child."

He blinks at me in confusion. "I have many healers at my disposal, and I can guarantee they will be discreet."

"They can't help me. It is the price I paid to travel through Strigula's swamp."

"Strigula?" He gasps. "Another servant's tale that turns out to be true?"

"Indeed. For one with such an extensive spy network, you know so very little about Ynys Luko."

"Blachstenius," he chides me, "everyone there can read minds. How am I supposed to get my people to the island and remain undiscovered?"

I know several ways, but that will have to wait until I need another favor.

I close my eyes and take a deep breath. "And Jebel is aware of this now. My only hope is that I can find some unrecognized child of my brother's before his assassins kill either the child or me. Otherwise, the great line of Mot Dariiks will end."

We both look at the Pretanni map while finishing our mead. The door creaks open, and the servant sticks his head in to check on us.

"Leave us!" Tilbert roars.

"I know that you have the best network of spies on the island," I tell him. "Don't bother to deny it. My price for being your secret missive to Solent Keep is any knowledge you can discover about my possible nieces and nephews."

"And just how am I supposed to find this child?"

"The mother is a local woman named Bara, and she has long brown hair. The child would be eight years or younger. She showed up at South Londinjon with her child to make the claim, so she can't be more than a couple days away and most likely in a Sorim-controlled city."

"That's more than a fair bargain. And Blachstenius, I'm sorry."

"Sorry enough to provide me with a wagon and some trade goods?" I smile tightly at him.

"Oh, look at you, changing the deal already." He smiles back. "When do you need your wagon?"

"Tomorrow would be nice."

"I can make that work."

I don't like how he agreed so quickly, but I can't negotiate when he gives me exactly what I ask for.

Chapter Seven

A New Wrinkle

I check out the wagon Tilbert procured for me. The wheels are thinner than the Pretanni style wagons and there are a lot of marshy areas ahead. No doubt this will work just fine on the official Wigestan roads, but the wheels won't fit in the wagon-worn groves to the west.

Tilbert is stroking the mane of one of the ponies. If we can get more leaders like Tilbert and Conwenna, this land will know peace and prosperity. If only.

"I've come to see you off because I need to ask for your help," Tilbert says.

"I am in your debt." I spread out my hands.

"Do you know anything about Loris?"

I scratch my chin. "Only a little. He's full of himself, he rules by dictate and he doesn't have much patience. When he was head of the druids, he was challenged by one of his own and fled rather than fight."

"And yet somehow he's in the running to be the Bretwalda." Tilbert laughs derisively.

"I forgot to mention, he's also a silvertongue, so that would explain his rapid rise in the Pretanni druids as well as the Wigesta."

"Yes, one of my spies mentioned this is a possibility. We know he has ties on the mainland as well, but they have been staying out of our struggle so far."

I give my friend a sidelong glance. I know what's coming, but I'm not going to volunteer for the job.

"Would you, by chance, be going through Verlamion?" he asks.

"I would. What in particular do you want me to find out for you?"

Tilbert scratches his thick brown hair. "My men have discovered that Loris is having hundreds, maybe thousands, of fyrian stones made. They're useful on the battlefield, since a fireball can be conjured in only a heartbeat, but it takes men to win the day. Is he so inept at warcraft that he's unaware, or is there more to it?"

"So, you want me to go up to the silvertongue and ask him?"

"You're more subtle than that," the Walda says. "Also, while you're there—"

"There's more?"

"There is, dear friend. The fyrian stones are now under the direction of a man named Shua. He's an ambitious druid, by all accounts. So no, you won't have to meet with Loris. But if you did, sticking a dagger in his neck would be greatly appreciated."

"So, I'm to be your spy and assassin and I dare say there is something else you wish to mention?"

Tilbert grimaces. "Yes, there is one more thing. I can't figure out why, but Loris is searching everywhere for a ghost orchid. I'm not even sure what one is, much less how to find one."

"And you don't know what significance it has," I finish for him.

"Exactly."

"As it turns out," I say, "I'm also going to add to our bargain."

We look at each other and laugh. Tilbert was my biggest rival before he swapped trading for government. We both know all the tricks to dealmaking.

"Any information about my possible heirs is to be sent to Lady Koni at once."

"Not you?"

"Your men won't be able to reach me."

He scoffs. "You're not going to Ynys Luko, so unless you're going to see Ganna the witch, my men will find you.

"Lady Koni. Immediately. She will be the only one who can reach me."

"You're going to see the witch?" Tilbert's eyes grow ridiculously large.

I shrug my shoulders.

"You're daft."

"Since I'm the one getting the worse part of this bargain, it's the least you can do," I say in a somber tone.

The weight of my failure at Regnorum and at southern Londinjon is hitting me hard. Tilbert's men will be hard-pressed to find my heir before true Sorim do, so now I'm seeking an audience with the most frightening person on all of Pretanni.

"Can you give me some coin to buy medjool dates?"

Tilbert claps me on the back. "It's not all bad. Loris' spies found a struggling merchant here with a ghost orchid. They were sloppy though, so the spies have been sent down the Thames with holes in their chests. Unfortunately, the merchant knows of his potential customer and he's not willing to part with the stupid flower for any price."

"Then why hasn't he been sent down the river after Loris' spies?"

Tilbert winces. "I hate to kill traders. For all their incessant complaining, they bring a lot of money to the city."

"What's the name of the inn where this merchant is staying?"

"The Mearh Heafod," Tilbert says.

"The Horsehead Inn?" I ask, disgusted. "Then I'm going to need some more coin. I'll need a good comb just to get the lice out of my hair."

Tilbert tosses me a coin purse before turning to leave. We've known each other so long that he had been expecting something like this.

*   *   *

The medjools and a fine comb were easy to procure. Now I must force myself to not eat all the dates, even if they are my favorite treat.

If only I were so fortunate with my traveling companion. The struggling merchant Tilbert mentioned is an unpleasant man with an unkempt beard and the need to clear his throat with every third breath. The way he scratches his head makes me wonder if I will indeed need a lice comb.

It takes me five leagues of nudging him before he mentions the ghost orchid. The man doesn't like to chat, which is fine. I'll just draw the rest out of his head while we travel in silence.

It's obvious he thinks the orchid is worth a fortune, but he has no idea why. Slowly, I plant the false memory of a glade near Camulodunon that is filled with the flowers. It's one which I've passed before, and it's plainly visible from the road.

Now that I have coaxed him to sleep, I can take the flower and strip it from his consciousness. Never before have I done such a thing to a fellow trader. I'll consider this theft my part in the coming war.

*   *   *

The entrance of Verlamion comes into view. I give my companion a mental jolt, waking him up. He sees the rows of statues that decorate the entrance as well as the earthen walls to either side and spurs the ponies onward at a trot.

"How long was I asleep?" He grasps his leather purse tightly, even though it's empty, and he has no conscious memory of what it held.

"It has been quite a while. Not that I blame you; I have always found the steady gait of ponies' hooves to be relaxing." I yawn once for good measure. "We should be inside Verlamion well before sundown."

The distrustful trader moves his purse to his other side, away from me, before he starts scratching his head furiously. I lean a little farther away from him.

A brown-haired Wigestan druid stares at us from atop the city wall. I sense no mental probing, but the man makes me uncomfortable all the same. He rushes down to greet us at the city gate.

"Hello travelers," he says with a false smile. "How are the roads?" He secures the reins with a practiced gesture.

"Thank you," I say. "The roads are good. I dare say that it is my aching bones that create most of my problems."

He leads the ponies off to the right, toward the stables. The ponies smell the water and it's all the Wigestan druid can do to stay out of their way.

"I'm Shua," he says, "And I take it upon myself to show off the best of Verlamion to new arrivals. Opportunities await!"

"I'm afraid that I am just passing through," I say.

"I'm not," my companion says.

Shua's eyes brighten at the news. "Once you settle up with this trader, I'll be happy to show you this fair city."

I wave off Shua's words. "Company on the road is enough for me. I hate to be parted so soon," I lie, "but I wish you well." I even bow to my mark as a sign of respect.

The disagreeable trader jumps from the box seat and rushes around the cart to Shua. I've done as Tilbert asked by acquiring the ghost orchid and making this disagreeable man forget all about it. Now it's up to Tilbert and his network to come through for me.

"Let me show you the wonders of our city," Shua says expansively.

A chill goes down my spine. I quickly read Shua's mind, and he's fixated on fyrian stones. As much as I'd like to believe the coming war can still be avoided, there's no doubt in that man's mind.

I've never liked this city. Many come and marvel at the statues placed throughout. If they only knew that the druids can animate the stones, creating a stone army in only a few breaths, they'd understand why the city has no gates. Attackers come in and the statues block the retreat. Spears and daggers aren't much good against hard stone.

I feel uneasy, as if every statue is watching me. No one in living memory has tried to take this city. I let the ponies have their water before I'm off to camp offroad. I want to be well past this place before nightfall.

Chapter Eight

The Griffin Hills

I wind my way through many small hamlets off the main roads and east of the Griffin Hills. Normally, I'd stop at each one and share pleasantries with the sturdy folk who live there, but now is not the time to dawdle. I have no doubt that Zianni and Jebel are looking for my unknown nephew, and their assassins are looking for me. The only way I can win against such odds is to get the location of the child before they do.

Zianni's man has the same information I do about Bara and her son. At least her name is a common one. Children's minds are wide open; learning to shield oneself isn't learned until age ten or later. If I were Zianni, I'd send whoever was familiar with my brother from town to town in hopes of picking up on a similar mental pattern. It's inefficient, but it's their only choice. I have a few more options.

Tilbert's spy network may be able to turn up something, but I can't put all of my trust in them, so I travel farther and farther away from my only family in order to reach the western side of the Griffin

Hills. I have one play that is open to precious few people on this island.

As I near the southern end of the hills, I look up and see that Ganna's seat is empty. Despite lush grasses, the area around here remains uninhabited. The people speak of a 'great crater' in these parts as a place of dark magic. In all my travels, I have failed to find such a place. If I were an unsuperstitious farmer, this land would serve me well.

I find the stream below Ganna's home meandering in the broad valley and follow it toward the hills. Just past the lazy waterfall is the path I've been looking for. I hobble the ponies and leave the wagon. Only a few would dare to venture into Ganna's lands. I grab the dates and make my way up the winding slope.

"I'm out of shape," I say between deep breaths in front of Ganna's cottage. There's no fire burning within. "Please do not be at the top of this hill."

A turtur dove croaks out its lamentable song behind me. I turn and locate the animal.

"How long have you been following me?" I ask Ganna.

The bird lands in front of me and transforms into the isle's most feared witch.

"I was wondering when you would figure it out," she says with a satisfied smile. "I was riding on your wagon while you kept staring up at my throne upon the rocks."

She extends her arm forward, and we walk together to her home that's been hewn from the hill.

"I have come to ask for a boon," I say.

It never pays to be formal or flowery with Ganna. I was too scared to try to read her thoughts that first time, and that's probably why I'm still standing; she has Vecti tattooed on either side of her head.

A Vectis consists of four interwoven circles, forming a perpetual knot. The glyph itself inhibits we Sorim from entering one's mind. It can be made more powerful by being carved into rowan wood or wrought with silver. My pity to the fool who would dare try to invade Ganna's mind.

Ganna speaks a word, and a fire begins. She moves a tripod over the flames and hangs a pot filled with water upon it.

"You would like an herbal brew."

It's not a question, but I nod my head, anyway.

"It has been several years, has it not?" she asks.

"It has been too long." I fidget with my pack. "And I've brought you a present."

I remove the bag of dates from my belt and open it.

Ganna's eyes go wide, and she smiles. She reaches for the bag, but I quickly pull it back.

"We need to discuss my boon first," I say, smiling back at her.

"This is a payment, then, not a present?"

"I hoped you would see it as both." I hand her the bag and watch her as she carefully selects the first fruit to eat. As she takes a bite, she gives me a contented grin. She quickly pops the second half of the date in her mouth.

"And what would you ask of me?" she asks, bouncing the bag in her hand.

"My situation is dire," I begin. "I am the last of the Mot Dariiks of Ynys Luko . . ." I wait for her to look up at me. "And Strigula, the marsh hag, has made me infertile."

"And how did she manage that?" She looks down at my crotch.

"Oh!" I close my legs. "Not like that," I manage to get out. "She gave me a choice of drinking a potion or fighting her right that moment in the swamp."

"She gave you no choice, then. Tell me about the potion."

"It was green and tasted sweet like honey and bitter like vinegar. Beyond that, I cannot say."

"Was it a smooth green, or were there little brown specks floating on top?"

I exhale slowly as I think back to that awful day. "There was some kind of solid that stuck between my teeth."

Ganna frowns and nods her head. "Then Strigula knows her herblore, not that I ever doubted it. You know, if I were to kill her, the effect would still remain."

"No! I did not come here for that." She looks at me, waiting for me to tell the rest of my tale. "I have begun searching for an undeclared child of my brother. I believe there is at least one, but other Sorim have learned of my plight, and they seek to thwart my efforts. I wish for you to divine whatever you can about my bloodline, so that I can protect it."

The witch rocks back and forth and bobs her head. She pokes the logs with a stick, sending the flames higher. "Wouldn't a child of your own be easier to find?" she asks.

"I have no offspring. It was the agreement that Rhunior and I made. I could live my life unencumbered as a trader, and he would continue the family line. He broke the agreement almost immediately by sending assassins after me, but I still held to my end of the bargain."

"Then you're a fool."

"No, my reasons were more practical. To have a child would mean that I would have to settle down. The moral high ground was only a side benefit."

The old witch ponders off into the sky for a time.

"It can be done, but not until I've made myself ready." She pops another fruit into her mouth. "If such a child exists, I can point you to them."

"Thank you. I can't be the one who fails my ancestors. All that I have learned is that the records say that a woman named Bara claimed her son was Rhunior's child."

"Bara," the witch says. "A common name. Did you get more?"

"Only that she had long brown hair. And since Zianni's man got there before me, it is a blessing that nothing more was available."

She goes to her shelves carved into the cave wall and selects too many herbs to keep straight. She splits them between two wooden cups and pours steaming water on top of them. She breaks off two thin sticks from her kindling and starts stirring the mixtures. She hands me one and returns to her seat.

"What news do you know of the druid Grahme or his nephew Figol?" she asks.

"I have not spoken to either in a handful of months," I say, surprised by the question. "Why do you ask?"

"They were both here three months ago. Indeed, Figol would have died if not for my ministrations."

"Died?"

"Oh yes, and they still might. My husband escorted them north to see the centaurs."

"What? Who but the mentally damaged would seek out the centaurs?"

"I had hoped that you had seen them. It has been a while, and none of the three have returned to me."

"Conwenna would know if her son had died, and I likely would have felt her grief, no matter the distance between us."

"Then I will have to take solace in that. Grahme is a bit stiff, but I am fond of them both."

"Since you mentioned Grahme, what can you tell me about this?" I open one of my pouches and hand over the ghost orchid.

She gingerly takes the crushed flower and lays it flat on one of the fire ring stones. "I haven't seen one of these since I left the Wigesta lands many years ago." She pulls on the stem and straightens the flower. "I will tell you about these rare flowers, but only for a price."

I spread out my hands. "You've seen my wagon. What would you want?"

Ignoring me, she retreats into the shadows. She brings back a glass bottle and a wad of beeswax. "What I require is already before me." A short incantation leaves her mouth, and the flower glows from the bottom of the stem. Slowly, the incandescence rises to the bloom. An intense green light emanates from the flower as a single drop of water falls into Ganna's bottle. She crams the beeswax over the top and holds it at arm's length.

"You can keep that," she says. "Someone will pay handsomely for it, I'd wager."

Following her gaze, I see a delicate stone flower. Too amazed to move, my mouth begins opening and closing. Formulating a question is beyond me.

"It's not brittle," Ganna says. She grabs the flower and whacks it against the stone a couple of times. To my amazement, it doesn't break. She tosses it to me, and I cradle it against my chest.

"This single drop of liquid you see," she says, holding up the vial, "is an elven tear. Ghost orchids only grow from where elven tears have touched the ground. They are magical flowers, and they don't require sunlight to grow. In fact, they are often found in the deep shadows of ancient trees." She gives me a curious look. "Where did you find this?"

"Tilbert learned that Loris has put out a call for the flowers. A trader had come across this and was headed to Verlamion. Tilbert asked me to keep it away from Loris, though he couldn't tell me why, just that if Loris wanted it, that was reason enough."

"This Tilbert shows remarkable understanding. The elven tear within each flower is capable of devastating magic. I did my best to wipe out knowledge of this flower, but it seems I wasn't totally successful."

"What can it do?"

"In the hands of an educated practitioner, terrible things. Even in the hands of the inept, like Loris, it's still dangerous."

"You speak of elves. Where did you learn of them?"

"I've met a few elves, many years ago, though I can't say that I ever really knew any of them."

I stare at her, mouth agape. "The druids . . . the druids say that all the elder races left this isle eight hundred and twenty years ago."

"Has it really been that long?" She cocks her head to the side. "That would make it almost five hundred years since Berhtric and I arrived here."

"Berhtric the Brave? He was here at the time of Dariik, my family's founder?"

"Yes," she says slowly, her eyes beginning to water. She sighs. "I haven't thought of my love in quite some time."

"How old are you?"

"Bah, what does that matter? Long ago, I learned how to tame the years."

"And Bodmin? Do you preserve him from the forces of time as well?"

She looks at me as if I'm a misbehaving child. "Bodmin is very capable of taking care of himself."

"So, you do not force him to remain a black leopard up on his moor?"

She chuckles. "Is that the current story?" She looks up at the fading light of Belenos. "Tomorrow, I will tell you a great story of which only tiny pieces remain in the locals' folklore before I perform the divination."

"Can you answer one more question for me?"

"That depends on the question."

"When I was in Verlamion, a druid named Shua met us at the gate. Before I even used my powers, I could sense something disturbing about him. I scanned him as I left, and he identified very strongly with being an erilaz. Do you know what this means?"

"When Berhtric and I came to this isle, I was his confidante and his right hand. It is I that taught the Wigesta of the giant runes. The runestones, once imbued with power, are called fyrian stones. Erilaz means apprentice rune maker. A master is known as a halvdan, and I have been the only one of those here since the giants left. It's impressive that the Wigesta have preserved this knowledge over all these years. This Shua is a man to be feared. If he can make enough fyrian stones, the war next year will go badly for the druids."

CHAPTER NINE

A Glimmer of Hope

"We will take your wagon today," Ganna says after we break our fast with herbs and nuts.

"Yes, of course," I agree.

"And we'll have to get several skins of water before we leave."

"Is it far?"

"No, but I will have need of them." She tosses me three waterskins. "Prepare the wagon and fill these while I collect my medicines."

Ganna arrives with the bag of dates and three filled pouches in her cooking pot. "I am counting on you today, trader."

"I appreciate the trust you put in me."

"You don't understand; I bring with me fools funnel mushrooms, bhelena and wild valere. The first two are poisons, and the third will cause a deep sleep."

"And dates," I add with a smile.

"And dates," she says as she cradles the bag of fruits. "I will be undertaking a visionary journey today. Afterwards, I will be helpless for a time. You must collect my unconscious form and bring me back here, to my cottage."

"How long do I need to stay?" My gut tells me I haven't much time, but I can hardly leave her alone and helpless.

"There are few enough who will come near my home. You need just bring me back, and I will wait out the stupor on my own."

"I'm not entirely happy with that arrangement." I purse my lips.

Ganna merely shrugs and samples another medjool date.

* * *

The steady clip clop of the ponies' hooves calms me. Ganna directs me around the southern end of the Griffin Hills and onto the plain. We stop next to a standing stone with vaguely human features.

I run my hand over the 'arm' and 'shoulder' of the stone.

"That was a stone elemental I summoned three hundred years ago," Ganna calls from the wagon. "That was before I met Bodmin."

I eye the stone closer.

Ganna cinches up a large leather bag and stares east toward a gentle depression in front of a small hill. The hills naturally rise and fall, but these two look out of place. They're too small to be natural features.

"Did you make those features as well?" I ask.

"I had a hand in it, yes. Give me a moment so that I can tell my tale properly."

She leaves the wagon and ambles up to me. I stand next to her and look toward the small hill.

"Three hundred years ago, Otsanda Bedia, an unbelievably powerful Vascone who was more powerful than me by a good measure, came here in hopes of taking over the isle."

"She thought she could best all the druids?" I ask.

Ganna rolls her eyes. "I have dominion here. No one can give me a challenge; none of the druids, none of the Wigesta." She looks pointedly at me. "And none of the Sorim."

"And do you receive tribute from all your subjects?"

"What could they give me? Medjools?"

I smile back at her. She has a point; she seems to have everything she wants. Besides, most everyone is afraid of her.

She stretches her neck from side to side. "We Vascones, we are all women. Never do we produce male offspring. The cities of our kind tend to be transitory."

She stares off at some distant memory and smiles.

"The most powerful among us learn how to defy time and live for as long as we wish. A few moved from our homeland to various cities in Hiberia, where the locals worship them as goddesses."

"But not you?"

"No. Over the decades and centuries, egos grow unbounded and feuds cull the Vascone demigods. I had no need to be worshipped, so I came north, to Pretanni. The last time I ventured back to my homeland, others learned of my good fortune, and that is why Otsanda sought to displace me. Not content to share, she wished to take the isle from me."

"Were there any witnesses?" I say in wonder.

"Hardly. By the rights of duel in Vascone, she got to pick the magic. She chose elementals."

"So that stone one was yours. What did you do with hers?"

"First, this is not Vascone. It is Pretanni, and it is mine, so I determine the rules of combat. That mound you see there," she points. "That is the remains of her earth elemental. It came from the giant hole before us. When I called forth my stone elemental, oh, how she taunted me so. What she didn't know was that I had also summoned Vozzir, a demon beholden to me. It appeared behind her and slit her throat."

"You don't play fair."

"Not unless I must. But let me finish my tale. Vozzir drank deeply from Otsanda's blood and grew in strength. It might have been too much for me to expel from our world, so I changed into a griffin and knocked the elemental on top of the demon and the corpse."

"Will burying a demon kill it?"

"No, but it will have to expend tremendous energy to climb free. I waited an entire day for it to emerge. Exhausted, it readily obeyed me and returned to the hell from whence it came."

"The earth elemental doesn't look way bigger than your stone one," I say. "Couldn't your elemental have beaten hers, if only by knocking the dirt free?"

"Ah." She nods. "Do you know what the locals call this place? They call it the 'great crater'. Don't let this gentle depression fool you. The land has been settling for hundreds of years. The elemental was thrice the size of what you see now."

"This is the mythical great crater of the plains?"

"It is, though only you and I know that name was bestowed upon it."

I smile at her for sharing her secret. "I appreciate you letting me know the origin of this place. But is that why you brought us here? To tell me that story?"

"No. I had hoped to find fresh fool's funnel mushrooms here. Using dried ones makes the magic more difficult." She sighs. "I knew all along that it was too early, but even I, from time to time, follow my wishes rather than common sense."

She kicks the grass before searching one last time. "I also had company not long ago, and I found it pleasing. Perhaps I'm just drawing out your visit, or perhaps I'm stalling. It's hard to say."

* * *

Ganna grabs one of the waterskins and drinks the entire contents. "Are you well?"

"When I eat those mushrooms, they will make me lose a lot of water." She tosses the skin into the back of the wagon. "We don't have much time to waste." She removes the pouches from her cooking pot and empties the second water skin into it. Holding the pot in her lap, she adds the dried mushrooms.

There is no road to follow in these hills, only tall grass that hides dips in along our path. One lurch either way, and the mushrooms could be lost. I don't want to broach the subject with Ganna about her stores of this ingredient. A pressure is building inside me, screaming that every moment we waste is one more opportunity for Zianni and his cronies to find the last member of the Mot Dariiks.

Mentally, I'm exhausted by the time Ganna directs me to a hill with a flattened stone circle atop it. All fourteen of the standing stones have been knocked down.

"This will do," she says. "Please start a cooking fire here." She points to a spot directly in front of a downed stone.

She sits on the next stone over as I get to work. Once the flames reach the height of her knees, she sets the cooking pot on top.

"No tripod to hold the pot?" I ask.

"This will bring the mushrooms to their full size faster." Off to the side, she opens her second pouch, pulls out a many-fingered valere root and cuts it up fine.

"Once the mushrooms are ready, I must start eating them. I may not remain right in the head, so listen carefully. The mushroom water must be poured out and rinsed well. After I've eaten my fill, the bhelena seeds need to be thrown on the fire and I must inhale them. It is known as the 'crazy plant', so you must stay away from the fumes."

She grabs my hand in a tight grip. "Promise me that you will do as I say."

"I will do so."

"Good. Once I inhale the smoke, I'll have the sense of flying. You must add the last skin of water to the pot and bring the valere root to a boil while I reach out to the Hooded Ones." She grabs a piece of kindling and, using tree sap, affixes a red stone to the top of the stick. "Give me this and draw my eyes to the red rock. It is only when both eyes cross at a single point that the journey will begin."

"When do I give you the root juice?"

"You will have to judge that for yourself." She pops a mushroom in her mouth and grimaces. "These are so bitter." She follows it up with a date.

That is in no way helpful, but I nod my head. "How soon will the magic begin?"

"Watch and see." She downs a couple more mushrooms and another date. Staring off to my left, she slurs her speech. "Start preparing the valere root now, my love."

The last three mushrooms are placed next to her, though my fingers are scalded for the effort. Ganna's fingers are likewise red and enflamed, though she doesn't seem to notice. Dumping the water out, I add the valere root to the pot. There's sizzling, and the burned root has a noxious smell. Quickly, I add the final bit of water.

Ganna's head has flopped to her left, and she makes no effort to lift it. Tears stream from her unfocused eyes and her spindly arms are covered in sweat.

There's something that I'm forgetting. I look at the fire, the stick with a red rock, and then I see the bhelena seeds. Carefully, I remove the cooking pot and throw the seeds into the fire. A foul-smelling white smoke curls up from the flames. The odor smells of rotten meat. I fan the smoke toward Ganna while holding my breath.

She sways from side to side, with her head rolling from shoulder to shoulder. A small, disturbing smile causes fear to grow in my stomach. She's just a small woman, but she looks . . . feral.

I hand her the stick and clap twice behind the stone. Her eyes lock onto the stone, and she starts to drool.

"I'm soaring," she says dreamily. "There is a town, a strange town."

"Is it Sorim, Wigesta, or native?"

Her whole body starts to fall to her left. I steady her shoulders and she glares at me.

"Don't break the trance," she snarls as her eyes focus on my lips.

Turning her hand so the red rock is in view again, I clap twice more. Her eyes reacquire the stone. The water is not boiling yet, but

I have to hope whatever is in the roots has been drawn out. I take the pot off the fire and step behind her. With a hand on either side, I'm ready to catch her should she fall.

"What is that strange town's name?" I ask in a whisper, hoping that by being more subtle, I can direct her vision.

"There she is," Ganna purrs. "That's Bara. She has a beautiful multicolored mantle."

"Where is she?"

"You can see me? How are you talking to me without your lips moving? Your voice is deep, like a man's."

She thinks my voice is Bara's.

"Where are you going, dear one? To the market?" Ganna looks off to her right. "Your market is long and stretched out along the wall between the two gates, the big one and the secret one." She chuckles quietly. "You didn't think I'd see that second gate, did you?"

Ganna leans forward. Much farther and I'll have to pull her out of the flames, but I dare not disturb her until I must.

"Why are you showing me your long brown hair? I want to see your face." Ganna stands up, yelling into the wind. "Come back here! I'm not finished talking to you!" She freezes for a couple of heartbeats, then she begins to slowly collapse to the ground.

I grab her under her shoulders and sit her back on the rock. Her hands reach up and caress my fingertips. In front of us, the red rock stick is burning in the fire.

Ganna looks skyward and begins to sway. "I'm flying," she says with a smile.

I wait, but her vision doesn't start again. While she's humming a nonsense tune, I pour the root water into a small cup. The water is clear. I smell the water and there's no scent. I take a couple pieces of the root and place them in Ganna's hand.

"Here Ganna, have a date." It takes a couple of attempts, but finally she chews on one of the roots.

"Here's some water to wash it down."

She drinks the water and sprays it into my face.

"Have another medjool date," I say.

She coos as she takes the root, humming her strange tune. In all, she eats half the roots before she falls unconscious. Her chest is barely rising and falling. Anxious and confused, I hoist her over my shoulder and place her in the back of my wagon.

Do I leave her alone as she instructed and hope I've guessed the right city? Or do I wait for her to recover and hope she can tell me more?

CHAPTER TEN

Venta

I've been in every city, town, village and hamlet on this isle over the years. Each and every city has their market just inside the gate. It's convenient for the farmers who must travel into the city, as well as the city's taxman, who imposes his fees on the traders. There is only one city that fits Ganna's description, and that is Venta.

Should I have stayed another day to ensure Ganna's safety and possibly gained more insight? I don't feel completely happy about leaving her, but my gut tells me I must hurry. Years of travel have taught me not to overstress the ponies, lest one come up lame. Every sinew within me demands I take to the whip, but I keep my head and spare my animals.

The hillfort of Venta looks much like any other Pretanni town, except it was captured by the Sorim at a tremendous cost of life. It guards the road to Solent Keep, and its sole purpose is to dissuade the Wigesta from marching southward. Otherwise, the people have been left to themselves.

The town has several elven bowl barrows in its center that the superstitious folk refuse to disturb. In the midst of the barrows is a wooden statue of Brigantia that is a head and a half taller than me.

Since the town is limited by the ramparts and the center is left open, the remaining area is filled with tight alleyways between the buildings. Only the mead hall and a few smaller buildings far from the front gate remain in the old style, with thatched roofs.

Lougha is still the gatekeeper for Venta. As far as gatekeepers go, he's one of the more suspicious. Even as a known Sorim trader, he stops me every time.

"Hello Lougha," I say with forced cheerfulness.

He waves at me to keep my voice down. I slow the ponies and lean down to hear what the man has to say. Looking inside the city, the market is quiet. In fact, there are very few people on the streets.

"Blachstenius, you're a fair trader, everyone says so." He bites his lip. "So, I'll tell you this because the other Sorim maggots treat us as less than human."

I drop to the ground and lead the ponies off to the side of the road, keeping the wagon between me and the rest of the town.

"What's going on here?" I ask.

"The Sorim leader, Zianni, he came here and demanded that every young child be brought to him. We are a peaceful people, but no parent will give up their child."

"Did they give a reason?" I ask.

"No, but we've heard of them going to the outlying villages and doing much the same. They inspect the children, then the Sorim get angry for not finding whoever they are looking for. Threats are made against the villagers, as if the people are holding out. In the small village just across the river, it came to blows. People are close to panic. Now those who can have hidden their children in Pretanni cities. Those who can't, well, they try to hide the fact that they have children, but the Sorim, they know."

"It's better if you don't know all the details, but I am also looking for a young boy," I say.

"So, the child being sought is a boy?" Lougha asks.

"Lougha, please, do not ask questions. Whatever you learn, they can take from you."

He nods. "They have mentioned you, too."

"I'm not surprised. All I can say is that I wish no ill upon this child. Zianni and his thugs cannot say the same."

"How can I help you?"

"Are you willing to hide in the forest from Zianni and his men?"

He anxiously eyes the empty road. Like all gatekeepers, his duty defines who he is.

"Until Zianni leaves, who would be fool enough to enter this city?" I ask. "With so few citizens about, they'd likely think a pestilence is within."

"Never say such things." He looks at me, incredulous.

"Sorry, but in many ways, Zianni resembles such a thing."

He looks through me and lets out a long, slow breath. "I will hide in the woods," he says finally.

"Then tell me before you go. I am looking for a four-year-old boy whose mother is Bara."

"Bara works for Grusta."

"Grusta the potter?"

"Yes."

"I know where his shop is. Thank you, now please leave while you can."

Lougha grabs his staff and haltingly rises from his seat. The years have not been kind. He limps off at a sluggish pace, and I wonder if he'll ever reach the tree line.

I lead my ponies into the tight streets. I know what I must do, but it doesn't make it any easier. To do otherwise is to see my honored house fall. Forever.

"Conwenna, I need you, in Venta," I broadcast as widely as I can.

Zianni and his men will know of my presence, but they were bound to find out soon enough.

I put my mental shields up and head directly to the potter's shop. Two women clasping toddlers in their arms run down the narrow road toward me. I lead my ponies off to the left, giving them room to pass.

One of Zianni's temple acolytes rounds the corner in pursuit. I keep my head down and wait for him to get close. A quick burst of mental energy, and the man is knocked from his feet. I drag him through the door of the nearest home. In the corner are several children's toys. Hopefully, the children fled the city in time.

"Spread out! Find him. We can interrogate the people after Blachstenius is dealt with!" Zianni yells from the next street over.

I pull my hood tighter, keep my head down, and fake a limp. It's not much, but as long as I don't run into four or five at a time, I have a chance.

"Blachstenius?" the blacksmith asks.

"Do you wish to help me?" I ask in a low tone. I know thousands of people all over this island, but for the life of me, I can never remember this man's name.

"Of course."

"Then open your mind to me and accept my apologies."

He furrows his brow, but it doesn't matter; I'm already in his head. I plant the false memory that he's just seen me hiding in his shop. It's on the opposite side of town. I regret the next step. I override his nature and make him *want* to share this information with the Sorim. He won't be able to explain why, but sharing this will be the most important task he's ever had. Finally, I turn him away from me and strip our conversation from his mind.

The big man shakes his head, gets his bearings, and runs straight for the city center. With luck, Zianni will be too excited by the news to investigate the man's mind.

I send out the lightest of feelers for my fellow Sorim. I'm not exceptional at this, like Conwenna, but I'm better than most. There are eleven Sorim in the city by my count, twelve if I count the one sleeping off his headache.

I encourage the ponies to take me through the narrow market street toward Grusta's shop. A mental attack nearly knocks me out of the wagon. To my right is a Sorim standing amazed that his attack didn't work. He raises his arms, as if that would stop my mental thrust if I made one. Instead, I grab a chisel from the wagon tools and throw it at his head.

His guard is down while he dodges, like I expected. I command his left leg to kick up as high as his head. He tumbles in a heap. Only now do I use my mental ability.

A *chanith* is the equivalent of a mental spear. It is tightly focused and can only be felt by you and your target. It's the perfect choice when you're trying to navigate a city filled with enemies. It's one of the few useful skills I learned when I was in the warrior caste.

Only ten Sorim remain. Still, I'll never make it out of here if I must duel every last one of them. I give the reins a quick tug, and the ponies whisk me away at a trot.

I enter the pottery shop and signal for the merchant to remain silent.

"Grusta, where are Bara and her son?"

"They're hiding in the back of my shop," he whispers.

"That boy is the one everyone is trying to find."

Grusta's eyes go wide. From behind him, a small woman emerges and throws a flagon at me.

I duck so that it only glances off the side of my head. The woman charges me and starts flailing with her fists. I grab her arms and urge her to be quiet.

"You must be Bara," I say.

She headbutts me and tries to pull free.

"Stop, Bara," Grusta says, placing his meaty hand on her shoulder.

She stops struggling, and I release my grip. I raise my hands up and step away from her. She's breathing hard and readying for another assault. I touch her mind. She's one step away from going berserk. She's wracked with guilt because a tiny part of her always knew that it was her son for which they have been searching.

"Please calm yourself," I say while nudging her mentally.

She kicks me in the shin and disappears into the back. My leg is throbbing, but I'm more concerned that my efforts have failed me. Grusta steps between Bara and me. He pulls out his rowan protection amulet.

"Don't try it."

"We don't have time for this," I say. "Those men mean to kill the child. The only way this doesn't end in tragedy is if I can get those two out of the city before Zianni can marshal his men."

"And they will be better off with you?"

My mouth opens wide in amazement. "You know me, Grusta. You've known me for twenty years. Have I ever cheated you?"

"We're not talking pots here. We're talking about a little boy who means a great deal to me."

I take a deep breath and slowly let it out through my nose. "That boy is my nephew and the sole heir to my noble family. That is why they are so desperate to find him. If they find him, they will kill him, and my family—the preeminent noble house on Ynys Luko—will fall. If I can get them both to Solent Keep, they will be safe forever out of the grasp of Zianni and his men."

"How do you know your brother is the father?" Grusta asks.

"I am never going back to that city!" Bara says in an angry, low voice. "Rhunior ruined my life."

"Who did that, mum?" a tiny voice whispers.

"Quiet, Corsi," Bara says. She bends down to her left, caressing a child in the shadows.

So she knows Rhunior and I were brothers.

"Bara," I say, "you'll get no games from me. You are going to have to choose between trusting me or facing that Sorim zealot alone."

I get only silence as a reply.

"Grusta can confirm that my brother sent assassins to kill me on more than one occasion. I am not like my brother."

There's some shuffling, but she doesn't come out of the shadows.

"Lady Conwenna is in charge at Solent Keep now. Just a few short months ago, she was but a blacksmith's wife. She knows of the commoners' struggles."

"Is she a Sorim too?"

I was so close.

"Yes, she is. She chose hiding as a wife and mother over marrying Rhunior, a man she could not love."

"Bara, Blachstenius speaks the truth," Grusta says.

"Then how do we get out of here?"

"We'll make for the west gate. If there is any trouble, you and Corsi run, and you don't look back."

I take the amulet from Grusta's neck.

Here is an amulet to keep Corsi safe. I will do all I can to lead them astray, or to fight them in the street if I must."

"Who's in there?" a man yells from the street. I can feel his mental energy building.

"I'm just cleaning up a mess so that no one injures their feet in my shop," Grusta calls back.

The Sorim strides into the shop and I take him out before he even sees me. Grusta goes to grab the body, but I wave him away. "You must be out front; I'll take him in the back."

"Is he dead?"

"No. I don't kill unless I have no choice. He'll recover by sundown. It would be best if you were not here when that happens." I grab the Sorim by the arms and drag him into the back.

Bara holds a reed torch near my face as she decides whether to trust me or not.

"He's old," the child says.

I chuckle. "Some days, I feel my years more than others. But today, I feel every single one of them." I smile at him.

"What did you do to him?" Bara asks.

"I stunned him. When he wakes, he'll have a terrible headache, nothing worse."

She looks down at the big innocent eyes of her child.

"We'll go with you," she says, her eyes refusing to meet mine. "Brigantia, I beseech you to smile upon us this day."

"Thank you for trusting me." I turn to Grusta. "Go out the main gate and head for the forest. We'll exit the west gate and find you."

Chapter Eleven

Escape Plan

Before Bara and Corsi can get in my wagon, a battle clarion sounds from the city center.

"Is that a carnyx?" I ask.

Grusta's eyes go wide in fear. "It is. And if they're blowing it, that can only mean that the city guard has been turned."

"Head for the main gate."

"Are you sure?"

"I don't have time to explain things again. Lougha is hiding in the woods already. Wait for us there. It will all be over tonight, one way or another."

"I should come with you."

Before I can argue, Grusta the potter is out in front of the wagon, clearing the road of clutter. By the look of the rubble, Zianni's men have already come down this street once.

"Toss me that rope," I say in a low voice. "And remind me to give the ropemaker two silvers for it once this is all over."

Grusta looks up and down the road before taking the rope. If I weren't in such a desperate strait, I'd laugh at him.

"Now go out the front gate while you can."

"I'll stay and fight," he offers.

"You don't have an amulet anymore; you'd just give us away. Sorry friend, but you'll do the most good if the Sorim don't enter your mind."

Grusta isn't happy, but he nods and heads for the gate.

Phew. Now the only two who know about Bara and Corsi will be outside of Zianni's clutches. We may actually escape this place.

"What's your plan?" Bara demands.

"It's better that you don't know." I give her an apologetic smile while pointing to the side of my head. "Your son must keep that on at all costs; it's the only way he'll remain hidden from Zianni and his men."

"So, we're just to ride in this wagon like cargo?"

"Sorim require a view of their target to work their magic. Both of you staying hidden is the only way we'll make good our escape."

"Why aren't we going out the front gate?"

"Too risky," I reply. "They'll be able to see us on the road and with their horses, they'll be able to run us down."

I shouldn't have told her that.

The only other exit is through the Shambles, at the west end of the market. From there, we'll find a woodsman's path and stay out of sight. The plan, such as it is, is a fairly obvious one, and now Bara—whose mind isn't protected—will piece together the plan if I give her time.

"Corsi, you heard the man," she says. "Let's both lie down and be quiet."

"Yes, mum."

I give the reins another tug. We don't have much time, but the Shambles is the long, narrow end of this street. It won't take much to create a suitable barricade.

"What do we do if they find us?" Corsi asks in a tentative voice. His quiet fright breaks my heart. No one that innocent should have to go through this.

"I have considerable powers myself," I say, glancing back at him. "If they find us, I'll give them a few bruises while you and your mum hurry on your way."

"You keep saying *if*, but I think you mean *when*." Bara gives me a nervous smile before throwing my blanket over her and her son.

Each step by the ponies sounds louder than the last to my ear. I don't know how we haven't been discovered yet. Probably because the west end of town is where the poor live. Amongst his many odious characteristics, Zianni is a pompous noble with all the prejudices one would expect.

I can see the Shambles ahead of us. There are only two intersections left before we reach it. The city changes at that point. The stores are dilapidated, and the second-stories encroach overtop the street, leaving it in shade except at midday. There's no crossroads in there, either. That's where I'll make my stand. With the city wall to our left, these last two streets are my biggest worry.

Two city guards run into the intersection, axes held clumsily. Whoever's controlling them is holding onto them too tightly, making the men useless.

"Halt!" they cry in unison.

Before I can even stop my ponies, their spears are raised next to their heads as they ready to throw.

I send a *chanith* at the first man, and he crumples to the ground. To Sorim, it would lead to mental scarring, but to the ungifted, it merely renders them unconscious, I think. I've never had to attack a regular in this way before.

The second man throws his spear at my ponies, but he's way short. Whoever is controlling these men is an absolute amateur.

"Run, Corsi!" Bara shouts. She throws the blanket off them and readies herself to jump from the wagon.

"Hold," I say, as I clumsily send a restraining arm back toward her.

The guard has turned the corner.

"This is your fight," Bara says. "We're innocent and we want nothing to do with it."

I tug at the reins to speed the ponies up to a canter.

"What are you doing?" she demands.

I touch only the outermost of her thoughts. She's scared and overwhelmed and angry. In that state, she's capable of doing anything.

"You're right," I say. "Can you and your son ride?"

"If we must."

"At the entrance to the Shambles, I'll overturn the cart to block their way. You and your son will ride the ponies to safety. Make for the west gate and look for Lougha and Grusta in the forest."

Bara brandishes a knife. "Try anything different and I'll stick you through the ribs."

"Hold on tight."

I tug at the reins again, and the ponies give me all they've got. At this speed, I'm as likely as not to wreck the cart before the Shambles, but I can't risk a hole in my chest.

There's debris in the road, and the wagon bounces off the wooden houses as it lurches to either side of the narrowing street. There's only one last crossing. I slow us down so we don't end up in a heap. A wide turn in the intersection allows me to position the wagon in front of the Shambles.

Bara helps me free the ponies from the harnesses.

"Keep your head down," she says to her son.

"I summoned Lady Koni from Solent Keep as soon as I stepped foot in this city. She'll be coming from the west, and if I know her, she'll have a score of soldiers with her. Seek her out. She will protect you from anything the mortal realm can throw at you."

Bara freezes in place, abject fear on her face. Someone is invading her mind. I search the side street and see her attacker. He can't relay our plan.

I send a *chanith* at him with all my anger attached. He grabs his head and falls backward.

"Is he dead?"

"I don't think so," I lie. "Maybe? I didn't have time to perfectly weigh my attack."

"You should kill him."

"Mum, why are they chasing us?" Corsi says in a small, shaky voice.

My heart breaks just hearing it.

"Corsi," I say, waiting for his eyes to meet mine, "I'm your uncle, Blachstenius. These men have been fighting with our family for years. It's nothing that you or your mother did."

"We don't want to be a part of this," Bara says.

I look directly into her big green eyes. "We both know it won't matter to them."

Bara grunts as she lifts Corsi out of the wagon. He immediately hugs her leg as tightly as his little arms will allow.

"Take the ponies." I hold out the reins to her.

"Neither of us can ride."

"Why didn't you say that before?"

"Everything was going so fast, I just agreed."

My head sinks into my chest.

"Fine." I steer the ponies back into the Shambles and give them a slap. There's no sense in them being harmed. "Then go out the secret gate and look ahead for the woodsman's trail. You know the one?"

She nods her head. A light touch tells me she has no idea what I'm saying.

"Go to the woods. Look for a trail that follows alongside the west road. When you see Lady Koni, wave her down. She will keep you safe."

"Come along," she peels her son off of her, even as he fights to stay clinging to her leg.

"Corsi," I squat down to look him in the eye. "I will delay them as long as I can, but I need you to protect your mother. Can you do that?"

"I'm scared," he says as he buries his face in his mother's thigh.

"We're all scared." I give him a tight smile. "But if we do nothing, they'll find us and hurt us."

Bara squeezes her son's hand. "Let's go, Corsi."

She leads the last hope of the Mot Dariik house away as fast as his little legs can run.

"Find a protection amulet for yourself!" I call.

So, it has all come down to this.

CHAPTER TWELVE

The Showdown

The wagon is surprisingly light. I'm able to tip it on its side without trouble. Sliding it against the shops on either side, well, that's a bit more of a challenge. Using a chisel and hammer from the wagon's toolset, I create two small eyeholes between the boards of the wagon's bottom. Trying them out, I see city guards forming up a block away.

That was fast. I was hoping for more time.

I weave the rope between the wagon wheels and tie either end off to the doorways of the shops. It's not much, but if they get close enough to remove my barrier, I'll be dead, anyway.

The shops on either side of me belong to a weaver and a shoemaker. Why couldn't one of them be a weapon maker's shop? As much as I'd like to let my thoughts wander, my desperation keeps me focused, and as the slow march of city guards begins, I can clearly see how this will end. As good as I may be, I'm no match for ten Sorim and ten guards.

But I don't have to win. I only have to stall until Conwenna arrives. The fact that I'll be able to see them but not the other way around is a huge advantage.

"Would you like some knives?"

I jump at the voice. Behind me is a smiling dwarf wearing a leather apron. Nothing, it seems, can flummox Alabaster the trader.

"Even for you, this is an odd situation," he says.

"Alabaster? Where is everyone? Why are you here?"

"Are you going to ask me the meaning of life, too?" He's enjoying my confusion. "We've all heard of the village raids of the Sorim. At first sight, the signal was given and the traders with children here in the Shambles fled to the forest."

"But you remain?"

"I have no children here, and I'm immune to your people's mental prying." He sticks his hands into the pocket of his apron. "I've found a new knifemaker; let me know if these are any good." He drops six Wigestan knives in the dirt at my feet.

"I'm likely to die here," I say.

Even as he gives me a lopsided smile, he begins backing up. "Try not to do so. I'd like to be reimbursed."

"What's the real reason you're doing this?"

"Your people harass me because they can't enter my head," he says in a low voice. "This is my way to address the problem."

"I could use some help."

Alabaster shakes his head. "I don't see any profit in that."

The lead guard yells at his men, telling them line up across the road. That's stupid. Any knife I throw is bound to hit one of them. Zianni must be in control of the leader; no one with any military training would do such a thing.

"But you'll arm me with knives?" I look out my eyehole and see the guards coming into range.

"If you die, I'll say you stole them." He bows slightly. "I must be going."

I pick up one of the knives and toss it over the cart. I hear a satisfying grunt from the other side as it finds a target.

"If I make it out of here alive, you're going to have to tell me what happened to get you ostracized from your people."

"Good luck," the dwarf says before he hustles back to his stall.

I check on the guards. There are only nine walking in a line now, with one man dealing with a knife in his gut. He screams out in pain, now that the mental connection with him has been broken. So, Zianni doesn't care about the health of his men. The more I manage to injure, the tighter hold he'll have on the rest. That will make them less and less affective.

I could wrest control away from whoever is controlling the guards, but it would consume too much of my mental strength, and there's still the ten Sorim out there wishing me harm.

The guards can't be controlled by a committee; so many mental auras would collide. And no Sorim can hope to control people unless they have a line of sight. I'm sure the person will be hidden, but if I can find him, then maybe one of Alabaster's knives can find its way there.

Right, so either I take out my friends in the Venta guards or . . ..

The guard on the far left is a stout man. I've seen him before, but I've never got to know him. Focusing my will, I knock the Sorim out of his head—Zianni. I recognize his aura. Before anyone can react, I compel the man to impale the guard next to him. His victim falls to the ground, and I have my man remove his spear. He kills another of his cohort before his wooden companions can act. I know a fair number of these men by name, and the thought of killing them is repugnant, but I harden my resolve.

If I must, I will kill in this manner to preserve my noble house.

The other guards break the formation and stab my champion multiple times. Where there were ten, now there are six.

Zianni must have realized his folly and reduced his control. The guards break for the nearby shops. No line of sight means I can't control them directly. Zianni must have enthralled them, since they still do his bidding. On a tactical level, why would he enthrall them *and* overtake their movement? I guess I should count myself lucky that Zianni is so hopeless. Enthrallment magic is slow but effective. It's not something I can hope to do while defending myself.

Zianni and the rest of the Sorim line up shoulder to shoulder and link their arms. They're keeping their distance, though, standing well behind the first wounded guard. I recognize several of the priests from the Melqart temple in Solent Keep. They begin chanting. They're too far for the Nimr Nissek to be effective, but I suspect that won't be the case for long.

Does he know any other formation besides a straight line?

Once the spell is activated, they'll continue the chant as they walk toward me. The oppressive mental weight will sabotage my concentration, inhibiting my powers. I look through my peephole. They're still well out of knife range.

I can feel the pressure in my forehead building. What now? My Sorim powers may soon be neutralized, but not my mind, so I need another way to engage. I dash into the weaver's shop with a knife and cut the long threads from the loom. The weights attached at the bottom are exactly what I need.

Spinning my makeshift weapon, I make two full circles before launching the weight over my barricade. It lands with a thud well behind them, but the pressure lessens. At least it worked as a distraction.

"Focus the attack!" Zianni yells, and the assault on my mind returns.

Alright, the first one was too long. I have five more weighted threads.

Let's try again.

The second one lands successfully, and one of the priests goes down while cradling his shoulder. I hope it's broken.

Despite the hit, their spell is still active. I take the next weight and repeat with another hit. This time, the spell dissipates. Looking out the peephole, the men break formation and scurry for cover. No wonder Zianni didn't join the Obsidian. He is spectacularly bad at attacking.

CHAPTER THIRTEEN

The End Game

The sun is beginning to descend into the trees, and it's an easy ride from Solent Keep. Knowing Conwenna, she'll push the horses and be here by sundown. I look out over the street. Only the four downed guards are visible; everyone else has hidden in the shadows.

I grab the shoemaker's stool and stand on top of it so I can peer over the wagon and get a better view.

"Zianni was repudiated by Melqart in Solent Keep!" I shout. "If your god has lost faith in him, why do you remain by the side of this disgraced priest?"

An arrow emerges from the shadows and lodges itself into the side of the wagon, just below my head. I hop off the stool before I lose an eye.

"Just because Zianni is stupid doesn't mean you should be too," I chide myself.

"I agree." A woman in light brown clothing walks out of the weaver's shop. Unlike the natives, she is wearing trousers with several knives prominently displayed.

"Hello Amma," I say with as much nonchalance as I can muster, even as a chill runs down my neck. Few who see the Yatiim Jabbur—the head of the assassins—anyplace other than her palace live to tell the tale.

"What brings you here?" I asked in a forced, light tone.

She struts out to the middle of the road. I turn my back on my cart and Zianni's forces. This threat is much more ominous.

"I detest that man and the entire dar Arqan clan," she volunteers.

"You still braid your hair, I see."

If we were to fight, I'd lose every time. She hasn't made an aggressive move yet, so I'll stick to my strength and bargain.

Amma whips her head around and the braid rests over her left shoulder. At the end of the braid is a short dagger.

"Do you often get a chance to use that one?"

She licks the side of the dagger and smiles at me. The effect is unnerving.

"That's very well done," I say. "I didn't even feel you invade my mind."

"It's my favorite ploy," she says. "It works better if the dagger has some blood on it. It sends my adversaries running in fear. A knife to the back is just as deadly, and I don't have to be wary of an attack."

Behind the leader of the assassin's guild, a quarter of the sun has fallen behind the trees.

I just have to keep her talking.

"Amma, you could have killed me that day in Regnorum."

"True."

"But you did not. You could have killed me from behind moments ago, your favorite way of killing no less, but you did not."

"Also true."

"I've barricaded this place to protect myself from Zianni and his cronies."

She nods.

"So, I'll ask you again, what are you doing here?"

"Watching the exploits of the legendary Blachstenius." Her eyes have gone large, and her voice takes on a dreamy tone.

She was always a strange child, but she couldn't have risen to the head of the Yam Mjann by being loopy.

I turn my back to her and peek at the intersection. The guards have taken up bows and are all ready to fire.

"Would you excuse me for a moment?" I ask.

Not waiting, I pick up a knife and throw it in the direction of the nearest archer. It lands woefully short. I set my eyes on the archer opposite my original target. With one great push, I sweep away the Sorim in the man's mind and take control of his body. Looking through his eyes, I take aim at my initial target and loose the arrow. It hits the man, and I've eliminated one more assailant. Before anyone can challenge me for supremacy of this man, I release my captive.

I turn back to Amma.

"That was impressive."

"Would you like to help me?"

She walks seductively toward me, her chest held up high. "You left the academy before I could count you as one of my conquests."

"Is it always about conquest with you?"

She walks past me and uses one of my peepholes. A guard screams in terror and flees the battlefield. "There, that should confuse the hell out of Zianni and give us a little peace."

"For the third time, what are you doing here?"

Amma struts over to me and rubs my chest with hers. Her right arm trails down my side and she grabs the top of my left leg, my *inner* left leg. She squeezes and releases, and my body responds. I feel a warmth from below like I've never experienced before. My breath quickens.

"I really do hate the dar Arqans."

Why is she talking about Zianni now?

"Three times you have defeated my assassins. The Arqans have threatened to depose me if we fail again."

I look down in horror to see my life blood staining my clothes. I try to gather my will.

"I wouldn't do that," Amma says. "If I release my hold, you'll be dead in the space of a dozen breaths."

"I'm dead, in any case."

"True, but this way I get to partake in your death's kiss."

I reach for the wagon to steady myself as my legs go weak. My strength is leeching away from me. The sun is half-obscured by the trees.

I was so close.

"I . . . I wish to employ your services."

"That's new," Amma says. "But with your death, the Mot Dariiks fall and I'll be sure to get my share. What can you possibly offer me?"

"No, my nephew lives, and he is under the protection of Lady Koni."

"You lie." She shakes her head. "Koni isn't here. My guess is that you're bluffing, and you haven't found the child, if there even is one."

"I did find him." I give her a triumphant smile. "And Lady Koni and her men are on their way."

"You lie!" she repeats, though I think more to convince herself.

"Read my thoughts. I called her as soon as I stepped foot in this town. I offer you your life as a commission. Pledge that you will protect Corsi Mot Dariik at the Vectis and I will tell Koni to spare your life."

"No!" she screams. "I get to win this time."

She lets go of my leg and a surge of blood leaves my body. I drop to the ground—the warm, blood-stained ground. I try to prop myself up, but my fingers are cold and numb.

"Swear it, before I die."

Amma crouches over me, grabbing my leg in a firm grip. "You do not get to win this time."

"The dar Surbys will lead another raid on Taht Qadah Mijdil if you don't. What's it been, two hundred years since they massacred the assassins?"

I can feel her mind racing through mine. She finds the memory of me calling out to Koni and the fierce, wordless response. Then she flits to the discovery of Corsi and his mother.

"I curse you, Blachstenius Mot Dariik," she growls. She looks at the sky and clenches her jaw. She returns her gaze to mine and I wonder if she'll spit on me.

"I pledge myself as the protector of Corsi Mot Dariik until he reaches adulthood," she snarls.

"No, it must be forever."

"No, that's all you get."

I've no more time to bargain. I look past my killer at the sinking disk of Belenos.

"Conwenna, I have loved you since the first time I laid eyes upon you."

I too will fade from this world like the Lord of the Sky. I smile. *Like the Lord of the Sky.*

Epilogue

Conwenna

Blachy can't be gone. He just can't be. I turn my head side to side to dislodge the tears from my eyes as I spur my pony to a gallop. Alur catches up to me, but I can't make out his words. He sees my tears and stares resolutely forward.

The unmanned gates of Venta are in sight. I lead my men through the gate and down the market street. Zianni peeks his head out of a shop.

"Kill all the Sorim!" I shout.

"Are you sure?" Alur asks.

"Do it."

My men dismount and head for the shops lining the street. They all wear silver vectis, so they are immune to Sorim mind tricks.

"No! No!" a man cries off to my right. He's soon silenced.

I see several dead city guards in the street, but no sign of Blachy. Ahead is an overturned cart blocking off a tight alleyway. That's not the cart I gave him.

Did he forsake my gift?

Alur sees what I see and nudges his horse toward the barricade. My countrymen's cries find no pity this day. I close my eyes and take a deep breath to ready myself for what's to come.

The ropes are sliced, and Alur pulls the cart out enough for me to slip through. There's Amma, the assassin queen, sitting cross-legged next to . . . Blachy. My thoughts flee from my head, leaving me to stare with mute anger.

He's lying in a brownish-red puddle of his own blood. I eye the assassin, but she doesn't move. Blachy's brown eyes stare down the street at the twilight sky. I close them and touch my forehead to his. There is nothing remaining. Blachstenius is truly dead.

"Before you order my death," Amma says, "I have a message from Blachstenius."

Cold fury builds within me, but I tame it until I can hear what this vile thief has to say.

"Alur, put your knife to her throat. Any sudden move and you're to kill her."

Extending my hand to her forehead, I relive Blachy's last moments. I see the promise that this assassin has made, and I feel her yearning for his death's kiss. My stomach pitches in revulsion of this woman. As much as I want to claim her life, her pledge to the house of Mot Dariik is too valuable to squander.

"You will keep your pledge to the Mot Dariiks for as long as you live."

"That wasn't the agreement," Amma says.

"It wasn't, but we are making an agreement now. If you refuse, then the day young Corsi Mot Dariik reaches his majority will be the day that the dar Surby declare war on the Yam Mjann." My arms tremble from the building rage within me. How dare she maraud through Blachy's mind as he lay there dying? If I could split her skull and rip out Blachy's memories, I would.

"And what do I get in return?" She sounds calm, serene even.

My left-hand flies on its own and slaps her face. "You get to live."

She slowly draws her right hand up to her cheek and wipes the blood from her lip. She licks her hand clean. "Then I guess I have no choice but to agree."

"Get her out of here before I kill her."

I look at the twilight sky.

An unprotected child such as Corsi won't be safe anywhere on Ynys Luko.

Curse you, Blachstenius Mot Dariik. We could have done this together and saved so very many lives.

"I will have to raise him myself."

"Who?" Alur asks.

I look around the street. Amma is nowhere to be seen. If I knew Blachy, and no one knew him better, then he has sent the child—hopefully with protection—toward Solent Keep.

"Amma is as slippery as an eel," I say, shaking my head. "Hurry, Alur, we must get on the road."

Book Four

Arthmael

Camulodunum

CHAPTER ONE

The Proposal

I grab Dalna's bowl as soon as she's finished eating her morning porridge. It's a game we play: who can clean up first after meals. She looks at me, cross. She thinks I have important work and shouldn't waste my time with menial chores. Clearly, she has never been an apprentice druid. I drop both bowls on the floor and let Shadow, my ever-present canine companion, lick them clean.

There's a thunderous rapping on the door and Dalna, and I look at each other. The townspeople all knock respectfully, not like this. Dalna kisses me and grabs the bowls from under Shadow's nose. She'll be the one to clean up after all.

"Whoever it is, you shouldn't keep them waiting," she says with an impish smile.

I grunt once to let her know she won this time. Before I can get to the door, the rapping repeats. Whoever it is, they're hitting the door with a stout piece of wood.

A little irked, I snatch the door open all at once. Cynbel, my old mentor, stands before me and my harsh words are forgotten. I gape at him in astonishment for an instant before lowering my eyes.

I'm not an apprentice druid anymore.

"May I come in?" Cynbel says with a smirk.

"Yes, of course." I nearly trip over myself as I get out of his way.

"You must be the beautiful Dalna," Cynbel says, bowing low. He pets Shadow at the same time.

"Arthmael won't be giving you any preferential treatment, no matter how kind your words are toward me."

"Dalna!" I say in surprise. "This is Druid Lord Cynbel, protector of the plains and Men Meur Kov Keigh."

"Oh!" Dalna's eyes go wide. "Well, I must be getting little Malry. He's a handful for mother to deal with." She ducks under my arm and is out the door before I can stop her.

"The rumors are true. Dalna is both gorgeous and clever," my old mentor says.

"Thank you, Lord Cynbel." I invite him to sit next to the fire as I add more kindling.

He waves me away. "Just Cynbel will do."

He grabs a stick and starts stirring the embers. "I like how you keep this place tidy. It was always so discouraging when Gwalather was here."

"Thank you, Cynbel." It feels unnatural to be so familiar. "But we both know that cleaning wasn't my biggest concern when I was in your camp."

"I was hoping you have time today to meet at Grahme's for dinner."

"That shouldn't be a problem," I say without any thought. One does not disappoint two druid lords. "Is everything alright?"

Cynbel chuckles. "Oh, there's much too much to go over now. Hopefully, you will agree with us and accept another opportunity to prove your worth to the druid community."

"The druid community is aware of me?"

My mentor gives me a look of disbelief. "Arthmael, you have studied under three sitting members of the Nine. Not once in our history has anyone done that. It's unclear if anyone has ever studied under two." He puts a hand up to keep me silent. "Furthermore, everyone knows how you and your party battled the Obsidian Lord and his army of warriors at Ynys Witrin. If it weren't for Grahme, your name would be sung by the masses."

"I'm fine with Grahme getting all the attention."

"But he doesn't." Cynbel wags his finger at me. "How do you think I knew Dalna's name and what your nighttime habits are?"

"Who's been spying on me?" I ask, bewildered. My thoughts go to last month, when Dalna and I bathed together under the moonlight.

"Old friends of yours."

I run through the possibilities in my head. I know exactly who the culprits are. "Anuc and Faigha." I look at Cynbel for confirmation, but I know I'm correct.

His eyes dance in delight. "They were telling the other apprentices about a certain moonlight swim, I believe."

"I'm going to kill them." I say with mock outrage.

"I'm sorry, I shouldn't gloat." He pats me on my shoulder. "Especially if I'm to have my way tonight."

"What is it?"

He smirks as he rises. "You'll know at dinner."

For the first time in my life, he shakes my hand. "If you succeed like I believe you will, you will be on a very short list for inclusion to the council when another opening arises," he says with a wink.

Mouth agape, I watch him turn into a red kite and fly off toward Dartmoor. Shadow runs hopelessly behind him, barking incessantly.

*   *   *

Dalna rubs my back and rests her head on my shoulder. I let out another sigh. Whatever they have in mind, it must be important, but not so important that one of them doesn't do it. I have nothing worthy to focus upon as the day slowly fritters away.

"This will be good for you," Dalna says.

"I know. It's the other thing."

"You still haven't told Grahme about us?" Her voice turns frosty.

I bounce my head back and forth. "I keep meaning to, but the timing is always awkward."

"That's it, I'm going with you tonight," Dalna says.

"What? No! You can't." I raise both arms to restrain her, as if she means to set off right now.

"You tell him tonight, or I'm going up on the moor tomorrow."

"I don't need this kind of stress right now."

"I see, telling your best friend that we're in love is too horrible to contemplate?"

"No, of course not. It's just that you and him . . .."

"Grahme and I what?" she asks. "I'm three years older than him, and while that may not mean much now, he was still a boy when Malry and I wed."

"But . . . never mind."

"Is it that you're ashamed of me?"

"That's not fair." I look down at my empty hands. "You're right, I'll tell him."

"And dear, don't hang your head like a child. You're a druid. There are only nine people in this world who rank higher than you."

That's not quite true. Druid masters are considered experts in their crafts and held in higher esteem, but that will be lost on everyone but other druids.

"Yes, and two of them are waiting for me on Dartmoor."

Dalna leans over, hugs me and positions herself to whisper in my ear. "It's a full moon tonight. We can go bathe each other in the river again when you get back."

"We'll see," is all I can muster.

*   *   *

Grahme and Cynbel are sitting comfortably at the fire. There's a hefty stack of kindling between them, so I know Grahme has sent Brehmne away for the night. I immediately scan the treetops. Ever since Grahme told us how he spied on Boswen as an owl, it's been a common practice. If Grahme knows we do it, he doesn't let on.

"Lords," I say once I retake my form.

"See, I told you it would be an owl," Grahme says.

"That makes me sad," Cynbel says, but with a smile on his face. "I was confident that you would choose a red kite."

"Red kites are not naturally seen on the moors."

"The Boswen doctrine." Cynbel rolls his eyes. "Not even Caradoc cares about that."

"Why have you called me here tonight?" I ask before they get into a meaningless argument. If I didn't focus their attention, I'd get saddled with bringing more wood for the fire and refilling waterskins while they argue over nothing.

Grahme smiles. He's the one that told us how important the tactic is.

Shadow makes his way up the path and lays in front of Grahme. The dog is panting heavily, even though I know he's not that exhausted. He's only dramatic when he knows he'll get attention.

"I don't know how much you know," Cynbel begins, "but the Wigesta are building their forces for war."

I shake my head, making sure I heard the words I thought I did.

"There are three men vying for leadership of their army," Cynbel says. "First, there is Rendell. He's in Camulodunon, the capital of Wigestan Pretanni. He's been a military man his entire life and would make a formidable opponent. The second is Tilbert, the Lord of Wigesta, in Londinjon. He's as crafty as they come. Though he has some military experience, he's more known for the unexpected. Rendell will meet us on the battlefield and trade blows until only one side remains standing. Tilbert would never do such a thing. Or if he did, it would be to set us up for attacks at our sides or rear."

"Both sound terrible for us."

"They would be," Cynbel says. He looks at Grahme, who gives a slight nod. "So it is in our best interest to have the newly emerging third candidate become the overall commander."

"Who is it?"

"Mind you, he has his own skills, but war planning isn't one of them."

He reaches over and pets Shadow. Cynbel is very direct. It's not like him to dance around an issue.

He looks me straight in the eye. "The third candidate is Loris."

I stare at my old master and Grahme. Is this some kind of hazing? They both look and wait for me to say something.

"But Loris left for the mainland," I offer, my voice rising slightly, questioning what I believed to be true.

"That's what we thought, but we have a sighting of him in Verlamion. Thanks to his silvertongue, he's in charge there now."

"And we haven't killed him?" I ask.

"That was my initial reaction," Grahme says. "But Cynbel is right. Loris can't lead men. If he's in charge, our chances of success improve."

"I don't understand why you're telling me this."

As if sensing my distress, Shadow walks over and leans against me.

"We'll get to that. But first, you should know that Bradan has gone missing."

"As in, he got lost?"

"As in, we believe he has joined Loris at Verlamion. The Nine met late last month to go over strategy for the impending war. It seems he was waiting to hear what we would do before he defected," Cynbel says.

"So he knows we were exploring the option of attacking this summer as a surprise," Grahme adds.

"With respect to you both, I don't know why you are telling me this. I have nothing to contribute."

The two men smile at each other.

"That's almost word for word what I told Cynbel earlier today," Grahme says.

Cynbel stands and paces. "We cannot send troops of any size into Wigestan lands now. Even if Loris gets overall command *and* we can unite all the Pretanni tribes, we will still be the weaker side."

Cynbel stops pacing and pulls on his robe. "For us to have any chance, Rendell and Tilbert must fail in their bids to become the Walda, the man in charge. I've talked over my plan and Grahme agrees. If you were to sabotage one or both of those two, we would have a chance come next warring season."

He raises his hand to stop me from responding. "And you would be on a very short list of people to replace Bradan at Brenin Cairn."

Disbelieving, I laugh at the men. "I don't know what is more ridiculous, infiltrating the Wigesta high command or becoming one of the Nine."

"I know how you feel," Grahme says. "But you are familiar with Wigestan territory, are you not?"

"My grandmother was from a small village outside of Camulodunon. I visited her a couple times before I became a druid apprentice, but I wouldn't say I'm familiar with the land."

"Arthmael," Grahme says, "how many people do you know that can travel to Camulodunon on their own?"

"I don't know. I never thought about it."

"Well, Cynbel and I have given it quite a bit of thought. Other than Blachstenius, we couldn't name another person we trust to do so."

"Then why don't you send Blachstenius?"

Cynbel laughs. "You've met the Sorim trader many times. Does Blachstenius take orders from anyone? But rest assured, you will have help. We're sending you to Solent Keep first, to meet with

Conwenna. She is our best source of information about both the Sorim and the Wigesta."

"The Wigesta business is an impossible task, so I can't even begin to worry about it." I stare at my two mentors. "But Bradan's position? Why do you think I'd have a chance at that?"

"Before Loris and now Bradan, we haven't had members of the Nine vacate their positions since Bodmin's time. Meraud is adamant that we are not going to have the best candidates kill each other for the honor. Instead, she wants the council to vote for someone before Bradan's defection becomes common knowledge."

"Is that how Vacea became a member of the Nine?" I ask.

"It is." Cynbel confirms. "It's also the price Meraud extracted from us in order to accept the head druid position."

"That makes sense; Vacea was always terrible with the staff."

"And she was Meraud's second at Keynvor Daras," Grahme adds.

"So that just leaves the impossible task for me to perform."

"Conwenna says she can help, but she won't say how," Grahme says. "Even to me, and I'm her brother-in-law."

"Me? Really?" Disbelieving, I laugh silently.

The two druid lords look back at me placidly. I wait, hoping an elaborate prank will be revealed, but they aren't budging.

"When do I have to go?"

This is sheer madness. Why am I even considering this?

"Very soon, but not right now," Cynbel says. "You can have a few days, but not much more. The Wigesta will only grow stronger as the year progresses."

"I will have to think on this."

I rise from my seat, nod at them both and transform into an owl. I fly a good distance away before animorphing back into human form and vomiting up the contents of my stomach.

Shadow is beside me, sniffing my mess. I move him away from it with my leg. "Come along, Shadow, I need to think."

I do my best thinking when I run, and it's been a long time since we ran as a pack. I change into a wolf and start down the trail.

CHAPTER TWO

The Confrontation

Dalna is leaning against the doorframe when I return. I give her a big, foolish grin before I kiss her. Together, we enter the cottage and she manages to close the door.

"I gave Malry some of your sleep draught," she says. "He'll sleep very soundly."

Malry used to get a sour belly when we gave him a nip of the draught, so I changed some of the ingredients. Now he sleeps through the night.

"So will Shadow," I add.

The pup is yawning already. He retreats to his bed by the fire and snuggles up into an impossibly tight ball.

"If I don't watch it, I'm going to be replaced as the potion master in these parts." I stroke Dalna's lovely blond hair.

"So how is Grahme?" Dalna asks.

"Grahme is good. He and Cynbel have a mission for me."

"Oh?"

"I don't want to have you worrying needlessly," I say as I kiss her cheek, "but I'll be gone for a while, maybe up to a month."

"That sounds serious," she says.

"It sounds impossible. But I'm going to give it my best effort and see what happens."

"Do we have time to get married before you go?"

I freeze for a just a moment, but it gives me away.

"You didn't tell him about us," she accuses me.

I grimace and try to think of the best way to minimize the damage.

"I guess I'll just have to go up on the moor tomorrow and tell him myself," Dalna says.

"Hon, it's not like that. They hit me with the mission to Wigestan lands as soon as I got there."

"Wigestan lands? What exactly do they want you to do?"

Her voice gets lower, and that's how I know I'm in trouble.

"Just to see what I can find out. You know that I spent a lot of time near Camulodunon at my grandmother's place."

"Camulodunon? They're sending you to the capital of the Wigesta?" Her eyes lock onto mine.

"The Wigesta are building up their forces, so we can't very well send hundreds of men into their lands."

"You're going alone?" she growls.

"I shouldn't even be speaking of this."

She laughs at me mirthlessly. "It's too late to try that now."

I put my hand on the small of her back and try to gently steer her toward our bed. She glares at me, and I raise my hands up to my shoulders and look away.

I don't have to worry about apprentice druids watching us tonight.

* * *

I wake to my shoulder being jerked back and forth.

"Dad, I'm hungry," Malry says. "When do we eat?"

My arms skims across the other side of the bed and encounter nothing.

"Your mum will have it ready in no time."

"She's not here," he says, plaintively.

I open my eyes and see that Belenos has risen quite a bit in the sky. "Where did your mum go?"

"I don't know. She was gone when I got up."

I bolt upright and look around for her mantle. It's not by the door. She chose her heavy leather shoes instead of her sandals. A shiver goes down my spine.

"I'm going to have to go help your mum," I say. "So, get dressed and we'll see if your grandmother can make any sweet oat cakes for you."

Malry runs across the cottage and attacks his shoes. His mantle is crooked, his shoes aren't laced and his hair resembles a hedgehog.

"Let's go see your grandmother."

After surprising Dalna's mother, I'm off to try to catch up with my beloved. Owls are too slow. I choose a red kite and head straight for Grahme's camp. Shadow barks at me in frustration, but he knows the way.

"Are you ready so soon?" Grahme asks as soon as I change to my human form.

I ignore him and search about his camp.

"What is it?" Grahme asks.

"He's looking for me," Dalna calls from behind.

"Dalna?" Grahme says, perplexed.

"Yes, noble one," she says as she draws up next to me.

"There's no need for titles," Grahme says, waving them away with his hand. "You look out of breath. Come sit by the fire."

She gives me a sideways look before sitting.

Should I sit with her? Should I stay where I am? I'm frozen with indecision.

"Hi Dalna," Brehmne's cheerful voice rings out. "Are you here to finally tell Grahme about you and Arthmael?"

"I am," she replies.

"You and Arthmael?" Grahme asks as everyone turns to look at me.

My mouth opens, but no noise comes out.

"What Arthmael was supposed to have told you months ago," Dalna starts, "is that we have been living together and we plan on getting married at Beltane next month."

Grahme looks at Dalna, then me, then back at Dalna again. "That's great!" He says. "I'm thrilled for you. How long have you two been together?"

Dalna glares at me.

I can't look at my master's face. "We met about a year ago, but we weren't really serious until recently."

"Oh?" Dalna says dangerously.

Brehmne is grinning foolishly at me.

"I mean, we've been very close for a while, but the time to tell you about us just never really presented itself."

Grahme glares at me until the sides of his mouth rise and he can't contain his mirth any longer. He laughs and Brehmne laughs too. I glance over at Dalna.

"You're an idiot," she says, shaking her head.

My head falls into my right hand and I drag my face across my palm. I look up and everyone is still smiling at me.

"You will have to pronounce us married," Dalna says to Grahme.

"I would be honored." He bows to my love.

"Of course, that'll be hard to do when you're sending him into Wigestan lands to get killed." She says with an iron tone.

Grahme looks at me. Brehmne's eyes go wide.

This can't be happening.

"Brehmne . . ." Grahme says.

"I know," he says, resigned. "Do you want firewood or a rabbit for dinner?"

"A rabbit, I think. Arthmael will get the wood today."

Brehmne turns into a tawny owl and launches himself into the air. He doesn't even try misdirection. He lands on a branch behind Grahme so he can listen in on our conversation.

Shadow barks, announcing his presence to us. He runs past me and straight to Dalna.

Not even my dog is on my side?

"Arthmael," Grahme says. "Would you like to start on the firewood? I'll be happy to prepare a small meal for Dalna and Shadow while we talk."

"Of course." I turn into a tawny owl as well, but I head off into the woods before I circle back and land next to Brehmne.

"I'm happy for you both," Grahme says.

"I told him that he was being stupid."

Grahme smiles as he grabs her hand into his. "Dalna, it is vitally important that Arthmael's mission remains a secret." His face turns serious. "We have to assume that the Wigesta have spies in our lands."

"If you're truly happy for us, why are you sending him on this dangerous mission? He tries to play it down, but he's a terrible liar."

"And that is one of the things you love about him most, I'd wager."

When did Grahme get so good at talking to . . . well, anyone?"

Dalna bites her lip and I feel as if a dagger has been thrust into my chest.

"His mission may, and I need to stress *may*, be dangerous, but it is vitally important to us. Cynbel and I sat here most of yesterday thinking of other candidates or other ways of accomplishing this. Arthmael makes sound decisions. You know I'm right about that."

Dalna nods, though she has to blink away her tears.

"Good." Grahme moves to sit next to her. "And I mean it when I say that I'm happy for you both." He put his arm around her protectively.

"I know that," Dalna says.

"But if I can be so bold as to give you one piece of advice?"

"Please do."

"We druids tend to be a nosy bunch. We think that animorphing will hide us in plain sight. I would suggest that you and Arthmael be . . . a little more private when you're being intimate. Owls are solitary by nature, so if you ever see two owls sitting together, like those two behind me, you can safely assume they are druids."

Shadow follows Grahme's pointing finger and begins enthusiastically barking at us. Brehmne and I flee from our perch. I hear Grahme's laugh and my traitorous dog's bark over and over as I fly far away from camp.

CHAPTER THREE

Seized by Si

I feel foolish for not telling Grahme about Dalna. If I'm honest, that's why I'm walking to Grahme's camp on Dartmoor instead of flying. I hope he can forgive me.

"I'm such an idiot." I tell Shadow.

"We know that," Brehmne says from behind me.

I swing my staff low and trip the apprentice druid. "See, you've already gone soft now that I'm not there to spar with you." I walk over and help the smiling fool up.

"I beat Grahme four to two yesterday," he says proudly.

"Did you let him win twice, or are you just that bad?"

"He better not hear you say that."

I grab him in a headlock and rub my knuckles across the top of his head. "He's not going to hear anything about it. Is he?"

Shadow starts running around us, tail wagging and barking in excitement.

Brehmne backs out of my hold and smiles at me again. "He might. It depends on what's in it for me."

"How about, I don't break your neck for spying on Dalna and me?"

His ears turn bright red and his cheeks aren't far behind. His head drops and he becomes very interested in his feet. I scratch Shadow behind the ears as I wait for Brehmne to recover his wits. After a hundred paces or so, he dares to look up.

"Arthmael?"

"What."

"Grahme sent me to find you and tell you to hurry."

"Why didn't you lead with that?" I ask, exasperated.

"Well, I . . ."

I don't wait, I change into a tawny owl and fly straight for the camp. Shadow barks once and races to catch up. I circle around to see his tail straight up and the big goofy smile on his face. Finally, I see Brehmne in raven form overtaking my dog. He must still be struggling with the initial transformation.

* * *

Brehmne is straining to beat me to Grahme's fire. Once he's animorphed, he has no issues with the magic. I push as hard as I can until the very last instant. Then I flair my wings and watch as Brehmne soars past me. If I could smile in this form, it would reach both of my ears. I land gracefully just outside the fire ring and cah several times, since I can't laugh. Brehmne tries to stop and singes his tail feathers in the fire. He lets out an alarm call and lands on a branch just above us. He transforms back into himself, rubbing his backside. That was a poor decision as the too thin branch snaps under his weight. Just before he lands face first on the ground, he changes back into a raven and flaps desperately. In the end, he still thumps onto the ground, but not hard enough to damage anything more than his pride.

"If you're done with . . . whatever that was," Grahme deadpans. "I'd like to go over some last instructions with Arthmael."

Brehmne limps over, holding his left hip. As he slowly sits down, barking announces Shadow's imminent arrival.

"Good, you're taking the dog with you," Grahme says. "That makes my extra condition on your mission less problematic."

"There's more?" I ask, disbelieving.

A quick smile flits across Grahme's face. "You are going over the same path I took to reach Solent Keep. What I haven't told you about my trip is that when I was in the Arden, I came across a thick stand of beech trees. I skirted around them instead of investigating, and I've rued that choice ever since."

"Do you identify with Fagus that closely?" I ask. He is always known as the grumpy beech tree god.

Grahme doesn't acknowledge my barb. "When Figol and I went to Eriu, we spoke to Gortor, the firbolg leader. He asked if the si were still well in the great Arden Forest. I told him that I had never seen them before, but I did mention the beech trees. Those trees are sacred to the si and their god, Fagus."

I nod, though I have no idea why this is important.

Shadow leaves my side and heads straight for Grahme. The dog leans into my mentor's legs and plops down at his feet, awaiting a belly rub.

"Since you won't be flying over the Arden, you should have no trouble spotting the beech trees and presumably the si as well."

"What are they like?" I ask, more than a little nervous about meeting a people I'm not familiar with.

"I have no idea. I didn't investigate."

"And you don't want to tell them yourself, so that I can get to my mission?"

Grahme's chuckling makes it hard for him to get out his words. "The war won't start until next year; you have plenty of time."

*   *   *

The wall of beech trees is unmistakable. Even Shadow is hesitant to enter. I consider animorphing into an animal and entering unnoticed, but they'd have to assume I was spying when I change back in front of them.

I give Shadow a couple of solid thumps on his ribs and jog toward the beech trees. The branches are thicker than I'd thought, making it slow going. Shadow is glued to my side. He's sniffing the air and keeping his tail between his legs. I do my best to weave through the tangled branches without breaking them. I have to assume I'm being watched, so I want them to see that I respect their lands.

I make it to a small clearing and drop to my knees before falling down to a sitting position. My body is racked with sweat. Shadow sits too, but his gaze is off in a different direction.

"Why have you entered our lands?" a voice calls down at us.

I scan the trees, but I see no one. "I am Arthmael, a druid of Pretanni. I have been tasked with meeting with the si in order to deliver important news."

"Speak."

I set my staff down and slowly rise to my feet. "With respect, I would like to see who I am speaking with."

A thin, blonde-haired man is pushed from his cover in the canopy. He grimaces at the instigator before leaping from one branch to another until he's on the ground not ten paces from us.

"I am Wranlen, a half-si. Speak your words to me."

The half-si looks the same age as me. Other than several brown, bony ridges on his nose, he looks human—an extremely beautiful human with bright hazel eyes and an impossibly lithe body, but human.

I bow at the waist to him. "I greet you, Wranlen, and wish only good upon you. However, I would ask that I meet with your leaders to share my news." I take out my bone knife and toss it next to my staff. "As you can see, I have disarmed myself."

Shadow lets out a startled yelp. Turning, I see a second si has snuck up on my dog and grab his back legs. Shadow wiggles free and turns to bark at the new adversary. He grabs his bow from behind him, but not an arrow. I take this as a good sign.

"The dog is truly a dog, not a shapeshifter," the second si says.

I mentally tell Shadow to settle down as I signal him to come to me. Once he is in contact with my legs, his hackles lower, although he's still unsure.

"We can take you to see our elders, but you may regret it," the second si says.

"Then please, lead the way."

"Your weapons seem crude."

"As druids, we reject the use of metal, since it must be ripped so violently from the earth." I stop walking. "If it is not considered rude, may I have your name?"

"I am from the Unblemished line."

"The true si will only give out their name when a bond has been formed. Until then, only the familial line will be given," Wranlen says. "I am a half-si, so this doesn't apply to me."

"I am honored to meet you both." Once more I incline my head before following Wranlen.

With the half-si leading the way, we avoid tangled branches and are an easy walk away from a new, larger clearing. There are two creatures, each a cross between a si and a beech tree. Neither approaches us.

"Wait here with me," Wranlen says.

We watch as the Unblemished descendant heads toward the tree-si. He converses with them for a bit before they approach us, each with a very stiff gait. Each step takes several heartbeats to make, and they seem to have the balance of a toddler just learning to walk. The true si remains in the center of the glade, now with an arrow notched, though pointing downward.

"How old are your elders?" I ask Wranlen.

"They are over one hundred and fifty cycles and are hardening off, as you can see."

"What does 'hardening off' mean?"

"There are none in the outside world who retain familiarity with our ways?" He waits for a breath before continuing. "As the mobile life ends, the body stiffens and one's feet begin to dig into the ground. The true si will begin the reaching phase as they slowly transform into our sacred beech trees, like those all around you."

"Then all of the trees we walked through?"

"They are our elders. That is why you found it so hard to move on your own. They were blocking you, testing to see if you would inflict damage upon them."

"And if I had?"

"You would have a dozen arrows in you. Possibly your dog as well, though I am just as glad that he was not harmed."

The elders are almost upon us. We crane our necks upward to see their bark-like faces.

"Well, speak your words," the short tree-si says. "Though our lives are long, we do not waste the time we have."

There's a chuckle from the taller tree-si. Up close, it's hard to tell which part, tree or person, is more prominent, as most of their skin has transitioned into a soft, movable bark.

"Elders, I am honored to meet you." I bow at the waist once again. "My master, Grahme Fairweather, Protector of Men-an-Tol wishes you to know that a tremendous battle is brewing on this island, and no one can count themselves safe from it. The Wigesta, who control the lands east of here, wish to do battle with the peace-loving people of Pretanni."

The short tree-si snorts in derision. "Is there not land for all?"

"He is from the land of the pixies," the taller one says. "If men have usurped the lands of the younger races, then it may be that the isle is filled."

"I am afraid the Wigesta crave power above land. The time for building up defenses is now. It will be next summer, the warring season, when the battles will commence. Though we would welcome your aid and alliance, if nothing else, we are honor bound to share this terrible news with you."

"Where would we go?" the taller tree asks. He sweeps his stiff left arm around the glade. "Most of us have hardened and cannot retreat."

"In truth, I do not know. My master felt that as protectors of this land, it was our duty to warn you."

"And warn us you have," the shorter tree says. It's a low, gravelly voice, yet it is definitely female.

"In better times, my master and I would wish to get to know your ways and live in harmony. But alas, these are troubling times and that luxury is not afforded to us," I say.

"More knowledge of these new peoples is needed, I think," the tall si says.

"Yes," the shorter one agrees. "It is Wranlen who should go."

"As you say." Wranlen bows with his hands moving from his forehead to knees.

So that is the proper way to show deference.

The slow, deep voices have soothed my dog's anxiety. Shadow lays down on his side, though he keeps his eyes open.

"I will gladly welcome you, Wranlen, as I make my way through the forest."

The two tree-si make a rumbling noise, and I know that I have displeased them in some way.

Wranlen looks at me apologetically. "It is the elders' wish that I travel with you for the duration of your mission. Only then will we have the knowledge we need."

"My path is a dangerous one."

"One's true self is seen when all is risked," the short tree-si rumbles.

"I cannot guarantee your safety," I say to Wranlen.

"Then we are all agreed," the tall one says.

Wranlen bows again, touching his head and knees. I mimic his gesture.

"Help Wranlen prepare," the short one calls to the true si in a powerful, low tone. The true si and Wranlen leave the glade at once.

"Wranlen is unhappy to leave," the tall tree-si says.

"It is for the best," the other responds. "Remain here. Wranlen will not be long."

I look at the two, confusion on my face, but they only lumber off and leave me with my dog.

CHAPTER FOUR

Unwelcome Addition

Shadow barks as I stop again on the road to Solent Keep. I don't care how many times I'm told the city is now friendly with the druids; this place will always bring me a sense of dread. The black stone gate certainly doesn't help.

Shadow rubs against my leg to comfort me, and Wranlen waits without comment. I don't know what it is about him, but he never gives offence. It must be the si in him.

"Let's run." I change into the spitting image of my dog and the race is on. Shadow is caught flat-footed for once and struggling to catch me. Wranlen gives a surprised, "Oh," before bringing up the rear.

At the last bend in the road, I change back into myself and gasp for breath. Shadow finds a muddy puddle and starts lapping up the disgusting water. Wranlen catches up to us before I regain my breath. He's not even breathing hard. Try as I may, I can't figure him out.

With the si's amicable nature, the guards are all too happy to wave us inside. It's midday, and the market is still quite active. Shadow is sniffing a little too much at the butcher's wagon. I go to one knee and call my companion before he gets in trouble. Shadow licks my face energetically. Still too excited, I receive a couple of headbutts as he scrapes off a couple layers of skin with his coarse, wet tongue.

Be still. I project.

A man takes my hand.

"Are you a real druid?"

"I am," I say, smiling.

"The druids have returned!" he yells.

His excitement builds as he repeats himself several times. More merchants leave their carts, surrounding us as they each ask for a blessing from me. The butcher lures Shadow over to him with meat scraps, and I'm forced to follow before the dog causes more commotion. It's not long before everyone is trying to get to me through my dog.

Wranlen's eyes dance at the spectacle. I must resort to mentally controlling Shadow so that we can make our way to the keep. The crowd is slow to give up. I send Wranlen and Shadow on their way before facing the small crowd and calling for quiet.

"You have been overwhelmingly kind this day. Not long ago, this city was not open to my kind." The crowd settles down, waiting to hear whatever it is I'm going to say next. "Know that I will report this generosity to my brethren, and more druids will make their way to this fair city."

"We need a druid to live here, in the city," a woman cries out.

I raise my hands in mock surrender. "When I return to druid lands, I will share that message with not one, but two druid lords."

The people rumble their agreement and close the circle around me as they dart forward to touch my robes. Being worshiped like this makes my skin crawl.

I know how to get out of this.

"Not all druids will enter like I did," I say. "In fact, you may not see them until they are in your midst."

I turn into a raven, fly over the city walls, and make a broad circle that ends next to my companions. Now a block away from the market, we can walk in peace. Shadow has been stuffed with food and will want a nap soon. That should keep him from causing trouble when we meet Conwenna.

We amble through what must be the wealthy section, as the homes are large stone structures rivaling the Llanmelin mead hall in size. No one passes us on the road. I can't help but wonder, was that the proper way to act? Grahme went on his missions and slew the Obsidian Lord, nearly single-handedly captured Laleah and strode boldly into a centaur city. I have to flee a market full of people.

A couple of white streamers hang from the roof of the keep, obscuring at least some of the ominous black stones used on the city gate. They can try all they like to soften the look, but it will always look foreboding.

The guards allow me to enter the keep unchallenged. A short lady, looking as uncomfortably heavy with child as one could be, greets us in the foyer. She nods before making some sort of apology. Her voice is little more than a puff of air.

Wranlen and I rush over, each taking an arm.

"You should sit," I say.

She grudgingly agrees. "May I ask your names and your business here?"

"I am Arthmael, a druid sent by the Druid Lord Grahme Fairweather, Protector of Men-an-Tol, to speak with Lady Conwenna. And this is Wranlen, a half-si from the great Arden Forest." I smack my dog's nose as he tries to sniff a little too close to her private area. "And finally, this is my rude dog, Shadow."

She reaches down and pets Shadow absently. "I am Nidda, the chamberlady of the keep," she says. Struggling to rise, she bashfully looks to us and she returns to her seat. "Can you call for someone to come to me? I'm afraid this chair won't let go of me just yet."

Wranlen goes to the door behind our host and opens it halfway. "My pardon, lady, gentle Nidda is feeling a bit sluggish. Could you inform the Lady Conwenna that we would be well pleased if she could meet with us?"

A lady in a simple white dress approaches and closes the door behind her. "Conwenna is happy to meet you," a warm smile lights up her face as she nods to us.

"Lady Conwenna?" Nidda asks, mortified.

"Nidda," Conwenna says, exasperated, "how many times must I tell you to stay home until that lovely child of yours is born?"

"It is my duty—"

"Do you want my guards to be the ones to deliver your child?" Conwenna cuts her off. "I'm afraid to even contemplate what a spectacle that would be."

"Yes Lady Koni, but—"

"But nothing. That child will come into this world any day now. Do you believe you can defend me in your current state?"

A guard opens the door behind Conwenna. "You called for me, Lady?"

"I did. Please find Nidda's poor husband and tell him to take his wife home and make sure she stays there for a month, at least, while they welcome this child of theirs into the world."

"Thank you, Lady," Nidda says humbly.

"I'll check in on you when I can." Conwenna pats her chamberlady's hand. "If you two and that lovely dog of yours would follow me," she says to us.

Am I supposed to bow or show some sort of deference? Grahme really should have told me how to greet Sorim royalty.

"We have no royalty, Arthmael," Conwenna says.

My chin nearly hits the floor.

"I apologize. 'Skimming' one's thoughts is rude. I assure you, it only happened because I just came from my Sorim children. They don't know the boundaries, so I have to be in the background of their minds or else they'll have the cooks bringing them sweet cakes until their tummies hurt."

"It's fine, my lady," I stammer. She's not a large woman, yet she seems rather imposing all the same.

She gives me a disappointed look that all mothers know. "You must call me Conwenna, or Koni. I was a simple blacksmith's wife for nearly two decades. Formal titles carry no charm with me."

We enter a room with tapestries covering all four walls. I don't recognize any of the people or scenes.

"I don't have to read your mind to see your confusion," Conwenna says. "These are all Sorim tapestries detailing ancient victories." Her brow furrows, and she seems to notice Wranlen for the first time.

"I apologize," she says. "I did not greet you as I should."

Wranlen nods his head at her. "We have a way of receding into the background when we wish."

"You're like no druid I've ever met," Conwenna says. "In fact, I don't believe you're entirely human."

"The full-blooded si are much better than I at this, but as a sapblood, I still have some of the talent."

"Si? Sapblood?" Conwenna asks. "Are all sapbloods male?"

"The pure race," I look over to Wranlen to see if he objects, "is pronounced 'shee'. The sapbloods are the half-human, half-si and always male, like Wranlen here."

He nods his head.

"The si are an ancient race that live in the Arden. If you've ever seen a stand of beech trees within the forest, you were just steps away from our realm," Wranlen says. "And sapblood is a pejorative term for the half-si, like me. At least, among the si it is. They would never call me that directly, but when no half-bloods are around, they use it exclusively to refer to my kind."

"That's terrible," Conwenna says.

"Not so much," he responds. "There is no ambiguity in our station. The humans, however, use sapblood as more of a statement of wonder."

He rubs his scaly nose. "Humans can't believe that in another twenty or twenty-five years, I'll have my reaching day, when I will put down roots at my desired spot and stretch my branches toward Belenos."

"That is when you settle down and have children?" Conwenna asks.

Wranlen smiles. "No. See my nose?" He rubs it again. "The nose is the first part to harden, as we say. I will become more and more tree-like until my reaching day, when I sink my very real roots into the soil and stake out my place in the forest."

"You become a tree?" she asks.

"I do. Since I'm not full si, the community won't honor my day, but family will always come by to greet me."

"What about children?" Conwenna asks.

"These are my seeding days. No full si will lie with me, so I find willing human women. Any children will be either sapblood or human. In some rare cases, humans will retain the si ability to persuade. They are what you call silvertongues."

"I had no idea," Conwenna says. "About any of this, or even the existence of the si."

"We are a very private people, and by necessity, we can't stray far from our ancestors."

"I would love to know more, but I'm afraid we must address the reason you came here."

"I agree, Lady Conwenna," Wranlen says.

"It's your turn, druid." She shoots me an annoyed look. "You first must tell me why you agreed to this fool's errand. Did my brother-in-law force you into it?"

I look at her in confusion. "Grahme would never do such a thing. My hope is that I can become half the druid he is."

"Are we talking about the same Grahme?" she asks. "The man from Dinas Gwenenen?"

"Oh, you're a precious one, aren't you?" A man whispers from behind a door. "Come here pup, and see what Jory has for you."

The room goes silent as Wranlen and I look toward Conwenna in surprise. Shadow barks once, then chases after the voice.

"I'm afraid that's Jory, my Master of the Hounds," Conwenna says. "His love for dogs of all kinds has no equal, I'd wager. I promise to make him give your dog back when we are finished."

Before I can answer, there comes a shrieking sound from the opposite door. "Mum!"

Conwenna closes her eyes and exhales. "Yes Berga, what is it?"

She shouts "I had that scary . . .." from behind the door. Once she sees us, she freezes and runs to her mother.

"It will be okay," Conwenna assures the little girl. Do you want to play with Jory and the hounds while I speak to these men?"

"Can I?" The girl's face brightens.

"Forgive us if we came at a bad time," I say.

"When is a good time?" Conwenna asks. "This is my every day, and I haven't even begun to govern the city yet." She escorts her daughter to the door where Shadow disappeared. Straightening, she dusts off her simple robe.

"I assume Grahme has told you of our plan?"

"He has."

"I'm not pleased with what we are asking of you, but I see no other way." She looks off to the left for a moment. "I have someone you should take with you on your mission. He'll be here in a bit. While we wait, what specifically are you going to do to get Loris promoted?"

"In truth," I begin, "I'm trying to recall how to get to Camulodunon. I was nine when I was last there."

"You have no plan, then?"

I shrug and raise my empty hands.

"Typical." Conwenna shakes her head. "You druids systematically refuse to plan. It's breathtaking just how unprepared you are on every single occasion."

She looks directly at me. "I am going to have to insist that you take my man with you."

I nod at Conwenna. I can't imagine going against her wishes.

"She summoned me," a new person says, out of breath.

"She's in there," the guard responds.

The door opens and the knave, Alfswich, enters.

"Get back, Conwenna, he's dangerous." I level my staff at the thief.

Conwenna places her hand on my elbow, and I lower my staff. "Alfswich is the companion I spoke of."

"You can't be serious. Cynbel's standing orders are for us to kill him on sight."

"You see, Lady," the thief says, "they will never be willing to give me a second chance."

"Your problems are of your own making, Alfswich, but I think you are wrong. Arthmael is willing to work with you, aren't you?" She turns to face me.

"Never," I say. "He's killed two of my brethren."

"Alfswich has had a change of heart since you saw him last," Conwenna says in a calm voice. "He's not the same man that you knew."

I look at Alfswich and he raises his right hand. His middle three fingers are missing. If he thinks that will make me feel sorry for him, he's wrong. It's likely better than he deserved.

"It's hard to thieve when you're missing the middle of your hand." He wiggles his thumb and pinky back and forth.

"I don't trust him," I say.

"Are you druids aware that the Wigesta are making fyrian stones by the hundreds?" Alfswich asks. "Now, I'm not entirely sure how, but I was told that with the proper rune carved into it, they can transform into fireballs. I was told that's how they are going to defeat your kind next summer."

"Where do they get these fyrian stones?" Despite my revulsion of the man, I can't help but ask. If his information, wherever it comes from, is correct, I will need to share this with Grahme.

"Your mentor is aware," Conwenna says.

Wranlen and I stare at one another.

"Sorry, that was rude of me to read your mind, but I'm afraid my time is limited, so I must forego some of the niceties," Conwenna says.

"The vlint comes from the grim graves mine," Alfswich says, "near Camulodunon, and they are shipped to Verlamion. That's where the runes are carved into the stones and some sort of ritual is performed. By the time it's all done, common vlint has become a magical fyrian stone."

"How are we to fight against this?" I ask Conwenna.

"No one knows. I have asked Cynbel as well as Vacea to meet with me several times, but neither will visit me here. As you've seen, I'm too busy to leave. Of your people, only Grahme is aware, and I made him hesitant to share the information. I fear without further details, Meraud and the council will not believe this to be true."

"Then I must go to Verlamion and find out what I can."

"You'll be captured and enslaved if you go to Verlamion," Alfswich says. "Not to mention that Loris and his cursed silvertongue will have you spilling all your secrets to him."

"Then what would you have me do?"

"Go to Camulodunon," Conwenna says. "Rendell has no life outside of the military. Ingratiate yourself to him and play his dislike for Tilbert against him. He is the only real threat to this island. Tilbert would be a more benign ruler. Rendell is more apt to kill every man capable of holding a weapon."

"But if nothing is done about those fyrian stones, we'll be overrun next warring season," I say.

"You will be overrun regardless," Alfswich says. "Lady Koni is telling you the best result you can achieve."

Conwenna motions for Alfswich to stop. "I believe you are making a mistake if you go to Verlamion, but I promised I wouldn't interfere. So I will simply beseech you to stay away from Verlamion. Furthermore, Alfswich has been all throughout the Wigestan lands. Neither of us will force you, but you would do well to partner with him. I will vouch for his good behavior."

"But you don't know the half—"

"But I do," Conwenna taps her head.

"What about it, Wranlen?" I ask.

Conwenna and Alfswich turn to the half-si.

"That *is* a talent," Conwenna says. "I had forgotten you were here."

"I don't like him," Alfswich says. "I can't find his mental presence, and somehow he managed to be unnoticed, even in plain sight."

"I am a half-si," Wranlen says, "so your talents aren't so reliable on me." He smiles apologetically.

"And you trust him?" I nod toward the thief.

"I do," Conwenna says without hesitation. "Your course is yours to choose, but will you listen to my council and forego Verlamion?"

"In truth, I don't know. But I will take Alfswich, assuming Shadow doesn't attack him. My dog is a great judge of character."

"You see, no one is willing to forgive," Alfswich says to Conwenna. "Once out of sight, he'll sic his miserable cur on me."

She gives him a motherly sigh. "As I've told you, establishing friendships takes time and consistency."

"For whatever good it does. Release me from our agreement and I'll take care of Shua and his fyrian stones," the thief says to Conwenna.

"Alfswich, you will need to tell my husband that you are leaving for a spell. You should do that now."

The thief mutters to himself as he leaves.

"Alfswich has had a hard life, and that has made him retreat into himself. I would advise you not to give him orders, or he'll just smile as he disobeys. Being kind to him without making a show of it is the best course," Conwenna says.

"Are you sure he won't stick a knife in my chest while I sleep?"

"My hope is that in time he can learn to make friends, or at least non-enemies. He is very much a work in progress. If he gets stressed, he'll return to his old habits, and no, that doesn't mean he'll kill you. You'll need to lead without commanding and to befriend him without being obvious."

"Oh, that's all," I say.

There's a crashing sound from down the hall.

"I hope that you return safely, no matter what path you choose." She throws her hands up and goes to investigate the latest calamity.

.. 311 ..

Chapter Five

The Perilous Path

I transform into a wolf, ostensibly to run with Shadow, but my real reason is to have time for unbroken thought. Both Conwenna and Alfswich are adamant that we not go to Loris' city of Verlamion, but that is where the fyrian stones are being made. We know so little about them, other than rumors of their destructive power, that I feel discovering whatever we can about them is just as important as our given mission. Also, it's my chance to live up to the Grahme standard by doing more than what was asked.

Shadow has caught two rabbits already, and my inner druid tells me not to be greedy, however I can't go on a hunt and produce nothing. My canine friend has just spooked his prey into the open. I watch the long, graceful arc the rabbit takes, waiting for my opportunity. I lunge at it and dispatch it in one fluid motion. Shadow leaps over both me and the rabbit and starts vocalizing his annoyance at the loss of his kill.

I retake my human form and pet him furiously. He's soon mollified. The exercise has been good, and we'll all have full bellies tonight. My larder bag has a pleasant heft to it. Now the hunt for herbs begins as we make our way back to the road and our hungry companions.

"Come on Shadow, we'll wait until after dinner to break the news that Verlamion is our first destination."

* * *

Alfswich tugs on the thumb and pinky of his bad hand and shakes his head. It's clear something is not right with him, but he isn't telling us anything.

"Alfswich," Wranlen says as he puts his hand on thief's shoulder, "you need to relax. Look at the dog. He knows you're anxious, and he's staying as far away from you as he can."

"You have a history in this city?" Wranlen asks. "We don't need to know all the details, but we need to know if we can rely on you." The sapblood's voice is warm and soothing. Maybe his way will get Alfswich to tell us whatever he's hiding.

"There are people there who wish me ill," the thief says at last. "And in my current condition," he holds up his mangled hand, "I don't know that I can protect myself from them all."

I'm quite confident he can say that about any city he's ever visited, but I keep my mouth shut. This is the first time he's answered any of our inquiries.

"But you won't be alone this time. Your friends will be with you," I say.

"Friends? What good are friends? Why would I let anyone else be in charge of my own protection? Maybe having friends makes sense for the weak and the timid, but I will choose death before I become either of those."

I start rotating my staff in my hands. The thief is infuriating. Maybe a good knock on the head will help somehow. Oh, how I wish that were true.

"Are you willing to enter the city?" Wranlen asks after casting a nervous look at me. There's no judgement in his voice, which is a tone I'm unable to match at the moment.

"I won't go in with you two. We're a strange party and sure to draw attention. I'll go in alone and meet up with you when you leave by the Camulodunon gate. Take care, it's close to the slaver's gate, and that one will take you on a one-way trip to the Grim Graves mine." Alfswich looks over at us, waiting for an argument. "And whatever you do, stay away from the man named Shua, unless you want to be walked out the slaver's gate."

"That's fine," I say. I don't want an angry thief in the party. "How will we find you at the Camulodunon gate?"

"I'll find you."

*   *   *

For all the insults thrown at the Wigesta, none can say they slack at the ditch work surrounding Verlamion. Only Sarum's ditches are deeper. The gate is two stories tall and made of fine white stone. From a distance, it looks mottled, but that is due to the sheer number of niches built into the wall, each of which holds one or more fine white statues.

Shadow, of course, is uninterested in such art. And why would he be interested when there's pungent black water at the bottom of the ditch?

"Shadow! Come here!" I bellow in a futile attempt to keep him out of the brackish water.

He finds something in the water to his liking and it's all I can do to have him return to my side without his prize. Once he's between Wranlen and me, he shakes his coat dry, drenching us in the process.

The druids on top of the gate all laugh at our misfortune. I throw my hands up and resign myself to my fate.

"So much for not being noticed when we enter," I whisper to Wranlen. He can't help but smile benignly as a reply.

Inside the gate are more niches and more statues. While I turn to speak to Wranlen, my faithful canine bounds off in the other direction and is busy peeing on a statue of a stern-faced soldier. As much as I want to yell, it would only cement the memory of our entrance, so I look the other way instead. When this mission is over, I'm going to have to instill some discipline into that dog. Until that time, I will not be giving out any extra treats. And I mean it this time.

"I've never seen a market like this before. Is it this way in all large cities?" Wranlen asks.

I see what he means. The area just inside the gate is empty. What few sellers we see are all pushed against the sides of buildings for at least two blocks. Above the sellers are more statues, but these rest on corbels, so they hang over the sellers.

"I've never seen a market with so much dread hanging over it," I say.

"Do you mean the statues?"

"They definitely add to it. They look like stern masters staring down at misbehaving children, but it's the merchants, too. None are overly loud or aggressively courting customers. I don't like it. Let's keep moving."

Past the market are the temples. They are built to the same gods we worship, Brigantia, Camulos and Sucellos, but they glorify the stonework, not the gods. Like every major building in the city, life-sized statues adorn their walls.

Only the dead would leave the beautiful, natural world to reside in one of these unsympathetic tombs of stone. And the druids within, they tax the commoners to enter these monstrosities. They could not be further removed from doing the gods' work if they tried.

The manor houses are more of the same, just not on the same scale as the city gate and the temples. The final home is the most ornate and largest of them all. Embedded within the walls surrounding the house are sheets of clear glass. Only after touching it several times can I believe anything can be made so clear. A guard comes into view opposite the glass and orders me away. Hands up, I return to the street.

"You're not planning a theft of that manor house, are you?" A man decked in Wigestan druid robes asks.

"What? No, of course not," I say, taken aback.

"That's good," the man says reassuringly. "A few months ago, a master thief attempted to do so, and he lost a hand for his troubles."

Wranlen and I look at each other. We're fortunate that Alfswich refused to accompany us into the city.

"I am Arthmael," I say as I extend my hand.

"Shua," the man replies.

Wranlen makes no attempt to join the conversation, so I assume he's trying to not be seen.

"Since you are not here for a heist, may I know why you have ventured to our fair city?" Shua asks.

Absently, he pats Shadow on the head. He's not watching what he does, and I can see the anger starting to build in my dog.

"We came here to find a stonemason," I say off the top of my head. "I'd like to have a statue made." I'm not sure where this is coming from, but I extend my arms to halfway between my shoulder width and full extension.

"You must not be well schooled in these things. The mason will cut the raw stone, but you will need a sculptor to bring the figure out of the block. Unless, of course, you are looking for a special type of stone slab."

"Yes, you've guessed it," I say convincingly, I hope. "I wish to speak first to a mason, then a sculptor."

"Andros is our best sculptor and his best friend Nikos is a well-respected stonemason. Would you like me to take you to them?"

Chapter Six

A Stony Path to the Almshouse

Andros is an excitable fellow, with a deep appreciation for stone types. Unfortunately, this is knowledge he is all too willing to share. After going over the differences in the rocks, he continues by describing his favorite hammer.

The man has a favorite hammer.

"Now that I have explained all the stones, you are ready to see my masterpiece. I haven't even shown the mason responsible for this remarkable find!" Andros says.

I look at Wranlen, but he's standing askance, which I'm beginning to see is one of the steps to not be noticed.

"This is called the *Siren Warrior*," Andros says breathlessly.

The excitable sculptor removes a cover to reveal a proud warrior woman. The stone itself is alabaster with a band of clear stone near the top. She is leaning forward, with her weight resting on her sword and shield. She wears armor up to her chest. It's at this point that the stone turns clear.

Andros has decided to have her breasts fully exposed, however, with the band being clear, the obvious female markers are not the first attribute one sees. But for the life of me, I have no idea what the woman's face is like, because once you see this feature, it's hard to pull your eyes away.

My thoughts race to Dalna, and if I am sure of anything in life, it's that I will never mention this statue to her for as long as I live. Wranlen is staring too, with a lop-sided smile. Searching for Shadow, I see the dog lifting his leg to mark a different statue.

"Stop!" Andros cries. "Your dog is ruining my work." The sculptor runs over, hurling his arms in random directions.

Shadow is quick enough to escape the kick. Mentally, I tell my dog to stay near, but out of sight. I can't help but smile.

By ones and twos, people begin to gather to see what the excitement is about. A couple of different people try to pet Shadow, but he's having none of it. As each bends down, he scurries away, always out of reach. One particularly persistent fellow doesn't give up, and it's not long before Shadow is sprinting up and down the street, barking up a storm. This only increases the size of the gaggle.

"Andros?" a stout man calls, concerned.

"Nikos, you're finally here. Let me show you my masterpiece," the sculptor says. He rushes to Nikos' side and bodily pulls him through the crowd until he's right in front of his work.

"What do you think?" he asks. His whole body is vibrating somehow. There are no grand gestures, but neither the sculptor's arms or legs can remain still, like he's dancing in place.

"She's naked!" Nikos yells. He gives Andros a look of disgust as he throws his hands wide. "That stone was a once in a lifetime find. Every single statue in this city is either a stern druid or fierce warrior, ready for battle. None of them are nude. Why did you carve a native woman warrior?"

"She's not a native," Andros squeals. "Look at the lion and stag image on the shield."

"Like any man is going to pay attention to the shield," Nikos clamors.

"It's a masterpiece," Andros says.

Nikos puts his hands to the sides of his head that shakes back and forth as if it might detach. "It will get us taken to the amphitheater, if not the grim graves mine. I'm going to have to destroy it," he says with an air of finality.

People have now encircled the front of the shop. Shadow is forgotten as a new, juicy drama begins to unfold.

"They'll talk about this statue on the mainland," Andros declares with some heat.

"That's what I'm afraid of," Nikos retorts. He sets his jaw and pushes his way through the crowd.

"You see the beauty of my art?" Andros says as he grabs my arm.

"I have never seen it's like," I reply, noncommittal.

"Wait until Belenos is free from the clouds. The effect of his rays upon this statue is beyond words."

Nikos returns with a hammer that is much larger than the delicate tool of the sculptor. The angry determination in his eyes is more than enough to part the curious onlookers.

Andros' arms and legs explode away from his body when he sees his friend's return. He rushes to the larger man and starts talking fast.

"Nikos, you can't do this," he says with his two hands on Nikos' chest. "You need to stop and think about this. There will never be a chance to repeat this work."

Nikos' gait is slowed slightly, but the resolve in his eyes never wavers.

"Don't do it," Andros says. "Spare it for me, for our friendship."

The smaller man is walking backward in lockstep with the mason. After nearly tripping, Andros is forced to spend as much time watching his steps as he is imploring his friend.

"Stand clear," Nikos says as he readies his hammer.

"No!" Andros rushes back until he's resting against the statue. He reaches back and places his hands protectively across the statue's chest.

For a second time, the crowd parts, but this time is quieter and with apprehension. One by one, they slink away.

"Halt!" a man cries. At his back are a dozen guards in full Wigesta battle gear. It's Shua.

Nikos' shoulders slump and he drops his hammer. Andros lowers his arms to the statue's waist as he watches in confusion.

"Leave," I whisper to Wranlen. "Find Shadow and get away from here."

The half-si walks nonchalantly past the guards and none of them register his passing.

"I told him it had to be destroyed," Nikos tells Shua. "I even brought my hammer to do the job." He reaches for his hammer, but quickly thinks better of it.

Shua eyes the statue. "Come away from it," he says while gesturing with his hand.

"Do you see the exquisite beauty?" Andros asks.

"I see her breasts. Is this supposed to be a native warrior woman?"

"Of course not," Andros says, indignant. "See the shield? It has the lion killing the stag." He pauses before his thoughts come pouring out. "It is not quite finished. In fact, I was going to look for fine sheets of gold to highlight the lion. And I was going to mix some murr in with my brown, to color the stag. Oh yes, this statue will not just appease the eye, but the nose as well." He flings his nervous hands behind his back and does his best to compose himself.

"I see," Shua grunts. "The three of you will come with me while I figure out this statue's fate."

"We'll happily go to our own homes," Nikos says quickly.

"No, then one or both of you will sneak back here tonight and my sleep will be interrupted. The guards and I are on our way to escort the amphitheater men back to the almshouse. The three of you can spend the night there."

"I can't go to the mines," Andros says. "I'm an artist, not a ruffian."

"I have an important job here in the city as well," Nikos says.

"I see." Shua looks at me, thoroughly disinterested.

"Do you have an excuse too?" Shua asks.

"I was just here to learn about the process of sculpting a statue, as you recommended," I say as I take a step backward.

"Very well. All three of you stand in front of my guards."

Slowly, we amble over to the newly cleared spot, all of us more than willing to give Shua time to reconsider. He doesn't.

Chapter Seven

Ending Carved in Stone

Shua leads the way to a vacant part of the city. There is a two-story structure in front of us, which I believe is the amphitheater. Like the rest of the city, niches with statues decorate the part facing us. In front of the wall is a life-sized sculpture of a lion dragging a dead stag. It's an image often repeated in this city. The lion and stag are sculpted from different stones; the stag is a lifelike dingy brown, while the color of the lion resembles the spent stalks of wheat or flax.

Shua caresses the lion's mane as he passes. He sees me watching him and turns his head away. Frowning, he beckons the guards to match his new, quicker pace.

What did I just see that he is embarrassed by?

"I sculpted that," Andros informs me.

"It might be the last statue you see," Nikos says.

"Oh no, there are many statues—"

"Quiet!" the head guard barks.

Humbled, we walk in silence across the empty street to the amphitheater. As we round the side of the wall, it's mostly empty space, save for rings of stone set into the grassy hill. Twelve men work their chisels and small hammers on palm-sized rocks. Half a dozen guards mill among them, keeping a very close watch on their efforts.

Behind the free-standing wall is a paved semicircle with a hearth in its center. This must be where the stage is located, in happier times. Now, four druids in Wigestan robes encircle a hearth, chanting in old druidic as they add and remove stones from the fire.

I was never very good at the old tongue, but mostly because I saw no use for it. I bow my head so that no one will notice me straining to decipher the words.

"I told you to stay away from Shua and the amphitheater," Alfswich says in my head.

I scratch my ear vehemently, hoping he'll get the hint to leave me alone.

"Three more men?" a druid near the fire asks Shua.

"At least one; I haven't decided on the other two."

Andros is on the verge of speaking, but Nikos stomps on his foot before he could.

"How many of your workers are disappointing you?" Shua asks.

"Just Viti."

"Which one is that?"

"This lazy little rat," the druid points to the man in the center of the first row.

Viti looks up, startled. He puts his head down and starts hammering faster. The rock he's working on splits in two. Viti swipes the rock off his table, sending it flying. Refusing to look up, he grabs another dark rock from his basket and begins again.

"Then just one it is," Shua says. "Andros, Nikos," he addresses us, "you two are free to go, but if I have to separate you again, it will be the last time."

"Thank you, Erilaz Shua," Nikos says as he bows his head.

"But what about the statue?" Andros asks. "You agree that it is a masterwork?"

Nikos stomps on Andros' foot again. "We'll be taking our leave now, sir."

The stonemason grabs his friend's robes and bodily hauls him out of view.

"That just leaves you," Shua says. He punches me in the stomach, doubling me over.

A push from behind sends me sprawling onto the ground. Before I can even speak, a guard's knee finds its way to the small of my back. He grabs my left arm and slams a manacle over it.

Shua says as he stands above my head. "Are you going to follow my orders, or does my man need to explain what happens if you don't?"

The guard adds more weight to his knee and my spine feels as if it will break in two. He grabs my right arm and pulls it until it, too, is bound in metal.

"I'll do as you say!" I blurt before my shoulders are broken.

The disappointed guard sighs and removes his knee. He rises and I savor the ability to draw one long, sweet breath as I get to my knees. The man grabs my hair, forces me to my feet and pounds my unprotected stomach. As my legs go weak, he jerks me upright.

Growing up, I learned how to both win and lose fights. Since this fight isn't winnable, my goal is to minimize the damage. Conveying my burning hatred will only result in more injury, so I keep my eyes down and my mouth closed.

"Get the leg irons on him and take him and the rest of the workers to the almshouse," Shua says.

*　*　*

It's been two days, more than enough time for me to perfect the carving of the stones and to memorize the fire ritual. I've tried to talk to my fellow prisoners when they walk us to and from our jail, the almshouse, but none are willing to engage with me. My fellow prisoners eat in silence, then wait to be escorted to their rooms. The doors are all locked behind us. Even at the amphitheater, looking around brings a swift response from the guards. I've never felt so helpless, so alone.

Where is Alfswich!? Has he abandoned me?

I finish another stone just as the roaming guard comes to collect my work. I've learned that as he passes, I'm able to look around without getting the lash. I look up at the theater roof and immediately lower my gaze. Alfswich is there, next to a statue. He's not even attempting to hide, yet no one but me has noticed him.

My arms tremble as I realize I will soon be freed from this wretched place. I shake my shoulders to release my excitement. I must do my part—namely, not draw attention to myself. I've learned how to make the stones and I've decoded the words of the druid's chant. Both of these will be invaluable to our cause.

My excitement of soon being freed causes my hands to become shaky. The obvious errors in my last several stones would bring the lash, if I were still here to receive it. I keep my head down and focus on my work. I don't know what Alfswich's plan is, but I'm already savoring my freedom.

I hear stone scraping on stone from the roof and it takes all my will to not look up. The scraping gets louder and I can't help but take a quick glance at the stage. Between their chanting and the cracking of the fire, the druids are oblivious. I cough to make sure Alfswich isn't discovered.

Shua turns abruptly toward me, getting his lash out. Our eyes lock for an instant and I know that this will not end well.

A statue from above crashes with a thunderous boom on the stage, right where Shua would have been had I not drawn his attention. The druids dive out of their seats and look toward the roof.

"I saw a head ducking away!" One druid says as he points to where Alfswich had been. Another druid grabs a finished stone and throws it toward the top.

"*Cweorth!*" he shouts, and the stone explodes into a fireball in midair. I close my eyes and try to blink away the white field in the center of my view. The heat scalds my throat, causing me to wheeze.

"Stop, stop!" Shua yells over and over. "There's only one way down from there. Secure the exits."

I look down at my stone. The blast caused me to scrape a mark across the entire surface. I chance it and throw it off to my left.

A guard hears it and screams, "Over there!" He and another run to investigate. They find the stone and point to one of the slaves several rows up. "He's trying to hide his mistake." One of them goes to beat the hapless prisoner. I keep my head down and mimic inscribing while my vision slowly comes back.

In all the confusion, my fellow prisoners and I are given a reprieve. Only the one unfortunate man's shouts of pain punctuate the air. Never have I stood by and let the unjust be punished, but neither have I been in chains before. It's a bitter potion to drink, but swallow it, I must.

"My Lord," the head guard says to Shua, "there was no one to be found. Whoever it was, they must have run as soon as they loosened the statue. They left nothing behind."

"Very well. Escort the slaves back early for their midday meal. We'll move the hearth underneath the stage's overhang, so this can't happen again."

"Erilaz, don't you want the prisoners to move the setup?" the guard asks.

"And let the prisoners handle fyrian stones? Are you daft?" Shua asks.

*　　*　　*

I would have thought that being sent back early was a boon. But being left in my miniscule room just allows me to wonder what could have been. After our thin gruel, we're marched back to the amphitheater by twice as many guards as normal.

The man who took the beating for my mis-carved stone is struggling to stay on his feet. He keeps stumbling on his gimpy left leg. After several threats, a guard knocks him to the ground and kicks him. A couple more join in on the beating. I keep my head down as I march past him, even as my jaw clenches shut. As one who protects, it galls me to not come to his aid. What I wouldn't give for a couple of Alfswich's deftly thrown knives in the backs of those guards.

The streets are empty of the thief, though, no matter how many times I discreetly scan my surroundings. I'm reseated at my station, and the leg irons are locked to the stone I am sitting upon. The scant amount of idle time I'm given before being given a hammer and chisel allows me to reflect. Whatever Alfswich was planning has failed. Now, with double the guard, it's unlikely I'll be rescued from here. Time to look to myself for answers.

Carving the stones has become second nature to me, allowing me to devise a plan. I know what I have to do, but I'm not looking forward to the inevitable beating. Since rescue from here is near impossible, I have to get myself sent to the mines. Then my companions will have opportunities both on the road and at the mine to free me. I'm easily the worst carver here, so it should be easy.

CHAPTER EIGHT

A Grave Mistake

My vision comes back into focus as I stare at the mine's enforcer's dirty feet. He doesn't have a sense of humor. He grabs my hair and forces me to rise before I catch my breath. I know what happens next. He'll ask me a question and I'll be unable to speak. He'll interpret that as obstinance and he'll knock me to the ground again.

"Am I going to have any more trouble with you?" he asks.

"Na . . . nah" I mouth with little to no breath.

He smiles at me. "Still too proud to answer?" He punches me in the stomach, then brings both his fists down on my back.

I think I can collapse to the ground now. Curling up in the fetal position too early will make him get the lash out. I moan as loud as my empty lungs will allow and keep my eyes closed.

He spits in my face. Good, that means the beatings are done for the day. "Viti, since you enjoy ratting him out, make sure his wounds don't fester."

So, Viti is the snitch.

"No dinner!" he shouts as he climbs up the ladder to the midlevel of the pit.

He's an expert at playing the slaves against one another. I get beaten to within a couple breaths of my life and the whole shift goes hungry. Someone less stubborn than me would have quit after the first time.

Twice I've tried to organize my fellow miners, and twice someone has squealed. I was given Viti's spot in the amphitheater, and he was sent here. It's not like I had any say in the matter, but he and his grudge are unmoved.

Alone in the center, I spit out blood from the overseer's first punch. Nobody wants to help me up this time. Beatings are mandatory viewing. My fellow captives mill around the walls of the entrance chamber. Whatever friendships I may have started are gone with our meal. Worst of all, if I'm honest, Alfswich was right when he'd said this whole idea was stupid.

Since I'd arrived, I was stripped and beaten with the lash "to set the proper expectations," and twice I've had every last breath knocked out of me. My peasant's robe from Alfswich's stores was taken and used to start a fire. Like everyone else, I'm left with only a loincloth and leg irons. My only other possession is a red deer's antler, which I use for digging through the chalk walls. Even if we wanted to attack the guards, we have no weapons and no way to hide them if we did.

I'm not sure why I'm standing in the entrance pit. If I'm spotted being idle, I'll get double the lash. Despite this, I feel compelled to remain. I shake my head; I can't be caught here.

"*Will you stop trying to run away?*" Alfswich projects to me.

"There you are," Wranlen says loudly from the top of the pit. "I've come to purchase some of the lesser performing slaves for an entertainment I'm planning."

The overseer comes into view, but he's concerned with Wranlen and not me for once. He nods his head energetically. "We have a number of candidates in this pit right here."

The main pit entrance has a small outcrop of stone jutting out about midway down the chalk wall. The only way to reach it is by ladder, whether from the bottom where we captives are, or at the top where my friends are now. Security is easy; just remove the ladders and no one can get out. Removing just one will do, but the overseer likes to gloat as all hope of escape is removed each time.

The head man points down toward me as an example. Anyone else nearby moves out of view. The overseer winks at me, and I know that he's keen on beating me again, so his customer will see how tough he is.

I wink back.

His left hand goes tight on his whip, and I realize that one way or another, this is my last day in the mine. He signals someone to retrieve the ladders before bowing low to his half-si customer.

"Come down to the mid-level. From there, you can pick the ones you want."

"Are you sure the ladder is properly secured?" Wranlen asks. "I wouldn't want to fall into the pit."

What my *friend*, the overseer, doesn't know is that directly below him, Alfswich is climbing down the pit wall. A white dust is loosened at every hand or foothold he makes. I'm dying to know how he is managing it, but if I watch him, he'll be given away. I scan the chamber for the rest of the slaves. Only one of us is dumb enough to stand in the light, where he can be clearly seen.

Wranlen keeps his nervous patter up, insisting on inspecting the sturdiness of the latter and even fretting about leaving his dog, Shadow, alone at the top. By the time he allows himself to be assuaged, Alfswich is standing in the shadows no more than ten paces from me.

"I'll happily pay double," Wranlen says, "if the men I choose make it up without injury."

Thank you, Wranlen. Now I won't feel the whip.

Alfswich signals for all of us slaves to be silent.

"That odor," Wranlen says, "are you sure they don't have a skin eating disease?"

"They do not. At the first sign of sickness, we remove them from the mines."

He doesn't add that the ill person is killed in the mine and the body burned, so only some of the person is removed from the mine.

"Let me blow my horn, and the workers will all assemble," the overseer says.

"What about that one?" Wranlen points at me. "He just puckered his lips as if he wanted to kiss me."

"Did he now?" The overseer smiles. "You won't want that one. He's too much trouble. But I'll fix him good."

The second ladder is set on top of the first and my torturer descends to the midlevel.

I blow him another kiss.

He bares his teeth as he smiles tightly at me. The second ladder is positioned on the pit floor in the small alcove, where no one can get behind him.

"You won't want this one, so I'm going to make an example out of him. I guarantee you won't have problems with any of the rest."

"Watch out!" Viti shouts, but one of the other men punches him in the stomach before he can give away Alfswich's position. The man stands over Viti's prone form, fists at the ready.

"After I dismantle him," the overseer nods at me, "you're next," he tells Viti's attacker.

The overseer steps onto the pit floor and stretches his neck to either side. His whip is released, and he spins it in a circle to add to the tension.

I back away to my right so he'll have to move closer to Alfswich.

He pulls the whip back past his head and I roll farther right. It was a fake. I barely make it back to my feet as the whip screams through the air and the crack reverberates off the walls. Only then does my stomach feel as if it's on fire. An angry red welt crosses my belly button and ends in an oozing open wound.

My eyes implore Alfswich to do something, and the overseer notices my silent plea.

"Someone over here?"

"You're a fool, druid," Alfswich says as he comes out of hiding.

"Who's this?" the overseer asks, and he tacks to his right to keep a distance between the adversaries.

Looking disgusted, my little thief friend points at the whip handler. "Freeze."

The whip tip drops to the floor behind the man as his whole body goes rigid.

"If you're done screwing up our plans, we can go now," Alfswich says, as he drives a dagger into my tormentor's neck.

"We still have one problem," I say, pointing to my manacled feet.

"Take them off," the thief scoffs.

"I don't have the key."

Alfswich takes a knife from the overseer's belt. "Everyone, watch this. Insert the tip in the keyhole, turn, step out of your shackle." He repeats the action again, and I'm a free man once again.

"Now stop wasting time." He turns to the men in the pit. "Once we're at the top, I will throw this knife down so you can all free yourselves."

"Why don't we just take it now?" a prisoner asks.

"Freeze." Alfswich points at the man as he says the word. "That's why." He turns to me. "Stop wasting time and climb up."

I'm grateful for the rescue, but Alfswich's superior attitude is still hard to swallow. Taking the form of a red kite, I soar next to Wranlen and Shadow. I screech at the thief to hurry up before I animorph back. I'm knocked over by my canine friend and we nearly tumble into the mine. The dirt and the uppermost layer of skin is removed before I can get Shadow to settle down and move back from the edge.

"What about us?" Viti yells.

Alfswich has made it up the first ladder. He tosses his dagger at the overseer's back.

"We'll come with you," the snitch says.

There's grunting behind him.

"No, I don't trust you at my back. After I'm up, you're free to do as you will."

The thief scrambles up to ground level as the slaves jump into action. Several go straight for the knife.

"I can't control all of their minds," Alfswich says. "We should go."

"Aren't we going to wait for them?" I ask.

The thief juts out his lower lip and nods. "This will be quite instructive for you, I think." He sits down at the edge of the pit, legs dangling. He taps the ground next to him, where he wants me to sit, but I'm not putting any part of my body in that place again.

One of the men caked in chalk grabs the knife and is tackled by a second. They wrestle for the knife until the first is able to stab the second in the chest. It's not an immediately lethal blow, but it gives the man distance.

"Anybody else want to get dead?" he says, holding the tiny knife in his big, meaty hand.

"Work together and you'll all be free," I call.

Several other prisoners leave the shadows and form a semicircle around the first.

"None of them will make it to the surface," Alfswich says to me. "They've forgotten what it's like to be human."

Another two men get stabbed. I'd never learned their names. They were always together and would scowl if anyone came too close. Now they both lay next to one another, dying on the ground.

The big man stares down at the rest before reaching to undo his manacles. Several slaves rush him at once and knock him to the ground.

"I've had enough," Alfswich says. He lazily tosses a black stone over the edge. "*Cweorth.*"

A deafening blast reverberates off the pit walls as the flames explode upward. The thief has to roll away from the edge before he too is consumed by the fire. My hands reach my ears too late to stop the constant ringing.

"What did you do?" I shout, though the thief doesn't react.

I grab his arm, and he sweeps my legs out from under me. I land with a thud and my head is left dangling over the edge. The flames may be gone, but I can still feel the intense heat rising upward.

"What did you do?" I shout again.

The thief releases me and helps me to my feet with his bad hand. He grimaces as I squeeze it tightly.

"Why didn't you give me your good hand?" I ask.

He turns his good hand over to reveal a hidden dagger. He waves Wranlen over and exaggerates his speech so we can both read his lips.

"I wanted to see what one of the stones would do, and we can't have them at our backs." Not waiting for a reply, he walks past us to our packs. He taps his foot, impatiently waiting for us.

I search for Shadow with my mind. He's taken off toward the road in a blind panic. It takes some coaxing, but he returns to us. Alfswich tosses me a new set of peasant's clothes and signals to go toward the road. I'd rather be wearing my druid's robes, but if the thief is giving me these, there must be a reason.

*   *   *

"What did we learn from this disaster?" Alfswich asks me.

"The fyrian stones are more deadly than we thought," I say.

"I was referring to your incomprehesiblly stupid actions," he says with a huff. "Why didn't you escape from the inn where they kept you at night? We waited for you to do something—anything—so that we could collect you."

"Have you seen those rooms?" I rub my arms to get warm in the usually cool night. "Where is my mantle?"

"Yes!" he interrupts me. "I broke out the first night I was there. All you have to do is pop out four nails on the boards underneath the tiny window. Then you can slip out into the night." He rummages in his pack and pulls out my mantle.

Why was that in his pack and not mine?

"I'm not a thief," I say, sounding defensive even to my own ear. "And I'm not likely to be anything but frozen if you don't hurry."

Alfswich snorts. "Then you created a spectacle right as I was going to kill Shua." He throws his hands up in the air. "What were you thinking?"

"I heard stone grinding on stone, so I started coughing so none of the druids would hear it."

Alfswich shakes his head in disgust. "And once you saw we were there to rescue you, why did you screw up and have yourself moved? I spent half a day determining that you weren't killed like that other guy in line."

"You saw us being marched to the amphitheater?"

"Of course I did. What do you think, that I was enjoying a leisurely sunrise meal with four beautiful ladies?"

"To answer your first question, I learned quite a bit. Vlint stones are more powerful than regular stones with the rune magic." I tick them off with my fingers. "I learned how to carve the cweorth rune correctly, before I started messing up on purpose." I used my thumb and pinky for the first two points, mimicking the thief's bad hand. Next, I extend my middle finger. "The vlint stones carry no extra power beyond the size of your palm, so there shouldn't be any inscribed boulders that they'll roll down hills before activating the magic. And finally, the black vlint stone they get from this mine is the most highly prized of all. No one knows why, but it is the best."

"You wish to use the giant runes then," the half-si says, nodding.

"If only I could have kept a couple to show the council."

"You're as bad as Grahme," Alfswich says. "You can't even keep your mind on your mission. You both have to go off on side adventures trying to right every imagined wrong you encounter."

Shadow snuggles up next to me, and with the addition of his warmth, I let my retort go unsaid. Alfswich shakes his head dismissively before he tosses two vlint stones in my direction. I rush to grab them, since I'm not sure if he means to incinerate me or not.

"Now you have your stones," he says.

I look to Wranlen, to see if he too was afraid of being incinerated. He remains unperturbed.

Am I the one going daft here?

"How far are we from Camulodunon?" I ask.

"Two days of brisk walking through the fens," the thief replies.

"Then let's plan on four days, so that I have a chance to heal a little first."

We keep to woodsmen's tracks as we head toward the military capital of the Wigesta. As bad as the mines were, at least I had a plan.

"You worry over the wrong things," Alfswich says.

"Stay out of my head," I growl before curiosity gets the better of me. "What do you mean?"

"I can read and to a limited extent control minds, and Wranlen can charm the pants off anyone, even in winter. Yet you're here feeling sorry for yourself because you don't know how we can possibly make friends with our mark. You would make a lousy thief."

"Well, I'm thankful to hear that."

I change into a dog and race through the fens with Shadow.

CHAPTER NINE

Infiltrating the Enemy

"How exactly are we going to get an audience with Rendell?" I ask again.

Even Wranlen's assurances don't satisfy me. Camulodunon's impressive stone walls are visible now. Only the River Colne is between us and the gate.

"It's easy," Wranlen says. "Alfswich dips into people's heads until he finds a suitable person. I explain that we're a traveling circus act and we would love to perform for Rendell. I use my best persuasion and Alfswich tinkers in the mind if he must. All you have to do is get Shadow to perform like you've practiced. Even then, it's only if the mark insists upon it first."

I look down at Shadow, but even he is smiling back at me. Without me even asking, he rises up on his hind legs and walks the three paces toward me. He rests his front paws on my chest, and I'm honor-bound to scratch his chest while he licks my face.

"Fine," I say, surrendering. "I still don't understand how this could possibly work, but it seems I'm outvoted three to one."

"Finally," Alfswich mutters.

The river is shallow enough to ford. Keeping Shadow from exhausting himself in the water is our only obstacle. We make it across and my dog decides to roll in the mud on the bank before shaking himself dry, all over my peasant's smock. While I'm grateful he didn't ruin my druid robes, it reminds me that I do need to train him.

As we approach the gate, Alfswich is dressed in tight leggings and a colorful top while Wranlen is dressed in the thief's finest linens. His smile is off-putting, since none of the wealthy would acknowledge the lower classes, but he's too irrepressible to change.

"This is never going to work," I say under my breath as we enter the city.

I feel a mental slap, and it's all I can do to keep my head down and not respond.

"People of your station don't speak unless spoken to," Alfswich projects into my head. Shadow lets out a low growl, but I calm him at once.

One of the guards steps in front of us. "And just who do you think you are? I'll have you know that impersonating a noble is a serious crime in this city."

Wranlen bows low to him. "I am sorry for this mistake. I am the leader of this band of circus performers, and I must dress the part."

"Circus performers?"

Alfswich starts coughing and looks away. This is the sign that we have our mark.

"That we are," Wranlen says as he bows again. That's his signal that he's turning on the charm. "Arthmael, show him what Shadow can do."

I bow low repeatedly. "Yes, master, at once."

I don't get a signal. As they explained to me over and over, I'm just a peasant who does as he's told, so I don't need to make strategic decisions. Alfswich is still second guessing my choice of being captured, despite all that we learned.

I give my best friend a short 'up' hand gesture, and he rises on his hind legs. I move my open hand forward as if to push him away, and he steps backwards two steps. I wave for him to come forward and he closes the distance until his paws are resting upon me. I reach into my robe and give Shadow a piece of dried rabbit jerky as a reward. He drops to all fours and bows his head at the guard.

The guard smiles at Wranlen, even though he did nothing. "Rendell has been in a foul mood since the last court entertainer was removed. Come with me and I can get you in front of the First Wickner tonight."

I look at the guard to gauge his honesty, at least until Alfswich gives me another mental slap. I go to one knee and scratch my dog's shoulders while thinking vicious thoughts.

Alfswich snorts at my thoughts, then apologizes to Wranlen for the interruption. The guard confers with his comrades at his station before leading us through the city. We breeze through the market and the craftsmen's buildings. The guard stops in front of a white stone building with columns too wide for me to fit my arms around.

"This is the trading hall. If your audience goes well tonight, you'll find any number of people who'll want to employ you. Just remember who it was that introduced you." He nods slowly before waving for us to follow him around the corner.

"Over there," he points to a two-story wooden building, "is where you can spend all the money you'll make."

There are several women waiting along the rail in the front of the house. As brothels go, this one is better looking than most. The next block contains an empty public square. Behind it is the largest fight ring I've ever seen.

"It's called a coliseum, and there's live sport inside there every day," Alfswich informs me mentally.

I visualize getting the little thief in a headlock and pounding on his face with multiple blows again. I'm not really angry with him, I only do this because he keeps entering my head unbidden. He snorts at the image in my head. We continue on our way, only to be stopped once we leave the open courtyard.

"This is called the noble's bathhouse, though in truth it's just a nicer, more discreet brothel. The only reason anyone ever goes to the public square is because Rendell shut down the brothels on either side and the coliseum behind the plaza. With all entertainment suspended, people come here and listen. Rendell is a good leader; he rarely addresses the entire city."

Camulodunon's coliseum is the only one of its kind that I've seen. Verlamion did not have one. As we pass, the crowd groans and roars at a pretty steady pace.

We pass ostentatious manor houses that are much larger than the ones I saw in Solent Keep. Once through the needlessly large homes, we arrive at another walled gate. Our escort speaks for a while with the very stern gatekeeper. Once mollified, the gatekeeper motions us to follow the guard through.

A short, thin man in outrageous colors intercepts us as we enter the palace grounds. Our guard waves off a handful of coins and a negotiation heats up. At last, the brightly clad man and guard shake. Our escort leaves his mark on two vellum sheets, followed by the fop. They each take one and our escort departs. The little man is clad in a bright white robe with purple sleeves and too many gold chains to count. He motions for us to come follow.

We reach an empty room with only a thick mat on the floor. Woven into it is a scene of a lion taking down a stag.

"Show me your act," he demands.

Shadow and I do our routine, followed by Alfswich and his lethal knife-throwing skill. The man says nothing, despite Wranlen's efforts to engage in a discussion. The man puts his hand up, stopping Wranlen in mid-sentence.

"You must relinquish all your weapons," he says.

"Of course," Wranlen agrees as he unbuckles his long dagger.

"And yours, thief."

"It would be very hard to put on a knife-throwing spectacle without knives." Alfswich says in his most sarcastic tone.

The man ignores him. "You will be given an equal number of tip-sharpened knives to work with tonight. No one brings weapons into the presence of the First Wickner."

* * *

The garishly dressed man leads us to the doors of the feasting hall. He has added a sash to his overly decorated clothing, also in the strange hue of purple. The sounds from within are akin to a battlefield. "Remember, stop halfway to the dais and all of you bow your heads low. Hold that position until Lord Rendell releases you." He points to Wranlen. "Be quick with your explanation. The Lord is easily bored."

He looks to Alfswich and me. "Think of this as a battle. You two had better have the best performance of your lives. Anything less would be unfortunate."

He leans into the double doors and, with considerable effort, pushes them inward.

The cacophony of noises and smells sends me reeling. The hall is the largest room I've ever seen. On a raised dais directly in front of us is a long table with twenty people seated above the rest. Only these people and the little man escorting us wear the purple, so they must be the royalty.

On either side of the room are two pairs of long tables running away from the dais. With the wall behind us, our stage is a large square. Each of the side tables seat men in richly adorned clothing. None of them look as if they've done an honest day's work in their lives.

My breath quickens. Despite the space, the crowd is making me gulp down air before it's all been claimed. I rub one cold hand in the other.

"How many people are in here?" I ask.

"A hundred and eighty," Alfswich says under his breath. The fact that he didn't mindslap me must mean that he's feeling pressure too. "In the old days, I'd leave here with the belongings of at least twenty of them."

"Focus," Wranlen says without moving his lips.

The little man pounds a heavy wooden staff on the cobblestone floor hard enough for several of his chains to bounce. "With the First Wickner's permission," the man bows low enough for his longest chains to touch the floor and holds it for a breath. "There is entertainment for you."

A gaunt man in the center of the dais rises and nods his head just a touch.

Is this Rendell?

He's the only one not wearing purple. He's wearing a plain red uniform that the Wigesta troops wear. His hands bear no rings. In fact, I can see no baubles upon him at all. That fact and his unusually tall, thin frame set him apart from his guests. If the man was capable of a smile, he'd look like a half-si.

"Begin before the First Wickner is bored," our guide says before slinking over to the side.

The silent room awaits Wranlen's words. If Wranlen is nervous, it doesn't show. With his same placid smile, he signals us to follow and walks halfway to the dais. He bows low and we match him. One breath, two, three . . .. Shadow has grown bored, so he starts licking my face. I squinch my eyes and mouth shut.

There's a booming laugh from in front of us. Three exhalations later, the rest of the crowd joins in.

"Rise," Rendell commands.

I hold my hands out between Shadow and my face. I feel lightheaded, so I can't focus enough to give him mental commands.

"I like the dog."

Wranlen makes a quick bow. "The dog is named Shadow, and he is a most wonderful performer." The half-si gives me a nod, and I lead Shadow closer to the only member of the audience that matters.

I give a quick bow and mentally command Shadow to run up my back and spring into the air. He lands right in front of the dais, so close, in fact, that Rendell stands and peers over the table. He takes a ham bone and drops it in front of Shadow.

"Leave it!" I give a powerful mental command, since I know my voice alone won't carry enough weight.

Shadow whimpers, but he obeys. He returns to me and I order him up on two legs. He falls twice, both times looking at the bone. At last, we finish the routine and it's Alfswich turn to amaze them with his precision knife throwing.

Rendell stands and pounds on the table. The rest of the room follows his lead. He raises his hands for silence and looks to Wranlen.

"It has been too long since entertainers have visited my hall. I am well pleased." His eyes narrow. "What do you require as payment for tonight's display?"

Still with the same detached smile, Wranlen places his hands behind his back and waits for the whispers to die down. "We request only a private audience with your Lordship."

There are a few chuckles from the crowd, but they quickly die away. Rendell cocks his head to the side, not unlike what Shadow does.

"A meeting? With me?" He looks to the half-si for confirmation.

"Yes, First Wickner, at your convenience, of course."

Rendell purses his lips as his head bounces up and down. "I tell you what, if that dog can retrieve the ham bone beneath me, I will grant your request." He sits down and places a mottled blue and white figurine at the edge of the table.

Wranlen gives me a perplexed look and signals that it is our time once again. I bend down and rub my dog's chest while resting my forehead on his. I tell him to retrieve the bone, but to go slowly, as if he was stalking it.

He's all too happy to scamper away toward the prize. Twice I bid him to go slow. He's only a handful of steps away and his whole body shakes as his discipline oozes away.

Rendell flicks the figurine off the table and yells some strange word as it falls. Straddling the bone is a giant warbird, one and a half times as tall as me. It squawks once and turns to Rendell.

"Sunshine, get rid of that Shadow!" He points at my dog.

The bird takes two quick steps and strikes the floor with its beak where Shadow had only just been. He had only just managed to jump sideways and avoid the strike. My dog dashes between the bird's legs, getting up to full speed in only a couple of strides. He races past the bone and under one of the side tables.

The bird races after him, kicking the table into the laps of the guests. Shadow sprints behind the food-splattered guests. The bird launches itself off the overturned table and nearly lands on my canine friend. Shadow scurries away before turning and bowing to his adversary.

He thinks this is a game.

My stomach sinks as I watch Shadow take off directly at the bird. It squawks once and readies a strike with its beak. At the last instant, Shadow veers left, and the beak hits the stone floor once again. The ridiculous helmet the bird is wearing flies off and clatters its way to the wall.

The bird rears up and begins the chase. As fast as Shadow is, he's no match for this monstrosity. The bird swipes with a talon and sweeps my dog's back legs out from under him. Shadow slides on the stone floor to just in front of the opposite row of guests. He barks at the bird as he regains his feet. The bird knocks over the table behind Shadow, but that wasn't where my dog was going. Seeing an opening, he races for the bone with the bird right behind him.

At the dais, all the men are standing and cheering the spectacle. The women, however, remain seated with bored expressions.

"Stop!" I scream mentally toward the bird, but it does no good. Shadow, however, obeys my command, and the murderous bird overruns its prey and hits the dais with a wallop. Shadow flies straight for the bone, sliding under the bird's attempt to kick him. There's a hollow boom from beneath the platform as the wood panel shatters. My canine friend grabs the bone and flees beneath Rendell and the guests at the central table. The bird straddles the hole, head peering into the darkness. From beneath our host, Shadow growls at his nemesis.

"My Lord," Wranlen shouts, "I do believe that the dog has recovered the bone, completing the challenge you set forth."

Looking perturbed, the first Wickner nods his head and says another nonsense word. The bird vanishes, and the mottled figurine reappears in his hand.

It takes a moment, but I'm able to reassure Shadow to come out from cover with his bone.

"Assassin!" Alfswich shouts.

The thief's good arm becomes a blur as he throws a dagger at the table to the right of our host. A man yelps in pain and he grabs his impaled right hand, confused as to what has happened. We all hear his dagger skid onto the cobblestone as the room falls quiet. Rendell rises from his seat and glares at his would-be killer. Knowing that he's a dead man, the assassin scrambles over the table and flees toward the exit.

"Guards!" Rendell says evenly as the commotion begins to swell.

"How can he be so stoic when his life was nearly lost?" I ask.

Alfswich motions for me to be silent.

The great wooden doors open and six guards pour through. The doomed man runs for cover behind the tables, but his fellow guests want none of it. The man is thrown into the center and surrounded by guards. The man wraps himself in a hug as his jaw starts to quiver.

"Search him!"

The guards ignore his shouts of protest, tearing every pocket and leaving him in tatters.

"Very well," Rendell says. "Tell me who convinced you into this sorry attack and I'll only take your hands."

The man looks at a man from his table dressed in fine green and blue linens. Surprise registers in the nobleman's eyes for just an instant before he looks to his right, as if his neighbor is the guilty party.

"Name your employer!" Rendell roars.

The man hugs himself tighter and stares at the stone floor below him.

"The entertainment isn't over yet." He drops another bone onto the floor. "Retrieve this and I'll make your death quick."

The petrified man stares, confused, as the guards leave him to close the hall doors. They stand with their spears at the ready.

Once more, Rendell throws the figurine, says his word and the battle bird reappears. "Kill him." He points to the man in tattered clothes.

The overwhelmed man does not try to move as the bird approaches. He looks up in disbelief at the bird's head as its left foot slams into his chest. The man tumbles like a child's doll across the smooth floor, only stopping when he collides with a feasting table.

The people crane their heads to view the dead man, staining their clothing on the evening's food.

Rendell rises and leaves the dais. The man in the rich green and blue clothing practically runs out of the hall.

The little man who showed us into the hall rushes out to the center, pounding his heavy staff. "The meal is concluded," he says, needlessly.

CHAPTER TEN

The Audience

I continue pacing. Even Shadow is tired of it, so he's gone to lie down instead of following and colliding with me at every turn.

"Maybe we should just head back to Solent Keep," I say.

"What, and not complete your mission? I thought you said you'd become a head druid if you're successful," Alfswich replies.

"*If*," I say emphatically. "We're no closer now than we were when we left. At least I can deliver the fyrian stones and how they're made."

"Careful now, those stones are mine," Alfswich says.

"Are you unwilling to let Grahme and Conwenna—"

"Lady Koni," Alfswich interrupts me.

"Fine, Grahme and Lady Koni. Are you unwilling to let them study the stones?"

"Depends on what's in it for me."

I push both outstretched hands toward the thief as if to push away his selfishness. "I can make the stones myself if need be. My point is, maybe we should just head back."

"My plan is nearly complete, and now you decide to lose your nerve?" Alfswich says. "What would Grahme say about that?"

"What is your plan?" Finally, we can get to what's really eating away at me.

"We're going to remove Rendell and Tilbert from the running of becoming the Walda of the Wigesta."

"I know what the goal is. How, exactly, are we going to accomplish it?"

"Oh no, you don't get that information. I told you to avoid Verlamion, and you went there anyway. I told you to avoid Shua. I told you to stay away from the amphitheater. You did the opposite of everything I said, so I'm not sharing the whole plan with you now."

"It's my mission."

Wranlen steps between us. "Perhaps you can share something with Arthmael."

The little thief alternates tapping the table with his thumb and pinky of his injured hand. "Fine, we're going to steal that battle bird from Rendell. After that, my plan is foolproof."

"The battle bird?" I look to Wranlen for an explanation, but he's as lost as I am.

"Yep, and you're going to have your dog filch it for us." He stretches his shoulder backward before readjusting to a new sitting position.

I start pacing again. If anything, I'm even less hopeful.

* * *

There are plenty of heavy footsteps approaching our room while we wait for our audience with Rendell.

"Remember your part in the plan," Alfswich projects.

"How can I remember what I've never been told?" I say as there's a rapping at the door. In all, there are twelve guards who escort us to Rendell's map room. They stand upright and look above our heads as their leader enters after us. It's a tight fit for sixteen of us.

The room is beautiful, and this is coming from a person who prefers the imperfect beauty of nature. A map of the mainland hangs upon the wall, filled with strange sounding cities, rivers and tribes. On the large table in the center, a finely prepared cowhide with southern Pretanni drawn in high detail stretches from corner to corner. There are a half dozen candles to light the room, but they all are against the wall farthest from us.

To my relief, much of the druid lands remains blank. Only two of our holy sites, Men Meur Kov Keigh and the Gwanwyns of Sulis are known to them. But Men Meur Kov Keigh is drawn in the wrong spot, so it's even better than I'd hoped.

"First things first," Rendell says, "I do appreciate your quick actions to thwart my assassination, but you were not to have weapons at my feast."

He looks directly at Alfswich.

"I can have my men tear your clothes to tatters looking for weapons, or you can surrender what you have now."

Shadow senses the confrontation and begins a low growl. I scratch his chest while sending messages to relax.

"And that dog can either behave itself or end up on a spit for my next feast."

I take in a breath. If I send commands while angry, Shadow will react to the emotion, not the order. I point to the corner and ask him to lay down.

Alfswich surrenders two more daggers, one from a pocket behind his neck and another from inside his thigh. Rendell nods to his man and two of the guards start feeling Alfswich's entire body from head to toe.

Wranlen, too, breathes a sigh of relief when they find no more weapons upon the thief. Mollified, Rendell walks to the opposite side of the large central table and places his dagger and the figurine of the battle bird before him. Only then does he send the guards from the room.

The first wickner looks at Wranlen. "You can tell me as many times as you wish that you are an oddities act, but I know an assassin when I see one." He points at Alfswich. "Only assassins are that accurate." He fingers the statuette protectively.

"Your men are not foolproof, as tonight showed," Wranlen responds. "In any case, we have not come here to inflict injury to you or anyone in your city, on that you have my word."

"I will hold you and your men to that oath, under pain of death."

Wranlen bows his head.

"The next question is why *did* you come to my city? What do you want?"

"We came at the behest of Bradan, the former druid lord of Pretanni."

"Bradan?" Rendell's eyes raise in surprise. "My sources have yet to confirm his presence in Verlamion."

"Oh, he's there," Wranlen says. "And this companion of mine," he places his hand on my shoulder, "is a former student of Bradan."

I gasp in surprise. No one told me that I was to be outed as a druid. And I was never a student of Bradan. I stand there, mouth open, as various fatal outcomes run wild in my head.

"It's alright," he says, patting my shoulder. "The time for subterfuge is past." He returns his gaze to Rendell. "Bradan is vexed at his demotion in duties. A truly capable man, and the one who managed the ascension of Loris to head druid, his contributions have now been dismissed by Loris."

"Loris is a pompous ass," Rendell says.

He takes his hand off the statuette and paces two steps in either direction. He may not feel threatened by us, but he doesn't entirely believe us either.

"And he has been propped up all this time by my master," I say. "What of it?"

"With the blessing of you and Tilbert, Bradan will remove Loris from the picture," Alfswich says. "With your tacit agreement today, we will journey to Londinjon and secure Tilbert's permission. We wish only to avoid any . . . complications after our plan is enacted."

"And Bradan is no fool. Being so new, he has no chance of being First Wickner. He only wishes to be given responsibilities commensurate with his abilities," Wranlen adds.

"So, you want me to put something down in writing?"

"No, nothing of the sort," the half-si says, surprised. "After the obstacle is removed, Bradan would like to meet you here to see how he can best help the cause."

"And after coming to me, what? He'll go to Londinjon for a better offer?"

"Who among the Wigesta would follow Bradan without the backing of the Walda? Whether you or Tilbert gets the honor,

Bradan wants to be well-placed when the war begins," Wranlen says. "He has no clout among your people, but he does have considerable skill. What harm is there in having a talented man in your ranks?"

"And I am to take your word that what you say is true?" Rendell asks.

"Are we likely to come unarmed in your presence and inform you that we want to kill a high-ranking member of the Wigesta for jest?" Wranlen counters.

"Yet you offer no proof that what you say is true."

"We can't very well announce our plan now, can we?" Alfswich asks, annoyed.

"So, you offer no proof," Rendell repeats. He rests his hands next to his dagger and the figurine.

"Bet him that you can convince him and make him offer up his silver necklace if you win," Alfswich projects to me.

I glance at Alfswich in annoyance.

"I can provide some surety," I say. "But I will need some room."

"What do we get for doing this job?" Alfswich asks.

Wranlen and I look at each other. Neither of us knows what game he's playing.

Rendell turns to the thief. "You'll get out of here with your lives."

"Not good enough," Alfswich says. "How about we get to keep that silver necklace of yours if my friend can convince you?"

Rendell fingers the chain. "I can have one brought to you, if you succeed."

"No," the little thief says. "It must be yours. If I can truthfully claim to my Sorim patrons that I got the protection necklace from around your neck, I'll be a legend."

"You're a Sorim?" Rendell eyes him carefully. "I don't see it. Sorim don't have such high cheek bones and they favor short hair."

"I definitely am not a Sorim," Alfswich lies. "And a really good protection amulet like yours will make for fairer negotiations."

Rendell stares up at the ceiling. "I'll give you a chance. Open that door and I'll tell my man to retrieve another silver necklace." He stares Alfswich in the eye. "If you can't convince me by the time he returns, I'll have him strangle you with it."

Alfswich shrugs. "Dead is dead."

Rendell looks at me, then at the door. "Will you take the necklace off once your men are in the room, so they know you do it willingly?" I ask.

He smiles at me. "Sure." I open the door and a guard nearly knocks me down.

"Sir!"

Unperturbed, the First Wickner looks past me. "I have wagered my necklace here in a contest with these men. Would you have one of your men retrieve a replacement?" He takes off his silver charm and lays it between his knife and ostrich statue. "If I'm not convinced, you are to strangle the little one with the retrieved necklace."

The guard's eyes flit over to Alfswich. "Very good, sir. How much time are you allowing?"

"Until your man gets back here."

The guard allows a fleeting smile before turning serious again. "It will be done," he says as he bows.

"My man is excited at the prospect," Rendell says. "I'd get right to it if I were you."

My stomach sinks as the gaunt man picks up the necklace and replaces it on his neck. I carefully close the door and step two paces into the room. Mentally, I tell Shadow to proceed. The plan makes me all kinds of uneasy, mainly because it will all depend on the dog.

"I can prove that I am a Pretanni druid, at least. No one else is capable of this." I gently push Alfswich and Wranlen away from me.

I envision a great cave bear and project the boundaries of its body around me. Next, I allow my essence to expand and fill the space. My head hits the ceiling and I let out a fearsome roar before dropping my front paws to the ground. My head is still a hand's width above the table.

The guards start shouting and try to enter. However, I keep the door shut thanks to my considerable backside wedged against it. I grunt a couple times to cover Shadow's theft before stepping forward and resting my head on the map table. The guards trip over themselves while entering, drawing all eyes toward their antics.

I revert back to myself while still on all fours. It's great that Shadow has grabbed the statue; but the last thing we need is for the prize to be seen in his mouth as he dares me to chase him.

Rendell recovers from his shock and raises his hands, calling for quiet.

I rise to my knees and shake out my mantle as if it contains bear fur. With the guards' view blocked, I mentally order my dog to come to me. I pick at some nonexistent fur with my left hand while taking the statuette with my right. I drop it into a pocket and finish adjusting my mantle.

Shadow emerges from underneath the table and slinks back to his spot in the corner. I give silent thanks to Nodons for bestowing a brindle coat upon my best friend. No one notices his movement in this poorly lit room.

"That will be all," Rendell says to the leader of the guards as he removes the amulet from around his neck and tosses it to Alfswich.

Reluctantly, the guards leave us again. Rendell starts bobbing his head up and down. If our lives didn't depend on this, I'd belly laugh at how ridiculous the man looks.

"I simply turn a blind eye?" he asks.

"And one of your rivals will be removed," Wranlen confirms.

"And if Tilbert doesn't agree?"

"Then there may be an accident," Alfswich says.

Rendell rests his hand on the dagger. "Should I be afraid, assassin?"

I hold my breath, fearing that he'll notice the missing statuette.

"Only if you wish to contend against both of your rivals for the title."

"Then I want you out of my city. Guards!" he shouts. Once more, they file into the room, filling the space on our side of the table. "This audience is over." He turns to his men. "Escort these men out of my keep at once."

"As you say, Lord."

*   *   *

Once we're turned out into the city, the guards leave us be.

"Quickly, we need to get out of view," Alfswich whispers.

Wranlen and I follow him and we turn at the first corner we see.

"What now?" Wranlen asks.

He doesn't know what the plan is either?

The thief signals for quiet. "He'll realize that we stole the statuette any moment now. We need to split up and exit the city on our own. Wranlen and I can manage with our powers, but you are going to have to change into a bird or bat or whatever and get you and your dog out of here."

"It won't be a problem," I reassure him.

"But first, give me the statue," Alfswich says.

I animorph into a herding dog and bark at him, letting him know that I have no intention of relinquishing the statue to him. In this form, his Sorim powers have no effect on me. I trot off toward the city gate with Shadow following me. I will not miss this city.

Chapter Eleven

Birdbrained Plan

The road gets increasingly busy as we approach Londinjon. We've been shadowing it from the fens and forest since we were free of Camulodunon. Alfswich didn't have time to change Rendell's memories, so he went with distracting his mind? I still don't understand exactly what he did, but he assured us it was very temporary.

There were several mounted patrols the first couple of days, but now that we're in the vicinity of Londinjon, they've tailed off. Still, we cling to the shadows of the forest. In a pleasing matter of divine justice, only Alfswich is uncomfortable surrounded by nature.

I summon Rendell's battle bird daily in order to get comfortable with it. Sunshine, as it's called, is at the center of our plan. Unfortunately, neither the great bird nor Shadow has forgotten about their first encounter. Having to give directions to both simultaneously is overly taxing. Unfortunately, Wranlen has had no luck in communicating with Sunshine, and Shadow's self-preservation instincts can only be overridden by me.

I shudder at the thought of giving the statuette to Alfswich, so that means I'm the one in charge of the bird. When we first saw it, it looked ungainly, deadly and angry. It's still all of those things, except it's more high-strung than angry. Reluctantly, Alfswich had shared the summoning and dismissing words, but only after it became apparent that the creature wasn't receptive to his commands.

Moving slower than we'd planned, it takes us a week to get to the outskirts of the great trading city. Londinjon is anathema to everything druids strive for. I thought Isca was huge back when I completed my quest to become a druid. Cunobel's entire city could fit several times over within the walls before us.

"I still don't like this plan," I say.

"Do you think we're going to let you come up with one?" Alfswich asks. "I don't care to be captured, imprisoned, beaten, shipped off to a work mine, starved and beaten again. I, for one, will not be entertaining plans from you."

Wranlen puts a hand on my shoulder. "Let it be. I don't like the plan either, but it does sound likely to work."

I stare at the forest floor. "But how do we know that you intend to come back and get us?" I ask the thief.

"I'm rehabilitated, remember?" Alfswich says with a nasty smile. "Neither of you know how to blend in with the people, and neither of you have any coin to pay for lodgings. Since you two practically danced your way through the forest, I don't understand why you would want to leave it now."

"Let him go," Wranlen says.

I throw Sunshine's statuette as far as I can from the road and shout "*Ifilf*," releasing the bird from wherever it was bound. Shadow growls at me.

"Sunshine and shadow have never coexisted together," Wranlen says.

I hate it when he gets philosophical.

"Sunshine! No!" Just that bit of inattention, and the bird is stalking my dog. I don't have time for this. "Sunshine, *tiwwut.*" I'll release him some other time when it's less hectic.

* * *

Wranlen and I watch as Alfswich leaves the city gate. I send Shadow to greet him and lead him back to our camp. The dog does him no favors as he sprints back to us. My dog is a good judge of character. Alfswich is wheezing as he makes it to the tree line.

The thief is bent over, gasping for breath. "Do . . . you . . . think . . . that was funny?" The last three words spill out all at once. He stands up. "Tilbert is going to address . . . the citizens today . . . in the town square . . . since it's Beltane." He sucks in another deep breath.

Wranlen and I look at each other.

"Why would we care about that?" I ask.

"You fools." He's still breathing hard. "He'll be out in the open. He's been in his palace or surrounded by a dozen guards for the past week."

He stops his panting, but he's still wiping the sweat off his forehead.

"Who knows how long before we'll get another chance?" he says.

"Then let's go," I say.

Alfswich gives me a dirty look. "I need some water first, and I'm too tired to get it."

I smile back at him. "I'll be happy to get it for you."

I look for Shadow, but he's gone off into the woods. I mentally send him a message to meet me at the stream. When he's done marking his territory, he'll turn up there.

*   *   *

I've collected the water before my canine companion appears. I squat down and raise my left arm in front of me. He rests his front paws on my arm and begins licking my face. Unsurprisingly, his paws are muddy again. I withdraw my arm and let him drop to the ground.

"You've been digging," I tell him in an annoyed voice.

He wags his tail and smiles at me in response. I can't help but smile back.

"One of these days I'll train him," I tell myself, again.

"We'd better hurry before Alfswich gets too out of sorts. He'll complain the whole way into the city if we make him wait much longer."

The thief is tapping his foot impatiently as we return.

"You have the statuette?" he demands.

"Always."

"Let's see it."

"And let you filch it from me, no chance," I say.

The thief throws up his hands and mutters something under his breath. He places his hands on his hips. "Then let's go before we're too late. Tilbert is due to speak at dusk."

To my surprise, the guards don't even move as we enter the city. Wranlen and I stare wide-eyed at the forest of buildings before us. There's a row of grass between the wagon tracks, otherwise plants are rare. Alfswich navigates us through the cramped streets, the cacophony of languages, and the myriad of smells.

If Camulodunon is rigid and formal and Verlamion is relaxed and beautified with statues, Londinjon is neither of those. It makes me think of birds in the spring, when they find whatever they can to build their nests. That's what this city is: a huge collection of people who, completely independent of one another, cobbled together building materials to suit their own purposes. There is no central plan, but rather hundreds of different competing, and most likely opposing, plans enacted upon this city.

We pass through the poor quarter and reach a bridge. A river runs through the middle of the city. There are three bridges over the river, and Alfswich has selected the middle one.

"Listen up," Alfswich says. "You two were fine when we were amongst the poor, but no one looks twice in those places. Now we're going to enter the nicer part of town, and the people are always weary of fragrant, strangely dressed people like yourselves. Don't look at anyone, don't talk to anyone, and follow me closely."

Wranlen taps my shoulder. "Look! Trees."

"That's where we're headed," Alfswich calls from in front of us. "And that's the last I want to hear from you two."

"If only they were beech trees," the half-si quietly laments.

We pass several manor houses before reaching a huge stone building. In front of the building are two guard towers, one on either side of the entrance. The walkway from the palace leads to a stone platform overlooking a tree-lined meadow. Thousands of people fill the grassy area with the lucky ones in the warm, full sun. We're more than happy to stick to the shade.

"Now remember," Alfswich says, "I can only make the people closest to us not notice you. So be quick, but be subtle when you throw the statue."

"Don't worry, I've already picked my spot." I ask Shadow to wander around the deeply shaded area and mark all the trees.

Guards emerge from the palace, lining the walkway to the platform. It's as high as Sunshine is tall.

I hope the bird can jump that high. Why didn't I test Sunshine's jumping ability?

Reaching into my mantle's interior pocket, I feel nothing but cloth. I pat the rest of my pockets, but there's no statue anywhere. I drop my pack and go down to one knee.

"Throw it now!" Alfswich screams inside my head.

I undo the last knot and check my pack. No statue there either. I spin around frantically.

"What are you doing?" Alfswich whispers.

"I can't find it," I say through clenched teeth. I look up and see Shadow sitting four paces from me, thumping his tail against the ground.

The muddy paws.

I slap my forehead. Shadow must have buried it while we were waiting for Alfswich in the forest. That was why he was late getting to the stream. I cover my eyes with my hands as I try to keep my temper reined in. It will do no good to yell at the dog.

Alfswich shakes my shoulders.

"What are you doing?" he demands in a barely audible tone.

"Shadow. He must have buried the statue in the woods."

"We'll never get another chance like this," Alfswich curses under his breath.

Wranlen comes over to see what the problem is.

"There may be another way." I shake Alfswich to pull him out of his blue streak. "How quickly can you get us out of the city?"

"Why does that matter?"

"If you can get us out of here immediately, I have an idea that should work."

He rolls his eyes and looks at Wranlen.

"How fast?" I demand.

"It's almost sunset, so that will help. What's your plan?"

"No time to explain."

I inhale deeply and slowly expel the breath. Grahme and Figol both turned into griffins, so I know this *can* work. I visualize Sunshine and project his body around my own. It feels awkward having my neck stretch so long, but I keep my focus.

Around us, people point in our direction.

"Go!" Wranlen says.

I break into a sprint and I'm at full speed before I leave the cover of the trees. Tilbert is busy reading his speech. My eyes allow me to take in details from an extra wide field. The podium is getting bigger and bigger, and I'm not sure I can leap that high. Thanks to my enhanced vision, I see a large rock next to the platform. If I jump off of that . . ..

I race toward Tilbert as fast as the commotion I'm causing. Placing my left foot on the stone, I push off with all I have. I beat my wings furiously for every little advantage I can muster.

My right talons land on the wall and I pull with all my strength. I tumble over the wall and lean into the roll. I'm able to pop up and survey the scene. The speaker and his guards have only just noticed me.

"What's Rendell doing?" Tilbert demands as he stares at me.

If ostriches could smile, I'd be the goofiest looking bird of all time. Three strides and I'm nearly on top of the pudgy man. I plant my right foot and kick Tilbert off the platform to the cobblestone street below. He will likely be dead before he lands, but the stone-lined road will insure the outcome.

The city goes quiet as their leader sails off his perch. His head hits the street, followed by a loud crunch and a quickly growing pool of blood. There can be no doubt that I've murdered the leader of Londinjon.

Behind me, a guard yells to his comrades a command to capture the bird. I look at the charging cohort and belatedly realize he means me. I see Alfswich dragging Wranlen off to my right, toward the River Thames south of the city.

I take two strides before leaping off the platform. This time, my outstretched wings steady me and I'm able to land on my feet. I take off towards my friends.

No one can catch me, not even horsed men. My companions dart into an alley, and I follow close behind.

"Change back! Change back!" Alfswich says, while waving his hands over his head.

"Where's Shadow?" I ask once I'm human again.

"Who cares? We have to keep moving," the thief says.

Closing my eyes, I reach out to Shadow and guide him toward us. It's slow going at first; he's obviously on the lookout for Sunshine.

Out of breath guards reach our alleyway. Before they can speak, Alfswich waves his hands frantically.

"It was so big!" he says, gesticulating wildly. "It could have killed us, but I threw those two against the wall and it ran right past us," he says in one breath.

"Which way did it turn?" the lead guard asks.

"It went straight for as long as it could, then it turned right. I guess it was going toward the middle bridge."

"Go home and stay there. There's a curfew until we find Tilbert's killer."

"Yes sir, of course sir," Alfswich grovels.

Once the guards are out of earshot, I give Alfswich a huge grin. "You did it!"

"That bought us some time, nothing more. Once they quit the worthless chase, they'll come back here looking for us. We need to move."

Shadow lopes around the corner, tail held high as if it's the best day of his life. My canine friend will get his scolding, but not now. Alfswich guides us to the fishing dock and unmoors a boat.

"Take your time once you're on the water. Remember, you're a fisherman who knows nothing about what has happened. Slowly work your way west past the city. Under the cover of night, beach the boat and make your way back to Solent Keep."

"What about you?"

I can just make out Alfswich's teeth in the fading light. "I wasn't cut out to be an honest laborer. Tell Lady Koni thanks, but I have to forge my own path." He turns from the river and disappears into the deepening shadows.

"Head east," I tell Wranlen.

He looks at me, confused.

"Alfswich is going back to get the statuette. I don't know about you, but it gives me chills thinking about what he'll do with it."

"He's been a good companion," Wranlen protests.

"Better than I could have possibly hoped," I agree. "The only open question is who would you rather see with that statue?"

Wranlen tosses me an oar and we head east.

I send Shadow to retrieve the prize for two reasons. First, he should know where he buried it and second, he's immune to Alfswich's mental skills. Just before Aine lights up the night, we hear the thief shouting at my dog.

"Do you think that Rendell will take the fall for Tilbert's death?" Wranlen asks.

"He has to. Tilbert named his killer, wrongly, of course, but he named Rendell right before he died. Besides which, who else would benefit from Tilbert's death and also happen to possess a magical ostrich?"

"Even if they can't kill him," I say, "there's no way the city of Londinjon will follow him into battle, and the Wigesta can't afford to lose the people and wealth of Londinjon."

For the first time in a long while, we can sit at a fire in peace. I've done Grahme proud, and I outsmarted Alfswich in the end. Now I can return home and marry the woman I love. Except, of course, we were supposed to wed today, on Beltane. I just hope she'll forgive me.

"It was a near thing, but we succeeded," Wranlen says.

I chuckle. "One could say that about this entire mission."

Shadow reaches the boat and we head west, having accomplished more than what was asked.

EPILOGUE

Wranlen suggested that we avoid the road back to Solent Keep, ostensibly to avoid running into Alfswich, but I'm not falling for it. Like me, Wranlen is tired of large cities and their lack of nature. We take four days to return, and in that time I have not managed to change the behavior of either my dog or my magical battle bird.

I can't get over the fact that I can just walk into Solent Keep now. I stare at the ground as if it's filled with quickearth that will drag me down and swallow me whole. For so long, this was a place of pure evil, and not the druid-friendly city that is now.

"One of those guards actually smiled at us," I tell Wranlen.

"Why wouldn't he? I smiled at him."

I shake my head. He just doesn't understand the history.

The keep still looks just as menacing, but now at least we know what to expect.

A tall woman with long brown hair greets us.

"Hello, I am Bara, Lady Koni's chamberlady."

"Where's Nidda?" I ask.

"At home with her three small children," Bara says.

"And who is this?" Wranlen asks as he notes a young child struggling to draw city glyphs.

"This is my son, Corsi. We haven't been in the city very long."

I encourage Shadow to go lay down next to the child, which makes the boy put down his writing stick and pet my dog. He looks apprehensively at his mother.

"You can take a break and pet the dog," Bara says.

"His name is Shadow," I say. "We have just returned from a mission given to us by Lady Koni. May we speak with her?"

"I am sorry, but no. She will not see anyone from outside the keep for another three days."

"Three days?" I ask, startled.

"A very dear friend of hers has died. She is in her seven days of mourning, as Sorim custom dictates."

"Who is the deceased?" I ask.

"As my son and I are learning, it is not proper to speak the dead's name for an entire month."

"Will you tell her that Arthmael and Wranlen have returned and that our mission was a success?"

"Oh, Lady Koni did tell me about you. She said that there would be three of you, though."

"Alfswich decided not to return with us."

"That will not make my lady any happier. She feared that Alfswich would not return, though she hoped she was wrong."

"Each of us must walk our own path," Wranlen says.

"That is true," Bara agrees. "My lady had hoped that friendship bonds would be enough to bind him to Solent Keep. I will tell my lady of your news. Where might she find you after the mourning period is up?"

"I will be at druid lord Grahme Fairweather's camp," I say.

She looks at her son and Shadow, who are laying on the floor against each other. "Thank you for your understanding."

"I will see them, Bara," the tired voice of Lady Koni calls from the hall.

"But Lady Koni—"

"Affairs of the city can't be put off, no matter what custom demands."

Lady Koni's swollen red eyes are the first feature I notice. She sniffs her nose once and looks at little Corsi while he pets my dog.

She waves for us to follow her back into the hall. Once we're through, she crumples into the door, closing it.

"Blachstenius is dead," she says in a monotone voice. "There, I've broken with even that custom and said his name." She looks at us. "Let's agree not to break it again."

We nod our agreement.

"Precious little Corsi," she pats the door that she's leaning against, "is the only living member of the Mot Dariik clan."

"I am sorry to hear about . . . the loss his clan has suffered," I say. "The deceased was a good friend of the plains druids."

Wranlen lifts Lady Koni's hand and kisses it tenderly. "Loss is always painful, and when the one is of great stock, the idea of going on without them is daunting. In our forest, we protect and tend our revered ones as best we can. In the end, all lives must end."

"I can see that you are tired," I say.

Koni's lips upturn for an instant of mirth before she is dragged back down by her grief.

"We did accomplish our mission, though I feel terrible speaking about it at a time like this."

"Tilbert is dead?" she asks in a monotone voice. "I'm sorry. Once again, I've entered your mind without your permission." She sniffles again. "No matter how exhausted I feel, it is wrong to do that."

"Yes, he is dead, and Rendell will take the blame."

She shakes her head as she sighs. "Can you read common?"

"I cannot."

We look at Wranlen, but he is unlearned in common as well.

Lady Koni pulls out a sheet of parchment. "This came yesterday." She hugs it to her chest as she struggles to keep her composure. "The deceased met with Tilbert earlier this month. The two of them worked out an agreement that would not lead to all-out war."

She lowers her head and rubs the tears from her eyes.

"These two traders bartered," she starts. "They agreed to avoid needless bloodshed and untold misery by negotiating a compromise." Spasmic gasping stops her from continuing for a moment. "And now they are both dead," her voice catches on the last word and she's quick to turn her back on us. "I'm sorry, I must go," she says as she flees from us.

"That's it then," I say as I turn to Wranlen. "Tell your people that there will be war next summer.

For once, I see my friend frown.

*   *   *

Grahme and Brehme remain silent as I finish my tale. Shadow lays over my feet, barely stirring. Only the fire is willing to be heard. At last, Grahme leans back and stretches with an audible groan.

"I don't know why I feel so tired; you're the one who went on this adventure."

I cross my feet at the ankles to keep from bouncing my leg. I've not been this nervous since the first time I was sent to Cynbel for discipline.

"How did Conwenna take Alfswich's departure?" he asks.

"She was disappointed, but I don't think she was surprised."

"I want to hate that man, but he keeps weaseling out of it somehow."

"Did you know?" I blurt out. "About the si?"

"I knew of them, and I felt they needed to know what is happening in the world around them, but no one I know besides you has met them."

"Then you didn't know that Wranlen would go back and marshal their forces for the impending battle?" I ask.

"I did not."

"How many warriors do they have?" Brehmne asks.

"No one knows. We don't even know if Wranlen will be successful. He's a sapblood after all. The full-blooded si may just ignore him."

"Then they will only have themselves to blame if this battle comes to their forest," Grahme says. "I'm amazed you put yourself in such danger to bring these back to us." He holds up one of the fyrian stones.

"Well, Alfswich did steal his stones back from me, but I was at the amphitheater long enough to memorize the carving and the necessary prayer."

"You made these?" Grahme looks at me. "How do we know that they work?"

"I didn't take multiple beatings only to be sloppy in the execution of that glyph."

Grahme looks like a child at the harvest festival. "We're going to have to test them." He tosses me one of them. "Come away from the camp and the trees."

We trudge well away from fire and the food that I so desire.

"On three, we'll both throw them above the moor and activate the magic."

I nod my agreement.

"One, two . . ." We both heave our stones. "*Cweorth!*" we yell in unison, as if more volume will have an effect. The moor lights up in reddish hues as the fireballs travel along similar paths.

"Brehmne, go make sure those flames go out," Grahme says.

The apprentice does his best to not pout, but he completely fails. It's the best thing about Brehmne. He's too honest to hide anything from you. We watch as he animorphs into a tawny owl and chases after the flames.

"Regarding Dalna," Grahme says calmly, "I want you to know that neither of you have need of my blessing, but I give it freely."

"My head knew that all along, but my heart feared the worst."

"Good. I'm glad that's settled, since I'm leaving in the morning to see Caradoc and Eghan."

"You are?"

"We have a reliable way of making our own fyrian stones now. Bradan's camp never really did much other than drink and fight. Once you're the druid lord there, they'll finally have a mission that validates their existence."

"Those stones weren't vlint, just regular river rocks," I say. "Where do we get our own vlint from?"

"That's the pivotal question," Grahme replies. "While you were gone, I spoke to Ganna and asked if there was any way to avoid the coming conflict."

"You didn't go to see Meraud?"

"I'm afraid," he says slowly, "that Meraud might not be the right person to lead us in the upcoming battle." He looks directly at me. "That is not to leave this camp, you understand?"

"Yes, Lord Grahme."

He gestures with his hands to take a seat. "No one wishes to replace Meraud. In fact, I don't know of anyone who would want the position, knowing what is to come. But there's no denying that she's a backward-facing leader. Everything must be preserved and every ritual must be performed as it always has been. That's fine in times of peace; it's desirable even." Grahme arches his back and stretches again. "But she's hampering our efforts to learn from the firbolgs. She's flat-out ordered that no one can go to Eriu. I haven't bothered to ask her thoughts on approaching Ganna or the centaurs because I don't want to defy her if I don't have to."

"What did Ganna say?" I ask.

"She was cryptic, of course, and she made no pledge of helping us when the time comes. But what little she did impart was a guarantee that this war cannot be stopped or even much delayed."

*   *   *

I leave a bit of food for Brehmne for when he returns from fire duty, but not a lot. I've been hungry for days. It will do him no harm. Wranlen is a fine traveling partner, except he ate next to nothing and he was always pained when I took an animal for our meal.

Brehmne wastes no time once he's back. He leans in close to me and whispers, "What did he tell you once he sent me off?"

"It seems you've been spying on people at night these last few months," I say in a loud voice. "And you've been going outside our camp and spreading gossip."

"What's this?" Grahme asks.

"This one," I nod toward Brehmne, "has taken to watching others at night, when he should be sleeping."

Grahme smiles. "Cynbel told me about that. It won't matter. You'll soon be moving."

"He doesn't care because he's got his own woman," Brehmne says, smiling.

"You've been spying on your own druid lord? And you admit openly to it right in front of him?" I can't help but laugh.

Brehmne's jaw drops open and he becomes very interested in anything that's not in Grahme's direction.

"Arthmael," Grahme says, "it seems I have been derelict in my instructions and I've given too much free time to young Brehmne. Would you be able to make time to train my charge further in staff work for as long as you remain in this area? I was thinking a good workout every day at sunrise would do wonders for his instructions."

"I would be happy to oblige." I look at the little sneak, who can't keep his mouth closed. "I bet Shadow would be all too happy to join as well." My dog stirs for a moment before dozing off again. "Be sure you've found some meat for us to tie onto the ends of our staves."

Brehmne looks at the finished plates before us. He'll have to get up before sunrise to hunt.

"But what about breakfast?" he asks, alarmed.

"You can have your breakfast afterward," Grahme says reassuringly. "Arthmael and I will wait and eat with you."

"But I'll have to go hunting before sparring. When will I have time to collect the wild berries and herbs? I can't do that in the dark."

He could do that, if he transformed into an owl or some other nocturnal animal, but Grahme always says you can't become a druid until you start relying on yourself to find answers.

"I'll wait a bit for breakfast, but you'd better not dawdle," Grahme says.

We look at each other. Poor Brehmne, he's too far lost in his own despair to see our mentor and I grinning at each other.

"I think it's fair to say that you'll not be having any late-night flights to spy upon others," Grahme says. He stands up and yawns.

"You're not getting off that easy," I say. "Who are you seeing these days?"

"It's Lura, the chiefess of Dinas Gwenenen," Brehmne says, tossing a playful smile toward the druid lord.

I smile at my mentor. I didn't think he had it in him.

Grahme glares at Brehmne. "It's complicated. Druid lords have always been able to take a spouse without issue, but no one has tried to marry a tribal leader or even a chieftain. I wouldn't actually be an impartial judge now, would I? And it's not as if having one of my druids rule instead of me would quell the suspicion."

"But if the other tribal leaders found out about this secret arrangement . . .."

"As I said, it's complicated."

Thank you for reading my book

Please consider signing up for my newsletter or find out more about me and my works at:www.AuthorMikeMollman.com.

My friend, fellow author and also my editor, Roe Bushey, and I have a YouTube channel:https://www.youtube.com/@BaldBalding-cv2mb

For the rest of my social links, go to my linktree: https://linktr.ee/mikemollman

Finally, ratings and reviews are the social proof that we independent authors desperately need to stay relevant. Please consider leaving one for me or any other author you read.

Thank you!

Pretanni Pantheon

Agrona	Goddess of Battle & Slaughter
Acasta	Local Goddess of the River Itchen
Aine	The Moon Goddess, her day is Godhvos Gras (the first full moon after Beltane).
Andrasta	War Goddess, Patron of the Iceni
Artaius Equinox)	God of livestock (His day is the Vernal
Lir	Lord of the Sea, one primary Merfolk gods
Belenos	Sun God (Beltane is his festival)
Brigantia festival)	Fertility and Prosperity (Imbolc is her
Camulos Solstice.	God of War. His day is the Summer
Cernunnos	Lord of the Wild Things. Called the Horned One, has antlers.
Cocidius	Goddess of the Hunt, Helghores Loor is her day (first full moon after Lughnasa).
Epona	Goddess of Horses, the primary goddess of the Centaurs
Fagus	God of Beech Trees, one of the Elven gods.
Hooded Ones	Gods of Mysteries and Oracles. Primary gods of the seers.
	(Opposed to Belenos, their day is the Winter Solstice)

Melusine	Goddess of the Merfolk, Lir's wife.
Ogmios	God of Eloquence, Music and Poetry, Patron of the bards
Sucellos	God of Agriculture and alcoholic drinks (Lugh is ancient name for god and Lughnasa is his festival)
Coventina	Goddess of Rivers
Nemetona	Goddess of Sacred Groves
Sulis	Goddess of the Healing Springs

Together Coventina, Nemetona and Sulis make up the Earhmother and she is celebrated at Autumnal Equinox. Her symbol is the triskelion.

Esus	Husband of the Earthmother – Human offerings by hanging
Taranis	Storm God – Human offerings placed in wicker cage and burned
Tettates	God of Male Fertility and Wealth – Human offerings drowned in lakes

If person suffers all three deaths (in one body), their soul is killed and they will not reincarnate.

Acknowledgements

The path to writing a book is a long and winding one. While much of the work is done alone, no one can finish a book worth reading without a lot of help.

My editors, Rosaire Bushey, Katherine D. Graham and my proofreader, Melissa Stone took my lump of a story and made it shine. I cannot recommend them highly enough. They can be found at:

https://www.rosairebushey.com/editing-services

https://www.fiverr.com/kritinia?source=order_page_summary_seller_link

https://www.fiverr.com/keverynn?source=order_page_summary_seller_link

The cover art was made by Dmitry Yakhovsky and the quality speaks for itself. You can find him at:
https://www.etsy.com/shop/DnDArtStore

No fantasy novel is complete without a map, and Theodor Andrei exceeded every single expectation. You can find him at:
theodorandrei4@gmail.com

Then there are those who provided services without payment.

For those of you upset with the fate of one of the characters in this book (no spoilers!), you can directly blame Ty the Reader Guy. He gave specific advice in a video meant to cheer on authors when they hit a rough patch, which I took. I told him I would deflect the blame onto him, and he said he was fine with it. Remember, blame Ty! Here's the video in question at the proper time stamp:

https://www.youtube.com/watch?v=HSDmnb39Vto&t=318s

Ask Jeff Davidson how a character would react in any given situation and he will paint a picture of mayhem and destruction. I did my best executing his ideas for the Dinas Gwenenen mead hall scene. And no Jeff, my druids will never be able to control fire, because with your ideas, they'd turn Pretanni into a conflagration reminiscent of the domains of hell.

My brother Danny had to listen to my trials and tribulations almost nightly, so I would be remiss not to mention him here. He had an opinion for every question I'd put to him, and sometimes he was even helpful.

Wyatt Johnson, Ph. D. once asked me why we are friends. I told him it's because he makes poor decisions. Not a fan of fantasy, he still read my first draft and patiently noted all the inconsistencies and gaping plot holes. First drafts are supposed to be lousy, and mine didn't disappoint(?). I should probably treat him better, but I won't.

My nephew, Johnny Mollman M.D. was uncomfortable but very helpful in deciding exactly what wounds my characters could receive and still survive. Something about a hypocritical oath, or something.

I cannot stress enough the value of SFF Discord channels. There is a real sense of comraderie amongst like-minded SFF nerds. There are so many great ones, but I have self-limited myself to only a handful. You can only join by invite, but if you reach out to me, I will get the invite to you. I personally vouch for:

Keymark

Indie Accords

An Unexpected Party

ToriTalks

Page Turners

Wizard's Enclave

Finally, there are too many BookTuber and Book Reviewers to thank, but I'm stupid enough to take a stab at it anyway. If your name is not here and you were clearly helpful, blame it on the forgetfulness of old age. You should check out their channels (in the random order they show up in my YouTube subscriptions:

Colin's Corner

   https://www.youtube.com/@ColinsCornerYT

Tori Talks

   https://www.youtube.com/@ToriTalks2

Beard of Darkness

   https://www.youtube.com/@BeardofDarkness

Niko's Book Review

   https://www.youtube.com/@nikosbookreviews

Books With Benghis Kahn

   https://www.youtube.com/@BooksWithBenghisKahn

Andrew's Wizardly Reads

https://www.youtube.com/@AndrewsWizardlyReads

An Erudite Adventure

https://www.youtube.com/@AnEruditeAdventure

Kay's Hidden Shelf

https://www.youtube.com/@KaysHiddenShelf

The Literary Apothecary

https://www.youtube.com/@TheLiteraryApothecary

Portable Magic

https://www.youtube.com/@trinforeman54

Liam's Lyceum

https://www.youtube.com/@LiamsLyceum

Boiled Jellyfish Reads

https://www.youtube.com/@BoiledJellyfishReads

The Next Chapter

https://www.youtube.com/@CNavo.TheNextChapter

Middle of Nowhere Books

https://www.youtube.com/@MiddleofNowhereBooks

and the infamous Ty the Reader Guy

https://www.youtube.com/@ty-the-reader-guy

Other Books by Mike Mollman

Protectors of Pretanni

Book One:	Becoming A Druid
Book Two:	Sins And Sorrows
Book Three:	To Speak With Elders
Book Four:	Desperate Dispatches
* Book Five:	Becoming A King
* Book Six:	Preparing For War
* Book Seven:	The Return Of Loris
* The Exodus of the Elders	

The Martian Saga

* Book One:	The Halley Traveler

* Upcoming

About the Author

Mike Mollman is a charming individual graced with good looks, undeniable charisma and humility. These descriptions come straight from his keyboard, so they must be treated as unimpeachable facts. Mike lives in the Richmond, Virginia area. When he's not self-aggrandizing, he likes to spend time with his two dogs and the many voices in his head.

9 781958 265017